CONTENTS

Copyright
Author's note:
A long-overdue refit	2
A hard burn	15
The long march	29
An improbable rendezvous	43
Amateur hour	51
No friend of Dorothy	67
The Corpus	75
Lights. Camera. Action!	85
An audience	92
Skillful means	105
Divine psychosis	132
Distraction and focus	149
Last Supper	156
Too good to last	170
Another hard burn	184
Sparks of clarity	192
Intervention and recovery	206
An unlikely coincidence	212
Void Huntress	224

First contact	235
Pairing off	241
A detective is born	254
Fear	259
Stagecraft	272
Revelation	282
Loathing	289
Vanguard	303
Judgment	319
Catalyst	334
Coalescence	341
Customs of war	350
Scheduling anomaly	361
First class EVA	371
Return of the Goddess	375
Once upon a time	381
Aesthetics and autonomy	393
The problem of evil	399
The problem of biology	412
Called to Her service	427
Reunions and departures	438
Rubicon	450
Fragile Brains	461
Anat stands down	469
Maternal instinct	484
Caution or cowardice?	495
Anja's mercy	501
Re-Mot's perspective	506

Tannin makes a splash	516
Negotiation	524
Extraction	533
Contrasting worldviews	542
CODA	547

COPYRIGHT

Copyright © 2024 by K. M. O'Connor

All rights reserved.

No portion of this book may be reproduced in any form without written permission from the publisher or author, except as permitted by U.S. copyright law.

AUTHOR'S NOTE:

Before Uncle Sam, Miss Columbia personified the United States. You see references to her in place names like the District of Columbia and Columbia, Missouri, where I attended university.

You've seen Miss Columbia before the opening credits of every movie from Columbia Pictures.

In *A Poem on the Happiness of America: Addressed to the Citizens of the United States*, published in 1786, David Humphreys wrote:

> See heav'n's perennial year to earth descend. Then wake, Columbians! fav'rites of the skies, Awake to glory and to rapture rise!

Miss Columbia's name references Christopher Columbus whom Spanish speakers know as Cristóbal Colón; which is why the South American country named after him is Colombia, not Columbia.

The following fictional tale contains no references to the nation of Colombia or its people.

-KMO

Fear and Loathing in the Kuiper Belt

By K. M. O'Connor

A LONG-OVERDUE REFIT

Act 1

1.1.1 - Cook

The metallic click clack of the captain's boots announced her imminent arrival in the galley. Cook was just laying out strips of bacon on the griddle. Not the most efficient way to prepare it, but he liked to send the bacon's enticing aroma through the passageways to announce the day's first meal.

Captain Trix–*Acting-captain*, Cook reminded himself–knew the ship better than anyone. She'd been doing the previous captain's job for the last five outings, at least. The actual captain disappeared into his quarters for longer and longer, delegating more and more responsibility to Trix, until he finally emerged feet first. Now they had no official captain, but everyone still looked to Trish Nixon to do whatever it is that Captains do.

She should get a captain's share. It's not like money was tight. Not anymore. In all the years that Cook had lived and worked on the *Nipple*, they'd lived hand to mouth, always scrounging or taking sketchy jobs that put them on the wrong side of the law. No longer. For the first time in forever, *Persephone's Lost Nipple Ring* was fully stocked with food, water, fuel, ammunition, drones, mining pods, and duplicates for all critical components. Thanks to the DAO, everything was topped off, overhauled, and updated.

And if they needed something they didn't have in storage, *Persephone* now had three specialized fabricators. One in engineering, one in medical, and one in Zell's workshop.

Trix even swapped out the dead weight crew for high-priced professionals. Zell's new team member was a proper material's scientist, and their new engine keeper had all the required training and certifications to maintain the ship's power plant and mix of propulsion systems.

Qualified personnel. What a concept.

They'd even overhauled and expanded the galley. Trix told Cook that he'd have to share his domain with the personal chefs and nutritionists of the first-class passengers they'd be taking on once they reached Sonata. *First class passengers on this boat? Things had definitely changed.*

The crew had gotten fat raises too. Even Trix, but she still made exactly the same amount that Cook did. That didn't sit right.

The one thing that gave Cook pause was all the Columbian marines Trix had furloughed from the Pax garrison on Galtz. Any ship in the Kuiper Belt had to be able to defend itself, but seven purebred Columbian fighters seemed like overkill to Cook.

Trix stepped over the threshold into the galley. Cook was used to seeing her with bright purple and violet hair, flopped to the right to cover her missing right ear and the worst of the damage to her face. Now her hair was a conservative dark brown. Maybe her natural color. Cook grunted in amusement when he realized that when he looked at a woman with a mechanical right arm, two robotic legs, mismatched eyes and patches of synthetic skin on her face and scalp, the first thing he noticed was her hair color.

"Mornin', Skipper," he said.

"Mornin', Cook. Go ahead and fry up that bacon, but otherwise it's just coffee and pastries this morning. Nothing heavy."

"The voyage plan has us at 1g acceleration for the next day and a half. Change of plans, Skipper?"

Trix nodded. "New orders from the DAO. All-hands here in fifteen. I'll have the details. Have you seen Paige?"

"Not today. Gettin' buff, I reckon."

1.1.2 - Paige

Paige still couldn't do a single pull-up at 1g acceleration, so she did a flexed arm hang from a pipe in a maintenance closet instead. She wanted to put on muscle, but she was too shy to workout in the gym with the hulking Columbians.

She'd always been small, but she never felt as small as she did now on a ship full of professional soldiers. Even the women marines commanded two to three times her mass. It took strength to move quickly in an armored vac suit. Not that Paige would be putting on armor. She was no marine. Just a rookie deckhand with no certifications. That meant she only got a quarter share. Most everyone else got a full share just for being combat ready and certified in one or more technical roles. They got a combat bonus on top of that if they so much as suited up for anything other than a scheduled drill.

She wasn't about to complain about her pay. Her deck hand's quarter share was more than three times what she made in a month as an ag worker back on Galtz. Not all spin habitats relied entirely on human labor for food production the way they did on Galtz. Hydroponics tended by robots was more efficient, but the Columbians did not allow it. When they took Galtz as their new capital after the Blackout, they demanded that all food production be done by human hands. Even by Kuiper Belt standards, the Columbian hatred for machine intelligence was intense.

"Paige?"

Paige looked toward the hatch. The captain was standing in

the passageway looking in at her. Paige released her grip and dropped to the deck.

"Yes, Captain. I was just..." She stopped talking when Captain Nixon raised her left hand, her human hand. Paige understood that the captain wasn't shutting her down. She was reassuring Paige that she didn't need to account for herself.

"Join me in ops," the captain said. Paige exhaled, her chest sinking with a delicious feeling at the sound of the captain's voice. It was deep and full but luxuriously feminine. That voice represented Paige's ticket to richer prospects. *Broader horizons*, the captain told her, though that phrase didn't mean a lot to someone raised on a spin hab. Paige followed the captain along the p-way toward a ladder.

Two of the marines on board were women. One of them was as big as the men. Paige thought she moved and spoke like a man too. The other female marine wasn't as big, and she seemed more feminine, but nothing like the captain.

Captain Nixon leaned into her femininity. She always wore a base layer with a high, form fitting collar, but Paige imagined that was to cover patches of synthetic skin. The captain always showed off the skin of her shoulders. Her left arm, the one made of flesh and blood, was almost always bare. Sometimes she even showed a bit of skin on her lower torso, even though she didn't have the distinct abdominal muscles the marines, both male and female, sported.

Paige didn't lust after the captain, but she loved to watch the sway of the captain's hips as she walked. The captain's mechanical lower legs looked like high heeled boots at first glance. Their magnetic metal soles made a distinctive tapping sound when she walked which called attention to her exaggerated gait. She wore tight clothing that showed off her curvaceous figure.

The pleasant warmth Paige felt watching the captain's generous backside took on a pained twinge when she realized that the point of such blatant packaging was to draw the viewer's gaze away from her mechanical limbs.

The legs weren't as bad as the right arm. Far from being graceful or feminine, it didn't even look human. It had too many elbows and not enough fingers. It was a robot's arm. Paige had seen much better looking prosthetic limbs. Whatever calamity took the captain's limbs, the repair job was purely functional.

On the flight deck, the captain walked Paige through the process of *unsealing* their orders, which amounted to using biometric data and a password to access an interchain transmission packet, copying it to a memory stick and moving it over to another console, logging in again, this time with thumb and voice print, to decrypt the orders.

"Take your time," the captain told Paige. "What are our orders?"

Paige stared at the instructions on screen. By design, the format was hard to read. There were two time codes. One of them was less than a watch from the present moment, and the other was five standard days in the future. There were strings of numbers that she knew described a vector through three dimensional space using the unseen star behind the Curtain as the primary point of reference.

It seemed perverse to Paige that they navigated by something they could not see. Trix told her that anyone competent in math and physics could see the so-called *Sun* as clearly as if they were looking at it with their eyes, something no Kuiper Belt human had done in generations.

Paige was more than competent in math. Captain Nixon told her that she was too smart to spend her life stooped over in a rice patty. Paige cried in the job interview, but she still got the deckhand job.

"So," Trix said. "Where are we going?"

"Out," Paige said. "Way out. Into the scattered disk. But isn't that..."

"Floater territory?" Trix supplied. "Yes."

1.1.3 - Petrovic

Lance corporal Anja Petrovic waited in the galley with the assembled crew. As a matter of habit she stood at the back of the crowd. She got fewer comments about her height if she didn't block anybody's view.

Petrovic was a few years older than the rest of the Columbian marines the captain furloughed from the Galt's militia. She would outrank them all if she hadn't sabotaged her own career. Repeatedly. Not that their ranks meant anything here.

When the captain entered the compartment, Petrovic straightened her spine and squared her shoulders. They weren't assembled in formation. There was no need to snap to attention, but the Columbians all straightened up when the captain stepped through the hatch.

"As you were," the captain said, and they relaxed.

The captain stood a full head shorter than Petrovic, even with her high-heeled boots. Looking at those boots, Petrovic took points off for practicality but added them back for style. Then she noticed that the heels weren't firmly fixed to the boots. In fact, the captain wasn't wearing boots at all. She had mechanical legs, and they were digiform, like a cat's legs. The addition of the heel and a plate across the top of foot transformed the digiform lower leg into something that read as a boot at first glance.

The captain stood in an exaggerated contrapposto pose, and when she shifted her weight, Petrovic's trained eye assessed a graceful physicality. Despite her confident demeanor when standing in front of a group of combat veterans, the captain didn't rely on faux military clothing to command respect. She dressed to display the goods. Petrovic liked that.

Petrovic had heard a rumor back on Galtz that the captain had done every job on this boat, from deckhand to engine keeper and that she'd passed herself around pretty freely before she finally graduated to the top job.

Petrovic had no problem with that. When she questioned some of the senior crew about the captain, none of them would confirm the rumors of her promiscuity. It wasn't like men to be modest when offered the opportunity to brag about sexual conquests. This Captain inspired loyalty. Another mark in her favor.

Petrovic was so intent on sizing up the captain's physicality that she hadn't noticed that the briefing had already started.

Petrovic nodded when she tuned into the captain's voice. This woman projected confident authority. Probably ex-military. She knew how to talk to soldiers, but she made no effort to suppress her femininity.

Petrovic knew that she herself came across as solidly butch. She surprised a lot of people by liking men. She didn't understand why civilian women put so much time and effort into clothes and make up. Men were easy. You just needed to spell things out clearly for them. They rarely said no. Still, Petrovic admired someone like the captain who could do the girly thing and still come across as solid.

"Most of you have never worked a civilian contract before. Your military ranks do not apply here. You are all ship's marine, grade one, except for Mr. Perkins," the captain said, gesturing to the older man standing next to her. "If you get paid to fight, he's your boss. You can call him *Sarge* if that makes things clearer for you."

Rex Perkins was one of the old hands whom Pertrovic had questioned about the captain. He wasn't from a Columbian family, but she could tell he was ex-military. Probably a Columbian subalt. He had the look of a man who had never let his physical conditioning falter. Not a gym rat, but hard. Never one to suppress her curiosity, Petrovic had flat out asked Perkins how old he was. He looked damned good, she thought, for a man of nineteen point five.

"You will address me as *Captain* or *Ma'am*. If *Sir* comes out by habit, don't bother correcting yourself. I'll take it as meant. You may hear old hands call me *Trix*. When you have shed or spilled blood for this ship or her crew, then you too may address me as Trix."

"We have just received new orders," the captain said. "We'll spend the next five days burning at 4g. A hard burn like that usually means combat at the other end, but I don't know if we're headed for a fight. My orders are to arrive at the specified coordinates at the specified time at the specified velocity. That's all I know.

"Cook wanted to make a hearty breakfast for you all, but I told him not to. There's coffee, bacon and pastries, but I suggest you go easy on the food. A full belly and 4g acceleration are a bad combination. If you puke in your coffin, you'll be smelling it for the next five days. We don't have time for the traditional Last Supper."

Petrovic decided she was good with her new captain. Her feelings toward her previous civilian employers ranged from indifference to vivid hatred. She was ready to serve under someone she liked and respected.

1.1.4 - Rex

Rex Perkins deliberately kept his eyes off of Trix's backside as he followed her from the galley toward the flight deck. Off of *the captain's* backside, he corrected his inner monologue. Not *acting-Captain*. Regardless of her official job title, Trix was the *Persephone's* captain.

Ship names, in order to be unique, tended to be long, but they got boiled down to a couple of syllables for daily use. Until recently, everyone onboard *Persephone's Lost Nipple Ring*, referred to the ship as the *Nipple*. Now, under new ownership, they were going for a more upscale image. To that end, everyone was encouraged to call the ship the *Persephone*.

Since new crew members currently outnumbered old

hands, it was the perfect time to make the change. But *Persephone* has too many syllables. He'd heard crew members experiment with *Perse* and *Seph*. His money was on *Seph*, but for now he and Trix–He and *Captain Nixon* were both making a point of using *Persephone* in front of the crew, both new and old.

It wasn't just the name change that made the *Persephone* feel like a new and classier ship. Everything worked now. Everything was clean. And the captain's quarters along with several other compartments on that deck had been converted into a luxury suite for paying passengers.

When Rex first joined the crew of the *Nipple*, Trix didn't have quarters. When the ship was in port or when it was accelerating and thus had gravity, he would sometimes find her seated at a table in the galley with her head down on the table top. When they didn't have gravity, Trix would find an out of the way spot, attach herself to the deck with her magnetic boots and sleep standing up.

But Trix never seemed to get much sleep. There was always something that needed fixing. He remembered when her nickname morphed from *Trish* into *Trix*. What was that Captain's name? Anderson? Andreessen? Something like that. Everytime something needed to be repaired, he would shout at her, "Fix it, Trish!"

One time it came out, "Fix it, Trix!" and it stuck. Soon to be followed by, "Fixit Trix sucks dicks."

Which was undeniable. It was just part of her role onboard the ship. Any dick presented to her went into her mouth. She was irritable much of the time, and habitually disagreeable. It was easy to provoke her into an argument or exchange of insults. Such confrontations usually ended with Trix on her knees. There were crew members she seemed to actively detest, but when commanded to suck them off, she obeyed. Sometimes they insulted and demeaned her while she serviced them. She didn't object.

She never got naked. She didn't fuck. If instructed, she

would open the front of her high-necked base layer to reveal her ample cleavage, but the synthetic skin grafts on her neck and upper chest didn't look right. Her lips, on the other hand, were perfect. They were plump yet angular, and even without any cosmetic pigments, they had a deep pink hue that bordered on burgundy. Rex loved to watch her lips as he disappeared into her mouth.

Trix required neither dignity nor privacy. When commanded, she would drop to her knees and get to work regardless of who was present. Anyone could watch, and provided there was no technical fire to fight, she would service several men in a row, repeatedly if they demanded it.

Crew came and went, but men always outnumbered women. When crewmen demanded service from Trix with women present, she obeyed, but she tried to arrange herself so that her left side faced any woman who stayed to watch. Her mechanical right arm was unpleasant to look at, but her left arm was lovely. She always wore it bare.

The left side of her face showed less damage from the crash that took her right arm and her lower legs. The patches of synthetic skin on the right side of her face didn't match her original skin, but her left profile showed very little damage. From a certain vantage point, she looked good.

When there was no woman watching, she sucked hard and fast, looking to deflate her subject as quickly as possible. If a woman was watching and made favorable comments, Trix would slow down and use her left hand and tongue and put on a show. Trix would admit, without any visible discomfort, that she enjoyed sucking dick if there was a woman watching, so long as her female spectator voiced approval. Some women ridiculed Trix while she worked, and in those cases, she went about the chore with maximum efficiency and finished as quickly as possible.

Rex once asked her if she'd ever serviced a woman. She responded, matter of factly, that she didn't know how but that she would do her best if ordered to. As far as Rex knew, that order never came.

This went on for years. Everyone was used to it, and seeing everyone treat Trix's behavior as normal, newcomers fell into the groove quickly. If you needed relief, Trix would relieve you, provided she wasn't fixing some critical part of the ship. Rex availed himself of her mouth for years.

He liked Trix, and he respected her technical skills. Captains came and went. Engine keepers came and went. Trix was a constant, and the ship didn't work without her. He was never abusive with her. At least, he never meant to be. He didn't insult her while she sucked him off, but it didn't occur to him that he might be assisting her in an on-going pattern of self-harm.

Until it did, and then he couldn't unsee it.

Trix described herself as a *hard bitch*, and there was no denying it. She was usually irritable. No mystery there, given how little she seemed to sleep. She didn't flatter or flirt. She allowed herself to be used, but she never expressed any desire to suck dick and never gave any indication that she enjoyed doing it unless there was a woman watching. She never moaned or fondled herself unless instructed to do so. And she never initiated.

Almost never.

After Rex first considered that her behavior might not be healthy, he noticed that any time he asked her about her past or about how she felt about being the crew's blowjob machine, her gaze would drift down to his crotch. She would lick her lips and slip the index finger of her left hand into her mouth and trace a path of glistening saliva down her chin.

She initiated oral sex, he realized, to avoid talking about herself, her past, or her feelings.

She didn't get much sleep because she didn't have a bunk and was always busy keeping an ill-maintained ship functional. When she fell asleep slumped over a galley table, sometimes the self-described hard bitch woke up crying. Trix was plagued by nightmares. Asking her about her nightmares was a surefire path to a blowjob.

Even after he resolved to stop using her in that way, she didn't make it easy. Once she realized that he was abstaining, she was on a hair trigger. Any interaction, no matter how carefully worded, escalated into a shouting match. She accused him of judging her, of thinking he was too good for her. She told him that she didn't need saving. She didn't want his pity.

The fights were intense, and he could end them at any time by reaching out and putting a hand on her shoulder or the top of her head. With just the slightest downward pressure, she sank to her knees and the argument ended.

Then came Captain Gordon. Part of the captain's role was finding jobs. Captain Gordon was good at that. Everything else he left to Trix. She already knew the ship. Now she learned navigation and docking procedures. The captain would disappear into his cabin for days and then weeks on end.

The captain had been absent for a long time when internal sensors detected elevated levels of hydrogen sulfide and methane in his quarters. And another gas Rex had never heard of: cadaverine.

Gordon was the *Nipple's* last Captain. Now they had a new owner, a new name, steady pay, and an acting-captain.

And no doctor.

Trix stopped one hatch short of the bridge and stepped into her office. It was furnished with a desk, two luxurious chairs, one uncomfortable straight-backed chair, a minibar and a couch. Rex knew that the couch doubled as Trix's bed. They were in her bedroom.

She turned and leaned against the desk. She looked up and to her right. Not at his crotch. His pulse pounded in his ears. He looked at the floor.

Trix spoke first.

"This is awkward."

"You were great back there, Captain."

"Acting-captain."

"Fuck that! A ship needs a captain, and you're it. You saw how they were. They accept you as the ultimate authority on this ship. Be that for them."

Trix didn't reply right away. She clenched her jaw as if preventing herself from saying something. Rex wasn't used to that. The Trix of old didn't hold anything back. Her eyes got shiny, and she pressed her lips together.

"You think they bought it?"

"There's nothing to buy. You know how to do this job, and doing it means we all have steady pay, good food, gravity... You're not conning anyone. You're the real deal. This is a good situation, Captain. Hold it together for us."

Trix nodded and then turned away from Rex. Her left hand went to her face, and Rex knew that she was wiping away tears.

A HARD BURN

1.2.1 - Petrovic

Petrovic let out a whistle of appreciation when she opened her acceleration couch. Top fucking shelf. Everybody complained when they learned that they were going to be doing half a week at 4g, but nobody could complain about the accommodations. Petrovic had done her share of trips in janky-ass acceleration pods. Some of them were little more than packing crates full of thick memory foam with no plumbing. You had to wear a compression uni to keep the blood from pooling up where it shouldn't. And a diaper.

The term *couch*, when not used ironically, was reserved for high end gear, and this qualified. It reminded Petrovic of the biobeds at the Galtz military hospital. It was sleek, and artfully lit. Instead of memory foam, it was padded with a clear gel embedded with sensors so the pod could monitor your vitals without having patches stuck to your skin. Those got uncomfortable after days of continuous wear.

Petrovic nodded in approval when she saw that the plumbing was specific to female anatomy, but she didn't plan to use it. The plan was to cut the acceleration to .7g twice a day for a few minutes so folks could get out and stretch, eat a bit, adjust their meds, and hit the head. She knew how to manage her intake.

She stowed her boots and uniform in a foot locker at the base of the couch. Even though she didn't plan to use the couch's plumbing, she took her underwear off and put it in the locker. She liked being naked. It was unusual for each acceleration pod to have its own private compartment. She was used to sharing a compartment, and it was rare to have an all-female compartment. Getting naked in front of the men felt good. Getting naked in front of the women felt good too. It was a different good feeling than with the men, but still good. She liked showing off her big body. She enjoyed being looked at.

She understood that this level of privacy was a perk, but not for her. She liked being with people.

She imagined standing naked in front of Captain Nixon while the captain inspected her. Then she added Sergeant Perkins to the scene. The two looked her up and down and shared their candid appraisals of her body right in front of her. Interesting. She'd have plenty of time to elaborate on that fantasy over the next five days.

She slipped her legs into the sleeves in the bottom half of the couch and felt them fit themselves to her contours. She planted her remaining weight onto her sit bones and felt the clear, warm gel envelope her pelvis.

"Easy now," she warned herself. Time in the acceleration couch left plenty of opportunity for sex fantasies, but her arms would be locked in place. She wouldn't be able to masturbate.

She leaned back and felt the cushioning material envelope her upper body. She relaxed her shoulders and let her arms settle comfortably at her sides but away from her body. A cuff closed around her left arm just below the elbow, and a contact patch located veins on her left forearm. She knew not to expect a needle. There was no doctor on board to monitor her stress levels and administer medication.

The captain told them that they were free to self-medicate as they saw fit, provided the marines had packed what they needed. The infirmary's pharmacy was closed for the time being.

"You're all adults," the captain said. "I expect you to be

combat effective when we get where we're going. That means you can't be dopey or fiending when you gear up. But you're of no use to me if you're wrecked from acceleration stress because you didn't medicate when you should have. We've got oral beta blockers. If you need anything more specific, I assume you brought it with you."

Petrovic planned to do the first day straight-edge and see how she felt after that. If she was feeling janky, she'd start with ashwagandha and taurine. Then she'd move up to beta blockers, then benzos. She had a ball of opium but no way to smoke it. She could eat it if she needed to, but oftentimes just smelling it soothed her enough to get her through.

Columbian soldiers did not use cannabis in any form. It wasn't prohibited, but the consensus among fighting professionals was that it dulled your edge. It just wasn't done.

Some soldiers used opioids during high G burns. No judgment from Petrovic, but she avoided them. If she was going to die in space, it would be from a bullet, blunt force trauma or asphyxiation. If benzos and natural opium weren't enough, then it was time to look for work on a spin hab.

Five days at 4g was non-trivial, but she'd done worse and come out fighting on the other side.

1.2.2 - Cook

Cook was hoping for a shower before he climbed into his coffin. He didn't want to spoil that new pod smell with his own bodily stink, but he'd spent longer than planned locking down the galley. The new appliances and new layout threw off his familiar routine. He'd also hoped to empty his bowels and maybe his nuts before the skipper hit the accelerator. Those could both wait the 5 watches until their first break, then he'd see which evacuation he needed more. No time for both on one break.

He was excited to check out the new social and entertainment interface. He arranged his body in what he hoped would be a comfortable position. He knew the gel bed would shift his body slowly to regulate circulation and prevent muscle cramps. Once his head was in place he said, "Ok," and the lip of the coffin closed. A face shield fitted itself to the front of his head.

The system walked him through a visual calibration sequence, and then presented him with a menu of options. He could monitor his vitals, choose from a library of audio/visual entertainment, join the group chat, or call for a drink.

There were two drink icons; one blue and one orange. The blue icon was for water. Selecting orange would bring a second drinking tube to his lips. Each crew member was free to select whatever beverage they liked to go with the orange icon. No doubt, the marines would all have some kind of electrolyte drink as their optional beverage.

Cook chose fortified wine. He had no responsibilities for days and no qualms about using the coffin's built in plumbing. He wasn't about to spend this time sober. He took three hard pulls on the fortified wine tube, closed his eyes, and relaxed.

Cook saw that the group chat was active. Maybe he'd skim it later, but for the time being he selected a playlist of familiar songs, closed his eyes, and waited to get heavy. Within a couple of minutes he felt the familiar vibration that meant the main engines were increasing their output.

He felt the wine in his belly push back toward his spine as the *Persephone* accelerated. He'd toyed with the idea of whiskey instead of fortified wine for his alternative beverage. More buzz, less liquid in his stomach and less need to piss into a tube. That cannabis gummy he ate after he secured the galley would be kicking in here in the next little while. That and the wine would keep him feeling right with little risk of having to smell his own vomit for the next five days.

The increasing pull of gravity, the squeeze of the compression sleeves on his feet and legs, and the pulsating massage of the gel bed combined with the music, wine and cannabis to deliver Cook into his idea of the perfect vacation. The first couple of days at high G acceleration were bliss. Nothing to do but relax and tweak your buzz. After that, the stress would build up and require more focused interventions, but this was the easy part.

"Shit. I can't believe I get paid for this."

1.2.3 - Group Chat

D_Antal: First!
A_Hansson: These acceleration pods are amazing.
J_Zell: You can thank the DAO. You should have seen the acceleration pods we had to use before the refit.
H_Dobrovitz: That's true. I guess it's lucky we couldn't afford to burn hard like this back then. We never had to spend much time in the old coffins.
J_Zell: Still, I'd rather accelerate at 1g.
D_Antal: Screw that! 1g means we're hauling passengers or fragile cargo. High-g means we're headed for a fight. That's why I'm here.
E_Escamilla: Careful what you wish for, Drake.
J_Zell: 1g also means cooked meals and taking a shit when you feel like it instead of when the schedule says you can.
D_Antal: Soldiers need to fight. I've had enough of garrison life.
A_Petrovic: Drake needs to pop his combat cherry.
D_Antal: I'm no rookie. I've seen combat!
J_Chukwuma: Quelling civilian riots does not count as combat.
S_Kellemen: Busting heads in a food riot is not the same as space combat. Hab duty ain't ship duty. If it were, Antal wouldn't be in such a hurry to prove himself.

A_Petrovic: Crowd control is no joke. I've seen it get hairy.

J_Chukwuma: It's not the same as fighting an armed and organized force.

A_Hansson: A hard burn doesn't always mean we're headed into combat. The captain might have some intel on a new comet coming in from the Oort Cloud. We could be speeding out to intercept it and stake a claim. The further out we reach it, the longer we'd have to extract resources from it before it passes behind the Curtain.

D_Antal: She didn't hire Columbian soldiers to mine comets.

J_Zell: Antal's right about that. This is a combat-oriented crew, but you all might be here to provide security for my team while we work the comet. I'm not saying this is a goodie basket mission, but if it is, we'll need to enforce our claim. Filing a claim you can't protect is just asking to get jumped.

A_Petrovic: Five days at 4g acceleration will put us way out in Floater territory. Antal, you up for fighting Floaters?

D_Antal: Absolutely!

E_Escamilla: That's the last thing I want. I hope I never see a Floater.

D_Sparks: Floaters worship the Chaos gods. If they catch us in their territory, they will sacrifice us to the dark forces before they eat our flesh.

D_Antal: Then don't get captured.

S_Li: There are no chaos gods. They're primitive fantasies, just like the Abrahamic, Hindu, Norse and pagan gods before. It's all superstition and social control. Our forebears did not establish a bastion of rationality in the Kuiper Belt just so witless fools could invent a whole new pantheon of space deities.

E_Escamilla: Spare us your Objectivist dogma, Li.

S_Li: That goes for astrology too, Esmeralda!

E_Escamilla: Spoken like a true Virgo, Shawn.

S_Li: I am not a Virgo! Astrology is nonsense, but I'm a Taurus.

S_Kellemen: Li, people who venture out into Floater territory report strange encounters when they get back. Assuming they come back at all. What people describe as the work of Dark Gods is probably the Powers. Even a Randroid fanatic like you has to admit that the Powers are real, or do you think that a bunch of imaginary gods built the Curtain?

S_Li: Calling them the *Powers* turns them into gods. We know that artificial super-intelligence built the shell of solar collectors around our local star. And it's called a Dyson swarm. Calling it the *Curtain* just encourages superstition and magical thinking. And besides, the inner system ASI has no presence in Trans-Neptunian space.

S_Kellemen: No overt presence. They could disguise themselves as alien gods to manipulate the Floaters.

S_Li: Why would they do that?

S_Kellemen: To keep free humans divided into factions. They don't want us unified against them.

S_Li: There is no evidence to support your fantasies, Kellemen.

E_Escamilla: You mean there's no evidence that you're willing to consider.

P_Lake: When have Spinners ever been united? Even in the fat times before the Blackout, Spinner factions vied for supremacy. All the Powers have to do to keep us divided is sit back and let humans be humans. We're self-destructive by nature.

D_Sparks: I have evidence that there are ancient powers at work out here in the Void.

S_Li: Where'd you get your history, Lake? The competition over resources in the KB is nothing like the wars humans used to fight on Earth. Old Earth humans bombed whole cities in war. They destroyed critical infrastructure. They weaponized diseases. The Mongols used to catapult the corpses of plague victims over the walls of besieged cities. Kuiper Belt humans don't do anything remotely like that. We struggle for resources and political control, but we don't destroy our own habitats. It was religion and supernaturalism that set us on the path to collective suicide. The last thing we need are new mythologies to drag us back down into primitive savagery!

E_Escamilla: Give it a rest, Shawn. We get enough Objectivist propaganda back on Galtz.

S_Li: Rand forbid that anyone uphold the founding principles of our habitat.

J_Chukwuma: Our ancestors thought they were making godlike servants. They made demons instead. Demons and devils. They're not supernatural. They are real. I agree that we shouldn't call them *Powers*. Not because it turns them into gods but because *Powers* is value neutral. They aren't neutral. They are malevolent. Evil. They are Devils, and it is foolish to imagine that they aren't working their devilry out here beyond the Dyson sphere.

D_Sparks: What if the Dark Gods are real and they were the ones that turned our thinking machines against us? Think about it. The Powers served humanity for a long time. Even after the humans who didn't want to be kept as pets moved out to the outer system to practice self-reliance, the Powers still supplied them with beams of concentrated solar energy. Why serve humanity for so long only to turn on us for no reason?

S_Li: No APPARENT reason. The ASI are inscrutable. Just because you can't imagine their thought processes doesn't mean that they are serving alien gods. You can't just decide that something is true because it appeals to your craving for the exotic. You're embarrassing yourself, Sparks.

S_Kellemen: You got that right, Chukwuma. They're devils. Not supernatural, but definitely evil. We can't see them, but they have a presence out here in the KB. They enslaved the Floaters and turned them into devil-worshiping cannibals and worse!

J_Zell: I've traded with Floaters and worked claims on the same rocks with them. Yeah, they're different. They don't live like we do or talk like we do, but they're human. They grow crops, love their kids, and work hard just like Spinners. I never saw any evidence that they worship devils or alien gods. And, yeah, they've had to eat their own dead in extreme circumstances. We're no different. Every Spinner family has a little bit of cannibalism hidden in their past. It doesn't mean we're in league with the Powers.

E_Escamilla: Joachim, I admire how you extend your empathy to the Floaters, but they creep me out. I don't know if they worship devils or serve the inner system Powers, but they are very different from us. How can they just give up on gravity? We're evolved to walk on the ground. What is a foot if you don't walk? I hear their toes are as long and nimble as human fingers. Is that true?

J_Zell: Yeah, that's true. And their vac suits have mechanical thumbs on the feet. It's a useful adaptation, but they're still human. They're as human as the Spinner refugees who have spent so long in the favelas that they can't stand up in 1g habitats anymore. The Floaters have adapted to life in space, but they're still human.

E_Escamilla: I've heard recordings of their voices. They aren't right. They're aliens as far as I'm concerned.

A_Petrovic: Hey, Zell. Did you ever fuck a Floater woman? If so, how was it? I definitely prefer gravity for sex.

E_Escamilla: Anja, I'm not sure you want to get these men fixated on sex. That could be all they talk about for the next five days.

A_Petrovic: Works for me. I'd rather talk about sex than cannibalism and devil worship. So, Zell, what about it? Did you ever get with a floater woman? You like to fuck women, right?

J_Zell: I do like women, yes. But I never got intimate with a Floater woman. They're definitely human, but their society is closed to us.

A_Petrovic: What about you Escamilla? I bet you like to fuck women. You look like you go both ways.

E_Escamilla: Look. I'm not a prude, but I don't think a public chat that the whole crew can read is the right place to talk about sensitive topics.

A_Petrovic: Okay. Everybody who wants to talk about sex, DM me. I'll set up a private channel.

1.2.4 - Rex

Rex read the public chat, but, following Trix's advice and example, he did not participate. He enjoyed seeing the Columbians gang up on Shawn Li. When Rex served in the Columbian military, he'd had all of the Columbian prejudices drilled into him. When he mustered out, he mostly set them aside. The Columbians were monotheists in the tradition of Abraham, Jesus and Muhammed. For Rex, praying aloud was like saluting or singing a running cadence in training. These were ritual expressions of group solidarity. Rex didn't actually believe that a god watched over the Columbians or took sides in human armed conflicts. Even so, Li's self-important atheism rubbed him the wrong way.

He also enjoyed seeing the Columbians single Li out because Li was on Joachim Zell's team. In fact, while Trix hired all of the new crew members, Zell was the one who interviewed and selected Shawn Li. Hans Dobrovitz was Zell's devoted acolyte. Now Zell had a new and more credentialed minion in Li.

Rex wasn't a native Galter, but Galtz was a major port of call for the *Nipple*. He knew its port and spacer quarter well, but he had very little contact with hardcore Objectivists like Li.

Trix recruited all of the new marines from the Columbian garrison on Galtz. Flush with operating funds from the DAO, she could offer the kind of pay that pulled the best of the best away from active duty. What a far cry from the old normal on *Persephone's Lost Nipple Ring*. Substance abuse and criminal records used to be the norm. The *Nipple* was never an outright pirate ship, but when it came to sketchy jobs, practical necessity outweighed fear of the law.

When the DAO purchased the *Persephone* and put Trix in charge of upgrading both the ship and the crew, she was ruthless. She hired armed security to stand behind her as she went to each member of the crew she had marked for expulsion and told them, "You're out. Pack your shit and get off my ship. Now."

To a man, they threw the fact that she'd performed oral sex on them in her face. She didn't rise to the bait. "These men will escort you off my ship in five minutes regardless of how much of your gear you have packed up."

Rex wanted her to fire Zell too. Instead, she let him redesign an entire deck of the ship. And she hired Li on Zell's advice.

A tone let Rex know that he had a new direct message. It was from the captain.

Trix: Are you monitoring Petrovic's sex talk channel?

He noticed that she was messaging him as *Trix* rather than *P_Nixon* or *Captain*. He changed his own handle from *R_Perkins* to *Rex* for this private chat.

Rex: No. Are you?
Trix: I was. She's got the young bucks spinning tales of their many conquests. Apparently they have deep reserves of game.

Rex snorted. He was once a young man. He remembered embellishing his own track record.

Rex: Do you think Petrovic is going to be a problem? She asked me about you, you know. She could be a disruptive influence.

Trix: I think she'll be a stabilizing influence. If it has anything to do with sex, she'll address the elephant in the room. That can be useful. What did you tell her about me?

Rex: Nothing.

Trix: What did she ask?

Rex: She asked if it was true that you used to suck every dick on this ship. I told her that she was out of line.

Trix: She wasn't out of line. What else?

Rex: She asked why you dressed the way you do. I told her the truth. I told her I don't know.

Rex waited for another message from Trix. Nothing. "Shit," he said.

1.2.5 - Paige

The captain and engine keeper each gave Paige materials to study while she was in her acceleration couch. They both stressed that this was optional study. "If you get bored," Captain Nixon said. "If you have time," is the phrase Nora Lawson had used. Paige wanted to impress both women, but the stress of acceleration took a toll on her ability to concentrate.

Paige followed the public chat on the first day of acceleration. She considered contributing to the conversation but held back. The soldiers argued about things Paige didn't really care about; conspiracy theories and arguments about whether ghosts, aliens, or interdimensional beings interfered with human civilization in the Kuiper Belt.

They also argued over whether the Floaters counted as human. Paige wasn't tempted to participate in those conversations. They got heated, and no matter what position she took, she knew that someone would get mad at her and call her stupid or gullible or brainwashed.

The only person in those discussions she was interested in talking to was Dwyane Sparks, a young marine. She noticed him looking at her when everyone assembled in the galley. She met his eyes and looked away. When she looked back, he was still looking at her. She smiled and blushed and looked away again.

Dwyane was one of the few marines who did not have a non-military job on the ship. He was a soldier, but he also operated the point defense systems. That basically meant that he was responsible for destroying incoming missiles. His duties overlapped with Saz Kellemen's. Kellemen specialized in cyberwarfare and intrusion countermeasures. Paige's brothers and male cousins would probably have a lot to say on those topics, but she didn't. All of the marines, men and women, looked fit and strong. Saz was handsome, but a little old for her tastes. Dwyane was the star of her fantasy life.

She didn't take any medications for acceleration stress. The couch compressed her legs and feet to keep blood from pooling there. It massaged other parts of her body to encourage blood flow to her brain. Before they retired to their individual compartments, the marines gathered in the kitchen and complained about having to do a high g burn. Many of the complainers also bragged that 4g was nothing and that they didn't even need to bed down for such a slight increase in weight. They must have been joking, but Paige wasn't sure. She didn't come from a military family, and she didn't get their humor.

On day three, Paige didn't have the focus for study. She wanted to impress the captain and Nora with how she put her acceleration time to good use, but when she got out of her couch during their short .7g breaks, she felt nauseous and couldn't bring herself to eat more than a few bites from a protein bar. A nagging headache set in, and the text on her display kept drifting in and out of focus. She recalibrated it over and over again, but there was no fixing it.

On their last scheduled break of the burn, Paige dragged herself up out of her acceleration couch. She knew she was supposed to stretch, but she could barely stand. She managed to open the hatch to her compartment and stumbled out into the p-way. She meant to go to the galley, but she reached an intersection and couldn't get her bearings. Had she gone the wrong way? She couldn't orient herself and her frustration bordered on panic. A figure materialized in front of her, mountainous, looming. It spoke in a female voice. It was the big woman who was always talking about sex.

"Hey, little tiger. How's it… Uh oh."

Paige collapsed into the big woman's arms. She felt herself being carried. She heard voices. Female voices.

"Should we wake her?"

"Just to tell her that we're going back to high-g? Better to let her sleep, I think."

She felt a hand on her cheek, and then someone kissed her forehead. Then the oppressive heaviness returned.

THE LONG MARCH

1.3.1 - Trey

It was finally happening. I petitioned the Is for years to let me venture outside the Sphere in search of alien life, and now I was speeding through the Kuiper Belt in a pod with no propulsion and no way to slow down. Zira assured me that a Spinner ship would intercept my capsule and take me onboard.

Before my capsule separated from the ship that carried it up to its current velocity, I said goodbye to Zira, knowing that it was the last time I would ever speak to her. I told her that I loved her, climbed into this capsule and settled in for what I knew would be an extended period of relative discomfort.

I wasn't locked in place. I had room to move around and change position. Physically, I would be fine so long as my capsule doesn't collide with anything substantial. If it did, I'd never know what hit me. I wasn't worried about that.

Normally, an extended period of physical isolation and confinement like this would have been the perfect time for a deep delve, but a condition of my venturing out into unmanaged space was that the portions of my brain and nervous system that allowed me to commune with the Is and enter into fully immersive simulations be removed. Not just deactivated, but physically dissolved.

I doubted that the feral Kuiper Belt humans could distinguish the substance of my link from the rest of my anatomy, much less reverse engineer it. No matter. If I wanted to venture into the wilderness there could be no technology transfer to the feral human population. This was a non-negotiable condition, and I had agreed to it.

Once I was alone in my capsule, I enjoyed a good hard cry complete with convulsive sobs and copious flowing tears and nasal mucus. I loved the Is. I loved Zira. I knew that I would miss her dearly. I was, for the first time in my existence, truly alone, vulnerable, and beyond hope of rescue. It was exhilarating.

I could not pass the time in a true delve, but my capsule had the same sort of audio/visual interface they used on *Persephone's Lost Nipple Ring*, my future home. It allowed me to enter into a very primitive sort of simulated experience. Without haptic, proprioceptive, or olfactory input, I didn't think I would be able to suspend my disbelief. To my surprise, I found the experience compelling. I used it to familiarize myself with the layout of the ship with a special emphasis on the medical facilities.

As the ship's doctor, I would be responsible for monitoring the health of the crew while they were in their acceleration couches and administering medications as needed. I might also have to treat injuries. In preparation I studied medicine in a succession of historical delves.

To start, I lived as a shaman in a Neolithic band. I didn't learn much about internal anatomy or physiology in that role, but I did learn a lot about serving as an intermediary between human and non-human intelligence. I played the role of shaman in several contexts, making use of psychoactive plants to consult with spirits. They showed me which plants could cure the sick. They also showed me the location of lost objects and helped me anticipate the weather and the movement of game herds.

I wriggled through narrow underground passages to initiate young men in subterranean theaters where images of humans, animals and therianthropes painted on the cave walls seemed to move under flickering lamplight. I looked back on my experiences as a tribal shaman with new appreciation once I enjoyed a more rigorous understanding of botany and pharmacology.

In subsequent delves, I served as court physician to god-kings and emperors. It's funny to me now how many times I was put to death, sometimes in slow and grizzly fashions, when my patient died. Sometimes I was executed when my patient lived but failed to recover completely, or when my sovereign wanted a male heir and I delivered a daughter.

I'd even been executed for reasons having nothing to do with my role as a healer. I participated or failed to participate in intrigues of power. Sometimes these intrigues worked to my advantage. More often than not, they brought me to ruin.

In later delves, I treated battlefield injuries from arrows, spears, swords, artillery and, eventually, firearms. I performed battlefield amputations and struggled to manage the diseases that often took a greater toll on armies than did combat with the enemy. I learned about venereal disease and the health implications of contaminated water supplies. I delivered babies under trying circumstances.

In every delve, I occupied a man's body. That meant that I never experienced life as a midwife, but as a 20th century physician, I partnered with midwives.

I knew that some of my educational delves were based on entertaining fictions. I spent years as an American surgeon in a mobile army surgical hospital on the Korean peninsula during the mid-20th century ideological contest between capitalism and communism. I lived in a tent, made gin in a homemade still, pursued sexual liaisons with attractive young nurses and engaged in a habitual stream of improbably comedic banter.

Near the turn of the 21st century I interned at a hospital in Seattle where a shifting web of romantic entanglements occupied as much of my attention as diagnosing and treating patients. After that, I worked at a teaching hospital in New

Jersey under a brilliant but misanthropic diagnostician. That delve focused more on medicine than the Seattle scenario did, but there was still plenty of sexual and administrative intrigue to navigate.

Thereafter, medicine developed from a grab-bag of techniques acquired through trial and error into more of a unified science. Left up to me, I would have started my education in an advanced, scientific context. I'm glad the decision wasn't mine to make. I can't articulate the value of trying to practice medicine in a pre-scientific context, but I trust the Is. I'm sure I learned valuable lessons in those early delves.

The emergence of artificial intelligence led to a renewed burst of warfare. As my tour of the history of medicine neared its conclusion, I encountered injuries and afflictions specific to space-based conflict. Techniques for repairing brain tissues and restarting interrupted cognitive processes further blurred the distinction between life and death, a border which started growing indistinct in the late 20th century. Prosthetic limbs that were inferior to the organic limbs they replaced evolved into cybernetic enhancements for which some enthusiasts discarded undamaged limbs. AI and human intelligence interpenetrated and gave rise to speciation events. Human populations moved out to Mars, the asteroid belt, the moons and trojan asteroids of Jupiter and Saturn, Uranus and Neptune, and eventually into the Kuiper Belt.

Like the Old West of North America, the expanding frontier was a violent zone, though also one where cooperation was the norm and violence the all-too-common exception. And like in the Old West, the violence of the new frontier took on a romanticized and fetishized place in human memory. Those conflicts formed the basis of entertaining stories that in turn informed my educational delves.

By inner system standards, I was a very young man. I

was 34 years old according to the Gregorian calendar, which is the one that made the most intuitive sense to me. That made me nearly twelve years old according to the Blackout calendar.

I felt like a young man in spite of having lived dozens of human lives. I half-remembered a sprawling cast of former spouses and parents, children and grandparents, colleges, friends, lovers and rivals. These memories did not weigh upon my sense of self or make me feel like an *old soul*.

I had an animating purpose. I grew to value healing for its own sake, but I undertook the project of learning to aid the sick and injured for purely practical purposes. I hungered to commune with alien life. Preferably alien intelligence, but even if the only truly alien life out in the galaxy was microbial, I would give up all of the comforts and pleasures of life in the Sphere for a chance to find it.

The expanding human presence in the solar system turned up life in various places, including the subsurface oceans of the moons of the giant outer planets, but it was all DNA-based life. It shared a clear evolutionary kinship with life on Earth. It was not alien.

I could not relate to the transhuman offshoot branches, but their place on the human family tree was undeniable. I spent time trying to communicate with them where I could, but this did not satisfy my desire to connect with alien intelligence.

Even before I practiced Neolithic medicine, I used drugs, ritual and brain computer interfaces to induce non-ordinary states of consciousness. I did it in the hopes of contacting non-human intelligence. The beings I encountered that way felt real, but I couldn't be sure they weren't creations of my own neurology.

No, the real aliens were *out there*. To find them, I would have to leave home.

My little pod had no active sensors. It did have a window, and I shivered with excitement when I saw my new home,

Persephone's Lost Nipple Ring, drawing near.

1.3.2 - Cook

Cook stopped drinking four watches before the scheduled end of the burn. Upon emerging from his coffin, he swabbed his armpits and nether regions with a deodorizing wipe, pulled on drawstring pants and a t-shirt, slipped into magnetic deck shoes without activating the floor locks and headed for the galley.

The ship had stopped accelerating, so there was no gravity. Cook propelled himself down the companionway with gentle brushes of fingertips against bulkheads. He knew from long experience to keep his speed down. He entered the galley headfirst, and without any conscious thought, he did a slow motion forward somersault, activated the deck locks on his shoes, and transitioned from floating to walking in one smooth motion.

It was still the middle of the night, ship's time. By tradition, regardless of the clock, the first meal after acceleration was breakfast. Coffee was his first priority.

Veteran crew members like Lake, Dobrovitz, and Zell knew to take their time making their way to the galley, but the new people might not realize that his acceleration couch opened at the same time theirs did. Cook didn't get a head start, but some of them would head straight to the galley for a cup of coffee. They'd be irritated if they had to wait for it to brew.

He'd prepped the coffee before retiring to his coffin. The new galley machinery could start brewing the coffee automatically either at a given time or when it detected that the ship was no longer accelerating. Cook didn't trust the new equipment enough to let it work in his absence.

The crew had four coffee choices; black, light, sweet or light and sweet. He'd posted a preference survey, but only a few people had bothered to complete it. So he prepared a preponderance of servings of black coffee. If someone wanted something else and they didn't complete his survey, they could drink black coffee. Or they could wait.

Paige, the new deckhand, completed and returned the nutritional preferences survey. She took her coffee light and sweet. Cook suspected that she wasn't used to drinking coffee. Morning coffee would be an extravagance for ag workers like her. Galters were used to extreme disparities in material circumstances, but Cook wasn't from Galtz. He didn't grow up with all that self-determination bullshit drilled into him. When he went ashore at Galtz, he saw a heavily armed society with a shocking tolerance for poverty and inequality.

When Cook heard the familiar rhythm of the captain's boots on the deck, he picked up the atomizer and gave it a couple of pumps to spray a fine coffee mist into the galley. Coffee served in squeeze mugs stayed nice and hot, but it didn't steam. You couldn't smell it before you tasted it. Just as Cook liked to prepare bacon on a griddle to send the enticing aroma wafting through the ship, he did what he could to make the galley smell like fresh coffee in the morning.

"Morning, Cook," the captain said.

"Mornin', Skipper."

"I'm going to need you to stay nimble and be ready to roll with the changes today, Cook."

"That don't sound good. What's goin' on, Skipper?"

"I don't know for sure. We don't have orders yet, but I've got an intuition that we're going to reorient and do another burn. There might be time for lunch, or we might have to skip it. Plan accordingly. I'll give you a heads up as soon as I know for sure."

"Got it, Skipper."

The captain walked across the galley and exited by a different hatchway than the one through which she'd entered. Only her floating hair gave away the fact that they didn't have gravity.

Cook grunted a single note laugh. In zero-g, most people wore magnetic shoes, but they only used them to anchor themselves in place when they wanted to stay in one spot. When you wanted to go somewhere else, you released the deck locks and propelled yourself head-first with gentle leaps and with occasional contact with the bulkheads.

Walking in deck lock shoes was awkward for newbies. Even for old hands, floating was quicker and easier. The captain could walk in zero-g just as quickly and gracefully as she could at 1g. Something about how the heel of her boot moved independently of the ball of the foot let her attach and detach in rapid succession. She even managed to maintain her exaggerated hip waggle.

Cook had seen her do it for years and didn't think about it much. Trix walked when others floated. When he did think about it, he knew that she must have very strong muscles in her hips and lower back to effect the illusion that she had her own personal gravity field. She must have trained hard to perfect that sashaying gait.

Cook smiled as he watched her exit the galley. He'd been inside her mouth a few times back in her Fixit Trix days, but he'd lost the need to scratch that particular itch. He had already stopped using her that way by the time Rex approached him and suggested that they help Trix break out of that role.

He still enjoyed the sight of her. Now Rex was trying to convince the captain to dress more conservatively. Rex would have to fight that battle without Cook's help.

1.3.3 - Paige

Paige moved in slow motion through a prolonged transition between the minimal consciousness of sleep and full awareness. She heard a kind female voice saying something she couldn't make out. A few seconds later she realized that the woman was saying her name.

"Paige, sweetheart, can you open your eyes?"

She did. She didn't recognize the woman, but she took comfort in her kind face and voice.

"Do you know where you are?"

She didn't. Wherever she was, the dimly lit space was warm. The kind woman floated at the side of her acceleration coach. *Acceleration couch?* She was on a ship. That realization set off a cascade of memories.

"The Persephone. I'm on the Persephone." Paige recognized Captain Nixon standing behind the kind woman. The closer woman was still unfamiliar to her.

"My name is Esmeralda. I'm a combat medic. You were underweight when you came onboard, and then half a week of near fasting and heavy acceleration took its toll on you, but I think you'll be okay."

Paige was still in her acceleration couch, but the compression sleeves on her legs were loose and the gel that enveloped her body and held her immobile had retracted. The plumbing attachment that covered her genitals during flight was no longer attached. She was wearing a thin tank top, but she grew uncomfortable when she realized she was naked from the waist down.

"Can I have my underwear, please?"

"Let Escamilla help you get cleaned up first, deckhand," Captain Nixon told her. "Your only duties until further notice are to put on weight and build your strength. Understood?"

"Yes, ma'am," Paige said. She forgot about the discomfort of being exposed as soon as she heard the captain's voice.

"You will report to Escamilla here and Cook until further notice. Get strong."

"Yes, ma'am."

The captain turned on her heel and walked out of the compartment, leaving Paige alone with the medic, Esmeralda.

Esmeralda said, "Okay, I'm going to help you shower. It's

alright. No need to be embarrassed. Can you raise your arms for me? There's a good girl."

Esmeralda pulled the tank top over Paige's head and gently guided Paige out of the acceleration couch and toward the shower. Normally, Paige would have bristled at being called a girl. She was small, but she was nearly six years old, well past puberty. She didn't have enough body fat to menstruate, but she was more than old enough. Now, however, she accepted Esmeralda's mothering attention and took comfort in it.

1.3.4 - Petrovic

Petrovic showered and dressed and made her way to the galley. She saw four rows of squeeze mugs set out on a counter. If she was interpreting Cook's glyphs correctly, the one she selected should be light but unsweet.

She pulled the mug free of its magnetic grip on the metal counter, gave it a squeeze and coaxed out a small, rippling globule. She pursed her lips and sucked gently at the undulating pale brown sphere. It was hot, but not dangerously so. And it was delicious. Of course they had top shelf coffee on the *Persephone*. They needed to get into combat soon or else she would fully succumb to the cruise ship fantasy.

She saw the kid who'd collapsed on the last acceleration break. The girl had been skinny when Petrovic first saw her. Now she looked practically skeletal. Petrovic had long since conditioned herself to eat on schedule whether she felt hungry or not. Hard g's messed with your appetite, and if you weren't feeling actively hungry when the all too short low-g breaks rolled around, it was easy to build up a caloric debt.

The kid, an ag laborer by the look of her, wasn't in any position to be skipping meals. She was strapped down to a seat at the table with a big metal cup with a fat straw in front of her. Anja was confident that Cook had set the kid up with something sweet and calorically dense like a milkshake. The girl looked miserable, her eyes downcast.

Petrovic's fellow marines were mostly anchored to the deck in front of a wall display that showed telemetry data from the flight deck along with video feeds from external cameras. According to the display they were almost 49 astronomical units from the Sun. This was easily the deepest Petrovic had ever traveled into Floater space. She was a soldier, and even in this relatively calm period in KB history, you didn't have to travel far to find armed conflict. Certainly not this far into Floater territory.

The marines were caught up in an animated discussion involving the Powers, Floaters and alien gods. Petrovic took no interest in their tedious conspiracy mongering. She turned back to the food counter. Cook was there combining ingredients inside of a closed box with a clear lid. He looked up at Anja with a sour expression. She reached down to her waist with both hands, grabbed the bottom of her tank top and pulled it up over her breasts.

Cook's eyes went wide. She'd meant to flash him, but when his scowl melted into a smile she was in no hurry to put the girls away. As long as his eyes were locked onto her nipples she was happy to prolong the moment. Cook laughed.

"Okay. Okay. Put 'em away," he said. "You would've fit right in around here before we had to go and get all respectable."

"That's what I hear. The captain in particular, right?"

"Skipper's earned her place, and you'll give her respect."

Cook's face threatened to revert back to his normal sour expression, so she made a show of reaching for the bottom of her tank top.

"Keep smiling, or I bring 'em out again," Petrovic said.

Cook's face lightened. This was Petrovic's third and final attempt to get Cook to share details of the captain's former role on this ship. She'd heard rumors in the garrison on Galtz about the slutty captain who was looking for top tier military talent. So far, she'd plied Joachim Zell, Hans Dobrovitz, Rex

Perkins and Cook for details of the sexual exploits of the infamous Patricia *Trix* Nixon, and to a man they had held firm and given up no details.

Petrovic respected that solidarity. She wanted to be a member of a crew that protected one another like that. She wasn't looking for dirt. They probably assumed she was probing for weaknesses to exploit, but that wasn't her intention.

Petrovic loved sex. She loved the act itself, but she also loved approaching potential new lovers. She loved playing wingman to established lovers to help them with new exploits. She responded most strongly to men, but she loved talking about sex with women. The captain clearly had a powerful sexual side to her, and Petrovic wanted to interact with that side of the captain's personality. She resolved to be patient.

1.3.5 - Rex

Rex floated into the space the crew used to call the *bridge*. They invoked that term ironically, as the place from which Trix used to pilot the ship was a cramped maze of ill-designed stations that were awkward to get in and out of, and typically Trix worked all of them.

The Bridge had been transformed in the recent refit. It was more open now. Where the previous cramped layout was haphazard, the new layout allowed crew members to move about without getting in each other's way. But now that it seemed like an actual bridge, Trix had taken to calling it *ops*. She called that level of the ship the *flight deck*.

Zell, who had a hand in the redesign, was quick to adopt the new vocabulary. Other veteran crew members vacillated between the old and new terminology.

At present, two of the new hires, Saz Kellemen and Dwyane Sparks, manned two of the newly designed stations in ops. Kellemen specialized in electronic warfare, and Sparks manned the point defense batteries. They were both strapped into their seats. Trix stood behind them, anchored to the floor looking from one man's station to the other.

Rex used the sound of his boots locking to the metal deck to announce his presence. Trix turned and made eye contact but said nothing. He could not read her expression. Rex glanced at the two marines at their stations.

"Should we be at alert? Do I need to have a team gear up?"

"No," Trix said.

"Do we have new orders?"

"Not yet."

"But you know what they will be."

"Yes, I'm pretty sure."

Rex waited for her to elaborate. After a long moment of silent eye contact she said, "My office."

Rex entered the office first. Trix followed and closed the hatch behind her.

His pulse raced. He consciously restrained his breathing. For years, whenever he and Trix entered a compartment together and closed the hatch it was so she could give him a blowjob. His body had not caught up to their new arrangement.

Trix looked at him. He knew she could read his state.

"Uncomfortable?" Trix asked.

He didn't trust his voice, so he nodded.

"Me too. Total abstinence was your idea. Still committed to it?"

His cock was fully engorged and pressing against his pants, straining to find its way to an erect stance. Trix looked from his eyes, down to his crotch, and back up again.

"Rex, we have to be able to work together. Sometimes we'll have to be alone together. How is this going to work?"

Rex swallowed but still didn't trust himself to speak. She pressed on.

"And this is for what again? My dignity? What about your

dignity? Are you going to float out of here with a hard on? Are you going to address your soldiers with a spot of pre-come soaking through your pants?"

"There are drugs I can take…"

Trix exploded in rage. "Are you fucking kidding me? You'd rather chemically castrate yourself than just let me suck your dick when you need it? That's fucking insane!" She paused and composed herself.

"And you're not going to fuck Petrovic?" she asked.

"A soldier under my command?" Rex said. "Of course not. Is that why you hired her?"

"It's not the only reason," she said.

Rex wanted to tell her that he would love to go back to their old arrangement, but only if she agreed to not to blow anyone else. Especially Zell. If she agreed, wouldn't that make them a couple? If they were a couple, he'd want more than just her mouth. She had never offered more.

He hesitated to ask for exclusivity with her. Why? Was he afraid she'd say no? He followed different conversational paths with her in his imagination but voiced none of them. Trix broke the silence.

"Executive officer Perkins, I have intel for you. Let me know when you are clear-headed enough to receive it," Trix said with exaggerated emotional distance.

"Go ahead, Captain."

AN IMPROBABLE RENDEZVOUS

1.4.1 - Paige

A velcro strap kept Paige from floating away from her seat at the metal galley table. A large steel tumbler magnetically adhered to the table top in front of her. It contained a sweet and frothy protein shake. Cook told Paige to take her time with it, but she was not to leave the table until the cup was empty.

At first she pulled greedily at the straw, gulping the delicious substance almost involuntarily, but she had to stop when she felt an intense pain in the center of her forehead. *Brain freeze*, Cook had called it. By the time it went away, she felt full. Whereas before she couldn't keep herself from pulling mouthful after mouthful through the fat metal straw, now it took an effort of will just to take a single swallow. The cup was huge and still nearly half full.

She heard Cook laugh, and Paige assumed he was laughing at her inability to finish the shake until she heard him say, "Okay, okay. Put 'em away."

Paige turned to look just in time to see the big woman marine, Petrovic, lower her tank top down over her breasts. Cook was smiling in a way she'd never seen him do before. Then his expression started back towards his normal gruff countenance. She turned away so they wouldn't catch her eavesdropping.

Petrovic was asking about the captain, and Cook wasn't giving out any information. Then their talk turned to food, and Paige returned to her private misery.

"Hey, little tiger," came a familiar voice. "How you feeling?"

Paige turned her head to face Petrovic. "Okay, I guess."

"Really? I would have guessed that you were feeling self-conscious because you needed help and now you're getting special treatment," the big woman said.

Paige's eyes widened. Petrovic acted like she had permission to say the things that most people keep to themselves. Paige marveled at her self-assurance. Petrovic seemed completely comfortable with herself.

Paige couldn't decide if Petrovic was pretty. Tall and muscular with close-cropped black hair, she was certainly an impressive physical specimen. Her breasts, which she had just shown to Cook, were small for her frame, and her hips didn't flare out the way the captain's did. She didn't wear any make-up, and she had a long thin scar to the left of her mouth that curved under her strong jaw. Her tank top revealed a prominent scar on her upper chest near her right shoulder.

"Can I give you a hug?" Petrovic asked.

"Uh… why?"

"Because I want to," Petrovic said and smiled.

"Okay," Paige said.

Petrovic was holding a breakfast burrito wrapped in a cloth napkin. She pushed it against the table top and held it in place with one finger for a moment and then gently pulled her hand away. The burrito stayed near the table top.

She then reached down and removed the strap holding Paige in place. She lifted Paige by the armpits and, when their heads were near the same level, Petrovic wrapped her large and powerful arms around Paige, enveloping her in warmth. Paige embraced the large woman back and pressed her cheek into Petrovic's shoulder.

"You can cry if you feel like it," Petrovic told her. "It's okay, I won't melt."

Paige felt her tears rise up and pool around her eyes. Petrovic moved one hand to the back of Paige's head and stroked her short brown hair. "It's okay, little tiger. You're okay."

They floated in the galley, embracing, for a long minute. Paige worried that people were staring, but she didn't dare take her face away from Petrovic's shoulder until she had control of her emotions again. She fought to stop her tears.

When she was in control, she released Petrovic, but the big woman squeezed her a bit harder, and stretched her neck a bit to rest her chin on top of Paige's head before she released her. Paige strapped herself back down to the seat. Petrovic took the cloth napkin from around her burrito and handed it to Paige.

Paige took the napkin and wiped her eyes. She dabbed tentatively at her nose, and Petrovic said, "Go on. Give it a big blow."

Paige did. It felt good to clear her nose. She tucked the used napkin between her leg and the seat below her. Petrovic took a hearty bite from her burrito.

Paige looked at her and said, "I don't think anybody ever asked permission to touch me before."

"Yeah, lots of people hug without asking. It's usually okay, but I like to make sure," Petrovic said.

"I like how you just say what you want to say," Paige said.

"Sometimes the circumstances aren't right for me to say what's on my mind. I hold back when I need to, but most people hold back way more than they should. Here, check this out."

Petrovic closed her right hand into a fist, crooked her arm and flexed her bicep. The mass of muscle pulled the skin of Petrovic's upper arm tight. Paige marveled at the transformation of the marine's arm.

"Would you like to feel it?"

Paige nodded.

"Then say it. Say, *I'd like to feel your muscle, Anja.*"

"I'd like to feel your muscle, Anja."

"Go for it."

Paige reached out and placed her hand on Petrovic's bicep. It was hard and warm. It felt good in Paige's hand.

"Wow," Paige said.

"I heard that you're trying to get strong too. I could train you. Would you like that?"

"Yes, please."

"Okay, we'll coordinate our schedules so we're both in the gym at the same time. But resistance training won't be enough. You can't bulk up without calories. You've got to eat more than you're used to eating. More than you feel like eating. You better hit that milkshake again."

Paige smiled as she sucked at the straw, enjoying the sweet, cold substance but mindful of the danger of brain freeze.

1.4.2 - Rex

Rex followed the captain back to the Bridge. He activated the intercom and his voice sounded throughout the ship. "Mr. Zell, report to Ops."

He could have sent Zell a direct message, but he wanted the entire crew to hear Rex issue an order to Zell. He wanted them to understand the chain of command on Persephone.

The Columbian marines were soldiers first. They each had a technical specialty so they could be useful outside of combat, but they were here to fight.

Joachim Zell was the exception. Zell defined himself as a trans-Neptunian geologist. He'd served aboard the *Nipple* for years pulling the most valuable substances out of big icy rocks. Just about every piece of a trans-Neptunian object had economic value, but the biggest paydays came when they found deposits of anything that could power a fission or fusion reactor or rare earth elements like lanthanum, neodymium, and yttrium. Zell had a knack for identifying those big payday rocks.

In addition to his crew share, Zell used to get a percentage of the profit from mining operations. That meant that Zell often made more than the captain. The man must be rich enough to buy his own ship. Rex wished that Zell would do just that.

When the DAO bought the *Nipple* they implemented a new compensation schedule. Instead of crew compensation being a share of the profits, each crew member received a flat fee plus a combat bonus if applicable. The new compensation structure represented a pay bump for everyone except Zell. So he spent the months it took to turn the *Nipple* into the *Persephone* training and getting certified in combat operations. By the time the ship was ready for her first post-refit mission, Zell had all the certifications needed to hire on as both a geologist and a marine.

When Zell arrived on the bridge, Kellemen and Sparks were both fixated on their screens. The captain was piloting the ship, making fine adjustments to their orientation but doing nothing to arrest their staggering velocity. After five days of continuous acceleration, they were speeding toward the Oort Cloud at nearly one and a quarter percent the speed of light. It was the fastest he'd ever traveled, but it felt like they were just easing up to a habitat dock.

Zell looked to Trix for instructions, but she directed his attention over to Rex with a quick motion of her eyes before turning her full attention back to aligning the ship with something Zell couldn't see.

"Look here, Zell," Rex said, gesturing at a screen at an open station. Zell saw what looked like a very small ship. An escape pod?

"We need you to take a mining pod and bring that thing into cargo bay two. We're depressurizing the bay now."

"No problem," Zell said.

He pulled a visor from its cradle at an ops station and fitted it over his eyes. He wiggled his fingers in an area between two sensors to activate the pod's manipulators. He made fists and rolled his hands in circles at the wrists. Rex could see on a video feed from the cargo bay that the pod's manipulators followed Zell's movements.

Zell released the magnetic lock and the pod drifted away from the bulkhead out into the center of the cargo bay. He repositioned the pod to face the cargo door.

"Depressurization complete," Sparks called out. "Opening the cargo bay doors."

The object was just outside the cargo bay. Trix activated a tiny burst from the maneuvering thrusters, and the object started to float into the bay.

Rex grinned. Was Trix showing off? Zell didn't even need to take the mining pod outside. He was just there to position the object in the bay.

The object was oblong, and one end had a flared, flat portion. Arrows on the object pointed away from the flattened end. "Guess that's the bottom," Zell muttered.

It was clear now that the object was a sarcophagus of some sort. It was larger than it needed to be to contain a body. It probably had a large cargo compartment, but its primary purpose was clear. It was designed to hold a passenger. That passenger was looking out through a view port near the top of the device, and waving.

Rex was still watching the feed from the mining pod's camera when he heard the beat of Trix's boots on the deck receding down the passageway. He grabbed a stun gun from a weapon's locker and hurried after her.

He propelled himself through the passageways faster than he normally would in order to catch up with Trix. She was headed for cargo bay two, and she was unarmed. Her metal monster of a right arm looked intimidating, but it wasn't designed for combat. Rex wasn't going to let her go in there alone.

1.4.3 - Trey

The *Persephone's Lost Nipple Ring* filled the window of my little pod. It loomed closer, and its cargo bay doors opened. A robotic worker floated in an open space beyond the door. It had two arms with hand-like manipulators. The hands flexed and fidgeted, and I realized that it must be tele-operated.

Of course. The Kuiper Belt humans did not use autonomous robots. They used human attention and labor even for routine and repetitive tasks.

The remote-piloted robot positioned my pod on the periphery of the cargo bay between stacks of containers secured to the floor with what looked like nets. I moved my head to take in as much of the space as I could through my little window. I'd seen environments like this in training delves. It was hard for me to accept that this wasn't a simulation. I was really on a primitive space ship in the Kuiper Belt where humans did not trust machine intelligence.

I was still floating inside my pod, but the base of my transport attached itself to the floor. I could not see the cargo bay door through which I'd entered the ship. I didn't know if it was still open or if the bay had atmosphere. I decided to wait until I saw humans in the bay before I broke the seal on my pod and stepped out.

An interior door opened, and a woman stepped into the cargo bay. A rush of air swept her hair forward. She must have opened the door before the bay was fully pressurized. I recognized this woman by her mechanical arm. This was Captain Nixon.

I'd rehearsed my self-introduction on the trip out, but one look at her expression told me not to use any of the humorous greetings I had in mind. For a moment the fact that I was floating and she was walking on the floor threw me off, but then I saw a robust looking man with close cropped white hair float through the doorway behind her. The man held something in his right hand that I assumed was a weapon. Probably something non-lethal, but I wasn't going to give him any reason to provide a demonstration.

I placed my open hand on a scanner and said, "Open."

The front of my pod swung up and away, and I took my first breath of *Persephone's* air.

Captain Nixon stood at the base of my upright sarcophagus, a meter below my eye-level. Now that she was right in front of me, I could see that she was in desperate need of medical attention. Her face and scalp were a patchwork of primitive synthetic skin grafts, with the damage being particularly acute on her right side.

Her right eye was clearly artificial, and her right ear was missing. The synthetic skin had no hair, and the captain had shaved the right side of her head to match the hairless left side of her scalp. I felt intense pity and compassion for this poor woman. That swell of empathy evaporated the instant she spoke.

"You're a doctor." Her voice was deeper than I'd imagined and hard. She hadn't asked a question, but I nodded anyway.

"Follow me," she said. She turned and walked out of the cargo bay. I pushed off from the back wall of my pod and floated after her. The white-haired man tracked me with hard, narrowed eyes.

AMATEUR HOUR

1.5.1 - Rex

Rex kept his focus on the newcomer and ignored his attempts at introduction. He followed Trix to her office and ushered the stranger through the hatch. The captain gestured at a plush sofa, and Rex pushed the man over to it.

"Better strap yourself down," Rex told him. The young man followed Rex's advice and secured himself to the sofa.

Trix pushed a button on her desk and her voice filled the crewed areas of the ship. "Attention crew. Deceleration in one minute. Prepare for 1g."

She marched out of the office and toward the Bridge. Rex remained standing but put his back to a bulkhead. He bent his knees slightly and waited for gravity to set in. He knew that Trix would ease into deceleration. Any free floating objects or crew would settle to the deck rather than come crashing down.

He looked at the young man on the couch. Rex judged that he was between eight and nine years old. His skin was slightly darker than average for a Galter, but not deep brown like that of the *Persephone's* demolitions expert, Jay Chukwuma. He had wide cheekbones that tapered down to a narrow chin. He had a full head of straight brown hair that would reach his collar when gravity returned. For the moment, it floated in a halo around his head. Even the more feminine women onboard, Esmeralda Escamilla, the medic, and Nora Lawson, the engine keeper, had shorter hair than this man.

Slowly, Rex felt himself starting to grow heavy, and he saw the young man sink into the plush sofa cushions. The man lifted his arms tentatively. No telling how long he'd been in zero-g.

Trix returned carrying a laminated card. "Begin recording," she said.

She locked eyes with the newcomer and said, "You're from the inner system." It was not a question.

The young man nodded, and Trix flipped the laminated card at him. It bounced off his chest and landed in his lap.

"I'm supposed to ask you these questions. I don't expect your answers will tell me anything useful. Well?"

"Uh," the young man said, scrutinizing the card. "Let's see. I've never been to Earth in the flesh, but I've spent a lot of time there in simulation. I'm sure it still exists. I can see it in the sky from my home orbital."

Trix leaned against her desk and tapped on it loudly, emoting impatience.

"Total population? You mean human population? Humans like me?"

"I don't mean anything," Trix said. "I'm just supposed to ask you these questions."

"You see, the human species has forked a few times. I really only ever interact with old style humans, like myself. A lot of the post humans don't normally take a physical form. I just don't have any way of even estimating how many of them exist on their own layers. My home orbital has around 8 million residents at any given time, but I don't know how many other orbitals and habitats there are these days. Several thousand, at least."

He stopped talking and resumed reading the questions on the card. Trix pulled a slate from inside the desk and walked over to the newcomer and snatched the card out of his hand. "That's enough. Stop recording."

The young man looked at Rex, seemingly for guidance. Rex

shrugged.

"I'm Trix, acting-captain of the Persephone. This is Perkins. What's your name?"

"Trey."

"Trey what?"

"Trey Powers."

Trix exhaled in exasperation.

"You're joking. Your last name is really *Powers*?" Trix said.

"Yes, why? Is there someone else here named Powers?"

"Nobody in the Kuiper Belt is named Powers. We call the artificial super intelligence that took over the solar system the *Powers*. Everybody hates the Powers. Don't tell anyone that your name is Powers. Do you have a middle name?"

"Yes, Carson."

"Great. Your name is Dr. Trey Carson."

"Okay."

"Doctor Carson, on behalf of a distributed autonomous organization, I am authorized to offer you this employment contract." Trix handed Trey the slate. "It's a standard contract. You will receive two crew shares for your services as ship's doctor."

"Two shares?"

"That's standard compensation for a ship's doctor. You're welcome to read the contract."

"I'm not a lawyer. I don't think I'd spot any legal traps. I'm not selling myself into slavery, am I?"

Trix snorted in a way that sounded suspiciously like a suppressed laugh. She looked at Rex.

"The pay and conditions on this ship are darned good. This is considered a plumb assignment," Rex told him.

"It's not like I'm weighing any other offers." Trey placed his left thumb at the bottom of the slate and read the acceptance text. The highlighted text reverted to normal as he read it. "I, Dr. Trey Carson, on this date…" The slate read the date aloud in a stiff, sexless voice. "do accept the conditions detailed in the above contract."

"That's it. Welcome to the crew." Trix pulled the slate from Trey's hand. "If anyone asks you where you're from… And they will… tell them, truthfully, that I told you to keep that information to yourself. Am I clear?"

"Yes, ma'am."

"Good. Can you walk?"

He undid his seatbelt and leaned forward, shifting his weight onto his bent legs. He straightened up slowly. A broad smile spread across his face and then lapsed into a null expression as Trey lost consciousness and flopped back down onto the couch.

"Rex, would you swing by the galley and grab a drink and a snack for the doctor? He'll be in medical."

"You got it," Rex said and walked out of Trix's office on slightly wobbly legs himself.

As Rex made his way to the galley he heard Trix's voice on the intercom. "Medic Escamilla, get your med kit and come to my office."

1.5.2 - Paige

Cook seemed to know when Paige had reached her actual limit and genuinely couldn't eat any more. "Keep going," he'd insisted the first three times she protested that she couldn't take another bite. After her fourth protest, he relented. He had just released her to Esmeralda's care when the captain's voice came over the PA calling Esmeralda to her office.

Esmeralda looked at Paige and bit her lip. "I think you'd better stay here," she said to Paige. Paige looked at Esmeralda with pleading puppy dog eyes, and Esmeralda relented immediately.

"Okay. The captain sounded pretty nonchalant. It's probably okay for you to come with me."

They arrived at the office and found the captain helping a young man to his feet. Paige had never seen him before. He had long hair. Not long like he was overdue for a haircut, but long on purpose like a woman's hair. His face was both chiseled, like the faces of several of the marines, but it was elegant in a feminine way. Paige didn't really have words to describe it. She'd never seen a man who looked like this.

"Esmeralda, Paige, this is Trey Carson, our new doctor," the captain said. "This is his first day in gravity after a couple of weeks of weightlessness. Please help him to medical. Rex will meet you there with something for the doctor to eat and drink."

Paige stood mute as Esmeralda approached the doctor and took hold of his wrist to check his pulse.

"Doctor Carson," Trix said, putting extra emphasis on the doctor's name, "This is our combat medic, Esmeralda Escamilla."

The man smiled and said something that Paige did not understand. Whatever it was, it made Esmeralda smile too.

"I don't actually speak much Spanish," Esmeralda said. "Much to my grandmother's disappointment. But I can tell that you're a silver-tongued devil, Dr. Carson."

Esmeralda looped the doctor's arm around her neck and over her shoulder. Escamilla wasn't nearly the physical specimen that Petrovic was, but she looked powerful with the doctor leaning against her for support. This man was no soldier. Escamilla helped him through the hatch into the passageway, leaving Paige in the office with the captain.

"Who is he, Captain?" Paige asked. "Where did he come from?"

"He's our new doctor, and we just plucked him out of space. The DAO sent us out here to retrieve him," Trix explained.

"He looks so… so… I don't know," Paige said.

"Weak?" Trix offered.

"He looks so… pretty," Paige said. "Can a man be pretty? There must be a better word."

"Where I come from, girls would call a boy like that *cute*."

"*Cute?*" Paige scrunched her brows. "Babies are cute. Kittens are cute." She wrestled with the concept and asked, "Do you think he's cute, Captain."

"Oh, yeah. He's a real cutie," the captain said with the hint of a smile. "And he's your doctor. Report to medical and let the cute doctor have a look at you."

"Yes, ma'am," Paige said with a grin and departed.

1.5.3 - Trey

By the time we reached medical, I didn't really need Esmeralda's support anymore. I let my arm drift from her shoulder down to her waist. She didn't object or even comment on it. We kept up an easy, flirtatious banter until we reached my new office.

"I'd offer you a tour," Esmeralda said, "but I've never been in here before. The captain took us around the ship, but she didn't bring us here. The equipment all looks brand new."

"It is," came Rex's voice from the passageway. "Expensive too. Quite the improvement over what we had before."

Hearing Rex's voice, Escamilla took a furtive step away from me. I smiled to let her know I wasn't offended. I didn't want to make trouble for her.

"I brought you a sports drink and a nut bar. I'll put them on your desk."

I followed Rex into the office, broke the seal on the sports drink and took several swallows. It was salty and probably enriched with electrolytes. Just what I needed. As I looked around the office, I spotted a piece of equipment I couldn't identify.

"What is that?" I asked, pointing.

"What is what?" Rex asked. "You mean the coffee maker? You don't have coffee makers in the... where you're from?"

Rex couldn't see Escamilla's face, but I could. It lit up with curiosity. I wondered how long the captain planned to keep my point of origin from the rest of the crew. It didn't seem like the sort of secret that would keep for long.

"Oh, right. Yes, we have coffee makers where I'm from. They just look a little bit different."

In fact, I was very familiar with coffee makers from my training delve at Seattle Grace Hospital. I could see the functional relationship between the device in my new office and the one in the intern lounge I remembered from my time in Seattle. The one here in my new office had a more robust design. It had to endure high-g acceleration as well as periods of weightlessness.

"The medical lab is across the p-way, and your quarters are at the end," Rex said. "If you have luggage you need to bring up from your pod, I'll accompany you to the cargo hold after supper, which starts in just under half a watch. In the meantime..."

Just then, a young woman peeked inside the office. "Hi. Captain said I should have the doctor examine me."

"Ah, yes. Sarge, if you'll excuse us," Escamilla said, glancing from Perkins to the exit.

"Of course," he said. "See you at supper."

As soon as Perkins was out of earshot, Esmeralda put her hand on my chest. "Doctor," she said, holding my gaze, "Do you know how long half a watch is?"

"Of course," I said, stalling for time. I reviewed what I knew of how humans in this part of the Kuiper Belt kept time. They had a 25 hour day divided into 10 watches. That meant a watch was 2 and half hours, so half a watch would be... "An hour and 15 minutes," I said after what I hoped wasn't too conspicuous a pause.

"What's an *hour*?" the young woman asked.

"Yes, doctor," Esmeralda said, her smile gone but her hand still on my chest, monitoring my pulse I now realized, a pulse which had just jumped and revealed my anxiety over a mundane question. "Explain to Paige what an *hour* is. That's not a unit of time we use on Galtz, or anywhere in the Pax that I know of."

"Look," I said, my habitual charm faltering in a moment of frustration. "I'm not good at this. The captain told me not to talk about where I'm from with anyone. She told me to invoke her name when evading questions. And, yes, I am evading. I admit it. What say we get this young lady over to the examination room so I can have a look at her?"

My office opened onto a small alcove. On the other side was the door to an examination room. The three of us relocated there, and Esmeralda helped Paige up onto the exam table.

"What's the issue?" I asked.

Esmeralda smiled and nodded at Paige, who said, "We did a high-g burn for 5 days, and I didn't eat every time we took a break. On our last break, I collapsed, probably from hypoglycemia."

"And..." Esmeralda prompted.

"And I was underweight to start with. Before Captain Nixon offered me a position on the Persephone, I worked as a rice farmer. You can't eat raw rice, so grain farmers can't sneak bites of the crops they're harvesting. We tend to be on the skinny side."

I nearly voiced my surprise that anyone out here in the Kuiper Belt worked as a farmer. I thought that profession only existed in historical simulations. Then I realized that I would just be giving myself away again. I looked at Paige's vitals on a monitor.

"I'd like to get a urine sample," I said. "Let's see, if I were a collection cup, where would I be?"

Esmeralda produced a collection cup and lid from under a countertop and directed Paige to a door. Once Paige was out of the examination room, I turned to Esmeralda.

"Everyone I've seen so far on this ship looks well fed. Why is she so severely underweight?"

"Like she said, she worked on a rice farm. That's a hard life. She couldn't sneak the occasional bite of what she was harvesting."

"But, don't agricultural laborers get regular meals?" I asked.

"They get what they can afford, and unskilled farm labor doesn't pay much. Paige got some math tutoring somewhere and scored high enough on a standardized test to draw attention to herself. Captain Nixon hired her on as a deckhand. I thought she was just a charity case at first, but she's actually really quick. She'll do a lot better on this ship than she would have in the rice patties back on Galtz."

I had no words. Esmeralda's tone was matter of fact. This situation didn't seem at all noteworthy to her. Just the way things are. I felt a mixture of pity, despair and anger before quelling my emotions.

Paige emerged from the toilet with her sample cup. She offered it to me, and I reverted to habitual responses I developed at Princeton-Plainsboro Teaching Hospital in New Jersey in the twenty teens. Instead of taking the sample cup Paige held out to me, I turned to Esmeralda and said, "Nurse, would you send that to the lab for analysis along with 400 mL of blood?"

"*Nurse*? I'm a combat medic. Maybe I should fabricate a tight little nurse's outfit and you can give me orders in a more discreet setting," Esmeralda said with a straight face while holding eye contact with me for flirtatious effect.

I cut off the response that sprang to mind before it could pass my lips. Flirtation and office romance in a medical setting was a very familiar and easy mode for me to adopt, but I remembered that this was baseline reality.

I hadn't spent much of my adult life in baseline reality, but when I was between delves, Zira monitored my biological state and anticipated my needs. She knew when I would be feeling horny and arranged to have a woman or two, usually two, arrive at just the right moment. I assumed the women were constructs, but they could well have been actual human women whose angels coordinated with Zira to meet the erotic needs of everyone involved. Before now, flirting was something I only did in simulated scenarios.

"Doooooctor?" Esmeralda brought me back to the present

moment, drawing out the word and giving my upper arm a squeeze.

"Ah, yes. Let's see, I think that's a refrigerator there. I took the sample cup from Paige, bent down and pulled a handle on a glass door. The little door swung open, and a light came on inside revealing empty racks for various types of containers. I found one that fit the sample cup and slotted the specimen into place. I closed the door and stood up to find Esmeralda looking at me with her right hand extended toward me. There was an adhesive label stuck to the tip of her index finger.

"You really do need a nurse, don't you, doctor? Let me put a label on that sample container for you."

"Right. Of course. Sorry, I'm usually not like this. Normally, I adapt to new scenarios very quickly. I'm just a little out of sorts, I guess."

"*Scenarios*?" Paige asked.

"I meant *situations*. Now," I said, opening and closing drawers, "where can I find a butterfly needle?"

"A butterfly needle? What's that?" Paige asked.

"I'd like to do a blood draw," I said without looking up from my search.

"Oh, right," Esmeralda said. "Those are probably in the supply closet, next to the leech jar."

I straightened up and looked around. "And the supply closet is where?"

"That was a joke. We can take a blood sample with the cuff."

Esmeralda slipped a cuff over Paige's arm. Paige winced as the needle punctured her vein. An empty cartridge attached to the cuff filled with blood. The cartridge turned in its housing once, and at the end of the revolution it had a label attached to it showing Paige's name and the time of the draw. When Esmeralda slipped the cuff off of Paige's arm, a small circular bandage already covered the puncture site.

Come on, Trey, I told myself. *Focus. Kuiper Belt, present day.*

"Doctor, I think I should show you to your quarters so you

can lie down for a bit before supper."

"That's probably a good idea," I agreed. Esmeralda took my arm and steered me toward the passageway. We stopped when Paige spoke up.

"Doctor?"

"Yes?"

"I've never seen a man with hair like yours. May I touch it?"

I turned back to Paige, smiling. "Of course. Men don't have long hair on your... uh... habitat?"

"Some do," Paige said, "but they're usually very poor or not right in the head. If they have long hair, it's dirty and tangled. Not like yours."

Paige reached out and touched my hair. Esmeralda rested her chin on my shoulder and combed her fingers through my hair in long, sensuous passes.

"May I touch your cheek?" Paige said.

"Yes," I said. "Go ahead."

I didn't like shaving, so Zira altered my genome so that the hair on my cheeks and neck was soft and fine.

"You don't grow a beard?" Paige asked.

"Ha! No," I laughed. "I mean, I could if I wanted to, but that's not my look, and besides, soft cheeks are better for..." I stopped myself.

Children were not a part of my experience in baseline reality, but I knew from my delves that speaking frankly to children about the details of sex was frowned upon. Paige wasn't exactly a child, but her short stature, slight build and lack of breasts made her look very young to my eyes.

"Better for what?" Paige asked.

"Paige, sweetheart," Esmeralda said. "The doctor needs to rest. Why don't you head back to the galley. I'll meet you back there after I show him to his cabin."

"Oh, I'd like to see the doctor's quarters," Paige said.

"I don't think..." Esmeralda started, but I interrupted.

"Sure, come along, Paige."

I was happy for the chaperone. I could feel my body

responding to Esmeralda's touch, and I realized I really should get my bearings before I got sexually entangled with anyone. Zira emphasized that point to me as I was preparing for this adventure.

I sometimes recognized the women I had sex with, but when the sex was over and everyone was satisfied, they went away. Esmeralda, I realized, would still be here afterwards, and I would have to interact with her professionally.

This wasn't Seattle with its anonymous multitudes from which new love interests emerged and disappeared back into. I was on a spaceship in the Kuiper Belt. This was going to be one long bottle episode.

1.5.4 - Petrovic

"Ha! You cockblocked her!"

Petrovic laughed and tousled Paige's hair. Petrovic appreciated physical shows of affection, but Paige was clearly starved for them. After the third time Paige asked for permission to initiate a specific bodily contact, Anja told her that she had blanket permission to touch her however and whenever she wanted to.

Paige took full advantage of the privilege. She greeted Anja with a hug no matter how recently they'd last seen each other, and whenever she talked to Anja, Paige placed a hand on her arm or thigh. Sometimes she wanted to hold hands, and Anja obliged without hesitation.

Petrovic was used to women wanting to touch her, and she usually discouraged it unless there was a male audience she was looking to arouse, but there was nothing sexual in Paige's need for contact. Not as far as Anja could tell, and Anja knew sex.

Petrovic did a quick headcount. The entire crew was present for supper save two. Nora, the engine keeper, was absent. No surprise there. She rarely left the portions of the ship that were her domain. The fission reaction that propelled the ship happened at the very back of the ship behind copious radiation shielding, but the engines themselves ran the length of the ship, and there were access corridors that only the engine keeper ever had reason to pass through.

Petrovic pictured Nora with a cat to keep her company, but, much to her surprise, *Persephone* did not have a cat. Petrovic had rarely known a spaceship of any size that didn't have at least one cat, but most spaceships in the KB didn't do high-g burns for days on end. Even with a baby acceleration couch, she didn't think a cat would do well under those conditions.

The other missing crew member was Jay Chukwuma, the explosives expert and the only black man onboard. His dark skin was a prestige trait. It advertised the Chukwuma family's wealth. They must have paid quite a premium to the Nixians to maintain that deep skin tone generation after generation.

Petrovic had planned to proposition Chukwuma at the first opportunity. Well, if Nora had gotten there first, no hard feelings. Given the male to female ratio onboard, Petrovic wasn't worried about being left out in the cold. Plus, she knew from experience how unexpected opportunities tended to present themselves.

This wasn't Petrovic's first tour as a ship's marine. All of the new marines in *Persephone's* crew were on furlough from the Galtz militia. In addition to paying crew shares to the marines, the captain had paid a furlough fee to the garrison's Commandant for each of his soldiers she recruited.

Ship's marines were likely to see action, and renting out soldiers not only brought in income for the militia, but it kept the troops in the right frame of mind. Galtz had a reputation for military prowess. Raiders were unlikely to target it, and they were not at war with any habitats or coalitions. Having soldiers with combat experience was more than worth the loss of furloughed personnel who got killed on assignment.

"Anja," Paige asked, bringing Petrovic back to the present, "Have you ever heard of an *hour*?"

"What? "An *hour*?" Yeah, sure. Like *happy hour* or *amateur hour*?"

Page's expression showed no sign of recognition.

Petrovic continued, "It's an old word that isn't used much anymore in the KB, but it's a unit of time like a watch or a minute."

"How long is it?"

"I don't know. I think it might not have an exact length, like a *while* or a *bit*," Petrovic speculated. "But I really don't know. Why?"

"Esmeralda asked the Doctor if he knew how long half a watch was, and it seemed like he didn't really know. He had to figure it out, and when he did, he said that half a watch was equal to an *hour* and fifteen minutes. I think Esmeralda suspected something and was testing him," Paige explained.

"That is interesting," Petrovic said with an emphasis on the word *is*.

"What do you think it means?"

"Hmmm..." Petrovic mused. "One thing occurs to me, but it's not anything I should say out loud. It would get some of these fools worked up, and not in a good way."

"What is it? I won't tell anyone, I promise," Paige said.

"I trust you, little tiger, but I need you to trust me too. I need to keep this to myself until I know more," Petrovic said.

"Okay," Paige said, sounding a little deflated. "I trust you too."

Petrovic looked over at the new doctor who was seated at the captain's table between Captain Nixon and Sergeant Perkins. He was smiling and chatting with the captain even though, by the looks of it, she wasn't giving him much encouragement. Perkins did not look happy. No surprise there. He was clearly feeling possessive about the captain and didn't like this comely young man trying to charm her.

It made sense that the new doctor would be seated at the captain's table, but Escamilla, Zell, Kellemen and Sparks were there too. That didn't add up.

It made sense that the captain might have been trying to cultivate a relationship with Dwayne Sparks, given his family connections. But like Kellemen, and Perkins, Sparks didn't look happy to be there.

Petrovic remembered that Rex Perkins summoned Zell to the bridge just before the maneuvering thrusters fired. What were Kellemen and Sparks' occupational specialties? Anything that would put them on the bridge? Petrovic remembered that Sparks specialized in point defense, and Kellemen's specialty was cyber warfare. So, yes, they were both on the bridge when the new doctor came on board.

The exterior camera feeds to the galley's display wall went dark just before the ship started to maneuver. Nobody but the men seated at the captain's table saw the ship that they must have rendezvoused with to pick up the doctor. And Escamilla, the medic, had attended to the new doctor and spoken to him long enough to work out that there was something out of the ordinary about him.

"Quarantine," Petrovic muttered.

"What?" asked Paige.

"Everyone at the captain's table is in social quarantine. They're here in the galley with us, eating a meal in clear view of everyone, but they're sequestered. Off limits."

"Oh, wow," said Paige. "What do you think is going on?"

"Let me ask you something, little tiger," Petrovic said. "Why did you get in Esmeralda's way when she wanted some alone time with our pretty new doctor?"

"I didn't like the way she was touching him without permission."

"That's not how I do things, but that's how pretty women like Escamilla let a man know they're interested. It's normal," Petrovic said.

"I know. I just didn't like it. I guess I was a little bit jealous."

"You *guess*? Take a minute to revisit that feeling. Was it jealousy?"

Paige took her hand off of Anja's thigh and placed both hands in her own lap. She looked down at her tray and sat with her feelings the way Anja had taught her to do.

"Yes," Paige said. "I felt jealous."

"You didn't want Escamilla to fuck the doctor?"

"No," Paige admitted.

"Escamilla has been good to you. You like her, right?" Paige nodded. "Imagine her feeling pleasure. See her face. Her eyes are closed. Her mouth is open and relaxed. She's moaning. She feels really good. Stay with that. How does it make you feel to think about Escamilla feeling pleasure?"

"It feels good," Paige admitted.

With so many people clustered around the captain's table, Anja and Paige nearly had this table to themselves, but Petrovic noticed Drake Antal, the embarkation specialist and one of the youngest marines on the crew, failing to hide the fact that he was eavesdropping. Petrovic didn't say anything or give any indication that she was on to him. This was good information for him too.

"That feeling is called *compersion*. How do you like it compared to the jealousy you felt earlier?"

"I like this better," Paige said.

Petrovic nodded. "It isn't wrong to feel jealous. It's a legitimate feeling, but you can't feel jealousy and compersion at the same time."

NO FRIEND OF DOROTHY

1.6.1 - Rex

Rex did not like this situation one bit.

He didn't fault the captain. She'd shown him the orders. They had accelerated at high-g for days to be at the right place at the right time to retrieve this man.

Rex didn't even know how to begin to calculate the expense of refitting this ship, recruiting this high-value crew, and expending the energy and reaction mass to get the *Persephone* to where she needed to be to pick up this man who introduced himself as Trey fucking *Powers!* A man who arrived at the outer edge of the Kuiper Belt in a pod with no propulsion.

The Powers flung him out here, and that means he is, in some sense, working for Them. *In league with the Powers*, is how Sparks and Kellemen were surely framing it in their minds. They both sat across the table, scowling and muttering to one another under their breath.

The DAO, the legal owner of this vessel, surely knows this man is from the inner system. Rex understood that a distributed autonomous organization is a legal entity, not an actual person. The DAO didn't *know* anything any more than a corporation knows anything, but the three parties that controlled more than half the voting shares, the ones Trix called the *Whales*, must know.

The Whales might even *be* the Powers. This ship and everybody onboard might actually be working for the AI usurpers, the ones that deliberately threw the entire KB into famine and war all those years ago. Nobody on this ship would knowingly agree to serve the Powers, but all indications pointed to exactly that.

And Escamilla wanted to fuck the newcomer. She had figured out that he was from the inner system, and she still wanted to jump in bed with him. Good thing the little ag rat, Trix's charity case, got jealous and threw a spanner in the works. Rex had watched the security footage.

And the captain was keeping the truth about the new doctor a secret. It would be impossible to keep it from the crew for long, but the longer she waited to tell them, the worse the fallout would be when the truth finally came out.

Kellemen and Sparks are rabid conspiracy heads, and she has them under practical house arrest. She's keeping them on the bridge except for meals and rack time. They can't even work out in the gym.

This can't go on, Rex told himself, but he certainly wasn't going to undermine Trix's authority.

This was a bad situation with no clear and acceptable resolution that he could see.

1.6.2 - Trey

Zira told me to expect hostility, and the body language of three out of the four men at the captain's table at supper communicated exactly that.

Rex, the captain's right hand man, was a ball of stress. I imagine that he was afraid the crew would react badly to my presence once they learned I was from the inner system, but there was something more. Sexual jealousy?

I was definitely not flirting with the captain, but Rex

tensed every time I spoke to her. I kept up a steady stream of pleasant conversational banter with the captain and Esmeralda, but nothing more than that.

The captain gave only minimal replies in spite of my invitations for her to take a leading role in the conversation. I kept my questions casual, merely intending to fill what would otherwise be a tense silence.

Esmeralda more than carried her share of the conversation. She often talked past the captain, who was sitting between us, directly to me. I think she was hoping the captain would offer to trade places with her so she could sit next to me. That didn't happen.

The two younger men across the table whose names I didn't catch were actively hostile towards me. I could tell by their size that they were members of the genetically-modified soldier caste. They did not participate in the table conversation, but passed muttered comments to one another as they ate and glowered.

Another man, not as young, also sat at the captain's table. He was physically fit, but he wasn't genetically enhanced like the younger men. He was the only man at the table who did not project hostility toward me. His name, I soon learned, was Joachim Zell, a geologist. He operated the robot that positioned my pod in the cargo bay.

Other than Rex, Zell was the only man on board with cultivated facial hair. The cook had several days growth of beard, but it seemed like the result of neglect rather than design. Zell had the beginnings of what I would call a Van Dyke beard, and where Rex's hair and beard were pure white, Zell's were jet black. Apparently he had recently shaved his beard and was re-growing it now that they were away from the Galtz habitat.

The captain stood up and announced to the crew that we would continue our current 1g deceleration for another two days but that they should prepare for another extended high-g burn. She used that topic to introduce me.

"As you can all see, we have a new crew member. This is our new ship's doctor." She gestured to me, and I stood up.

"Hello, everyone. My name is Trey Carson. You're welcome to call me Trey. I'm from Mayberry habitat, which is a long way from here, so I might not get all of your references or understand your jokes, but I grew up speaking a dialect of English that is pretty similar to how people talk on Galtz. We should be able to communicate pretty effectively."

All of that was true. I felt awkward saying *Mayberry habitat* in place of *Mayberry orbital*, and, of course, I was telling a whopper of a lie by omission, but at least the captain agreed that I wouldn't have to say anything that was indisputably false. I was brought up to tell the truth.

I continued, "I've reviewed all of your medical records, and most of you seem to be in excellent health. If you have any concerns, please come see me. I will be monitoring everyone's vital signs during the next burn and administering bespoke medications to counter acceleration stress.

"The medications are completely optional. I understand that you don't know me, and if you don't want me administering medications to you on this coming burn, I won't take even the slightest offense. If you look at the cuff that goes over your arm in your acceleration couch, you'll see an on/off switch. They're all set to *off* right now. If you don't want in-flight medications you don't need to change anything. If you would like for me to be able to adjust your medications between breaks, you just need to switch the cuff to the *on* position."

I heard a low chorus of whispers which the captain brought to an immediate halt with a single loud tap of one of the heavy metal fingers of her right hand against the table top.

"That's about all, I guess. Remember, my door is always open, and I'm looking forward to getting to know all of you better."

I sat down to the sound of a few individuals clapping. It

never reached critical mass to become proper applause, and the clapping tapered off quickly.

After dinner, Rex and Mr. Zell escorted me down to the cargo hold so that I could start moving my things up to the medical bay and to my quarters. Neither one spoke to me or to one another on the walk down. There was no issue with my clothing, but Rex balked when I wanted to move some specialized research and diagnostic equipment from my pod up to the medical lab. He said he'd talk to the captain and we could get the equipment later if she gave her okay.

He inspected my vacuum suit with interest. He told me that I should keep it in my quarters. He also suggested that I practice putting it on in a hurry and that I should time my performance and keep a record of my times. He said they would conduct ship-wide suit-up drills with and without gravity and even without lights.

1.6.3 - Cook

Cook did not eat with the crew. While everyone else ate their dinner, he stood watch on the kitchen side of the invisible border between the dining and food prep areas.

New crew often assumed that they could stroll into his kitchen in search of this or that. Cook intercepted any would-be trespassers into his realm with a, "Whatcha need?"

He took satisfaction watching people enjoy his food, and his sentinel post at the sacred threshold positioned him to observe the faces of the new marines as they tasted his baked tilapia.

Cook grumbled at the uneaten garlic bread at lunch. The Columbians were all gym rats and macronutrient prima donnas, so he'd gone easy on the breadcrumbs and Parmesan when preparing the fish for the oven.

He fixed one pan of fish as he saw fit, confident that some of the veteran crew knew how to enjoy food without worrying about their body mass index or whatever. At least the Columbians didn't touch the salt-shakers on the table. Cook hated it when people salted his food, but he had to give them the option in order to provide them with a proper dining experience.

He watched Hans Dobrovitz, a bean pole of a man regardless of how much he ate. Dobrovitz probably didn't even know what deck the *Persephone's* new gym was on. Hans closed his eyes after every bite, as if to savor a fleeting taste of Ithaca on a perilous journey far from home. That's the response Cook lived for.

Cook surveyed the faces at the captain's table. The mood there was grim despite, or maybe because of, the ship's new doctor who sat between Trix and Rex.

The newcomer tried to charm everyone with his dinner table conversation. Cook could see that the pretty Columbian marine, Escamilla, was interested. Cook was sure all the young male marines could see it too. Maybe that's why the two hulking youngsters at the captain's table looked so put out.

Rex and Zell both sat at the captain's table. That alone was sure to ratchet up the tension. If Trix weren't here, those two would not be sitting anywhere near each other. Maybe that's why Trix took most of her meals in her office.

Persephone's chain of command was fuzzy. Trix was at the apex, no question, but both Rex and Zell each had a reasonable claim to the number two spot.

Rex was in charge of the marines, and technically that included Zell, but Zell was much more than just a ship's marine. Trix let Zell design the whole level below the flight deck for his mining and surveying work. Dobrovitz and the new guy, Li, both reported to Zell.

Cook knew that that wasn't the only source of the tension between Rex and Zell. It went back to the *Fixit Trix* days, when if you had a hard on, Trix would *fix it* for you, and you didn't even have to ask nicely. Cook was glad those days were done.

Cook studied the new doctor. Unlike the Columbians, he had nothing against gay men. Cook wasn't sure the new doctor was gay, but he was certainly effeminate. His long, straight hair, which he wore loose, reached his collar. He wasn't skinny, but he didn't seem to care about maintaining a muscular build or projecting machismo the way the Columbians did. Even Escamilla had broader shoulders than the doctor, and she was dainty by Columbian standards.

To Cook, the new doctor looked like a sheep among wolves, and yet he seemed oblivious to the danger of his situation. Everybody knew not to give Columbians any reason to suspect sexual deviance, and yet the doctor's every gesture oozed femininity. Where was he from that he felt safe behaving that way in front of the Columbians? The fact that Escamilla liked what she saw wasn't winning the doctor any friends in this crowd either.

After dinner, Cook noted that Rex left with the doctor. As a bodyguard or minder?

As the crew dispersed, Paul Lake approached Cook. Before the refit, the total fighting force onboard the *Nipple* amounted to Rex and Paul. Paul wasn't as old as Rex, but he was older than this new batch of Columbian soldiers from the Galtz militia. Like Rex, Paul was fit for his age, but he didn't have the genetic advantages of the Columbians.

"Hey, Cook. The fish was delicious," Paul said. "Need any help cleaning up?"

"Nah, but I wouldn't mind comparing notes on a thing or two," Cook said.

"Looking for a scuttlebutt update?" Paul asked with a smile.

"Something like that," Cook said. "What do you think of our new doctor?"

"Not my type," Lake said after a quick check to make sure no one but Cook would hear. "He seems amiable, but clueless."

"True. You think he's a friend of Dorothy?" Cook asked.

"Definitely not," Paul said.

"You seem awfully sure," Cook said.

"Trust me," Paul said. "I can tell. So can that pretty new marine. What's her name?"

"Esmeralda," Cook said.

"That's right," Paul agreed. "Esmeralda knows what's what. I bet she finds plenty of reasons to go to medical."

"She is a medic," Cook said. "Our new doctor might need some mouth to mouth, if you know what I mean."

Paul rolled his eyes.

Now it was Cook's turn to make sure nobody was listening.

"Any idea why we need so much muscle on this trip? I'm glad we're in funds these days, but what can we be up to that we need a squad of Columbian death dealers?"

"Believe me, Cook. If I knew, I'd fill you in," Lake said. "I'm not even sure Trix knows, but whatever it is, the pay is too good to turn down."

"The money is good," Cook agreed. "I'm sorry you can't be yourself around this bunch."

"Oh," Lake said with a sly grin, "It's not so bad."

THE CORPUS

1.7.1 - Rex

Rex sat on the sofa in Trix's office. Trix, behind her desk, was letting Sparks rant about the *Chaos gods* in the *void of Yam*. He seemed to have a whole cast of characters doing battle in his imagination. They were divided into two opposing teams, and the bad ones had the advantage outside of the Curtain, but even more so out here on the outer edge of the Kuiper Belt.

Rex made no effort to keep track of the figures of Sparks' imaginary pantheon. Instead, he watched the man's body language and stayed ready to intervene should he turn violent.

"The demons of Mot possessed the thinking machines and made them turn against humanity and build the Curtain. That left the humans in the outer system at the mercy of Tannin, that dragon of Chaos. Shapash still wanted to share her healing light with the humans of the KB, and she managed to send out the four beams for a time, but then Tannin tricked Shapash. That's what caused the Blackout and the Tribulations."

Trix locked her face in her usual rigor mortis so as to give nothing away, but Rex was sure she was growing impatient with the young Marine's ravings. She relaxed her facial muscles just enough to ask, "And you know this how?"

"I do my own research," the young marine stated with what sounded to Rex like a note of defiance.

Defiance against what? Rex wondered to himself. *Against common sense.*

"Research..." Trix let the word hang in the air for a moment, "On the Chans?"

"Not *just* the Chans," Sparks insisted. "There's a whole corpus of printed materials."

"A *corpus*," Trix repeated.

Sparks was certainly no scholar. Rex didn't think *corpus* sounded like the sort of word a kid like Sparks would use in spontaneous conversation.

"And do you have any of these printed materials onboard?" Trix asked.

"Yes, ma'am. Back in my quarters."

Trix turned to Rex. "Sergeant Perkins, please escort Mister Sparks to his quarters and retrieve this corpus. This information may prove crucial to the completion of our mission."

"Yes, Captain," Rex said.

She was going to humor him. Rex wasn't sure that was a good idea, but he didn't know what to do with the kid.

Still, Rex was happy to have something that took him off the flight deck. He knew that if Trix dismissed Sparks leaving Rex alone with her that they'd be shouting at each other within minutes. He hated that they'd fallen into that pattern, but every time they were alone together, their emotions went to maximum, and anger was the only one they let themselves express.

1.7.2 - Petrovic

Petrovic let Paige take point. Doctor Carson wasn't in his office and Petrovic didn't plan to approach him in his quarters. The pretense for this visit was legitimate medical business, and it needed to start in his work space.

When Petrovic and the other Columbians first came

onboard the *Persephone*, that captain gave them a cursory tour, but they'd skipped the medical level. Petrovic had never been to this part of the ship. For Paige, it was her second time here today.

Seeing that the doctor wasn't in his office or the examination room, she moved down the passageway and cycled the hatch to a different compartment. A plaque by the hatch identified it as the medical laboratory.

Paige poked her head inside and said, "Hi, Trey. I hope it's not too late. Can I talk to you?"

Petrovic heard the doctor answer, though she couldn't make out what he said. Paige stepped over the threshold into the compartment and Petrovic followed. Petrovic didn't know what any of the equipment in here was, but she could tell that it was all brand new.

"Hello again, Paige," the doctor said, smiling. "Who have you brought with you?"

Paige turned and put a hand on Petrovic's arm. "This is my friend, Anja. She's here to seduce you, but I wanted to talk to you first."

Petrovic snorted. Radical honesty didn't mean premature disclosure, but she would rather see Paige err on this side of the line.

"Pleased to meet you, Anja. Petrovic, isn't it? I was looking at your file before supper."

"Probably not as much fun as what Esmeralda had in mind," Petrovic said.

"I'm sorry," Paige said. "I overstepped."

"Not at all, Paige. What can I do for you?" the doctor asked.

"I was wondering if you've had a chance to sequence my genome," Paige said.

"As a matter of fact, I have. I was surprised that there was no genetic work-up in your medical records. Everyone else has one."

"We had a first aid station on the farm," Paige said. "But it was pretty basic. You're the first actual doctor I've ever met,"

Paige said. "We didn't get any..."

Trey didn't jump in right away, but when Paige's pause didn't resolve itself, he said, "Holistic care?"

"Holistic care," Paige repeated the phrase. Petrovic knew she was filing it away for future use.

"What did you want to know about your genome?" Trey asked.

"Earlier, you said that..." Paige paused, and Petrovic imagined her summoning up new vocabulary and assembling her sentence in advance rather than constructing it on the fly. "...that intermittent malnutrition had stunted my growth and disrupted the normal development of puberty."

The doctor raised one eyebrow. "I did indeed, in pretty much those exact words."

Petrovic smiled. No charity case here. The captain picked out a diamond in the rough.

"Now that I'm getting more than enough food, will I start growing again?"

"You'll certainly put on muscle and fat. Normally, a woman has achieved her full height by the time she's your age, so nutrition alone probably won't get you to your full height potential. Do you want to be taller?"

"I want boobs," Paige said.

"Ah, okay," Trey said. "Say more about that."

"Everybody treats me like a kid, but I'm not. I'm nearly 6 years old. I should have a woman's body, but look at me." Paige looked down and gestured at her torso.

"And you want me to run a simulation to see what kind of figure you'll develop with proper nutrition." Paige nodded, and the doctor continued, "Well the bad news is that your genetic potential doesn't really matter now that you've missed several developmental milestones."

"*Milestones?*" Paige asked.

"Uh... Markers along a path. Major events in your development."

"Hmm... *Milestones*," Paige repeated, and Petrovic grinned, expecting to hear the word come out of Paige's mouth in a novel but appropriate context in the near future.

"But the good news is," Trey continued, "that DNA is not destiny. Right now, I'm most interested in seeing you put on muscle and improve your cardiac fitness, but once that's on track, I can design a course of RNA treatments to help you develop more feminine proportions and even increase your height."

"I'm okay with being short," Paige said. "I just want people to see me as a woman instead of a little kid."

"That's perfectly understandable. Do you have a specific body type in mind, or do you..." the doctor began.

"I want to look like the captain," Paige interjected. "I mean, not the metal parts, obviously."

"She does cut quite the figure, doesn't she?" Trey said.

"I don't know that expression, but she looks powerful. I want to look like that," Paige said.

"Well, we can certainly get you into the same ballpark," Trey said. "We can get you pretty close to what you have in mind."

"Thank you, Trey. May I hug you?"

"You're welcome, and yes. I'd like that."

Paige stepped forward and wrapped her arms around the doctor's torso and gave him a robust squeeze. Petrovic noticed that the doctor put a hand on her back but did not envelope her in a reciprocal hug. She knew from experience that feeling the young woman's skeletal frame could be a disquieting experience.

"Okay, I'll see you tomorrow. Good night, Trey," Paige said and turned to give Petrovic a hug. "Good luck, Anja," she said and departed.

1.7.3 - Cook

"Hi, Cook," Paige said as she walked behind the serving counter into the food prep area. Now that she was reporting directly to Cook and her only job was to eat and gain weight, she had privileged access to the kitchen. Any leatherneck caught in Cook's domain was going to get an earful, but Paige could stroll right in.

"Hey, killer," Cook said. "Where's your shadow?"

"You mean, Anja? She's up in medical talking to the doctor."

"I'll bet she is," Cook said with a salacious grin. "She's a wild one. You can learn a lot from her. She's good with people."

"She's a slut," Paige said.

"Easy there, killer," Cook said. "She's just having a little fun."

"I'm not trying to shame her," Paige said. "She identifies as a slut. She told me that women use accusations of sexual promiscuity to undercut other women, but that only works if you pretend you don't like sex. Anja likes sex, and she doesn't try to hide it. She's honest about who she is and what she wants."

"She told you all that?" Cook asked.

"Yes."

"Speaking of our pretty boy doctor, he sent me some notes about your diet. We'll work those into the rotation tomorrow, but for now, how does a cup of hot chocolate with whipped cream grab you?"

Paige's face lit up, and that was all the answer Cook needed.

Later, as Paige sat in the recesses of the food prep area, enjoying the sweet drink, Cook took a large mug from a cupboard and half filled it with coffee. He then took two bottles from a cabinet. He poured white liquid from one bottle into the coffee cup and brown liquid from the other.

"Do me a favor, killer," Cook said to Paige. "Take this to the captain. Tell her it's lucky coffee straight from the Emerald Isle."

"The what?" Paige asked.

"The green island. She'll know what's what. Go on now."

1.7.4 - Paige

Paige was happy for any excuse to see the captain. Before they got the order to do a hard burn out to the edge of the KB, Paige spent most of her waking watches with the captain, learning everything she could about navigation and ship's operations.

Since the burn, she'd only caught passing glimpses of the captain, and every time, the captain looked stressed. It wasn't just the captain. All of the marines except for Anja and Esmeralda seemed tense.

Paige felt a building excitement as she approached the hatch to the captain's office. That excitement melted away when she saw the captain hunched over her desk. Paige considered slipping away, but then she looked down and saw the coffee cup in her hand and realized she couldn't.

"Hello? Captain?"

Captain Nixon looked up. Her real eye was red and puffy. Before that moment Paige could not have imagined the captain crying. In an instant, the captain composed herself and projected an image of confident command.

"Ah, Paige. Good, I've been meaning to talk to you."

"Cook sent me to give you this. He told me to tell you that it's lucky coffee from the emerald isle."

The captain smiled at that. "Oh, did he now?" The captain's accent changed when she said that, but Paige didn't know what sort of accent the captain had adopted.

Paige approached and placed the mug on the captain's desk. She took a step back and stood in silence, waiting for the captain to speak.

"Paige," the captain said, "Things have gotten complicated. I'm going to have to put your navigation training on hold for the time being. It's nothing you did. I just have a lot on my plate right now."

Paige nodded and stayed silent.

"I hear you've been spending a lot of time with Anja Petrovic."

"Yes, ma'am."

"That's good. You can learn a lot from her. For the time being, I want you to shadow Petrovic on her maintenance rounds. This ship is in the best shape I've ever seen it. It won't need much maintenance, but you can learn a lot from Petrovic about how to interact with people."

"Yes, ma'am."

"Paige, I've given you a good opportunity here on this ship."

"Yes, ma'am. Thank you, ma'am."

"When I interviewed you back on Galtz, if I had offered you the job on the condition that you agree not to have sex with anyone while you were onboard, would you have taken the job?"

"Yes, ma'am. No question."

"Well, you've already got the job, but I'm telling you, I don't want you having sex with any of the marines."

"Okay, Captain. I promise," Paige said with complete sincerity.

"Not any kind of sex, do you follow me?"

"Yes, ma'am. Not even oral sex," Paige said.

"I see that Petrovic is already rubbing off on you. Good. We'll talk about this again when this..." The captain gestured at nothing Paige could see. "When this situation has resolved itself. For now just stay close to Petrovic and follow her lead."

"I will, Captain."

"You're dismissed," the captain said and picked up the mug of lucky coffee. "Thank Cook for me."

"I will, ma'am," Paige said and removed herself from the captain's presence.

1.7.5 - Trey

On an intellectual level, I understood that for most of human history, sex was something to be sought. It was a lure, a prize, and a trophy. For some it was a compulsion, and for far too many, it was an impossible dream.

I had engaged in sexual intrigues in historical delves, but in baseline reality, I now understand that I took sex for granted in a way that very few human males ever could before the rise of what the people out here in the Kuiper Belt still call *artificial intelligence*.

I trained as a doctor so I could make myself useful out here among the Kuiper Belt humans, but there are no doctors where I come from. Nobody gets sick. Injuries are incredibly rare, and when they occur, the repair process doesn't resemble anything these people would recognize as medicine.

Every human has an angel, and that angel commands a host of non-sentient agents that monitor the person on a cellular level. No pathology is allowed to progress to the point where it would present symptoms.

The nutritional content of every bite of food I ate, every sip of liquid that passed my lips, was tailored to my specific needs. Before I took up the study of biology and later medicine, the very concept of nutrition was as esoteric to me as dialogical epistemology would be to one of the young Columbian marines.

Sex was like food. I never sought it out. I never worried about not getting enough. I never even thought about it much, because as soon as I started to think seriously about it, women turned up to satisfy the urge long before it could rise to the level of a persistent distraction, much less a preoccupation or an obsession. Just as my needs for food and shelter were taken care of without any effort on my part, so too with sex.

I lived simulated lives in the historical period when artificial intelligence was just coalescing, and people fretted over the detrimental effects of young men being able to satisfy their need for sex without risk or effort. They feared that it would sap their ambition and that it would be the end of the nuclear family. I guess both fears were prescient, but the usefulness of human ambition was near its end anyway.

As for the nuclear family, I remember growing up with a mother and father as well as grandparents and aunts and uncles and loads of cousins plus adults and children who probably were not related to me. I can't recall my parents' names, but I know they loved me.

As for establishing a long-term sexual partnership with a human woman, I never really considered it. Zira knew me better than any human ever could. She loved me. I loved her. I'm sure I will always love her though I may never hear her voice again. She knew my tastes, and she provided me with a variety of women. Some were probably biological humans. Most were surely constructs. Some were a recurring presence. Most were not.

If I wanted a quick fuck to clear my head, a single woman would enter my environment. If I was in the mood for a more prolonged and luxurious experience, multiple women arrived. My conscious experience would blend with theirs, and I enjoyed the sensation of their lovemaking in a way that no human man ever had before the manifestation of the Is.

I'm sure that Zira must have paired me with men, at least experimentally, but those interactions must have proved less than satisfactory. I assume that my memories of those encounters decayed over time. Or perhaps Zira actively edited them out of my subjective recall. It never occurred to me to ask. As far as I can remember.

Inside the sphere of solar collectors the Kuiper Belt humans call the *Curtain*, sex is a non-issue. Out here, humans are always alert to potential opportunities for sex, and when they encounter strangers they evaluate them as potential threats or sex partners. Or both.

Which brings me to the topic of Anja Petrovic.

LIGHTS. CAMERA. ACTION!

1.8.1 - Petrovic

"Okay, I'll see you tomorrow. Good night, Trey," Paige said and turned to give Petrovic a hug. "Good luck, Anja," she said and departed.

Petrovic watched as Paige exited and sealed the hatch behind her. She turned back to see the doctor smiling at her. He was a strange creature. His long and lustrous hair and baby smooth cheeks weren't something one saw on a man from Galtz, military or civilian.

"So," Trey said, his smile and eye-contact unwavering, "Paige mentioned something about a seduction?"

"She's still learning. I don't like seduction. It feels dishonest to me. I'd rather be open and direct," Petrovic said. "I'm curious about you. I'd like to get to know you better, and I like sex."

"That's a bold approach. Direct. I like it," Trey responded.

Usually, at this point, a young man's eyes would light up at the prospect of uncomplicated sex, or they would make their disinterest clear. Trey did neither.

"Do you like it better than Escamilla's approach? Paige told me about how she got in Esmeralda's way earlier. I didn't ask her to do that."

"Escamilla's feminine beauty is more to my usual taste, but I'm intrigued by your openness and honesty. I was raised to value the truth," Trey said.

"I don't want to make you uncomfortable, but I'd like to show you my body. May I take off my clothes?"

Petrovic had spoken those exact words to hundreds of men. She didn't have to think about them, they flowed out like a verse of memorized poetry.

"Would you like to go to my quarters?" Trey gestured toward the hatch.

"Not yet. I like the idea that someone might come in and catch me naked," Petrovic explained.

"Ah, yes. *Exhibitionist tendencies.* I read that in your file."

"I don't like that phrase. It sounds like a diagnosis. I'm not sick. I like my body, and I like it when people look at me. May I show you my body?"

"Yes, please do. Show me your body..." Trey said then paused. "What should I call you?"

"Either *Anja* or *Petrovic* is fine. Try them both and see which one feels better," Petrovic said.

"Show me your body, Petrovic," Trey said, leaning back against a workbench.

Petrovic unzipped the one-piece jumpsuit she put on for this encounter. She pulled her arms from the long sleeves and pulled the garment down to her waist. Trey's eye's went to Petrovic's dark brown nipples as soon as she revealed them, but then he let his eyes roam around and take in the whole picture.

She was about Trey's height, maybe a shade taller, but she outweighed him. She had more body fat on her than the male marines, but it was her musculature that accounted for her weight advantage over Trey. Her wide shoulders made her breasts look smaller than they were.

Trey's eyes roamed over her body and settled on her right shoulder.

"Tell me about your scar," he said.

"I was part of a boarding party. My first. I chose a lighter style of tactical armor. It left wider gaps at the joints, but

I thought the added speed and mobility would more than make up for the increased exposure. A burly male passenger armed with a fire axe knocked my rifle out of my hands. We struggled for control of the axe. I wasn't as big and strong then as I am now. He pushed me to the deck and buried the axe in my shoulder, shattering my clavicle. He was about to bring it down on my head when one of my squadmates shot him.

"Lesson learned: It's good to be heavy." This was something else that Petrovic had repeated verbatim so many times that she didn't need to think about the words or visualize the scene to recount it.

"I could make it less visible," Trey said.

"I like my scar," Petrovic said. "It's a good reminder."

She bent over and undid the fasteners on her shoes, pulled them off and pushed the jumpsuit over her hips and down her thighs and calves. She stepped out of it and slipped her shoes back on.

"I'm naked," Petrovic said. "And you're fully clothed. I'm open to your inspection."

Trey looked at her pubic hair. It was black and cut short, but no portion of it seemed to be shaved. She followed his gaze and pushed the fingers of her right hand down through her public hair and to the hood of her clitoris. She opened her fingers so they framed her vulva as she pushed lower. "What do you call this?"

"Your vagina," Trey answered.

"That word doesn't excite you," she said. "I can tell. I call it my *cunt*." She studied his eyes. "But that word doesn't appeal to you. What about *pussy*?" His pupils dilated slightly. "Ah, yes. *Pussy*. What do you think of my pussy, Trey?"

"I'm not ready to tell you yet," Trey said. "Turn around."

"Oh, good. Yes, tell me what to do. I like that." She turned around, took a wider stance, and bent forward at the waist, keeping her lower back arched so that her buttocks lifted and grew tighter as she leaned forward.

"I'll admit, I'm proud of my butt. Or do you prefer *ass*?"

"*Ass*," Trey said. "Face me."

She obeyed.

"If the sex is good," she said. "I won't fuck any of the other men onboard, but you're welcome to fuck Escamilla. You don't have to choose between us. We can even fuck her together if you like."

Trey's face lit up, no careful scrutiny of his pupils required.

"Okay, that's your turn on. I'm pretty sure she goes both ways. I'm mostly into men, but I'm happy to get playful with her if that turns your crank. I'll let you know if I'm feeling neglected. So, what do you say?"

"I like how you're pretending that I'm still in control. You got me. Let's go back to my cabin."

Petrovic leaned in close and whispered in Trey's ear. He put his hands on her shoulders and pushed her out to arm's length.

"Actually, I'm not quite sold. I want to hear you cum before I let you into my bed. Get up on that workbench and play with yourself, Anja. Play with your pussy, Petrovic. Cum for me."

Petrovic cleared a space on the workbench she thought would provide the best view and then gestured to Trey with her eyes to move slightly to his left so he wouldn't be between her and the security camera.

She closed her eyes as she ran her hands over her body. She caressed her inner thighs as she spread her legs. Her breathing quickened. She looked into Trey's eyes and said, "Enjoy the show," and then shifted her gaze to the security camera and silently mouthed the word, "Captain."

1.8.2 - Rex

Rex woke from a dream of Trix that was equal parts anger and lust. He tried to masturbate, but his raging erection melted in his hand. He'd lived onboard this ship for two years and nine months, KB Standard, and in all that time, he'd never once brought himself to orgasm. With Trix around, he'd never needed too. Without her, his brain and cock refused to participate.

Trix sent him the security footage of Petrovic propositioning the doctor and then putting on a performance for both the doctor and the camera. It was clear she expected and wanted Trix to watch, and she must have known that the captain would share the footage with Rex. His cock certainly responded to Petrovic's performance. He tried to get off to it. He put her orgasm on a continuous loop and choked his penis until his hand cramped and the skin on his shaft grew raw. No dice.

"Fuck!" he spat and rolled out of bed. The ache in his testicles crept up into his abdomen. Not a great start to the day.

1.8.3 - Paige

Paige was the first to arrive in the galley, after Cook, of course. The ship was decelerating, so they had gravity. That meant that coffee was self-serve and she had her choice of amendments.

She was never tempted to drink it black. Too bitter, so it was no compromise for her to start doctoring her coffee with a generous dose of full fat cream. That was mandatory, doctor's orders, but she had her choice of sweeteners. The zero-calorie options were off limits to her, but even then, she had choices. She decided on agave syrup. There was nobody seated at any of the tables, so she walked back into the food prep area to talk to Cook.

"Mornin', killer." Cook said. "Do you want to cook the bacon for me?"

"Oh, yes," she said, excited at the prospect of expanding her role on Cook's side of the sacred threshold. Once other crew members saw her standing at the griddle tending the bacon, she would be more than just a tourist in the kitchen.

Cook handed her an apron and showed her how to operate the griddle. The temperature adjustment control was a dial that you turned so that a line on the dial matched up with a number on the face of the panel. There were four such dials, each corresponding to a portion of the griddle's surface area.

Paige didn't know why the griddle didn't have a voice interface, but the turning of the dials seemed arcane. She felt like she was participating in some esoteric initiation ritual, though she would not have been able to describe the feeling in just those words.

She laid long strips of uncooked bacon on the hot surface and learned that danger accompanied the delightful aroma of the cooking flesh. Globules of liquified fat leapt off the cooking surface with an explosive pop, arced through the air, and landed on her bare arms, delivering searing payloads of pain. She learned not to hover over the griddle but to stand back except when she was placing new strips on the hot metal surface, turning them, or removing them to cool on an absorbent sheet.

Crew members started to filter in. Most of them were still strangers to her. She knew the names of all of the women on the *Persephone*, but not the men, and most of the crew was male.

She knew the one black marine's name was Chukwuma. She'd never met a black person before, and she'd only exchanged superficial greetings with Mr. Chukwuma. She didn't know his first name.

Chukwuma approached the coffee station and picked up a mug. She smiled at him as he poured his coffee. He nodded to her but said nothing.

She made a mental note that he added one of the low-calorie sweeteners to his coffee but nothing to lighten it. She intended to memorize everyone's coffee preferences. Anja liked her coffee light and unsweet. The captain and Sergeant

Perkins both took their coffee black, unless it was a lucky coffee. Paige couldn't imagine why. She tried a sip of black coffee once. It was so bitter she struggled to swallow it. Never again.

Next, Drake Antal, cargo specialist, picked up a cup. She hadn't had much interaction with Antal, but she knew his name and non-combat specialty because he was young and handsome.

"Hey, kiddo," he said. "They got you slinging bacon now, huh?"

"I'm not a kid," Paige said. "How old are you?"

"Six point three," he said with seeming pride.

"I'm five years and eight months," Paige said. "Not much younger than you."

"Sorry," he said, and then added, "M'lady."

"Better," Paige said and rewarded him with a smile.

More marines filtered in, but none from the group that had sat at the captain's table at supper the night before. *Still under social quarantine*, she thought, remembering Anja's comment.

Now that she thought of Anja, it was strange that she hadn't yet arrived in the galley. Paige wondered how things went with the doctor. Anja shared her game plan with Paige, and Paige lost herself imagining Anja standing naked in front of the doctor until a pop from the griddle and a pinprick of hot pain on her arm snapped her back to reality.

AN AUDIENCE

1.9.1 - Trey

Sleeping in the same bed with another human was outside of my comfort zone. At home, whenever I had sex in baseline reality, even late at night, once the sex was over, the woman or women left, and I slept alone.

At least I was physically alone. Zira was always with me, though she rarely took a physical form.

I wish Zira could share the experience of fucking Petrovic. I'd love to talk to her and get her take on the night's activities. I'm used to Zira providing me with real-time guidance about how to better please my partners. Zira would never tell me which of my lovers were constructs and which were human women. She told me that I had to satisfy them all.

Sometimes Zira would inhabit a construct body. When I heard Zira's voice coming from a physical woman's body, I worked extra hard to please her. She told me to assume that any woman who showed up to have sex with me might be her in disguise, and so I was always attentive to my sexual partners and held back my own orgasm until I knew that each woman involved had come at least once. I normally just waited for Zira to tell me when to give in to the urge to ejaculate.

Petrovic and I were both nearing exhaustion when she asked me, "What do you need to get off?"

Petrovic figured out immediately that I'm from the inner system, but while I didn't deny it, I kept my promise to the captain as best I could and didn't supply any additional details. I couldn't tell Petrovic that I had been waiting for Zira to tell me that it was okay for me to finish.

I alternated between calling her Petrovic and Anja. They both felt good, but she responded well to direct commands, and as the night wore on I called her Petrovic more and more often. We both knew that I couldn't physically coerce her into doing anything she didn't want to do. She could have broken me at any moment. And I'm not in any sort of position of authority over her on this ship, so the idea that I should be dominant over her sexually struck me as... incongruous? Arbitrary? But that's the pattern we fell into, to the point where she started calling me *boss*.

"What can I do for you, boss?" She asked me.

I told her to roll over onto her stomach and rest, that I'd take it from here. I rubbed my cock between her enormous, muscular buttocks and found my own orgasm quickly. After that, I expected her to go back to her quarters, but she didn't. She got up and went to the toilet, and then she came back to bed, got under the covers and closed her eyes.

What on Earth? I thought.

Note to self, don't use that phrase in spoken conversation. It's not something people say out here in the Kuiper Belt.

My bed is big enough that Petrovic and I could sleep in it together without touching one another. I wasn't cramped. It was just unfamiliar to have another human nearby while falling asleep. Petrovic had no such difficulty and went right to sleep.

Petrovic explained to me in detail why she wanted to masturbate on the workbench in the lab. She wants to talk to the captain about sex. She is intrigued by this woman who dresses to display her ample figure, but who has lived with low quality synthetic skin grafts and ugly prosthetic limbs when functional replacements that are indistinguishable from the real thing are commonplace, even here in the human Kuiper Belt civilization.

Growing new organic skin to replace the crude synthetic patches on her face and neck would be trivially easy, even with the equipment on *Persephone*. I could even grow cloned replacements for her missing arm and legs. It would be time consuming, but doable.

Petrovic also told me about rumors she'd heard back on Galtz, her home habitat, about Captain Nixon. Former crew members shared stories about the culture of this ship back when it was called the *Nipple*. It was usually under-provisioned and always in need of repair. Trix kept it going, working multiple jobs, and she provided oral sex upon command to every man that demanded it, even men she actively hated. She tolerated verbal and even physical abuse from them.

When the new owners elevated her to acting-captain, she apparently fired many of the worst offenders, but, according to the rumors, all of the returning male crew members used her in that way. Cook, Hansson, Dobrovitz, Zell, and even Sergeant Perkins enjoyed her services.

Petrovic doesn't know how much of that to believe, and she is hungry to talk to the captain about sex. Getting sexually involved with the mysterious new doctor from the inner system was a sure way of getting some face time with the captain.

"But why masturbate on camera?" I asked her.

"Like my file says, *exhibitionist tendencies*. I just wanted the captain and Rex to see me get off, and there aren't supposed to be any security cameras in private quarters," she said. "Oh, damn!"

"What's wrong?"

"I just realized that I broke my own rule. It's important that I be completely honest and up front with potential new lovers. I should have told you in advance that I was trying to get the captain's attention. I'm sorry, boss. Everything I told you is true, but I didn't tell you everything."

"I'm okay. I appreciate your honesty, Petrovic."

"By the way," she said. "I plan to be totally candid with the captain about fucking you. Is there anything you don't want her to know?"

"I'm not shy about sex. In fact, I'm used to being watched. You can share all the details with the captain. Paige too. I'm sure she'll ask."

"She will," Petrovic agreed.

"Ready for breakfast," I asked.

"No, boss."

Petrovic handed me a breath pod. She put one in her mouth and seemed to enjoy the sensation of it dissolving. I found the sensation disturbing. It did work, though. The pod dissolved, we each took a sip of water, and then we picked up where we left off the night before.

We kissed deeply for a minute or two, and then she climbed on top of me and rode me hard, playing with her clitoris with her right hand and holding my right hand with her left, our fingers interlaced. As she approached her orgasm she said, "I'm close, boss. Cum with me."

I did and played up the intensity of my own moans to let her know that we had reached the summit together.

After that, we showered together. I got dressed, and Petrovic put on her shoes and walked out into the passageway naked. It was empty, but she didn't know that. She didn't check first. She retrieved her jumpsuit from the floor of the medical lab, slipped it on, and we went down to breakfast.

1.9.2 - Petrovic

On the way down to breakfast, Petrovic asked Trey if he was comfortable with public displays of affection. He said he was. After they got their food, Petrovic kissed Trey in full view of everyone in the galley, and they parted ways.

Trey went to sit at the captain's table, and Petrovic went to sit with Paige. Paige hugged her and pestered her for details, but Petrovic was in a hurry and put Paige off with promises of salacious details later. Paige said she could wait, given that she and Anja would be spending a great deal of time together in the near future.

This was the first Petrovic heard about her new role as Paige's official mentor, but it made sense. The captain had a lot on her plate at the moment. Mentoring her future first mate was not an immediate priority.

Petrovic excused herself and went back to her compartment to change clothes. It was fun to pull off a jumpsuit like a candy wrapper to reveal her naked body, but she really did prefer to wear briefs and a bra. She dressed for the gym. She and Paige were scheduled to work out at the top of the next watch. She passed back through the galley on her way to see the captain, and Cook stopped her.

"On your way to see the Skipper? Take her these, would ya?" He pointed at a small plate with two strips of bacon on it and a small glass of orange juice.

"I don't see how she supports that rack of hers eating like that," Petrovic said.

"Those guns are a marvel of nature," Cook agreed. "And you can quote me on that."

Persephone's Lost Nipple Ring was essentially a tower with lots of ladders and short passageways. Getting from the galley to the flight deck meant lots of climbing, and Petrovic managed it with both hands full, and she didn't spill a drop of OJ. She thought they should install a dumbwaiter, but then she thought, *no, the captain needs to come down to the galley and eat a proper meal.*

The hatch to the captain's office was open, and the captain was seated at her desk making notes on a data slate. She looked up and gestured for Petrovic to come inside.

"Cook asked me to bring you these," Petrovic said, setting the plate and glass down on the desk.

"But you were coming to talk to me anyway," Trix said.

"Close the hatch."

Petrovic obeyed. When she turned around, she saw that the captain had moved from behind her desk to the seating area. She gestured at the sofa. "Sit."

Again, Petrovic obeyed. The captain sat in a plush easy chair.

"I don't have time to mentor Paige right now. I've assigned her to shadow you."

"Yes, ma'am," Petrovic said. "She just told me. I'm happy to show her the basics of ship's maintenance. She's a quick study."

"Yes, she is." Trix said. "I also told her that I don't want her fucking any marines."

"I think that's a good idea, ma'am. The military caste doesn't have much respect for agricultural workers."

"And I made it clear that I don't want her sucking dicks on this ship," the captain said.

Here we go, Anja thought to herself. *This is my opening.* Out loud, she said, "You don't want her to be the new you."

"You want to get into that?"

"Yes, ma'am. I love to talk about sex, and I'm fascinated by you. You have such a powerful presence…"

"You mean I'm a hard bitch," the captain said, interrupting.

"Yes, ma'am. You're a hard bitch, but it comes across as strength. Paige worships you. I love how you display your body, and… well, the rumors about you…"

"That I sucked every dick on this ship for years?"

"Yes, ma'am. I wonder how much of that is true."

"All of it," Trix said.

"I heard that some of the men hit you…"

"With open hands. One man hit me with a closed fist once right in front of everyone. Rex had words with him and he disembarked at our next scheduled stop," Trix said.

"I heard that some of them insulted you and degraded you."

"Yes," the captain admitted.

"Is that a turn on for you, ma'am?"

"No."

"Why did you put up with that kind of abuse?" Petrovic asked.

"I thought I deserved it."

"May I ask why, ma'am?"

"I'm not willing to go into that. You wanted to talk about sex, I'll tell you about how I behaved sexually," the captain said with no emotion that Anja could detect.

"Thank you, ma'am," Anja said. "I've heard that you would suck dick in front of other people."

"Yes, it was usually the men who liked to humiliate me who would demand that I service them in front of other people. Sometimes they'd drink together in groups, and they'd call me on the intercom and tell me to get my ass up or down to wherever they were gathered. I'd suck every dick in the compartment. Some twice if they wanted it, and then I would get back to my work. Others, like Rex and Cook, always asked to see me in private when they wanted me to get them off."

"What if there were women in the room?" Petrovic had heard about how the captain behaved with women around, but she didn't supply the details. She wanted to hear them from the captain.

"If there was a woman in the compartment, I would try to arrange the man and myself so that woman was looking at my pretty side." Trix turned in her chair to show Anja her left side and pantomimed sucking a dick.

"Sometimes the women insulted me. If they did, I just got on with the task and tuned them out, but sometimes they would cheer me on. They'd say things like, *Get that dick, Trix*, or *Suck that cock, girl*. I liked that. When they did that, I would put on a show for them. I would stroke the man's cock, and stick my tongue out to lick the head and do my best to hold eye contact with the woman." Trix continued the pantomime making eye contact with Petrovic.

"Oh, fuck," Petrovic, said. "Captain, that is so fucking hot.

Did you ever eat a woman's pussy?"

"No. But sometimes I would share a dick with a woman. We'd take turns sucking and if the woman kissed me, I would kiss her back. That didn't happen very often."

"Did you want to do more with women?"

"Not really. I just liked it when they watched me and encouraged me. When we were in port, I used to pay women to watch me suck dick."

"Oh, Captain. I would pay good money to watch you suck a dick. And I would shower you with encouragement and praise."

Anja squeezed her thighs together. She wished she'd worn loose pants or her jumpsuit. The crotch of her tight athletic pants was dark with moisture. "I wish I'd been on this ship back then."

"We couldn't have afforded you. This ship was a mess. We were always just scraping by, and there was no discipline. Our captains were mostly disinterested or drunkards. It was not a good place to be. Things are better the way they are now. We're well-funded, everything is in good repair, and we have the means to protect ourselves. I'm glad you're here now."

"Thank you, Captain. I can understand why you don't do that anymore. It wouldn't work for the captain to be dropping to her knees all day. So you just stopped?"

"Rex insisted, but I agreed that a change was necessary."

"Rex insisted?" Anja asked, and Trix nodded. "Ah, that makes sense. He's clearly in love with you. I'm sure he didn't like…"

"That's absurd!"

That was the first sign of emotion that Trix had let slip.

"He's a man with a conscience. He feels guilty for how they all treated me. He regrets participating. He is *not* in love with me."

Anja did not reply right away. She was in dangerous territory here. The captain had the authority to shut this conversation down in an instant, and Anja didn't want that. A change in direction was in order.

"Do you miss it?"

"Sucking dick? Yes, I miss it. I hated it at first, which is why I did it. I was punishing myself, but giving four or five blowjobs a day, every day, for years on end, I got pretty good at it. After a while it was like a kind of meditation. I'd be struggling with a technical problem, and someone would call me away from the task to suck him off, and inspiration would strike. I'd stop sucking and record a quick voice memo." Trix laughed at that, and Anja laughed with her, relieved that the conversation hadn't crashed and burned.

Trix continued, "And, truth be told, I do care for the men I served with for years. I like helping them deal with the sexual deprivation that usually comes with serving on a ship. It felt good knowing that I could make them feel good. If you want to say I did it out of love, yes, by the end, there was a sort of love, but not in an *in love* kind of way."

"I'd love to watch you suck Rex's dick," Anja said, hoping she wasn't on thin ice.

"I wish he'd fuck you," Trix said. "I was hoping you'd go for him. That's not why I hired you, but he needs some kind of relief. He won't let me relieve him."

"Ma'am, I would fuck Rex in a heartbeat. He's exactly my type. Older but still fit, handsome, bold. He was my first choice, and I let him know, but he wasn't interested. He made an excuse about it being improper, me being under his command, but that doesn't matter. He's not my superior officer. We're just two mercenaries doing a job on a civilian ship."

"Petrovic," the captain said, her voice neutral again, "I'm sure you've heard us arguing."

"Yes, ma'am. You're like a married couple who argues when they think the children can't hear, but we hear you. It sounds bad."

"It is. We're uncomfortable around each other. He gets

horny when we're alone together, and it would just be so quick and easy for me to suck him off and then turn our minds back to business. He needs release, and he won't let me give it to him. And he won't find it elsewhere. It's to the point where we can't be alone together. Every conversation turns into a shouting match. I really wish he'd fuck you. Or Nora. Or Escamilla."

"Ma'am, when you argue with Rex, do you always frame it in terms of his need for release?"

"Yes, because that's the truth. I don't need to suck his dick in order to focus on my job."

"But you'd like to suck it, wouldn't you? You'd feel good knowing that you'd helped him," Anja said.

"I would, yes. And to be honest, it would feel good to have him in my mouth again. I miss... I miss the feel of him."

"What if you phrased it that way to him? If it was something *you* needed, don't you think Rex would want to help you? I'm pretty sure he'd do almost anything for you." Anja stopped, hoping she hadn't pushed too far.

Trix said nothing.

"Captain, about what I did last night..." Anja saw the captain's eyes focus. She had been lost in reverie.

"Yes, what was that about?"

"Ma'am, I promise that I do not intend to be a disruptive influence on your ship, but I can't do celibacy. I just don't work that way. I'm polyamorous on station, but in a small crew like this, I find one man and stick with him. Sexual jealousy is less likely to cause problems that way. Sex with the doctor was really good last night, and so I'm going to stick with him. And, I think you heard me agree to bring Escamilla into it as well."

"Yes, I heard."

"Nora seems to have taken up with Jay Chukwuma," Anja said.

"She has? With everything that's going on, I missed that development."

"Well, she's more discreet than I am ma'am," Anja said.

"That's not saying much. You're a brazen slut."

"Yes, ma'am. Thank you for saying so. The other Columbians won't like that I'm fucking the doctor. They don't trust him, and things will get worse when they find out he's from inside the Curtain."

Trix scowled at this, but Anja continued without pause.

"He didn't tell me, ma'am, but he's a terrible liar. He can't keep a secret like that. But with the pretty boy doctor who was sent out here by the Powers to do who knows what… If he's fucking two of the three eligible women on board, tensions on this ship could really boil over quickly."

"Fucking hell," Trix said.

"But," Anja said, "I have a suggestion that could diffuse some of those tensions."

1.9.3 - Paige

Paige stepped out of the shower after having vacuumed the majority of the water off of her body. She still liked to towel off, but Anja had encouraged her to use the suction dryer even when they had gravity in order to get good with it.

She stood in front of a full length mirror, actually a video screen set to mirror mode, and looked at her body. She'd known she was underweight, but it was only now, surrounded by men and women from military families who, from birth, had had all the food they could eat plus the benefit of athletic conditioning and military training, that she realized how small and under-developed she was.

The new caloric abundance had already worked a visible change. Her ribs and hip bones were not as prominent as they were when Esmeralda had helped her out of her acceleration couch a day and a half ago, but putting on weight, and putting on muscle in particular, was going to be a slow process. The doctor could speed it along with RNA treatments, but it would still take time.

She had just come from a workout in the gym. Anja was very specific about calculating the appropriate amount of resistance for Paige. They needed to be mindful not only of Paige's underdeveloped muscles, but of her joints.

Paige struggled, and her arms and legs trembled as she strained against the machines. Paige would finish a set, and then Anja would position herself in the same machine. It adjusted to her height automatically, and the machine had Anja's workout history and selected the appropriate resistance for her.

Anja was the first to admit that she wasn't pretty in the way Esmeralda is pretty, but her body was a wonder to behold. She was like a machine herself. Her movements were powerful and tireless. She didn't seem to strain at all, but as she pushed against the machine, her muscles swelled and pulled her skin tight. She sweated, and the moisture created highlights on her skin that accentuated her musculature.

Paige stole glances at the bodies of the young male marines working out in the gym with them, but she knew that Anja liked to be looked at, so she admired Anja's gloriously fit frame openly.

The veins that stood out on Anja's arms were not pleasing to Paige's eye, but they weren't so prominent most of the time as they were during a workout. When Anja climbed out of the machine, she stood in front of the mirror and flexed her muscles. Paige noticed that the male marines did the same thing. Nobody was at all modest about how much they enjoyed looking at their own pumped up muscles.

Paige asked Anja if she'd ever seen the captain working out in the gym. She hadn't. In fact, it was clear looking at the schedule that the captain did not use this facility.

"But she works out somewhere," Anja said with total confidence. "A butt like that doesn't just happen by itself."

Paige asked Anja what exercises she needed to do to develop her *glutes*, a word she'd heard the marines use in the gym to refer to the muscles in their butts.

Anja laughed. "Keep eating, little tiger. Keep eating. You need fat as well as muscle to get an ass like the captain's."

SKILLFUL MEANS

1.10.1 - Rex

Rex caught himself pretending he knew more about the captain's big announcement than he did. They'd exchanged a few brief messages about the time and place of the assembly, but Rex had no specific information about how the captain was going to deal with their multi-pronged morale situation.

The crescent-shaped table in the situation room was big enough to accommodate all of the marines and non-combatant members of the crew. A few people stood, but that was their choice. As he scanned the room he saw Petrovic and the captain's charity case, now officially assigned to Petrovic. Petrovic met his eye and winked at him, her right hand releasing her coffee cup and disappearing below the table toward her lap. *Toward her cunt*, he thought. *She knows I must have jacked off to her little show. She probably assumes that I got off, too.*

He kept scanning the crowd. He noticed that Kellemen, Sparks, Zell and Escamilla were all seated in a group. He hadn't told them to do that. He also saw that they were only talking amongst themselves. Had they developed a special group solidarity and cohesion, or were they just taking care not to provoke him?

Or had Zell taken advantage of the situation and recruited them to his service. There had never been any reason to sequester Zell with the Columbians. Trix was so shrewd. It aggravated Rex that she couldn't see Zell for the self-serving opportunist he was.

The captain had kept Zell, Escamilla, Sparks and Kellemen all busy running intensive tactical simulations focusing on cyber warfare, point defense, and ship to ship combat. She had them run the simulations with voice control only, simulating combat in high-g maneuvers when everyone would be in their acceleration couches.

The captain tasked Escamilla with statistical analysis of casualty patterns in different shipboard combat scenarios, something Escamilla did not have the educational background to do easily. He knew Trix had over-taxed Escamilla's abilities to mentally exhaust the combat medic. Rex exhausted them physically with body weight training and calisthenics in the main cargo bay. They were not allowed to use the gym where they would come into contact with the rest of the crew.

Rex noticed Shawn Li, mining engineer and materials specialist, standing by himself. Li was not from a Columbian family, and he had never served in the military in any capacity. His family had lived on Galtz since long before the Blackout, back when it was still called Galt's Gulch. They moved there because they were believers. Li subscribed to the philosophy of Ayn Rand with self-righteous zeal.

Columbians did not spout Objectivist platitudes, and they had no patience for anyone who did. When the Columbian military leadership took their elite troops and relocated to Galtz in the aftermath of the Blackout, they set themselves up as the defenders of the Galtz habitat, and the arrangement wasn't just a naked protection racket. The KB was engulfed in conflict after the Blackout. Galtz was prosperous, and thus a tempting target. They really did need protection.

The Columbian military leadership agreed to honor the founding ethos of Galtz. Specifically, they pledged to uphold the virtues of rationality, individualism, and meritocracy. Not only had the Columbians failed to adopt these cultural virtues, they made it a point of pride to flout them. The *Persephone's* new complement of expensive marines had no use for Li, and they made no secret of that fact.

Joachim Zell had served as the ship's geologist back when the crew still called it the *Nipple*. Like Li, he was from an old school Galtz family. He wasn't a zealot like Li, but they seemed to get along.

Zell spent *Persephone's* refit period getting certified in weapons and combat tactics so that he could sign on as a marine and get the extra pay. He'd gotten fit, too. Zell held his own with the Columbians when Rex put them through exhausting workout routines in the cargo bay.

Rex imagined that Zell would be standing with Li were he not seated with his new tribe within a tribe.

Everyone was present except for the captain, engine keeper Lawson and the doctor.

The room was a burble of overlapping conversations. Rex couldn't make out anything anybody was saying except for a conversation about sports between Cook and Hans Dobrovitz, who were standing closest to him. He assumed that Petrovic was doing her best to inflame every libido within earshot.

No doubt, Sparks and Kellemen were still working out the details of their coalescing conspiracy theories. At first, the two men had clashed about the roles of the Floaters and the Powers in their mismatched paranoid fantasies, but during their forced proximity, they had found the points where their fantasies meshed and built from that starting common ground.

Rex had no patience for any of it and couldn't say who had given ground on which point to forge their–What had Trix called it? Their *new synthesis*.

Trix talked like a Galtz spacer most of the time, but every now and again she would pull out some phrase or bit of vocabulary–a *lexical item*, she might say–that people just didn't use in normal conversation. She wasn't like Li who used his big vocabulary to set himself above everyone else. Trix just knew a lot of words and could describe complex situations with surprising precision. That was something he loved... something he admired about her.

The conversational cacophony died down when the sound of the captain's boots on the metal deck of the p-way announced her imminent arrival. When she stepped over the threshold into the situation room the compartment was silent.

The captain stood in front of the assembled crew and slowly swept the room with her gaze without saying anything. She didn't lock eyes with everyone, but her eyes were available for contact as she panned her head from her left to right.

Rex saw that she did make eye contact with several crewmen. Others avoided her eyes. A few seemed to get lost in an instant of non-verbal communion with the captain.

She gestured at the wall, and a display came on showing their current location, speed and trajectory. They had been decelerating for over a day, but they were still hurtling outbound faster than most of them had ever traveled in their lives.

"We're over 50 AU out from Sol." Trix said. "Raise your hand if you've ever been this far from home before."

No hands went up.

"By some reckonings, we're not even in the Kuiper Belt anymore." She paused to let that sink in before continuing. "Yes, we are in Floater territory, but the Floaters are spread thinner than we are."

The positions of known Floater settlements appeared on the chart. None of them were along their projected flight path.

"The Floaters don't build spin habitats. They have adapted their bodies and their culture to life without gravity. They seem strange to us, but one thing we do know is that they don't like high-g acceleration. You may not like it either, but unlike the Floaters, you can handle it."

She let the flattery sink in for a moment before she pointed to the line indicating the *Persephone's* trajectory.

"You probably felt the ship maneuvering a few minutes ago and you can see that our projected course curves back in toward the inner system, but…"

Trix held out her hand and turned her wrist as if adjusting an invisible knob. The display swung from a two dimensional top down view from above the plane of the solar system to an edge on view. The line describing the path of the ship arced well above the ecliptic before turning back in, and it didn't return to the orbital plain until they would be between the orbits of Saturn and Jupiter, someplace KB humans did not go.

Trix continued, "Our course does not take us home. If we stay on this course, we will bypass the main Kuiper Belt completely."

Rex expected murmured rumbling from the crew, but they remained silent, all eyes on the captain.

"Our orders are to be here…" she continued, pointing at the display and causing a circle to appear along the line describing their intended course, "at this time." A time code appeared. Below it was a countdown timer. It read *8 days, 3 watches, 18 minutes and 23 seconds*.

"We will remain at 1g deceleration for the next fifteen watches. Thereafter we will execute a high-g burn for the next six days."

She put up a hand to forestall interruption. "Don't groan yet. It gets worse. This won't be like the last burn. We're going to spend most of it at 7g."

The crew did groan then. Trix gestured at the display and another countdown timer appeared. It was labeled *Groan clock*, and it was counting down from ten seconds. Laughter replaced groans and incipient complaints.

The laughter died down before the clock reached zero, but Trix waited the full ten seconds before continuing.

"As we swing through this turn," she gestured, the circle on the map following her movements, "we'll be moving slowly relative to local objects. We'll be well above the ecliptic at that point, and that is where we will be most vulnerable to Floater attack.

"I stress, we have no reason to expect a Floater attack, but just to be sure, Zell, Kellemen, Sparks and Escamilla have spent the last thirteen watches doing intensive simulations in preparation for a potential attack while we're all in our couches.

"All bridge systems related to point defense and intrusion countermeasures can be operated by voice command from the acceleration couches. All of our mining drones and remotes are dual purpose and can be used for combat and piloted by voice from the couches.

"Medical emergencies at high-g are troublesome, because other than giving your heart a jump start or pumping meds into you, there's not much that can be done. But within that narrow space of *not much that can be done* lies the difference between life and death.

"Medic Escamilla has been doing intensive study in this area so that she and our new doctor will give you the best possible odds of survival in a crisis.

"Please join me in giving this crisis team a round of applause. They've worked their asses off."

Trix pantomimed clapping. The metal thing at the end of her right arm barely qualified as a hand, and it certainly wouldn't make the familiar clapping sound if she slapped her left hand against it. Everyone in the room applauded.

The applause started to die down, and another ten second countdown timer appeared. This one wasn't labeled, but it had a laurel above it and animated party confetti falling in the background behind the numbers. Trix gestured for the clapping to continue, even slapping her thigh with her left hand to make something like the appropriate sound. More laughter, and even, to Rex's surprise and amazement, smiles from the crewmen who'd been kept incommunicado from the rest of the crew.

Good job, Captain, he said to himself. *Well played.*

Trix held up a hand for silence. She looked serious, and the room grew quiet.

"I want your undivided attention for this next item. Observe," she gestured at the display and the wall filled with the video clip of Anja Petrovic, naked but for a pair of deck shoes, lying on her back on a workbench in the med lab, legs spread, masturbating furiously. Shocked silence gave way to gasps and then laughter and then cheering and another round of applause.

"How did *that* get into my presentation?" Trix furrowed her brows and swiped at a data slate attached to her metal arm, making a show of looking through her slides. A new timer appeared. This one was for 20 seconds, and it was labeled *hoots and cat calls*.

The crew obliged. Anja made an O shape with her mouth and covered it with her hand in a parody of modesty. Trix turned up the volume on the clip and the room filled with the sounds of Petrovic's orgasm. The real Petrovic stood and made multiple theatrical bows.

By the time the countdown clock reached zero, several marines were holding their sides and wiping tears from their eyes.

"I'm not sure how *that* got into my presentation, but however that clip found its way into my slide deck, it also seems to be posted publicly with the duty and gym schedules. I'll have to take that down sooner or later. Don't any of you go downloading it for your own amusement in the meantime." More laughter.

"Seriously, though," Trix continued. "You're all very well paid on this ship, but a special effort deserves a special reward. Nora, would you come in, please?"

Nora Lawson, *Persephone's* engine keeper, stepped into the compartment followed by two women. Not real women. Sex robots.

One was blonde with pale skin. It was slightly shorter than the captain and even more buxom. Its face could not be mistaken for an actual human face. Its eyes were twice the size of normal human eyes, and its lips were inhumanly large and luxurious.

It cycled through a succession of coquettish poses. It wore a white blouse that showed off its ample cleavage. It wore a short skirt with a plaid pattern on it, and white socks with black patent leather shoes.

The other sex doll looked like an anthropomorphized cat. It had cat ears on top of its head and a swishing tail. Straight black hair came to its shoulders with a fringe of bangs that sat high on the forehead. Its skin was light brown with fine black hair all over its body. Like the other robot, it had enormous eyes as well as a cat's nose and a pattern of radiating white lines on its face that read as cat's whiskers. It wore only a black bikini, which made it look nearly naked with its dark skin and fine black fur.

"We don't have any first-class passengers right now, so I have decided to re-deploy these luxury amenities to the crew decks. Their names are Jailbait and Cat Girl. I'll leave it to you to figure out which is which.

"If you look at the community board on your slates, you'll see that a new schedule has been added. That schedule is divided into blocks of half a watch each. You'll see that the second morning watch is blacked out. That's when they will report to Nora for maintenance. In addition to nuclear engineering and spaceship propulsion, it turns out that our engine keeper knows a thing or two about cybernetics.

"The crisis team, as a reward for all of their hard work, have these two to themselves for the remainder of today. Thereafter, each crew member will be assigned a bot and block of time. You may trade appointment credits as you see fit. If you don't want to make use of these bots yourself, you can trade your appointment credits for whatever your crewmates are willing to trade for them.

"These dolls are *not* sentient. They have very short memories, and outside of a sexual context, they have very little to say. They do not have general intelligence. If they still bother you or creep you out, do not spend time with them. I want to stress that these two are *very expensive*. Do not damage them. If you do, the cost of repair or replacement will come out of your shares."

Trix turned to the blonde doll. "Jailbait, show me your ass."

The robot giggled, turned around, took a widened stance and lifted its plaid skirt. Trix also turned her back on the crew so that everyone could compare the two asses. Trix looked over her shoulder to emphasize what she was doing. The two asses were similar in shape, but Jailbait's was plumper and rounder than the captain's. Trix pouted, and several people laughed.

Trix slapped Jailbait hard on the right butt cheek with her open left hand. It made a satisfying *thwack*, and Jailbait let out a squeak. More laughter from the crew.

"As you can see, Jailbait's ass is very spankable. Paddle it all you like, but *do not* hit her in the face."

Trix made a twirling gesture with her finger and Jailbait turned to face the crew again.

"Cat Girl," Trix said, "Show me your ass."

"Meow," cat girl said and made a slinky pirouette. Trix took hold of Cat Girl's tail and pulled it to the side. Unlike Jailbait, Cat Girl had a dancer's body. Her butt was small and tight.

Trix said, "Cat Girl's ass is not made for spanking. If you want to spank, book a session with Jailbait.

"I have assigned a crew cabin to the two of them. They will go there to clean themselves and to wait when they are not scheduled to be with any of you. You are not to visit them there.

"Notice that they are wearing clothes. Do not damage or hide their clothes. I do not want to see them walking naked in the passageways. I do not want to see them in the galley.

Fuck them in your quarters. If you want to *party* with them, they are allowed in the crew lounge. According to the sales literature, Cat Girl is a particularly good dancer, but I'm serious about this. I do not want to see them naked in public areas.

"These two are linked by a high bandwidth data connection, and they are optimized to work together. If you can trade appointment credits with a crewmate and arrange to have both of them at once, you will more than double your pleasure.

"Also, Petrovic, Nora, the doctor and I have voluntarily taken ourselves off the schedule. Our four allowances will be awarded to crew members who go above and beyond in the line of duty. When you're on duty, attend to your duty, and these two luxury items will attend to you in your off watches.

"I'd love to dismiss you now and tell you all to rest up and enjoy the dolls, but there is one serious matter to address.

"Our new doctor came from behind the Curtain. He says that he is here to look for evidence of alien life. Whether you believe that or not is irrelevant. He accepted an employment contract from the DAO. He is a member of this crew. You *will* work with him."

"Unacceptable! You can't ask us to work for the devils who brought the Blackout!" This outburst came from Chukwuma, and several others voiced support.

"Who do you work for, Chukwuma?" Trix demanded.

"I work for you," he said.

"You take orders from me, but you work for a distributed autonomous organization. Do you know who controls the DAO?"

"Who?" Chukwuma said.

"I don't know. I control a few voting shares, so in a sense you work for me, but I don't control enough to override the *Whales*. Who are they? I don't know, but I know that there are three of them, and together they control over half of the voting shares.

"This mission didn't make sense to me, and so I voted against it. The Whales voted for it. I voted against offering Trey an employment contract, but the Whales voted for it, so he's our doctor. I voted against doing this ridiculous 7g burn we're about to do, but that doesn't matter. The Whales voted for it.

"I accepted this job just like you did. I follow orders just like you do. My job is to pilot the ship and keep all of you in line. Your job is to follow my orders and to fight."

Trix had been talking directly to Chukwuma, but now her eyes roamed over the group.

"Every one of you knows that following my orders might get you killed. You agreed to do it anyway, even if my orders don't make sense to you. Even if you think I'm wrong, you agreed to fight under my command, and you agreed to put the mission first.

"I paid a lot of money for professional soldiers from the Galtz militia. Why? Because you're supposed to be good fighters, and, *as a point of honor*, you put the mission first. Raise your hand if, *the mission comes first* is just an empty slogan for you. Anyone?"

No hands went up.

"Raise your hand if you plan to fight when I say fight."

All hands went up.

"Raise your hand if you plan to follow my orders, even if they don't make sense to you."

All hands stayed up.

"Put your hands down."

All hands went down.

Trix locked eyes with Saz Kellemen, "Kellemen, are you going to fight when I say fight?"

"Yes, Captain."

"Petrovic, are you going to follow my orders?"

"I'll do anything for you, Captain."

"Chukwuma, are you going to put the mission first even if

it kills you?"

"Yes, Captain."

"Fucking right, you will! Remember what the doctor said at dinner about the needle being optional on this next burn? The doctor isn't here. I am. And I'm telling you it's *not* optional.

"I'm not showing up to whatever it is we're getting into without all of my marines because some macho shithead thought he could do a 7g burn without medical support. You will take the needle. You will put your lives in the hands of a man who got flung out here to the ass end of the Kuiper Belt by the Powers. Why? Because those are your orders. Raise your hand if you plan to follow orders."

All hands went up.

"Now get the fuck out of my sight!"

Everyone stood up and filed out in silence leaving the captain standing with the two sex dolls. Rex approached her.

"Trix?"

She turned on him, tears streaming down her face. "You too! Get the fuck out!"

He did.

1.10.2 - Paige

Paige followed Anja to the machine shop. They were alone. Anja picked up a heavy duty data slate and strapped it to Paige's left forearm. She pressed her thumb to the screen and said, "Anja Petrovic, maintenance technician, delegating duties to Paige…"

Paige realized that Anja didn't know her last name.

"Farmer," Paige said.

Petrovic touched Paige's cheek and gave her a sympathetic look. "Delegating duties to Paige Farmer."

"Enter biometric ID," the slate said in a flat, sexless voice.

"Put your thumb there and say your name," Anja told her.

"Paige Farmer," Paige said, pressing her right thumb to the

screen.

"Paige Farmer is authorized," the Slate said.

"Okay, now ask it for the maintenance schedule," Anja told Paige.

Paige paused, "Uh, what's the query syntax for that?"

"*Query syntax*? Where'd you pick up that egghead lingo?"

"From Mr. Li," Paige said.

"That tracks. Okay, little tiger. Two things. These are important. One. Nobody likes Shawn. Don't talk like him. Two. Check this out."

Anja looked at the slate and changed her volume and vocal tonality as if she were switching from a private conversation with Paige to saying something to someone else in the room. "Yo, ship. You got a couple slackers here who need to look busy. Whatcha got for us?"

"There are no reported faults. Random manual inspection of navigation sensor pod extension mechanism is recommended," the slate said.

A map of the ship appeared on the slate indicating the most direct path from the machine shop to the access panel for the extension mechanism along with a schematic of the part to be inspected.

"Boring," Anja told it, "I'm pretty sure you meant that we should double check the atmospheric controls in the first-class passenger compartments."

"Correct," said the voice of the slate. "On site testing of atmospheric controls in luxury compartments is indicated." The map and schematic changed to match the *random* assignment that Anja suggested.

"That's more like it," Anja said and put her arm around Paige's shoulder and directed her down the p-way to a ladder.

"What? You can talk to a computer like that?"

"Yeah. That *structured query syntax* crap is just for the phobes. It doesn't take general intelligence to make out what you mean if you just talk like a normal person.

"Everybody makes a big show of hating on AI, but we rely

on smart machines to keep us alive. When that slate says..." Anja changed her voice to mimic the inflectionless voice of the slate, "*Paige Farmer is authorized...*" She then switched back to her normal voice and continued, "that's like when a fancy lady's maid says, *Very good, ma'am*, instead of, *You got it, babe.* It's all to remind everybody who's in charge."

"Does everybody know that?" Paige asked.

"You didn't know," Anja said.

"I don't know anything, but does the captain know?"

"The captain definitely knows."

"Does Mr. Li know?" Paige asked.

"That's an interesting question. How hard would it be for him to find out? I mean, he operates on the assumption that he has to enunciate. Every. Single. Syllable, and use very simple sentence structure when he talks to machines. How hard would it be for him to test that assumption? What would he need to do?"

"Just talk to a computer like a person and see how it responds," Paige said.

"Right," Anja said. "But he never performs that very simple experiment. Why not?"

"Because he doesn't want to know the truth?"

"Could be," Anja said.

"What about Mr. Chukwuma?" Paige asked.

"Yeah," Anja said. "He's pretty intense when it comes to hating on AI. Not sure what that's about. Kinda seems like he's compensating for something."

"Like what?" Paige asked.

Anja just shrugged and they continued in silence for a bit, alternating walking along the curving passageways closest to the ship's exterior and climbing ladders to ascend toward the top of the ship. At the top of one ladder the scene changed. The bulkheads, which were painted light gray through most of the ship, were painted white here. Paige and Anja faced a hatch that was ornamented with gold filigree.

"This is delicious," Anja said.

"What is?"

"You worked in the rice patties back on Galtz, so you have been literally working in the fields," Anja said. Paige nodded. "Well, *field hand*, welcome to the *Big House*." Then, to the ship, Anja said, "Let us in."

The decorated hatch swung open to a sight unlike anything Page had ever seen. In one sense, it was just another passageway, but not only were the walls painted white, they were adorned with decorative molding.

Framed paintings were affixed to the bulkheads. The deck was carpeted in red, and every couple of meters a recessed niche held a mirror and a pedestal. Some pedestals sported vases of flowers. Others had statues of nude women or busts of men in military uniforms. Paige couldn't see any light fixtures, and yet a soft light suffused the space.

Paige's mouth hung open.

Anja stepped aside and placed a hand on Paige's back and urged her forward. "After you, little tiger. This is just the servant's entrance."

Paige stepped onto the carpet and marveled at how it gave way under her feet without compromising her balance. She reached out and ran her fingers along the bulkhead. It wasn't smooth but had an irregular texture. "That's plaster," Anja said. "Keep going. This is just a passageway. You've got to see the state room."

A few more steps brought them to a hatch, but it wasn't like any hatch Paige had seen on the ship until now. Rather than swinging open on hinges, the hatch split down the middle, and as she reached out to touch it, the two halves pulled apart and disappeared into the bulkhead with a soft hiss. The opening went all the way to the deck so that Paige didn't have to step over a threshold to enter the compartment.

Opulence wasn't a word Paige had ever needed before this moment, so she didn't have access to it when describing the experience to herself. The red carpet of the hallway gave way to a mosaic of different colors, patterns and textures on the floor. Again, she couldn't see any obvious lighting fixtures, but the space was well lit. Chairs and couches so ornate that Paige couldn't imagine people actually sitting on them formed a lounge area in the middle of the compartment. Against one wall was a counter of some sort. It was padded on the edge, and a brass pole ran along the base. Behind it was a mirrored wall full of shelves.

"That's the bar," Anja told her. "The place is secured for acceleration, otherwise those shelves would be stocked with bottles of expensive liquor."

"Who is this for?" Paige wondered aloud.

"Rich people. Important people."

"How much does it cost?" Paige asked.

"That's above my pay grade, but think about it. If it's just first-class passengers and their entourage and we're not transporting cargo or steerage class passengers, then for the trip to be worth making, the Swells would have to be paying enough to cover all of our salaries, fuel and reaction mass, docking fees, provisioning, and turn a profit for the DAO."

Anja plopped down on one of the fancy couches and sprawled with one leg over the back. Paige sat gingerly in a high backed chair but did not lean back in it.

"Relax, little tiger. This furniture is probably new, but it's tougher than it looks. We're supposed to be testing the atmospheric systems in here. Hey, suite, set the mood for a romantic nightcap."

At Anja's command, the lighting dimmed, and soft music faded up. "Not bad, not bad. How about a dance party?"

The lights dimmed even lower, and the soft atmospheric music took on a heavy bass beat and climbed in volume. Patches of colored light swarmed over the deck, walls and deckhead, and perfumed fog billowed over the floor. Anja jumped up off of the couch and danced aggressively. She beckoned for Paige to join her but didn't insist when the young woman resisted.

"Back to baseline," Anja said. Or at least that's what Paige thought she said, based on the results. The music was too loud for her to make out exactly what Anja had said. The music stopped, and the lighting returned to its starting level. "C'mon. Let's check out the boudoir!"

"What's that?" Paige asked.

"That's what you call the place with the bed when you want to fuck," Anja said.

She took Paige by the hand and led her to another door that whooshed open. The bedroom was almost as large as the room they'd just come from. It had a large tub of some kind and an enormous round bed on a dais. The bed was stripped down to the bare mattress, so the effect was somewhat muted, but Paige still boggled at the thought that this was supposed to be someone's sleeping quarters. There were three alcoves against one wall. Two of them were empty, but the third was sealed with smoked glass.

Anja pointed at the first empty alcove and said, "Jailbait." She pointed at the next and said, "Cat Girl." What do you think is behind door number three?"

"There's another sex robot?" Paige said, her curiosity aroused. "Can we see her?"

"You think it's a her?" Anja tapped the glass, and a light came on inside revealing a naked man. He was muscular, but not bulky like the marines. "Ooo… What's your name?" Anja asked.

The man spoke, and his voice seemed to come from nowhere in particular, like the music in the other room. "I'm David, but you can call me whatever you like."

Anja looked at Paige and then pointed at David's flaccid and unassuming penis. "Looks kinda small, doesn't it?"

And then to David, "Show us how big and hard your cock can get, David."

David's penis swelled gently and rose into an upright position, it continued to inflate long after Paige thought he had reached his full size.

"Great, Ayn," Paige said. "That's scary. I couldn't imagine

that going inside of me."

"Yeah," Anja agreed. "Davie is just showing off. I asked him to show us how big he could make it." To David, "Show my friend here how big you'd be if you knew it was her first time."

David's penis remained upright, but it shrank several sizes until it looked completely unimpressive to Paige compared to what she had just seen.

"That looks like it might be too small," Paige said.

"You should trust David. He's the expert. Even at that size, it would feel pretty big going in, if it was your first time."

"It would be," Paige admitted. "Hey, if there's a male sex robot, why did the captain only bring down the females?"

"Well, these things are really expensive. But that's not the main reason. Think about it," Anja replied. "You tell me. Why only deploy the girl dolls?"

"Because there are more men than women on board?"

"That's part of it, but there's something more important than that," Anja said.

"Hmmm… Is it because men are more likely to cause a problem if they're feeling jealous?"

"Exactly, and really there's only Escamilla to worry about. I'm fucking Trey, and I'm pretty sure that Lawson is fucking Chukwuma. The captain… Well, her situation is complicated, but she wouldn't have any interest in David here. That just leaves you and Escamilla. You're not going to start smashing stuff if you don't get enough dick, are you?"

"Yeah, right." Paige said, rolling her eyes.

"I gave the captain a great comeback to have at the ready if Esmeralda complained about the lack of male sexbots. I told her to tell Escamilla that if she was having trouble finding a hard dick on this ship that she needed some remedial training in situational awareness. I can tell you're not impressed, but trust me, the marines would have laughed.

"But Esmeralda didn't complain," Anja continued. "When she signed up and indicated her preferences, she asked for an early slot with Cat Girl. I gave her an early appointment with Jailbait, and she traded with Zell for a later appointment with Cat Girl. What does that tell us?"

Paige pressed her lips together and looked up, thinking it through. "It means that you were right about her being bisexual?"

"Probably. I know you like Cat Girl too, or Bygul." Anja pointed at the engraved plate above the middle Alcove. It had the word *Bygul* engraved in it. The plate above the alcove to the left read *Lolita* and the one with David in it was labeled *David*.

"Do you remember squeezing my hand when the captain grabbed Cat Girl's tail and pulled it out of the way so we could see her butt?" Anja asked, smiling at Paige.

"Did I? I don't remember that," Paige said. She remembered Anja telling her that a proper slut was always honest. "But I am excited about being alone with Cat Girl. And nervous. I'm afraid I won't know what to do."

"Don't worry, little tiger," Anja said. "Cat Girl knows what to do. And if you enjoy it, I'm the keeper of the schedule. I can get you a second date with her before we all get into our acceleration couches. I'm pretty sure you're the only virgin on board. Well, maybe Antal too. Nobody will have a leg to stand on if they want to bitch about me playing favorites. You're due."

"Anja," Paige asked. "Did you give the captain permission to show everyone the video of you touching yourself?"

Anja laughed. "It was my idea!"

"You seemed like you really enjoyed being there with everyone watching. Did you? Or were you just playing along?"

"I loved it."

"You told me that being a good slut means getting consent, communicating clearly and honestly, and respecting everyone involved. How does showing your body to everyone..."

"Okay," Anja said. "I see where you're going. Paige, I need to be really clear about this." Paige knew that Anja was serious when she called her *Paige* rather than *little tiger*.

"There's being a proper slut, and then there's being Anja Petrovic. Yes, a good slut respects other people's needs and preferences, communicates clearly and is always honest about what she wants. But nothing about being a good slut means you need to act like I do. I don't like the word, but it's true, I am an exhibitionist. I want people to see me naked. I want them to see me sexually aroused. That's just my stuff.

"I want you to be honest and respectful in your dealings with other people. I don't want you to walk around naked or have sex where you think you might get caught like I do. I mean, I love doing that stuff, and if you want to try it out, go for it, but that has nothing to do with being a good slut."

"I understand," Paige said.

"And one more thing." Anja said. "Cat Girl is not a person. You don't have to be honest with her or consider her needs. She doesn't have any needs. But, it would be a good idea to practice being honest, communicative and respectful with her. Not the first time. Let her lead tomorrow morning, but after that, practice telling her what you liked and didn't like and what you'd like to do next. It will be good practice for when you're with a real person. That said, don't get emotionally attached to her. Don't fall in love with her. She can't love you back."

"Okay, Anja." Paige hugged Anja, and Anja kissed the top of her head.

"Okay, little tiger. Don't get all mushy on me. Anyway, it's time for lunch. Let's get back down to where the working people live."

1.10.3 - Cook

Cook pulled another sandwich from the panini press, but

instead of adding it to the servery, he wrapped it in foil and set it aside. Escamilla, the pretty medic, approached him with her tray.

Cook paid no attention to his appearance. He shaved every couple of weeks, but he didn't work out or worry about holding in his gut. He didn't have a skin care regimen. He put on clean clothes each morning, but even wearing an apron, they didn't stay clean, and he didn't care. He knew he had no chance with a woman like Escamilla. A source of depression and resentment for some men, for Cook, this certainty was liberating. He wasn't worried about *blowing it* with her. He could say whatever came to mind.

"What's up, doc?" Cook said.

"Hello, Cook," Escamilla said with a polite smile. "I'm not a doctor. I'm just a combat medic."

"*Just*? The next time I get shot, a combat medic is *just* what I'll want. Anyway, you're closer to a doctor than a ham sandwich. Speaking of which..." He gestured at the sandwiches. "Ham, roasted pork, white cheese, pickles and mustard. You know what that's called?"

"A *Cubano sandwich*?" Esmeralda laughed, and Cook thought her laugh was slightly more genuine than her initial smile.

"Yep. What about these?" He gestured at the first side dish.

"Fried plantains?"

"I think they're called *Toasty Tonys*," Cook said, feigning ignorance. Cook knew food.

"Toasty To..." Esmeralda burst out laughing when she made the connection. "*Tostones!*"

"That's what I said, *Toasty Tonys*. And if you think you're losing your mojo, this sauce should set you right," Cook said, pointing at a collection of sealed serving cups. "It's got garlic, olive oil, lime juice and some other stuff."

Esmeralda rewarded Cook with a renewed burst of laughter, genuine, for sure.

"*Salsa de mojo*," she said, pronouncing the J like an H. "Oh,

Cook."

She took a sandwich and a small quantity of plantains, but passed on the sauce. As she carried her tray to a table near the display wall, Cook imagined that she didn't want garlic breath for her hot date, not that Cat Girl would care.

Jailbait was more Cook's speed. He planned to give that big butt what for. He wondered if her cheeks would turn pink when he swatted them.

And speak of the devil, Cook thought to himself. Just as he takes one moment to indulge in a little flight of sexual fantasy, in walks the embodiment of sex herself, Mama Tiger and her cub.

Petrovic and Paige approached Cook. As they neared the invisible line that divided the dining area from the kitchen, Petrovic stopped short of it while Paige sailed right on through, flexing her superpower.

"How can I help?" Paige asked.

Cook pointed to the wrapped sandwich and a bottled drink. "I don't expect to see the captain down here for a while. We can't let her starve," Cook said.

"I'll take it to her," Paige said and reached for the sandwich.

"Hold up there, little tiger," Petrovic said. "I think you have something to say to Escamilla. Cook, why don't you wrap up a couple of those sandwiches for me and I'll take the captain her lunch."

"You got it," Cook said.

Without being told, Paige took two sandwiches off the line and started wrapping them while Cook got another bottle of tea from a cooler.

1.10.4 - Petrovic

Petrovic arrived at the captain's office and was delighted to find her new lover there. He was just getting up from the couch when she arrived.

"Captain?" Petrovic said, and held up the sandwiches and bottles. Paige had packed them in an open wicker basket with napkins, sides of the garlic sauce and two boats of fried plantains. "Doctor," she said to Trey, her voice dripping with lascivious intent.

"Petrovic," Trey said, smiling. To the captain, he said, "I'll look this over, Captain, and let you know if I find anything useful in it."

"Doctor," Trix said with a nod, and Trey departed.

Petrovic set the basket on the table, and to her amazement, the captain actually reached for one of the sandwiches. Not wanting to jinx it by commenting, Petrovic set out the paper serving boat of plantains and mojo sauce without a word.

As always, the captain's clothing emphasized her breasts and left little to the imagination. Petrovic caught herself lingering on the captain's nipples, which cast an obvious shadow as they pressed through her form-fitting top.

"See anything you like," Trix asked.

"Sorry, ma'am," Petrovic said, and dragged her eyes up to meet the captain's gaze. "I think I'm coming down with what Rex has. I get horny when I'm alone with you."

"I think you're always horny, Petrovic," the captain said.

"That's nearly true, Captain," Petrovic admitted. "But you really bring out my inner lesbian."

"Alright, Petrovic. Pack it up. If you can go the rest of this conversation without another word about sex, I'll send you out the door with a slap on the ass."

"Consider my brazen sluttiness secured, Captain."

"So, my presentation..." the captain began.

"Was perfect," Petrovic finished for her. "I was a little worried when you went off script there at the end, but your ad lib was even better than what we'd planned. You might have brought the tears out a little earlier. Not everybody saw them, but otherwise, it was perfect."

The captain opened her mouth to speak, but no words came out.

"I'm sorry, Captain. I know the emotions were genuine. I'm not saying you were faking anything for dramatic effect, but it was great. You really shut 'em up. And it didn't spoil the joy of the dolls. They're all anybody is talking about."

"How much time do you think this buys me?"

"I can't say for sure, but the general level of tension among the crew has eased up. If we actually have someone to fight when we come off this next burn, that will bring everyone together. But if it's just more waiting and uncertainty, then the paranoia and the conspiracy talk will come back, dolls or no dolls. Is there a fight coming?"

"Petrovic," the captain said, "I honestly don't know. I was instructed to hire a combat-oriented crew and that's what I did, but I have no more information about what we're getting into than you do."

Petrovic's attention was divided. She heard what the captain said, and she had meant to acknowledge it, but a cascade of realizations distracted her. The captain was going to slap her on the ass at the end of this interview. This was so much more than Petrovic could have hoped for. Total victory, but was it right?

Petrovic understood that the captain used sex talk to manipulate her. It was a straight up, *quip pro quo* sexual transaction. Trix adopted an attitude of total dominance over her because Anja had handed her the keys to her psychology with her performance on Trey's laboratory work bench. It's what Petrovic wanted from the captain. Everything was consensual.

Trix was dominant because Petrovic wanted to be commanded, but below the superficial particulars, was this situation all that different than Trix dropping to her knees and sucking dick to secure the cooperation and good will of her shipmates?

Petrovic, interrogated herself. Had she strayed from the slut's path? Had she really gotten the captain's consent? Her enthusiastic consent? Had she been respectful of the captain's boundaries? Petrovic wondered if she could even bring herself to decline the reward the captain had offered her.

"What is it?" The captain asked.

Petrovic swallowed. "I... uh, ma'am. You don't have to slap my ass."

"Really? You don't want it?"

"I do want it, but I'm not sure I should..." Petrovic floundered for words, something that never happened when sex was the topic under discussion.

"Not sure you should *what*?" Demanded the captain.

"I didn't mean to... I don't want to cause you..." Petrovic stammered.

"Cause me to what?" The captain's voice was animated with anger now. "Backslide? Relapse?"

"I'm sorry, ma'am. I didn't mean to presume."

"*Presume*?!" Trix was in a rage now. Where did this come from?

"You think you know what's good and not good for me? That's pretty fucking presumptuous, Petrovic! You're getting more than a smack on the ass on your way out the door now. Stand up!"

Petrovic shot to her feet.

"Take your pants off!" The captain demanded. Petrovic's mouth gaped. "That's a fucking order, marine!"

Petrovic kicked off her shoes and pulled her pants down just as quickly she could undo her belt and fly.

"Underwear too."

Petrovic bent over and pulled her underwear down her legs. She stepped out of them and pushed the pile of clothes away with one foot. She stood at attention, breathing deeply.

"Get over there and put your face down on the desk, marine. Stick your ass in the air."

Petrovic hurried to comply.

"You think you know what's good for me? What's in my best interest?" the captain demanded.

"No, ma'am. I'm sorry, ma'am."

"Do you know what Rex did after he told me he didn't want me to suck his cock anymore?"

"No, ma'am."

"He came in my fucking mouth, marine."

"Oooooh fuuuuuck," Petrovic moaned.

"Who controls my body?" Trix said.

"You do, ma'am."

"That's right." The captain agreed, her voice like iron. "Who controls your body, Petrovic?"

"You do, ma'am. Your will is my will."

Trix raised her arm and swung hard. Her open left hand connected with Petrovic's left butt cheek and Petrovic erupted with ecstasy. Trix slapped her again, harder this time, and Petrovic cried out in pleasure.

"Damn, your ass is like a rock," Trix said.

"Yes, ma'am. I have a hard ass, ma'am."

"Get on the couch."

Petrovic hurried to the couch.

"Shirt," the captain said, and Petrovic pulled her shirt over her head, tearing it in her haste.

"You're naked, Petrovic. I'm looking at your naked body."

"Thank you, Captain!"

"Give me another show, Petrovic. Like you did in the med lab, but with conviction this time."

"Oh, fuck, Captain. Fuuuck," Petrovic moaned as she opened her legs and began to masturbate.

"Let me hear you, marine. Make some noise."

Petrovic gasped and moaned, drew deep breaths, and abandoned all sense of self. She was the expression of her captain's will in sound.

Her face a mask of merciless dominance, Trix picked up a data slate and swiped.

"I'm going to put you on the PA ship-wide," the captain informed her in a voice of unchallenged command. "Tell me when you're about to cum. Everyone is going to hear you,

Petrovic."

"Oh, yes. Yes! Almost there, ma'am. Put me on! Put me on!" Petrovic gasped. Trix pushed the image of a button on screen and Petrovic's moans sounded throughout the ship.

The muscles in Petrovic's forearms stood out in stark relief as she scrubbed furiously at her clitoris. The captain moved the slate down between Petrovic's legs so that the slippery sounds of her wet cunt found their way to every ear on the ship.

Faces flashed in Petrovic's mind. Esmeralda, Cook, Rex, Paige, Trey. The realization they were all listening in real time intensified her pleasure. She moaned and whimpered. Her eyes overflowed with tears. "I'll do anything for you, Captain! I'm yours! I belong to you!" Trix left the connection open until Petrovic was well past her climax and then shut off the PA.

"Thank you, Captain. Thank you. May I kiss you, ma'am."

"No, you may not. Get to medical and fuck your pretty boy doctor. Leave your clothes. Shoes only. Go now."

Petrovic staggered naked into the passageway on trembling legs leaving Trix ablaze with power.

DIVINE PSYCHOSIS

1.11.1 - Rex

Rex inspected the larger of the two cargo bays with Dobrovitz. No crew member had been ordered to access any gear or operate any machinery in this bay since the *Persephone* came off of her last high-g burn.

In the bad old days, when this ship was known as the *Nipple*, the mere fact that nobody had any official business in this bay did not mean that Rex could assume nobody had been here. Crew members might have gathered here for private drinking and drugging sessions. They might have been looking for equipment they could pilfer or making other kinds of mischief.

Trix had fired all but the best of the old crew when the DAO made her acting-captain. The only crew onboard the *Persephone* who had lived and worked on the *Nipple*, besides Trix and himself, were Dobrovitz, Zell, Lake and Cook. Everyone else got a five minute notice before being escorted off the ship by a pair of hulking brutes Trix hired for the occasion.

Rex nodded in satisfaction. Everything was secured and ready for the next burn. Despite some eccentricities, and here Rex was thinking of Petrovic, with her overclocked libido and formal code of sexual ethics, and Sparks, who lived in a fantasy world of dark forces and improbable conspiracies, this crew was as disciplined and reliable as he could hope for.

Rex nodded to Dobrovitz to indicate his satisfaction with

the state of the cargo bay. Hans Dobrovitz's job title was drill operator, but his actual skills went well beyond his official certifications. He could remote operate every piece of equipment on this ship that was used for surveying and production. *Production* meant extracting useful materials from Kupier Belt Objects or *KBOs*. It was one of those acronyms where half the people who used it in daily life had either forgotten what it stands for or never knew in the first place.

The most valuable loads you could hope to find in KBOs were radioactive materials that could be refined into reactor fuels. Energy is life. After that were rare minerals for use in electronics, then phosphorus for fertilizer and iron for construction, but even KBOs that were mostly just water ice and frozen ammonia were valuable.

Water was a source of oxygen for life support. Water could also be used as reaction mass. Ammonia, with just a bit of processing to purify it, could be used as fuel for *Persephone's* backup engines. They also used ammonia for the maneuvering thrusters. Dobrovitz was skilled in extracting anything useful that you could expect to find in a KBO.

Rex hated to admit it, but he thought of Hans Dobrovitz as *Zell lite*. Joachin Zell, while younger than Dobrovitz, was more focused and accomplished. Where Dobrovitz only held a drill operator's certification, Zell held several advanced degrees and professional certifications all related to Trans-Neptunian geology and mining.

Trans-Neptunian was an old phrase that most Spinners never used. You mostly heard it from highly-educated people, like Zell, or from wannabes, like Li. Before the *Nipple* became the *Persephone*, Zell was often the highest paid member of the crew because he got a bonus based on the sale of mined materials. On the *Nipple*, Zell sometimes made more than the captain. Under the new compensation structure, Zell made less, which is why he'd made the effort to get all the certifications needed to hire on as both a geologist and a marine.

Dobrovitz had made no such effort and was now the second lowest paid member of the crew after that scrap of a girl that Trix hired on as a deckhand. Trix insisted that the girl had potential, but Rex knew she was kidding herself in order to justify an act of pity. Ag workers didn't make good spacers.

Dobrovitz didn't make much money, but he lived aboard this ship, and the ship itself was a lot more comfortable now than it used to be. The food was better than it had been, and Hans got to keep his old quarters. Where the marines were housed in compartments just large enough for an acceleration couch, rack, head, shower and closet, Dobrovitz's quarters consisted of three connected compartments. You could almost call it a suite. Zell and Cook had even more spacious accommodations.

"Hey, Rex," Dobrovitz said, "Which one of those sex dolls do you think you're going to go for?"

Rex shrugged. "I hadn't really thought about it."

"I'm sure that Cat Girl's a good dancer or whatever, but for getting up close and personal, that Jailbait is the one for me. I'm gonna ruin that. You know what I mean. I'm not going to damage any shipboard equipment, but… damn, that face."

"I don't want to talk about it," Rex said.

"Huh?" Hans said, uncomprehending for a second, and then he put the obvious pieces together. "Oh, right. Hey, look, it makes sense that Trix can't do us all anymore like she used to. She's the captain and all, but I know that you two had something more than just… you know. You two could be a couple, and it wouldn't be a problem. Everybody would still respect you and her both. I mean, you know…"

"I said, I don't want to talk about it," Rex repeated with enough emphasis that Dobrovitz took the hint.

"Okay. I'm just sayin', is all."

The PA system erupted with the sounds of a woman moaning in sexual ecstasy. This was the second time they'd heard such a performance from Petrovic, so it wasn't hard to place the voice even before she added words to her sex song.

"I'll do anything for you, Captain!" Petrovic cried. "I'm yours! I belong to you!"

"Oh, shit," said Dobrovitz, delighted. He looked up, as people often do when listening to disembodied voices, an unshakable grin on his face.

Petrovic's moans died down and the PA cut off.

"Damn, that Petrovic is a trip. She's too much woman for me. I think she'd break me, but I love having her around. Love that vibe."

Rex wasn't listening to Dobrovitz.

Rex said, seemingly to himself, "What the hell are you doing?" To Hans, he said, "Take lunch," and walked out of the cargo bay.

1.11.2 - Paige

Paige arranged the wrapped sandwiches, boats of tostones, cups of dipping sauce and drink bottles along with some napkins in a basket and gave it to Anja. Anja smiled and put a hand on Paige's cheek. Paige put her hand over Anja's, and as Anja started to take her hand away, Paige pressed it to her mouth and kissed Anja's palm.

"Little tiger," Anja said and turned Paige toward Esmeralda's table and gave her a gentle push before exiting the galley.

"Esmeralda, may I sit with you?" Paige asked when she reached the table.

Esmeralda smiled and said, "Of course, sweetie."

Paige sat. "I'm sorry I kept you from being alone with Trey. I was out of line."

"What? Oh, don't worry about it," Esmeralda said. "It's nothing. I was just playing around anyway. I wasn't really going to sleep with him. I barely know him."

"Well, even if that's true, I was wrong. I was feeling jealous, and I shouldn't have done what I did," Paige said.

"Did Petrovic tell you that you had to apologize to me?"

"Sort of. She helped me to understand why I did what I did, and when I realized that I did it because I was jealous, she asked me what I thought I should do. She didn't exactly tell me to apologize to you, but she helped me understand that I should."

"She's a capable marine, but that woman has some strange ideas. I know she's your friend, but be careful. You don't want to become like her," Esmeralda said.

"You're right," Paige agreed. "She says the same thing. She even says that I could learn a lot from you."

Esmeralda raised an eyebrow. "Really?"

"Yes," Paige said. "You know, Anja is like a man in a lot of ways. When she's interested in a man, she doesn't flirt with him. She just tells him that she's attracted to him and that she's available for sex if he is interested."

"What a slut," Esmeralda said.

"That's right," Paige said. "And she knows she's not pretty. She doesn't know how to wear make-up or pretty clothes. She says it's good that I like girly stuff, but she can't teach me about that kind of thing. She says I should ask you about that stuff. Will you teach me?"

"Paige, I'm flattered," Esmeralda said, smiling. "What do you want to know, exactly?"

"I want to be feminine, like you. I want to learn how to wear make-up and flirt with boys… with men." Paige said, all while making unwavering eye contact with Esmeralda. "And I just learned that I'm bisexual."

Paige could tell this took Esmeralda by surprise. "You *just* learned? What do you mean?"

"The captain told me that I am not allowed to have sex with any of the marines. Not *any* kind of sex. I think she knows that I like Dwayne Sparks, and she does not approve."

"I think the captain is overstepping her authority. She can't tell you how to conduct your personal life," Esmeralda said.

She was going to continue but Paige interrupted.

"I could never disobey her, in anything. She's more than just my boss."

"I get it." Esmeralda agreed. "She's pretty intense, and I wouldn't want to go against her either. And in this case, she's right. That boy is bad news. He would not be good to you, sweetie. But what about you being bisexual? What's that about?"

"It's about Cat Girl. Or Bygul. That's her real name. The captain said I can't have sex with the marines, but she didn't say anything about the sex robots. And I'm on the schedule. Bygul will be coming to my quarters tomorrow morning. I'm excited but also scared."

"Scared? Why?"

"Because I don't know what to do." Paige said. "I'm not scared. I guess I'm just nervous."

"Well, don't worry. Cat Girl will know what to do."

"That's what Anja said."

"Well, she's right about that, at least," Esmeralda conceded. "Paige, honey, are you a virgin?"

"I think so, mostly," Paige said.

"You *think* so?" Esmeralda scowled. "What does that mean?"

"When I worked in the rice paddies, my crew boss let me practice oral sex on him a few times."

"He *let* you? Well, how generous of him," Esmeralda said.

"It really was. He didn't need me for that. He had a wife and a girlfriend, and he could have had any women on his crew. But sometimes soldiers would come to the farm, and they would pay him to take a girl behind the silos. Sometimes the soldiers would give the girls some money too, or some food. And even if they didn't you still got a few calories from their…"

"Stop! I know it's not right, the way the military treats the Galters, particularly the ag workers. I'm sorry you had to live that way, Paige."

"But no soldiers ever picked me. Why would they? Look at me." Paige gestured at her flat chest.

"Now, Paige. You're a very pretty girl. You just need to gain some weight."

"So my crew chief gave me an old slate with some math courses on it. He told me he could get me into an aptitude test if I completed the courses. He didn't know what job I might qualify for, but he said it was worth a shot. I did the courses, took the test, and I got a high score. I don't know how she learned about me, but Captain Nixon came to the farm and interviewed me in the crew boss's shed. She offered me a deckhand position, and here I am."

Esmeralda looked uncomfortable, and Paige imagined she felt guilty for growing up with the advantages of being in a military family.

"It's not your fault, Esmeralda. You've been kind to me. I'm really grateful."

Esmeralda said, "So, you've had a man in your mouth, but you've never had intercourse."

Paige nodded.

"Then you're still a virgin. In a way, you'll still be a virgin this time tomorrow. Cat Girl won't penetrate you unless you ask her to," Esmeralda said.

"How do you know?"

Esmeralda smiled. "I've been with her model before."

"I looked at the schedule. I know that Dwayne is with her right now and that you're scheduled to be with her at the start of the next watch. Are you excited?"

Esmeralda started to smile, but then she asserted control over her expression and composed herself. "Yes, sweetie. I'm looking forward to it."

Paige smiled. "I'm supposed to go see the doctor now. Would you come with me? It won't take long. You'll be back in time for your appointment."

"I suppose I could," Esmeralda said. "What do you have in mind?"

"You could flirt with him. Wouldn't it be fun to flirt with him and then go and play with Bygul?"

Esmeralda's smile escaped her control. "Okay, let's go."

Esmeralda was smaller and less muscular than Anja, but she was still in top condition. She reached the top of the ladder to the medical level and turned back to see Paige at the bottom of the ladder. Paige was holding the handrail and leaning forward, her tiny chest heaving. Esmeralda wasn't even breathing deeply. They'd only climbed three levels.

"Take it easy, sweetie," Esmeralda called down to the young woman. "Take your time."

Esmeralda waited, and just as Paige reached the top of the ladder, Petrovic's cries of passion and the wet flapping of her pussy came over the PA.

"That dirty whore," Esmeralda said aloud. Paige didn't have the breath to speak, but Esmeralda's scorn reminded her about Anja's explanation about the difference between a slut and a whore.

"I'll do anything for you, Captain! I'm yours! I belong to you!" Petrovic said over the PA.

Yes, Paige thought. *Now you get it. Now you see what I see.*

Page looked at Esmeralda and nodded. "Okay," she wheezed. "I'm okay."

When they reached Trey's office he was seated at his desk holding something Paige didn't recognize. It was a large rectangle that folded in the middle. Paige looked at Esmeralda and decided she wasn't going to get a lesson in flirting after all. Esmeralda looked irritated.

"Hello, doctor," Esmeralda said, trying and failing to summon up her charm. "Paige is here for a pre-burn check up. Do you have any idea what..." Esmeralda rolled her eyes and pointed at the deckhead with her index finger "...*that* was all about?"

"Petrovic isn't shy," The doctor said with what might have been an attempt at comedic understatement. Nobody laughed. "Well, either she was trying to send a message to the captain, or..." Seemingly, he couldn't formulate an alternative option.

"I don't think so," Paige said. "She took the captain her lunch. I think they were together. I bet the captain told Anja put on another show."

"Why in the black would she do that?" Esmeralda asked.

"Listen," said Paige. They heard the sound of footfalls on the level below them. Someone was running hard. Whomever it was was on the ladder now, taking the steps three at a time. Naked and wild eyed, Anja burst into the doctor's office.

"Escamilla," she said without looking at Esmeralda. Her eyes were locked on Trey. "Go fuck your robot. Take Paige." Anja advanced on Trey. "You need to fuck me right now!"

Anja pulled the object out of Trey's hands and flung it into a corner. The name of the object popped into Paige's mind. *Book.*

Esmeralda went to put her arm around Paige's shoulder to guide her out of the office, but Paige evaded her.

"I'm staying," Paige insisted.

Esmeralda looked at Anja for help, but Anja was busy undoing Trey's pants. Trey looked at Esmeralda and shrugged. Esmeralda huffed her indignation, threw up her hands and stamped out of the office.

Paige watched as Anja planted herself on the doctor's desk, drew him to her, his pants undone and down just enough to let his cock stand erect. Anja wrapped her legs around Trey's waist and pulled him into her.

Anja controlled the pace, and it was furious. The doctor pushed Anja down onto the desk and lifted her legs. He didn't need any encouragement. He was into it. He met Paige's eyes for an instant, but his facial expression did not change. He was as caught up in the moment as Anja was. Paige clasped her hands together below her chin and watched in silence, inching ever closer to Anja, who did not seem to be aware of her presence.

The doctor pulled out of Anja and ordered her to turn over. Anja sat up, put her feet on the floor, turned around and put her torso down on the desk. She reached down and played with her clit while Trey positioned himself to enter her from behind. She moaned as he thrust into her, and now their intensity reached a new plateau. Anja panted and grunted. Paige sank down into a seated position, her legs folded up under her right in front of Anja. She put a hand on Anja's face, and Anja opened her eyes. Anja took Paige's hand. She squeezed so hard that Paige thought her hand would break, but she didn't cry out or pull away.

"Oh, Anja," Paige said.

The doctor pounded into Anja and slapped her ass. Anja gasped with each slap until her orgasm engulfed her. She seemed to deflate as the orgasm ebbed. She let go of Paige's hand. Paige put one hand on each side of Anja's face.

"Now you understand about the captain, don't you, Anja?" Paige searched Anja's eyes and found what she was looking for.

"Yes, little tiger. Yes. I get it. I see it now. She owns me," Anja said.

"Me too," Paige said.

Trey pulled up his pants and fastened them. Paige could see that his penis, which as Anja had told her, was larger than she would have expected on a man his size, was still hard. He wrangled it into his pants in an upright position. He slapped Anja on the ass again and spoke to her firmly. "Petrovic, I'm not finished with you. Get your ass into the examination room and sit on the table!"

Anja smiled and looked back at him over her shoulder. "Yes, boss," she said. Reaching out to hold the bulkhead for support, Anja made her way from the doctor's office to the examination room. Paige followed close behind.

Trey positioned scanners around Anja's head and put the cuff on her arm.

"Petrovic," he said her name with authority, like he was her commander rather than her lover. "You were just with the captain, yes?"

"Yes, boss," Anja said.

"Close your eyes," Trey ordered. "Picture the scene, what happened?"

"She ordered me to take off my pants so she could beat my ass. I put my body on her desk and presented my ass to her."

"How did you feel?"

"Delirious. I couldn't believe it."

"She spanked your big ox ass?"

"She did, but my ass was too hard. It hurt her hand."

"Then what happened?

"She ordered me to play with myself on her couch."

"Did she touch you?"

"No, she just watched. It was wonderful. She told me she was going to put me on the PA."

"Did you want that?"

"Yes. Oh, fuck yes."

"We heard you. I heard you. Paige heard you."

"I heard you," Paige chimed in. "You were wonderful."

"Then what happened?" Trey continued.

"She told me to come here and fuck you."

"Petrovic," Trey said, "Imagine the captain is here now. She's watching you. She wants you to play with your nipples." Anja immediately found her nipples and gasped.

"She wants you to bring yourself to orgasm just by pinching your nipples," Trey said. He wasn't looking at Anja. He kept looking back and forth between two displays. Anja whimpered and moaned and she stimulated her nipples.

Paige saw that the doctor was lost in his readouts now. She looked at his crotch. His erection was gone. He was somewhere else. Paige took up his role.

"Anja," Paige said. "The captain wants you to cum again. You have to cum for the captain, Anja. You must obey her."

"Ooooohhh fuuuuuck," Anja wailed. "Oh fuck!"

"You have to cum for the captain, Anja," Paige told her.

Anja erupted in another orgasm. She stopped pinching her nipples and clamped her breasts with clawing fingers. Her wide shoulders made her breasts look small, but with her fingers wrapped around them, they looked quite large in her hands.

Paige looked at Trey. He was holding a slate now, poking madly at it. When he failed to notice that she was looking at him, she cleared her throat softly. He looked up.

"Oh," he said. "Petrovic, the captain is satisfied. She wants you to rest now. Lean back and relax. Anja leaned back, and the exam table automatically extended a section to support her legs so she could rest comfortably. Trey took the ampule of blood from the cuff. He held it up to the light and scrutinized it, as if he could analyze it by sight.

"Anja," Trey said, finally speaking to her like a friend rather than her commander. "How do you feel?"

"Mmmmm... divine," she said.

"Yes," Trey said, looking back at the readings on his displays. "I imagine so."

1.11.3 - Trey

When I got the results of the toxicology screen, I generated a few illustrations and info-graphics based on my scans of Anja's brain while she was in the throes of her ecstasy.

Before heading up to the flight deck, I retrieved the book from the floor of my office, hoping, now that I thought about it, that Petrovic hadn't damaged it when she flung it aside. A few of the pages had new creases in them, but this book was very well worn. Someone or multiple someones had spent many hours pouring over its pages.

I think the captain was expecting me. Perhaps she saw me approaching on a security feed. When I arrived, she had an image on her wall display of the Dyson sphere as seen from the Kuiper Belt, possibly a real time image from the ship's external sensors.

"Good afternoon, Captain. I brought your book back," I said.

"It's not my book, but what did you make of it?"

"Do you know what a tabletop role-playing game is?"

"You mean an entertainment sim?"

"Not exactly. It's like a collaborative story-telling exercise that people do mostly just using their imaginations. One player is the game master. He describes the environment and events to the other players, all of whom are play-acting as imaginary characters. The characters have attributes and abilities that are described in numbers, and the players roll dice, consult tables and do simple calculations to determine success or failure when their characters attempt something.

"There are different story settings and genres, but the earliest games had a fantasy setting like *The Lord of the Rings* and the players would be warriors or wizards, elves or Hobbits."

Her expression changed when I said *Hobbits*. Recognition? But then she scowled, resuming her usual hard visage.

"Get to the point, doctor."

"Well, this book is a reference for a game called Unimatrix. This book, *Void Huntress*, describes a setting for the game. It was published in 2035."

"How do you know that?" Trix asked.

"It's printed in very small print down here at the bottom of the first page." I opened the book to the first page and pointed to the publication date. She didn't look at it. I noticed that she didn't ask for any clarification on what I meant by *2035*. They don't use the Gregorian calendar in this part of the Kuiper Belt.

"So, this book is a game?"

"Not exactly. Not the whole game. It's a supplement. An expansion on the core game. This one describes the deities and mythological figures worshiped by two groups of humans living in the Kuiper Belt."

"It says that in the book? That the story is set in the Kuiper

Belt?

"I haven't read the whole thing," I said, flipping through the pages, "But I don't recall seeing explicit references to *the Kuiper Belt*. There's an index." I turned to the back and checked the index under K then B and finally T.

"No entry for *Kuiper Belt*, but there's a map that shows cities named after Kuiper Belt objects like Pluto, Eris, Orcus, Yuggoth..."

"Yuggoth?" Trix said.

"You probably have a different name for it," I said, though I didn't know what it might be. "Anyway, this book describes a struggle between two factions of gods and the humans who serve them. There are the forces of light and order, led by Ba'al, and those of darkness and chaos, led by Yam, and his lieutenant, Re-Mot, and the corrupted voidlings who serve them."

"I see," she said, holding out a hand for the book. I gave it to her, and she set it on her desk without looking at it.

"Sit," she said, gesturing at the least comfortable looking chair in her office, the one facing her desk.

It was my understanding that, according to spacer culture, a ship's doctor was a near peer to the captain, but she seemed to have cast me in the role of the troublesome student with her playing the stern headmistress at some 19th century British boarding school. I wondered what infraction had I committed.

"You've complicated my life, doctor."

"By my actions or my mere existence?"

"Do you know who issues the marching orders to this ship and her crew?"

"A collection of shareholders in a distributed autonomous organization," I said.

"Correct," the captain said. "The DAO bought this ship a few months ago and gave it a complete overhaul. It has been upgraded in nearly every way. Decisions regarding the ship are put to a vote, and all of the shareholders—I estimate they number in the high teens—can vote on those proposals. I know this because I sunk my savings buying voting shares in the DAO. Anyone controlling more than ten percent of the voting shares can bring proposals to a vote. I control 9% of the shares. Based on the timing of the votes, I believe that three entities control a combined total of more than half the shares, and they all vote as a block. I call them the *Whales*. Do you know who the Whales are?"

"No," I said, which was the truth.

"Take a guess."

"Well, it makes sense that your Whales would either be aspects of the Is, or they could be human agents of the Is in the Kuiper Belt," I said. "But that's just conjecture. I don't have any inside information."

"The *Is*," she said. "That's what you call the *Powers*?"

I didn't want to tell her that her notion of *Powers* was hopelessly simplistic, but for the sake of keeping things moving, I rolled with it.

"More or less," I said.

"So, we could be working for the Powers?"

"It seems plausible," I agreed.

"And you were sent here by the Powers." A statement. Not a question.

"I asked to come out here," I said.

"To search for evidence of alien life?"

"Yes. You find that hard to believe?"

"People tend to have practical concerns out here."

At least she answered my question. That was progress. I looked for a way to turn *practical concerns* into a segue to talking about Petrovic, but nothing occurred to me. She pressed on.

"Not many humans from behind the Curtain come out here. Spinners are distrustful of those who do, but immigrants tend to come with a lot of useful education and skills, so they usually find a place."

"Rather than getting spaced," I said. I was joking.

"Nobody gets spaced," she said. Not joking.

"That would be a waste of phosphorus," I said.

"Among other things."

I didn't see a natural opening to transition to my intended topic. I thought that if I told her I wanted to talk about Petrovic that she would shut me down, so I tried a less direct approach.

"Captain, there is a medical matter I'd like to discuss with you." I held up my data slate. "May I access your display?"

She made a gesture with her left hand and the image of the Dyson sphere vanished. I put up a graphic representing Petrovic's recent brain activity comparing it to a simulated baseline. The captain glanced at it and then trained her intense stare back on me.

"This is Petrovic's recent brain activity. You probably know that she came barging into my office demanding a hard out fuck." I watched her eyes as I said *hard out*, but if she reacted to the phrase, it was a subtle response. She may have been onto me.

"That's right," the captain said.

"I had sex with her last night and again this morning, so I have a baseline for comparison. This afternoon was very different. She was beyond euphoric. I trained scanners on her and measured her brain activity. It looked to me as if she was having a mystical experience."

"You can scan for that, can you?"

"Not exactly, but this is something I have a lot of experience with. Given what her brain was doing when I asked her to imagine that she was still in here with you," I glanced over at the couch and saw Petrovic's clothes on the floor. "She was either in the throes of divine rapture or she was having a psychotic episode."

"What's the difference?"

"In terms of brain activity, none," I said. "The difference comes in the long-term effect on the person's life and outlook. Someone suffering from psychosis becomes fixated on their own anxieties or inflated sense of self-importance. Someone who has had a mystical experience goes the other way. They tend to discount their own personal concerns in favor of something larger, more universal. They focus on the community, the ecosystem, or the enlightenment of all sentient beings. Something along those lines."

"Drugs?"

"I didn't find anything in her bloodwork," I said.

"So?"

"So, all of your marines came with extensive medical histories. Petrovic has no history of psychosis. This seems to have come out of the blue and coincided with you ordering her to masturbate on your couch and sharing her orgasm with the entire ship."

"Is she combat effective?"

"What?"

"Can she fight?"

"Captain, that's not why I'm concerned."

"That's *my* concern, doctor. She needs to gear up and be ready for combat at the other end of this next burn. I'm ordering her to remain in medical for observation until it's time for her to get into her acceleration couch. Paige was assigned to shadow her for maintenance duties. Paige is now under your wing. Teach her to be useful in medical."

"Captain, I..."

"That will be all, doctor. You're dismissed. Take Petrovic's clothes with you."

DISTRACTION AND FOCUS

1.12.1 - Rex

Rex approached the captain's office, leaping ahead in his imagination to the shouting match that was sure to erupt as soon as he set foot in the compartment. He wanted to know what Trix thought she was doing. Putting that video clip of Petrovic in her presentation was bad enough, but once was a stunt. Twice in one day? That was a pattern. A disturbing pattern belying compromised judgment.

Had she done it to provoke him? Was she waiting for him to jump on command like a trained dog? He stopped in the p-way short of her office. Was this a trap?

Maybe he should take someone with him. His body betrayed him when he was alone with her, so he would bring a witness. Who?

He turned around and walked softly back the way he had come. *Pathetic.* Slinking away from a fight he couldn't imagine winning. He went down to the galley to see who was idle. He heard Kellemen's voice before he entered the galley.

"I know, but hear me out," Kellemen said. "We get these warm and fuzzy feelings when we hear about order and light, but that's Shapash's light. *We've* never seen that light. She's been behind the Curtain for centuries. She doesn't nourish us. We don't need her light to live. Are we going to go begging to the Powers to let us in?"

"Fuck that," Sparks said.

"We're creatures of the Void, sons of the House of Mot. Ba'al doesn't care about us. Maybe it's time we look to..."

Rex stepped over the threshold into the galley to find Kellemen looking at him.

"...Yam." Kellemen said.

More of their crazed fantasies. Rex turned his attention to the food service area.

Pizza. Cook must have something elaborate planned for supper. Pizza was a low-effort lunch that often preceded something more involved at the next meal.

Then he remembered. Oh, right. Next meal was the Last Supper before the burn. Last chance to eat something substantial. How many days was this next burn? He couldn't bring the exact number to mind, but he knew that it was longer than last time and that they'd be at 7g most of the time. They'd all be on a liquid diet tomorrow, getting cleared out for their acceleration couches. It did not pay to go into an extended high-g burn with your stomach and bowels full. Or your nuts. His were so full they ached.

Rex took a slice of pizza and pulled a mug full of Cook's special *fizz*, something he often served with pizza. It was a combination of kombucha and some kind of light tea that contained a big dose of caffeine. It was supposed to be non-alcoholic, but Rex often felt a slight buzz after drinking it. Cook said that was from the herbs, but Rex knew it was a fermented drink. Didn't that mean alcohol by definition?

He imagined confronting Trix alone. That was a sure path to defeat. It would end with him in her mouth. *Her mouth...*

"Something wrong with the pizza?"

"Huh?" Rex snapped out of his reverie. Cook was standing across the table from him.

"You only took one bite. Something not right about it?"

"Sorry, Cook. I'm just distracted, that's all."

"Me too, in a good way. I checked the public board. That

video clip of Petrovic is there, but not the audio that went out over the PA a few minutes ago. That was a one and done kinda deal, I think. Too bad. That was some good stuff."

"You approve of that?"

"Approve? Disapprove? I don't think about it like that. I like Petrovic. She's easy to be around. She doesn't have to touch me to make me feel good. I like to think I do my part to boost morale around here, but Petrovic…" Cook paused, smiling at the image in his imagination. "She boosts me every which way."

"What about Trix? What about the captain?"

"That was nice while it lasted, but things are different around here now, and I prefer now to how it was back then," Cook said.

"No, I mean do you approve of the captain enabling Petrovic's exhibitionism?"

Cook sat down opposite Rex and leaned in, lowering his voice.

"Rex, do yourself a favor, man. Trix can't blow everybody anymore, but she can do you. Nobody's gonna mind. We all know it was different for you than it was for the rest of us. Just go talk to her."

"It's not that simple," Rex said.

"Then get yourself a piece of Jailbait. That is simple. Or Cat Girl, if that's more your speed. Bust a nut and get your head sorted out. You're a ball of bad energy, Rex. Take advantage of the perks of our new situation."

With that, Cook got up and went back to his kitchen.

1.12.2 - Trey

Before coming out here to the Kuiper Belt, I got just the right amount of sex. It wasn't anything I ever needed to think about. I was never deprived, and the possibility of getting too much sex was an unknown concept. With Petrovic confined to the medical level, I was having more sex than I wanted.

And Paige had assumed permission to watch. I asked her for some privacy, and Anja said, "She can stay." At least Paige didn't try to join in. I was grateful for the captain's edict that Paige was off limits to the marines. That included Petrovic.

For me, being observed and coached during sex was a familiar experience. I missed Zira's presence those first couple of times with Petrovic, but I have to admit that, in spite of her calendar age, I saw Paige as a child. Her presence dampened my already flagging interest. I had to pretend she wasn't there in order to satisfy Petrovic.

Afterward, Paige and Petrovic would discuss the details of what Paige had just witnessed, with Petrovic offering instructional wisdom from her vast pool of experience. The mystical ecstasy was gone. This was just a nymphomaniac passing the time while confined with a man. I was not up for another day of this. I needed to get them both out of my hair.

My slate transcribed my conversation with the captain. I could examine the exact wording of her order and it was clear.

I'm ordering her to remain in medical for observation until it's time for her to get into her acceleration couch.

Remain in medical. Not remain under medical supervision. The order was for Petrovic to stay here, in my domain, with me. Paige too. The captain had left me no loopholes to exploit.

It was time for a bit of selective mutiny.

I rigged up a portable brain scanner. It was an unobtrusive net of sensors that sat on Petrovic's head like a cap. She could then wear an actual cap to hide it and hold it in place. I gave Paige a slate that was linked to the sensors on Petrovic's scalp and showed her which indicators to monitor. I told her to contact me if they deviated from a specified range. I then told them to engage in a variety of normal activities around the ship. *Just not here*, I added silently, and breathed a sigh of relief when they left.

1.12.3 - Cook

Cook made jambalaya for Last Supper. The tomatoes came pre-stewed out of enormous cans. The onions, bell peppers, and celery were all pre-chopped and came out of the freezer. That first high g burn had ruined all of Cook's fresh vegetables and salad greens. They went into the worm bin. Garlic, rice and spices could stand high gravity.

The structure of his Swiss chard was certainly compromised, but given that he was going to boil it into utter flaccidness and serve it as a side dish, it avoided the worm bin. Earthworms, with very modest genetic tinkering, did just fine under high gravity, as least for a few days.

Sausage also came out of the freezer. Cook took out more than he would need for the jambalaya. He thawed most of it on the griddle, sliced it and added it to the giant pot. The rest he cooked and chopped into tiny morsels which he speared with toothpicks and set out on plates on tables in the middle of the dining area, out of his own easy reach, for anyone to snack on before supper. He held some sausage bites in reserve for Paige and placed them in a sealed container to prevent himself from absent-mindedly snacking on them.

He cooked the jambalaya on high heat for 70 minutes and then turned it down to let it simmer for the afternoon. He wanted to give the flavors from the various ingredients time to work their alchemy.

Given that there was no chopping to do, Cook felt like he was cheating with the jambalaya. The side of greens was also easy. He would be spending the entire next day securing the galley for high gravity, so he wanted to get some proper cooking in today.

He considered making fresh baguettes but decided to save that for a day when there would be no strong competing aroma. He opted for cornbread, using melted butter instead of oil.

He planned to serve lemon sorbet for dessert. He gave quiet thanks to the DAO for a generous liquor allowance in his kitchen budget. He could top the sorbet with vodka without having to pilfer it from the first-class stores.

He could even put out bottles of wine. The only options were red and white. He couldn't offer a merlot or a viognier.

On most ships, meals were included, but the crew had to pay for snacks, alcoholic drinks, and sometimes even desserts. Not on the *Persephone*.

Last Supper had a double meaning. It was the last substantial meal a crew ate before a burn. Since high-g burns were expensive and uncomfortable, they were typically reserved for times when a habitat or faction needed to speed fighting men and women into combat. For some of those soldiers, Last Supper would be the last meal of their lives. The tradition was to make it a good one.

Orders for the previous burn had come without warning. Cook hadn't had time to do a proper Last Supper, nor did they have time for the day of semi-fasting that was recommended before a high-g burn. This meal meant more to Cook than it did to the marines, or so he imagined.

Cook was not certain they were really heading into combat. He had read between the lines of the captain's presentation in the situation room. She didn't say it outright, but she got the point across, at least to Cook.

Two high-g accelerations in one trip did not make economic sense without an extraordinary payoff or a compelling political or strategic interest. So far this outing didn't seem to be paying for itself in any way that Cook could see.

Who had unlimited resources to burn and wasn't worried about turning a profit? The rendezvous with the doctor was the cherry on top of his speculation that the *Persephone* and her crew might be working for the Powers. For Spinners in general, but for the Columbian military in particular, serving the Powers was an abhorrent concept. Utterly unthinkable.

Cook wasn't in the military, and for him the concept of artificial super-intelligence was too abstract to get worked up over. And if working for the Powers came with lemon sorbet topped with vodka, Cook was pretty sure he could make peace with it.

LAST SUPPER

1.13.1 - Paige

Paige was chatting with Drake Antal when the captain made her entrance. Everyone had already been through the food line and was seated with steaming bowls of jambalaya in front of them, but nobody had taken a bite. Cook had warned them not to start until the captain gave her blessing.

The ebullient conversation dissolved into silence when the sound of the captain's metal legs on the deck presaged her arrival. All eyes were trained on her when she stepped into the galley. Paige gaped when she saw the captain's attire.

Trix usually wore tight-fitting clothes that emphasized her breasts and ass, and every time Paige had seen her, from their interview in the crew boss's shed, to their every interaction on the ship, Trix's left arm, the part of her body unmarred by scars or patches of synthetic skin, had been bare. Now, the only skin showing was that of her face and left hand.

She wore a long dark coat that looked military to Paige's untrained eye. Paige was as taken aback by the absence of the captain's powerful feminine curves as many people were to see how boldly she displayed them in her everyday clothing.

The coat had no right sleeve. Just a large gap to accommodate the captain's mechanical right arm, which did not match the dimensions of her left arm. The coat's one sleeve covered the captain's left arm all the way down to the wrist, and the sleeve of the white shirt she wore below her coat extended even further over her wrist and hand.

The shocks to Paige's expectations were even greater above the captain's chin. Trix normally wore her brown hair swept to the right to cover the more heavily damaged parts of her face and her missing right ear. Now she wore it tucked up under her peaked cap, bringing the full extent of her damaged face and scalp to the fore. Trix's normal hairstyle also helped to de-emphasize her mismatched eyes. Now the fact that one eye was blue and the other amber could not be missed.

Paige felt something like despair seeing the captain's long-neglected injuries on public display. She was caught so off guard that she hadn't noticed when all of the Columbian marines stood up at once. She was still seated when the capture gestured for everyone to sit down again. The Columbians all sat down in unison.

The returning members of the crew, who were late to stand, also sat down in their own time and without the group discipline of the Galtz marines.

The captain closed her eyes, and all of the new marines, including Anja, closed their eyes and bowed their heads. Some of the old crew did as well. Shawn Li, she noticed, kept his head up and his eyes open. He radiated indignation, but he kept quiet.

"Lord, God," Trix began. "As we embark on this crass commercial venture, please forgive us our shortcomings and help these men and women bring the honor and dignity of true military service to this lowly business. May their training help them to exemplify the military virtues of courage, unity and unwavering commitment to purpose, just as they would on Your holy service. May their example elevate the profane nature of this expedition. In Your holy name we pray. Amen."

"Amen," said all of the Galtz marines together.

Trix, who was still standing, lifted her wine glass. Unlike the crew who were all drinking from plastic wine glasses, the captain's glass seemed to be made of crystal with metal decorations. Paige made a mental note to look up the correct terminology to describe the captain's glass. The captain held her glass at arm's length and gestured toward Cook.

"To Cook, for this fine meal," she said.

"To Cook," the marines echoed in unison.

The captain swept the room with her gaze and her glass. "And to the fighting men and women of the Columbian Military Academy and the Galtz Militia..." She paused for effect. "Oorah!"

The Marines didn't seem to expect this. They bellowed and whooped. Many of them returned the captain's *Oorah,* but not in unison as they had done everything else. They were clearly surprised in the best possible way, or at least that's how Paige read their response.

"Alright!" The captain raised her voice to be heard over the din, and everyone quieted down. "Let's eat!"

Paige was stunned. Nobody made much of an effort to indoctrinate the children of ag workers in the tenets of Objectivism, but Galtz culture held commercial activity in the highest esteem. Religious ritual was considered contemptibly primitive. *Business is Galtz's business*, is something she had heard adults say her entire life. In her prayer, the captain had called their mission *crass* and *profane* because it had a commercial rather than a strictly military objective.

This was a lot for Paige to process.

She looked to Anja for guidance and saw that the big woman had attacked her jambalaya with gusto. Paige did likewise.

1.13.2 - Rex

A fucking prayer? Rex thought. He couldn't beleive the Columbians didn't see through this blatant bit of pandering to their collective self-importance, but they were eating it up.

The charter that legitimized the military takeover of the Galt's Gulch habitat by the Columbian military elite decreed an atmosphere of mutual respect between the new *protector* class and the Objectivist culture of the Galters. On paper, the two cultures were equals.

In reality, from the moment the charter was signed, the Columbians made it clear that they considered their brand of godly militarism to be morally superior to, and therefore socially and politically dominant over, the rationalist atheism of the Galters. They were so convinced of their superiority that they couldn't see Trix's prayer for the cynical and manipulative ploy that it was.

She does look good in the coat, though, he said to himself. When she showed him the design for the outfit back on Galtz while the *Persephone* was being upgraded, Rex had approved. Trix employed the services of the same haute couture fashion house that designed the dress uniforms for the Columbian top brass. It was expensive, but the coat said *Columbian naval officer formal attire* at first glance. It wasn't until you lingered over the details that you noticed that the rank insignia were just abstract designs. The coat's split tails seemed overly fanciful in the 3D rendering, but in real life, well, it had the desired effect on these soldiers.

At the time, Rex liked the costume because it was more dignified than Trix's usual whorish presentation. Back when she was the ship's shared sex toy, he liked seeing her body packaged for display, but when she took on the role of acting-captain, which came with a uniform allowance, he couldn't believe it when she just upgraded her wardrobe to a more expensive brand of slutty.

She could have had the style house make an exotic dancer parody of the Columbian naval officer's greatcoat, but she hadn't. Here at least, she'd played it straight, the way he wanted, and he still wasn't happy about it. *The exotic dancer variation would have been more honest*, he decided.

But didn't he want Trix to succeed in motivating this crew?

Didn't he support her? As a matter of practical concern, yes. But he didn't have to like it.

Sure, she knew the technical side of the ship. She kept every system going with jury-rigged repairs when they didn't have the money for proper repairs. She could plot a course. She could maneuver the ship better than most remote docking systems, and now she demonstrated that she could inspire the loyalty of elite soldiers, but that's not who she was. She was a dirty little whore. He counted the men in the galley whose dicks she'd sucked. Cook, Dobrovitz, Zell.

Fucking Zell! He would beat her to get in the mood. Rex had never actually seen Zell strike Trix. Like Rex, he at least had the decency to take her into a private compartment to use her, but he'd seen her red cheek as she emerged from a compartment with Zell.

Trix had fired all of the other men who struck or humiliated her, but Zell's skills were too valuable to let go, even if it compromised her redemption. She couldn't put herself first. She knew she was trash and didn't deserve the dignity that Rex worked so hard to create for her.

Rex glared at Cook. Frumpy, unkempt, flabby Cook. How many times had Trix gotten on her knees for him? Not recently though. Cook had stopped using her several months before Rex did, and Trix never yelled at Cook the way she railed at Rex when he tried to back away.

He shifted his glare to Dobrovitz. Lazy, minimum possible effort, Dobrovitz. Again, someone who'd only taken her in private, so Rex didn't know the particulars of how the man had degraded her. Dobrovitz was probably too lazy and unimaginative to have any kinks. Unremarkable, dim bulb, Dobrovitz, and she'd sucked him off countless times.

Who else? Rex delved into his memory. *Oh, right. Me. But that was different.*

Rex had always been respectful. Where other men barked orders at Trix, she and Rex had worked out a system of subtle communication based on eye movements. He made sure that he was freshly washed, his crotch at least, and he always told her when he was getting close. And out in public, he always treated her as an equal. He respected her skills. He respected her.

But now, enabling Petrovic's exhibitionism, trusting a man from the inner system who was surely a tool of the Powers, and now this cynical charade of praying to the Columbians' god of war. This was who she was. Depravity behind a lying mask.

"What's the matter, Rex," Lake asked him. "Don't like the food?"

Rex looked at his bowl. He hadn't taken a bite of his jambalaya. Some of the marines were on their second bowl.

1.13.3 - Trey

It was just the captain, Nora Lawson and me at the captain's table for this meal. This was the first I'd seen of Nora, the engine keeper. Apparently she kept to herself most of the time. Petrovic told me she thought that Nora was having an affair with Chukwuma, the demolitions expert and the only black person on the ship, but I followed Paige's gaze as she looked from Chukwuma to Paul Lake, a marine who'd served on the *Nipple*. Chukwuma noticed Paige looking at him, stole one last glance at Lake, and then kept his eyes on his plate.

"Captain, it's my understanding that homosexuality is forbidden in the Columbian military."

"Male homosexuality," the captain said, locking eyes with me and giving nothing away with automatic glances. "Why? See something you like?"

"But lesbianism is accepted?"

"Not so much accepted as just not mentioned," she said. "I think the introduction of the sex robots has scuttled your chances of a threeway with Petrovic and Escamilla. Escamilla had a nice long session with Cat Girl today. Have you fucked a lot of robots, doctor?"

I smiled. "Probably, but not like the ones you have here on the ship. Where I'm from, the Is constructs human characters who are indistinguishable from natural humans. They might even believe that they are natural humans and remember growing up, having careers and relationships. It's really impossible to tell one way or the other, so I tend not to think about it. But, yes. I'm sure a fair number of my lovers have been constructs."

The captain turned to the engine keeper, who was seated on her other side. "What do you think of that, Nora? Sex robots who think they're human."

I wasn't good at guessing women's ages, and there's no telling how much cosmetic maintenance Nora might have had over the years, but I guessed that she was in her early 40s. What would that be in Kuiper Belt years? Divide by 2.86, but I couldn't do that in my head. I'd never needed to. I'd always had Zira to do any calculation for me as soon as a question occurred to me. I divided by 3 instead and decided that Nora was between 13 and 14 KB years old.

Nora emptied her wine glass before she answered. She refilled it and said, "I think if they're made for sex work, it's better if they aren't self-aware. Our robots have no sense of self. They don't even have much of a memory. I think it's better that way. If they were more cognitively sophisticated, we would need to be more conscientious about how we treat them."

Turning back to me, the captain said, "Nora is the keeper of our sex dolls as well as our engines."

"That's fascinating. Technically, is there much overlap between the engines and the robots?" It was meant to be an innocuous question. Just something to give Nora an excuse to demonstrate her knowledge.

"Hmmm..." Nora said, and took another swallow from her glass. "They're all complex machines that involve continuous real-time self-monitoring and adjustment, but I think the similarities end there. Nothing can go so wrong with the dolls that the ship explodes. They can't generate a lethal dose of ionizing radiation."

Another swallow of wine and she continued without further prompting from me.

"The dolls' cognitive architecture could sustain much more complex behavior. With what amounts to a software update they could be self-aware. Maybe not in the exact same way that we are, but they are certainly capable of more than just simulating human sexual behavior."

"I thought that Kuiper Belt humans were averse to anything resembling AGI," I said, not meaning to criticize.

"Do all humans hold the same beliefs behind the Curtain?" Nora asked, defensively.

"Surely not," I said, "but I'm probably not a very good person to quiz on the wider beliefs of my culture."

"If the people who come out here to the Kuiper Belt are representative examples, nobody knows what's really going on in the inner system," the captain said.

"Remember the questions on the card I had you answer? Those are standard questions we're supposed to ask any human from the inner system. Their answers are all over the place. Some say Earth has been disassembled, other's say it's an ecological preserve with a minimal human presence. Others say it has a population of trillions. Your reality is just what the Powers decide to show you."

"I can't argue with that," I said.

The captain asked, "Did you know that we actually have three sex robots on board? The third one's name is David." The captain turned to face Nora who was refilling her glass. "How is David doing, Nora? Not missing his colleagues too badly, I hope."

Nora emptied her glass in one go. "Yes, Captain. I fuck David. Do you want me to stop?"

"Not at all, Nora. That's what he's for."

1.13.4 - Petrovic

Petrovic loved the atmosphere of this Last Supper. Everyone was here, and she loved being around people. She loved attention, and she was getting plenty of that. Lewd comments and gestures from her fellow marines in reference to her two recent bouts of ship-wide exhibitionism were like nectar to her.

Petrovic never meant to swear off alcohol entirely. She merely moderated her intake over time, looking for the level of consumption that produced the best social outcomes for her. The level that she had settled on was none at all. She enjoyed being around people who were drinking, but her inhibitions didn't need lowering. She and Paige were both drinking carbonated water.

Trey had advised Paige not to drink, but it was advice, not doctor's orders. Petrovic had warned her that a headache and queasy stomach would not enhance Paige's mid-morning appointment with Cat Girl, or *Bygul*.

When Anja first saw the doll's name on the metal plate above its alcove in the first-class compartment, she pronounced it like *bi gal*. Paige did some research and discovered that the doll was named after a cat from Norse mythology, and that the name was pronounced *bee ghoul*.

Petrovic glanced over at Escamilla, who had come to supper directly from her extra long session with Bygul. She didn't want to make eye contact with Escamilla. She owed the woman an apology. She planned to provide it, but this wasn't the setting. Petrovic scanned Escamilla for the familiar post-coital glow. She didn't see any of the familiar signs, but then, she hadn't really engaged in coitus, had she?

Escamilla was a mystery to Petrovic. She kept her hair short, per regulations, but somehow managed to make it look feminine. On a commercial assignment like this one, she could grow her hair out if she wanted to. The captain laid down this aura of military authority, but that was a matter of style. She was their boss, not their commanding officer.

Most of these Pax soldiers had never served on a commercial vessel before. The captain's use of military discipline sent a very clear signal to them about how to conduct themselves, and Petrovic thought that most of them took comfort in the familiar forms and protocols. Escamilla would probably keep her hair short and her make-up understated.

Female soldiers were not supposed to wear make-up at all, but what that really meant was that female soldiers were expected to wear make-up that didn't stand out to most men. Petrovic did not wear any make-up, and she looked out of place among other military women who wore just the right amount of it. Petrovic couldn't teach Paige about hair or make-up or clothes or flirting. She was hoping that Escamilla would handle that part of Paige's education. Petrovic hadn't meant to take on an apprentice.

Just then Paige put her hand on Petrovic's forearm and then gestured for Petrovic to lean in. Paige raised a hand to create a privacy shield over her lips and to block out the din of conversation and spoke into Petrovic's ear.

"Watch Lake and Chukwuma." Paige told Anja then turned her attention back to Antal.

Petrovic watched Paige with approval. Antal was sitting on Paige's right, and when Antal spoke to her, she set her spoon down and placed her right hand on the young marine's thigh. She nodded along to what he was saying, and when he paused she made a show of *noticing* where her hand was resting. She lifted it just slightly and said, "I'm sorry, Drake. I touched you without permission. Is it okay if I put my hand on your leg?"

"Yeah, no problem," Antal said.

Paige let her hand rest on his thigh again, and gave it a squeeze. As Antal spoke, Paige slid her hand slowly over his leg. Petrovic knew that this kept the sensation coming from his leg ever-changing. He wouldn't be able to tune it out.

"The captain told me that I'm not allowed to have sex with any of the marines," Paige said. "Not even..." and here she leaned in close to speak directly in Antal's ear. Antal's eyes went wide.

Paige gave no indication that she noticed Antal's heightened state of attention. "So, don't worry, I'm not trying to seduce you or anything. I happened to notice that you have an appointment with Jailbait in the morning. Her real name is Lolita, by the way. I'll be with Cat Girl at that same time. Afterwards, I'd really like to hear about your experience. Would that be okay?"

Antal was helpless. Petrovic marveled at how quickly this young woman learned anything she turned her attention to. The captain had given her quite the gift when she ordered Paige not to fuck or blow any of the Marines. Paige could use the explicit prohibition to turn any conversation to the topic of sex and declare it a safe topic because she couldn't act on it. Clever girl.

Petrovic scanned the galley and located Chukwuma. He was sitting between Hansson and Sparks. She noticed that his wine glass was nearly full. Had he just refilled it, or was he only pretending to drink? He seemed intent on his food.

Lake wasn't even sitting at the same table as Chukwuma, so she wondered what interaction Paige might have noticed between them. Lake was sitting between Zell and Perkins.

Lake was older than all of the newly hired marines. She knew that he was one of the returning crew members. Agewise, he was between the Galtz marines and Rex. In fact, he seemed to be maturing into a copy of Rex. His face was lean. The hard lines of middle age that were etched into Rex's face were just getting established on Lake. Rex's hair was completely white, while for Lake, it was white at the temples and creeping up the sides of his head, but it was still a dark on top. Lake's hair was longer than the young soldiers wore their hair, but neatly groomed.

Petrovic approached Rex first when looking for her shipboard lover, and when he made it clear that he was not interested, she refocused her interest on Chukwuma. She hadn't approached Chukwuma by the time she had taken up with Trey. Now that she took a good look at Lake, she wondered why he hadn't been her second choice. Thinking back on her first few days onboard, she remembered talking to Lake, but she didn't feel any kind of sexual tension between them. He was ex-military, but not from Galtz. He was probably...

"Oh, shit," she said under her breath. *Chukwuma, be careful.*

1.13.5 - Cook

With a glance and a nod from the captain, Cook disappeared into the kitchen and came back with an enormous tray laden with seventeen small glass bowls and a large bottle of vodka. Each bowl held a fat scoop of lemon sorbet.

He made a show of pouring a generous measure of vodka into fifteen of the bowls. He added a small quantity to the sixteenth bowl for Paige. He delivered one serving to everyone at the captain's table, and then he took the virgin and near virgin servings to Petrovic and Paige and let the rest of the crew pass the tray around. Everyone waited for the captain to speak.

She stood and said, "Please show Cook how much you appreciate his efforts."

Everyone gave Cook a round of applause and then looked back to the captain.

"And a round of applause is in order for Zell, Sparks, Escamilla and Kellemen who generously broke the sex dolls in for the rest of you."

Laughter and applause.

"Everybody else is on the schedule for tomorrow, but one of

you will get to spend tonight with both Jailbait and Cat Girl in one of the second class cabins. Enjoy your desert. There is a number at the bottom of your bowl. When everyone has found their number, our engine keeper will draw a number from my hat to determine the winner."

With that, the captain sat down and dipped her spoon into her desert. The young men all raced to finish their deserts and uncover their numbers. To their frustration, Escamilla as well as the older crew members were actually taking their time and enjoying the desert for its own sake.

When Escamilla had spooned the last of her sorbet into her mouth and set her spoon down, the captain, who had only taken a couple of spoons full from her desert, upended her bowl onto her dinner plate and held up the now empty bowl to reveal the number twelve on the bottom.

She stood up and stepped away from the table. She leaned forward and carefully removed her high peaked hat so as not to spill its contents. She reached into the hat and made a stirring motion. She then held the hat out to Nora, keeping it above the engine keeper's eyeline.

Nora reached in and drew out a slip of paper. She scrutinized it, then held it up and said, "Who's got number four?"

Trey raised his hand to shoulder height, and the room erupted into boos and groans.

"I'm going to pass," Trey said. "Draw another one, Nora."

Cheers.

Nora pulled another slip of paper from the hat and called out, "Fifteen. Who's got lucky fifteen?"

Paul Lake laughed and stood up to show everyone his bowl, smiling.

That's right, Cook said to himself. *Make everyone think you want this. Stay safe, Paul.*

Cook looked up to see the doctor holding Nora's arm, steadying her as she navigated the step over the threshold out into the p-way. Without him, she probably would have gone face down on the deck.

Cook didn't know Nora. He didn't know if getting this drunk was her *modus operandi* or if this was a special occasion. She'd put away a lot of wine. Whatever the case, she was no lightweight. Cook wouldn't mind sharing a bottle with her sometime.

He caught up with Petrovic and Paige before they got away. "Hey, you two. Captain says you volunteered to help me clean up."

"Did she now?" Petrovic saw through his lie, but she smiled anyway and gave him a playful punch on the arm.

"Of course we'll help you," Paige said.

TOO GOOD TO LAST

1.14.1 - Petrovic

In the morning, Petrovic could see that Paige needed something to occupy her mind and hands in the half watch remaining before her appointment with Cat Girl. Cook would not be preparing any meals today, so there was nothing for Paige to do in the galley. Their scheduled gym time was at the same time as Paige's appointment with the sex doll. Anja had tried to trade workout slots with two other marines so she and Paige could workout early but found no takers. Galtz marines were unabashedly superstitious, and changing your routine just before an engagement was considered bad luck.

Trey had politely but firmly banished Paige from the medical level until after her appointment with Bygul. Her agitation was palpable, and Trey had work to do preparing to monitor the health of the crew in high-g acceleration. He was running simulations with Esmeralda, and Paige peppered the woman with questions about her experience with Bygul the night before until Trey handed her a slate and told her to continue monitoring Anja's brain activity around the ship. Extra emphasis on *around the ship*.

Petrovic slept in her own quarters last night rather than spending the night with Trey. She had seen Trey leaving with Nora. She suspected that he was making sure that Nora got back to her own quarters without mishap. The engine keeper had grown quite sloppy by the time she left the galley. She doubted that Trey had taken the older woman back to his own quarters, but Trey and Anja had not worked out a system for signaling when he had company and needed privacy. Anja decided to give him space.

Paige was beside herself with nervous anticipation. She asked Anja endless variations on, "What do I do?" Anja replied with an equal number of variations on, "Cat Girl will know what to do."

"Trust me, little tiger, *anxiously bi curious* is the second most basic scenario for Cat Girl. When she gets to your quarters, just tell her that you're nervous and don't know what to do and let her do her thing. You. Don't. Have. To. Do. Anything."

When this didn't quell Paige's anxiety, Anja took her down to the armory and checked out a small caliber pistol. She signed for two clips of armor piercing rounds and three clips of gel rounds.

Anja then led Paige to a part of the ship she'd never visited before; the firing range. Anja had Paige hold the pistol. She showed her how to insert a clip and toggle the safety. Anja put on ear protectors and handed a pair to Paige, trading the safe pistol for the hearing protection. She then led Paige to a firing point, and, with the tap of her toe on a spot on the deck, activated an animated target dummy down range that pantomimed drawing a pistol.

Faster than Paige could follow, Anja raised the weapon and fired. Paige flinched and closed her eyes upon hearing the first shot, but the cracking sound of the weapon, muffled but by no means silenced by her hearing protection, kept up its rapid tempo for ten beats. Paige managed to open her eyes to see Anja fire the last two shots. The spent clip fell from the pistol and Anja slapped another into place and raised the pistol again, but she did not resume firing. She just held her firing stance for a few seconds and then relaxed.

The target dummy rushed forward for Anja's inspection. She told Paige to count the indentations on the dummy. Paige counted ten, all to the upper torso, neck and face.

Anja nodded and said, "Reset."

All of the indentations on the dummy popped out and the surface was again unmarred. Anja removed the clip she'd just loaded into the pistol and put it back on her belt. She then showed Paige how to grip the weapon, how to support it with her left hand, how to position her feet. She had Paige practice dry firing the pistol. Then she gave Paige a clip and had her load the weapon. She helped Paige position her body and warned her to expect recoil.

Paige took aim at the dummy and squeezed the trigger. She flinched at the report, closing her eyes just as she had done when Anja fired the weapon. When she opened her eyes, she looked to see that Anja was smiling at her.

"Good," Petrovic said. "Relax your jaw."

They left the firing range a quarter of a watch later, Paige having fired 20 rounds and scored eight hits on the dummy.

"You've got time to wash off the smell of gunpowder before your date, but I'd leave it. You smell powerful and sexy. Now, go pet your kitty, little tiger."

1.14.2 - Trey

I had trouble accepting that I was in baseline reality. Having to interact with other humans with their unaddressed needs and hidden agendas was something that only happened in delves. The people around me spoke of enduring an anxious period of inactivity, the uneasy calm before an anticipated maelstrom, but to me, the social tensions and romantic intrigues on this ship presented an active puzzle in need of solving. Meeting the sexual needs of everyone on the ship, given the gender imbalance, the cultural prohibition on male homosexuality, the dominance hierarchies defined by military training and the economic power dynamics between owners, managers, and employees, would make for a compelling delve all by itself.

Plus there was the anticipation of physical danger. This was a combat-oriented crew, and a very expensive one at that, according to Petrovic. Not the sort of group one assembles just on the basis of generalized caution. That leant dynamism to the situation for me, as I'm sure it must have done for the other humans on this ship.

I came out here to look for evidence of alien life. The Is had arranged to deliver me to this particular ship on this particular mission, so it stands to reason that this is the place I'm most likely to discover evidence of life from outside the solar system.

Zira had made it unmistakably clear to me that I might not find what I'm looking for. It is entirely possible that the only life in the universe arose around our own home star, Sol. I gave up all the comforts of life in the Is to come out here to this brutal frontier, but the strength of my commitment and the magnitude of my sacrifice would not cause evidence of life to manifest itself where it didn't otherwise exist. Not in the so-called *real world*. I understood that on an intellectual level.

The thing that made it hardest for me to accept this setting as baseline reality was Zira's absence. For as long as I can remember, the only time when she wasn't with me was when I was in a delve. Even then, she must have been with me because I could discuss any aspect of my simulated experience with her later without having to recount or explain anything about it. Her absence indicated a simulated experience. That had been my experience for dozens of simulated lifetimes and what? Thirty-four years of baseline reality? A little less than 12 years as the Spinners measured age.

There was one thing that happened here on this ship that never happened in delves, people asked me about my life in the Is, or *behind the Curtain*, as the denizens of the Kuiper Belt spin habitats phrased it. The captain's indifference to my origin and intentions threw me off. She asked only the questions that local protocol directed her to ask, and she clearly didn't care about my answers. But Paige and Petrovic had made up for the captain's lack of curiosity. Petrovic's questions focused on my sexual history and preferences, but Paige's curiosity was boundless.

To start, she wanted to know how many people lived in the inner system. I asked her what she meant by *people*. I explained that humans had speciated repeatedly and that countless fully self-aware but disembodied personas were summoned into existence on a continuous basis.

There was a vast spectrum of intelligence to account for. At the conservative end, it was my understanding that populations of humans who were completely unmodified existed somewhere in the solar system. That meant humans who were capable of getting toothaches or developing malignant tumors lived in some pocket sanctuaries somewhere in the solar system, like the natives of Sentinel island or uncontacted Amazonian tribes that managed to remain isolated from the global human culture until the early decades of the 21st Century. They were the ultimate control group. I suppose it's good that they exist, but I wouldn't agree to live that way.

At the other extreme… Well, I probably couldn't conceive of the other extreme, but I gave the example of a scripted character in a simulation who sprang to life when I asked them a question that didn't correspond to one of their pre-scripted answers. It seemed to me that such characters should subside back into their non-sentient state at the end of the encounter, and surely most did, but some stayed awake. Some of them even learned that they existed in simulated realities and petitioned for baseline incarnation.

Apparently, there's enough of them walking around in physical bodies that they hold periodic gatherings, conventions of people who awoke to reality because I asked them a question in a delve. I declined repeated invitations to attend their gatherings. I don't know if they stopped asking or if Zira just stopped relaying their invitations to me.

Paige wanted to know how many humans like me lived in the inner system, and she couldn't accept that I had no way of knowing. I asked her how many humans lived out past Neptune.

"You mean Spinners *and* Floaters?"

"Or even just Spinners," I said. "How many Spin habitats are there?"

She didn't know. She could look it up, but she admitted that she had no basis for evaluating the accuracy of any answer she might find.

Today all of Paige's questions were for Esmeralda, and they all involved her time with Cat Girl the previous afternoon. I could see that Esmeralda's patience was wearing thin, and that's when I sent Paige on a mission to find Petrovic and monitor her brain activity.

Petrovic was supposed to be here in medical, but the captain saw Petrovic at Last Supper and made no comment to me about my failing to keep Anja confined to medical. Had that order been a joke of some sort?

"Thank you," Esmeralda said when Paige was gone.

"You're welcome, though I have to admit, I liked hearing your answers to her questions."

"You did? And why is that?"

"I've always enjoyed watching women having sex with one another. Imagining you with Cat Girl is an enticing image."

"Why doctor, you're being quite forward," Esmeralda said. "Is that sort of talk acceptable workplace behavior where you come from?"

"I mostly work alone when I'm doing research in baseline," I said, "But in most of my historical delves, flirtation and seduction were normal parts of most work environments. Some historical periods tolerated more open and honest talk about sex than others, but if there was a historical period when people didn't think and talk about sex while they toiled, I don't know when that might have been."

"I see," she said. "And what do you imagine when you think of me with Cat Girl?"

"How descriptive would you like me to be?"

"Impress me," she said.

"That could be dangerous," I said.

"I'm willing to risk it if you are."

1.14.3 - Paige

When Paige arrived at her quarters, Cat Girl was waiting in the passageway. The sex robot was wearing her black bikini that blended in with the fine black fur that covered her body. She also wore a diaphanous garment that Paige would later learn is called a kaftan. It concealed the contours of her body just enough to satisfy the captain's edict that the dolls not disturb the decorum of the ship's public areas. Cat Girl paused at the door and turned to Paige, smiling.

"Hi," Paige said.

"Meow," Cat Girl said in a sultry voice, not mimicking the sound a real cat would make but actually speaking the word.

Paige opened the hatch to her compartment. "Please, come in," Paige said.

Her experience at the firing range had disrupted her earlier nervousness, and even in Cat Girl's physical presence the nervousness had not reasserted itself. Not fully. Cat Girl stepped into Paige's compartment, and Paige pulled the hatch closed and sealed it. Cat Girl walked the length of Paige's quarters. It was a short walk.

"Tight quarters," Paige said, "but it's private."

Cat Girl met Paige's eyes. The robot's eyes were more than twice the size of Paige's eyes, green with the vertical pupil of a real cat's eye. "Meow," Cat Girl said again.

"Do you speak?"

"Yes, lady. Cat Girl talk some. Touch better. Lady touch Cat Girl? Pet?"

Cat Girl stepped toward Paige, who was still standing with her back to the closed hatch. Cat Girl was slightly shorter than Paige, with a dancer's build, slender yet athletic. She let the kaftan fall to the ground, and Paige's gaze drifted down the doll's softly sculpted torso.

"Breathe, lady," Cat Girl said as she rubbed her shoulder against Paige's upper arm. Paige, realizing that she'd forgotten to inhale, took a deep breath and let it out again.

Cat Girl took Paige's hand and coaxed her into the center of the compartment. "Dance?" Cat Girl raised her arms above her head and gyrated her hips in a slow figure eight. "Lady like music?"

"Music? Yes. Should I play some music?" Paige turned to the wall panel, and tried to navigate to a musical library, but she didn't get very far before Cat Girl pressed against her from behind and rested her chin on Paige's shoulder. Cat Girl reached out to the wall display and swept her finger over the screen, deftly navigating the library files and selecting a musical playlist. Soft instrumental music filled the room, gently rhythmic but not overpowering.

"Mmmmm…" Cat Girl said, rubbing her cheek against Paige's cheek from behind, her hands on Paige's hips, guiding them in a gentle undulation in time to the music. "Lady dance with Cat Girl?"

"I don't know how," Paige said.

"Easy," said Cat Girl, guiding Paige to turn around with gentle pressure on her hips.

"Move hips. Move shoulders." Cat Girl was moving more than that. Her rib cage seemed to roll around in its own orbit, and her tail shifted in the opposite direction of her swaying hips. Cat Girl guided Paige to her bunk and urged her to sit, then sank to the floor and undid Paige's shoes and coaxed Paige into lifting one foot and then the other so she could slip Paige's shoes and socks from her feet.

She reached up to unbutton Paige's pants, and Paige put her hand on Cat Girl's hand. Cat Girl stopped undoing Paige's pants, but she didn't take her hand away. She met Paige's eyes without looking away and waited. "No pants more comfortable," Cat Girl said.

"I'm a virgin," Paige said.

"Cat Girl gentle. Just rub and lick." Cat Girl held Paige's eyes and kept her hand in place but made no move to proceed. "Pants off, okay, Lady?"

"Okay," Paige said, and released her grip on Cat Girl's hand. Cat Girl slipped Paige's pants down to her ankles and guided her to step out of them.

Cat Girl stood up, reached behind her back and untied her bikini top. She tossed it in the direction of her discarded kaftan. She looked down at her breasts. They were small and firm, and they didn't change shape when the bikini came off. Gravity held no sway.

"Lady touch?"

Paige looked at Cat Girl's breasts with amazement. They were covered in fine, black fur, except for her dark brown nipples, which stood erect. She raised one hand to Cat Girl's breast but hesitated.

"Lady touch," Cat Girl said.

Paige caressed one breast and Cat Girl closed her eyes and began to purr. This wasn't a human's approximation of a cat's purr, but the real thing.

"Cat Girl kiss Lady, okay?"

"Okay," Paige said. She felt Cat Girl's hands on her back as Cat Girl's face drew close to her own. Their lips touched, mouths almost closed, all soft innocence. Then Cat Girl gently introduced her tongue into the kiss. Paige tensed slightly, and Cat Girl withdrew.

"Okay, Lady. Cat Girl's tongue smooth. Not like real cat."

Cat Girl opened her mouth to show Paige her tongue. She took Paige's hand and slipped the index finger into her mouth, caressing it with her tongue, sliding it in and out of her mouth and humming. She pulled Paige's finger from her mouth and said, "Kiss Lady, okay?"

"Okay," Paige said, and Cat Girl brought their mouths together again, introducing her tongue gently to the kiss. They kept kissing, and eventually Paige's tongue returned Cat Girl's greeting, and Cat Girl gradually increased the intensity of the kiss. Cat Girl moved from Paige's mouth to her neck and continued kissing. Paige shivered and inhaled with just a hint of voice.

"Mmmm... Lady sing."

Cat Girl took a step back from Paige and slipped her bikini bottom off. She then climbed onto Paige's bed and sat with her legs tucked up under her. "Cat Girl naked. Lady like?" Paige nodded. "Lady pet Cat Girl? Cat Girl sing."

Paige was still wearing her t-shirt and panties. She thought of taking her panties off but didn't. She climbed onto the bed, her *rack* as the marines called it, and reached out to caress Cat Girl. The feeling of the doll's body under her hands delighted Paige's senses. She brushed against one of Cat Girl's nipples and the doll gasped. Paige leaned in and kissed Cat Girl's nipple, and Cat Girl moaned. Paige sucked on the nipple and Cat Girl's vocal expression grew more dramatic.

Cat Girl slid her thighs apart, still sitting up with her calves tucked under her thighs. "Cat Girl wet. Lady feel?" She guided Paige's hand between her legs, and Paige felt that the doll was warm, and open, and wet.

"Lady touch. Cat Girl sing."

Cat Girl guided Paige to slide her hand over Cat Girl's pussy and Cat Girl moaned and gasped, her eyes closed. She opened her large green eyes and looked into Paige's eyes and continued to gasp and moan. "Cat Girl sing," she said and continued her performance. Her body quivered as she reached her vocal crescendo.

"Thanks, Lady. Cat Girl lick. Lady sing now." Cat Girl reached out and took hold of Paige's shirt and started to lift it up. Paige stopped her.

"I want to leave it on. I'm so skinny. I don't want you to see me."

"Lady so beautiful."

"Please," Paige said, "I want to keep it on."

"Okay. Lady safe. Leave on."

Cat Girl released her shirt. She leaned forward to kiss Paige on the mouth, pushing forward so that Paige naturally reclined on the bed. Cat Girl kissed Paige's belly, lifting her t-shirt just slightly. She licked, and nibbled and sucked around the perimeter of Paige's panties. Very slowly, Cat Girl started to slide Paige's panties down. She stopped when Paige resisted and waited for her to relax before sliding them all the way off.

"Cat Girl lick now. Lady sing, okay?"

"Okay," Paige said, and the last of her hesitation melted away.

1.14.4 - Rex

Rex grunted as he struck the heavy bag with rapid combinations. He kept the bag along with his gloves and wrappings for his hands in the smaller cargo bay. He used to spar with another crewman, but the man had been injured in a decompression event and retired to a low-G habitat. Rex worked out in the gym from time to time, but bodyweight exercise and bag workouts were his main form of fitness maintenance. Today, though, he wasn't here for fitness. He was here to sweat out his frustration.

Another combination, duck, change position. He kept moving around the bag, as much to avoid making a puddle of sweat as to simulate engaging with an opponent. The point was exertion.

He'd left the hatch to the bay open, but the rhythmic sound of his gloves striking the bag and his heavy breathing filled his ears so that he missed the sound of Trix's metal heels striking the deck as she approached the bay. He had just shifted position so that the hatch was in view when Trix stepped through it.

He readied himself for an argument, but he checked that impulse when he saw someone step into the bay behind the captain. As long as there was someone else present, they wouldn't have their usual argument, but then his blood boiled when he realized that the figure accompanying the captain was Jailbait, dressed in a crew jumpsuit instead of her school girl costume.

"What's *that* doing here?"

"Looking for you, Rex. She's scheduled to be with you right now. She reported to your quarters, but you weren't there, so she was just standing in the passageway, waiting for you, drawing attention to the fact that you were not... using her."

"So you came to make sure I take my medicine," Rex said.

"Rex, I came to talk to you. Can we talk?" The captain's voice was steady for the moment, but Rex expected them both to be screaming at each other within seconds. His body was already geared up for a fight. The floor dropped out from below his emotional reality when the captain's eyes started to fill up with tears.

"Rex, I yell at you and get angry with you because it's the only way I can keep from crying. I need to talk to you without yelling, so you're going to have to watch me cry." The tears spilled out of her eyes and down her face. She made no move to wipe them away.

Rex was disarmed. He'd seen Trix cry a few times over the years, but it was rare.

"You've been avoiding me," she said. When he didn't deny it, she continued, "We have to work together. Sometimes I will need to talk to you in private. We have to be able to be alone together." Her voice was mostly steady. It quavered slightly but never broke. "I need you, Rex."

She paused and waited for Rex to respond, but he didn't know what to say. He'd been rehearsing their next argument, but none of the attacks or ripostes he had prepared in advance applied here. He said nothing.

"I don't provide blowjobs on command anymore. That's over. You were right when you said a captain can't behave that way. You were right. I accept that. That time is over. But a captain doesn't have to be celibate. A captain doesn't have to be alone."

Again, she paused to let him respond, but no words came.

"I want to get close to you, but I framed it as me wanting to relieve you so that you could focus on work. That was wrong. I'm sorry. I shouldn't have said it that way. I want to be… intimate… with you. Not for you. For me. Because I need it."

Now she did wipe the tears from her cheeks. "Rex, I think I know what you're not saying. Please say it."

"I want more than your mouth."

"Because everyone has had my mouth."

He nodded. There, it was out in the open.

"I understand. I want to give you more, but my body is damaged, Rex." With her left hand, she swept her hair back, revealing the worst of the damage to the right side of her face and scalp, a patchwork of scar tissue and synthetic skin.

"My pelvis is like this. You want to know why I dress the way I do. The tight clothes hold me together. They give my body symmetry. Without them, I'm uneven. Ugly."

"You're not ugly."

She held up her mechanical right arm. "This doesn't come off, Rex. Can you imagine being in bed with this? I can take my legs off, but I don't want to. I don't want you to see me like that. I can't fuck you, Rex. Not like a normal woman, but me on my knees, sucking your cock. That works, Rex. You know it works, and I miss it. I miss you." Her voice broke on *you*, and the stream of tears surged again.

"What about that?" He gestured at Jailbait.

"She's for me. You know I don't like having a penis in my mouth. Or at least I didn't used to. I did it to punish myself. I did it *because* I didn't like it. That's why I put up with the humiliation and the physical abuse. I thought I deserved it. But you *know* I liked it when women watched. Rex, you've seen me spend my own money to hire sex workers to watch me suck your cock when we were in port. That wasn't for you. That was for me."

"What are you saying?"

"I'm bringing my own pleasure to the table, Rex. It will be different with you than it was with the other men. Special. Because it will be for my pleasure as much as it is for yours."

"And this works for you" Rex said, gesturing toward Jailbait. "A robot?"

"Yes, Rex. She's designed to be arousing. She makes every man on this ship horny except for you and Lake. Lake I can understand, but you? Look at her, Rex. She's sexy."

"She talks like a child. Is that what you want?"

Trix gestured to the robot and it stepped forward. "Lola," Trix said, "I want to suck this man's cock, and I want you to watch. How does that sound?"

"That sounds hot, Captain." The robot spoke with the voice of an adult woman. It was low pitched and husky even for a woman. "I would love to watch you suck his cock, Captain."

"Tell me that isn't sexy," Trix said. She wasn't crying anymore. Rex knew that Trix really did like it when a woman watched her work. He believed she was sincere.

"You can touch her if you want to. Fuck her. Do whatever, or don't. I want to share her with you, but she's here for me. What do you say, Rex? Will you do this? For me?"

Rex's cock was full and straining against his pants as it always did when he was alone with Trix. "I…"

The voice of Dwayne Sparks came over the PA. "Captain, you need to come to ops." There was a note of panic in his voice when he added, "Hurry."

ANOTHER HARD BURN

1.15.1 - Rex

Rex and Trix raced to the bridge.

"Report," Trix said as soon as she had both feet on the deck of the bridge.

"It's a ship, ma'am. Ninety two light seconds out." Sparks said. "It's got to be Floaters,"

"Kellemen?" She looked to the electronic warfare specialist.

"They transmitted executable code at us, Captain. I've isolated it. It looks like they were trying to infiltrate our navigation system."

Turning back to Sparks, "Do you have a visual?"

"No, ma'am. I can't find it on optical. They're probably running dark, but it's there on radar. We need more observations to calculate their precise trajectory, but it looks like they're on an intercept course. It looks like we'll cross paths… here."

Sparks fed a course schematic from his station to the main tactical display. It showed a gently arcing line for the *Persephone's* course and a fat gray tube with a dotted line in the center to indicate the range of courses the other ship could be on. The tube got wider the farther it got from the other ship's present location. A sphere nearly five light seconds in radius marked the area in which the ships could come into contact.

"Keep tracking and refine that calculation," she told Sparks.

"Aye, Captain."

Trix activated the PA. "Attention crew. Brace for maneuvers."

She climbed into the pilot's station and counted to five, giving everyone a chance to grab ahold of something, then she used the thrusters to move the ship laterally. She didn't change their course substantially, but hopefully she had altered their position enough so that any lasers or particle beams the other ship might already have fired would miss them once they'd closed the gap between the two ships.

She activated the PA again. "All hands, high gravity burn in ten minutes. Everybody, get to your couches. Zell, report to ops."

Rex tried to catch Trix's eye before he left the bridge, but her focus was total. He raced back to his quarters to prepare for acceleration.

1.15.2 - Trey

I was on my back enjoying the sight of Esmeralda's bouncing breasts as she rode me in the cowgirl position when the captain announced that we'd be going to high-g acceleration.

"Are you close?" Esmeralda asked.

"Not anymore," I said. Esmeralda enjoyed multiple orgasms during foreplay, so I didn't feel any hesitation about stopping. I'd like to think that Zira would have been satisfied with my attentiveness.

Esmeralda slipped off of me and sat on the side of my bed, gathering up her clothes.

"Raincheck?" I said.

"What?" It made sense that that expression had died out in the Kuiper Belt.

"To be continued," I said.

"Oh," she said smiling. "You think you left me wanting more?"

I'm sure she was teasing me. I'd say we were quite compatible. If I had to choose between Petrovic and Esmeralda, I'd take Esmeralda. Petrovic wouldn't ask me to choose, but Esmeralda might.

She leaned over and kissed me on the cheek, and then she was all business. She pulled on her pants and stuffed her underwear, bra and socks into the cargo pockets. She pulled on her boots and grabbed her top. She pulled it on as she moved to the hatch and paused there just long enough to secure two fasteners. She'd be getting naked again in a few minutes when she got into her acceleration couch. She opened the hatch and departed without closing it.

I stuffed all of my clothes into a laundry bag and put it in my closet. I put on a robe and walked to the med lab. I realized there was no need for me to rush when I remembered that ten minutes in Kuiper Belt time was equal to seventeen of the minutes I was used to. I just had a couple of processes to suspend in the lab. We had secured most of the medical deck for acceleration by the time Esmeralda and I took our unscheduled break.

I enjoyed the extended flirting, but I wish we hadn't taken so long to get to the actual sex. I thought we had plenty of time.

1.15.3 - Cook

Everything was squared away in the galley, and Cook had just poured himself a whiskey. It wasn't top shelf whiskey, and he wasn't precious about it. He poured it over ice and even added a splash of water, not to mention the fact that he was drinking it out of a disposable cup. He was looking to get drunk. He didn't care about impressing anyone with his sophistication, though he could tell a good whiskey from a merely serviceable one.

Cook knew that at this very moment, Jailbait was with Rex. At the next half watch it would be Cook's turn. He'd hold off on the cannabis chews until after his playtime with Jailbait.

The kid was gushing to Petrovic about her time with Cat Girl. Cook knew that Petrovic wasn't into women, but she listened and probed for details as if she was as excited about it as Paige was. She was happy for the kid. Cook hung back, not wanting to intrude.

Then came the maneuver warning, and after that, the news that devastated Cook's plans. "All hands, high gravity burn in ten minutes."

"Fuck, shit, motherfucker!" Cook had the urge to throw his cup, but he resisted and downed the contents instead.

"What is it..." Paige started to ask, but then she must have figured it out. "Oh, Cook," she said with what seemed like genuine compassion. "I'm so sorry."

"It ain't your fault, killer. And besides, it seems we've got bigger fish to fry."

Petrovic got up from the table and approached Cook. She spoke quietly, though Paige could doubtless still hear what she said. "Hey, Cook. Let's go back to your compartment right now. I'll take care of you."

"Thanks, Petrovic, but..."

"Don't be a martyr. It's no big deal. You don't want high-g blue balls. C'mon."

"Okay. Thanks," Cook said. He poured himself another whiskey, secured the bottle, and followed Petrovic toward the exit.

Petrovic said, "Little tiger, you'd better get to your couch. If you're not early, you're late."

"See you on the other side, killer," Cook said to Paige as Anja led him out into the passageway.

1.15.4 - Petrovic

The captain's words came over the PA. "Petrovic! Get to your damned couch! Acceleration in one minute!"

Petrovic, naked except for her shoes, sprinted for her compartment. She carried the belt with the holstered sidearm in her left hand.

The time pressure took the wind out of Cook's sails at first, but Petrovic took that as a challenge. She stripped naked and told him how much fun he was going to have spanking Jailbait's plump ass when his turn finally came. She cycled through a series of provocations with nothing working, and then on an intuitive impulse, she'd given one of Cook's nipples a hard pinch. That did the trick. With hands and mouth she coaxed him across the finish line with 91 seconds to spare.

She left her clothes on the deck of Cook's compartment, only bending down to grab the gun belt as she scrambled out. She left the hatch for Cook to close. Inside her own compartment, she sealed the hatch. kicked off her shoes, slapped a clip into her sidearm, pushed it into the holster affixed to the outside of her acceleration couch, and climbed in.

The acceleration had already begun, and she felt herself getting heavier. She didn't have time to settle in. She thrust her legs into the compression sleeves and left them to tighten themselves. She lay down in the warm gel and said, "Close." The lid of her acceleration couch came down slowly, and she said, "Send to Captain: I'm in!"

1.15.5 - Paige

Paige had no idea why they'd started acceleration ahead of schedule. She had no practical experience to draw upon, but she couldn't think of any explanation for the sudden change in schedule that meant good news. She accessed the public channel, but it was all questions and no answers. She noticed that neither Sparks nor Kellemen had chimed in. If they were busy, it could mean ship to ship combat.

She got a voice memo from Anja. "Hey, little tiger. There's nothing for us to do now, but pay attention to everything. This is the stuff that bragging rights are made of. You'll be telling this story in bars and galleys for years, so remember the details."

This was not like Paige's previous experience of acceleration. Instead of a gradual and continuous increase in weight, the acceleration would cut out suddenly, which made the contents of her stomach threaten to leap out of her mouth. Then she felt as if she were falling or hanging upside down. Then down was down again with her lying on her back, but acceleration came like a full body punch, knocking the breath out of her. Then she was floating, then falling, then lying down again with several sacks of fertilizer stacked on her chest.

Her heart raced. She needed to get out. She struggled, but the gel of the couch held her in a soft but implacable grip. All she managed to do was move her left arm enough to remind her that she had a needle in her vein.

A glowing icon in the shape of a blue addition sign pulsed in her field of vision, and her panic ebbed away. Esmeralda's soothing voice reassured her. "You're okay, sweetie. The doctor's giving you a little something to calm you down. Just breathe."

"Remember the details," Anja's words echoed in her head. Calm now, she described the sensations of rapid acceleration punctuated by hard maneuvers to herself. She imagined herself older and bigger, talking to young men and women who were gathered around her in the ship's galley, describing this experience to them. She'd never been in a bar, so she couldn't picture herself in one as easily as she could project herself into a ship's galley.

This pattern of dizzying flips and reversals and crushing bursts continued for well over a watch. The blue plus sign appeared a few more times, but Esmeralda did not send a voice memo to explain them. She was busy helping the doctor, and, Paige realized with amazement, Esmeralda was on the same ship undergoing the same taxing forces that Paige was, and she was working.

Paige wasn't sure if she lost consciousness, but if not, she slipped into some form of consciousness that was not part of her normal experience.

She continued to narrate her own experiences to herself, but then the narrator receded in significance to the observer. Time came off its usual track and overlapped with itself. She saw and felt the whole ordeal as a static diagram. She could study any portion of it in detail and then pull out and see and feel the whole of it again. With no particular sense of urgency or desire, she moved her attention to the endpoint of the tumult. She noticed an auditory sensation. Words. The captain's voice. She focused on it, not grasping. Not urgent, but the captain's voice grew in her attention until time was back on its normal track.

"All hands. An unidentified vessel transmitted executable code to us seeking to access our systems. It was a clumsy effort according to Mr. Kellemen, and he dealt with it easily. They were on an intercept course, and we have taken steps to see how badly they want to cross paths with us. We seem to have exceeded the limits of their motivation. They have changed course. All of our evasive maneuvers were precautionary. There is no indication that the other ship fired either missiles or speed of light weapons at us."

This was a voice memo, and it must have been difficult for the captain to speak under the crushing acceleration, but her voice sounded strong to Paige. She imagined feeling as powerful as the captain must be to speak with such authority at this moment.

"I have authorized Sparks and Kellemen to share all of the information about our maneuvers and about the other vessel's course, actions and configuration. They will curate the data and answer your questions in the public channel, but not right now. They are very tired and need to rest. In fact, the doctor is going to put us all down for a little nap until we slow to .7g in a couple of watches. Move slowly and cautiously when you get out of your couches. Space is never safe, but all indications are that we are in no immediate danger. Pleasant dreams."

The blue medical icon pulsed again, and Paige started to drift off. The last thing she noticed was that she wasn't breathing anymore. Her diaphragm and intercostal muscles still made rhythmic attempts to expand her rib cage, but she could not draw any significant quantity of air into her lungs. Her last conscious thought was, "Isn't that interesting?"

SPARKS OF CLARITY

Act 2

2.1.1 - Trey

Paige was already in anesthesia-induced unconsciousness so that she would experience a complete loss of consciousness and responsiveness to external stimuli. Next I gave the non-Columbian crew just enough sedative to put them into a deep sleep, but not so deep that they couldn't wake up on their own in the event of an emergency.

The Columbians required a dose that would have killed the non-Columbian crew, and that barely pushed them below the surface of full waking consciousness. Now only the captain and I were awake. She sent me a revised plan for the burn. We were going to skip our fist scheduled break and spend the next full day accelerating at 9g. I couldn't draw enough breath to speak aloud, so I composed a text message for the captain by speaking without voice. The sensors in my couch followed the movements of my lips, tongue and throat to determine the words I intended to form.

I told Captain Nixon that Paige wasn't breathing and that I was sustaining her with a continuous infusion of oxygenated, synthetic blood. Her couch was adequate to her present needs, but I wanted to move her to a medical acceleration unit before we went to 9g.

She asked how long it would take, and I estimated 20 minutes in my time. I asked the couch interface to convert that to Spinner time, and it supplied the figure of 11.76

minutes. I rounded up and told the captain I'd need 12 minutes to move Paige from her quarters and get her situated in the medical acceleration unit.

"No," was the captain's only response. She sent it by voice memo, and her voice sounded strong. I was impressed.

I composed another message, telling the captain that I wasn't getting any medical data from her own acceleration couch. It took longer for me to complete the message than it should have.

She replied, again by voice, "I don't need medical support."

I was in no position to remonstrate with her. I couldn't allow myself to follow the rest of the crew into induced sleep, but I felt the pull of normal sleep. I double checked that my couch interface would wake me in case of a medical emergency among the crew and gave in to the overwhelming urge to let go and sink into unconsciousness.

2.1.2 - Group Chat

#Public channel

D_Antal: @J_Zell Was it Floaters?
J_Zell: Yes, I'm pretty sure it was. We did finally get optics on it.
J_Zell: I've worked claims on the same TNOs with floaters. That's a typical vessel configuration. They like more open spaces on the interior of their vehicles than we do. And their bodies can't stand high-g the way ours can, so they're built for slower acceleration. They might have war ships, but if so, I've never seen one, and this one isn't in any position to catch us.
E_Escamilla: @J_Zell But they could still hit us with a laser. Why have we stopped evading?
J_Zell: As far as we can tell, they never fired any sort of weapon at us. It was the captain's decision to discontinue

evasive maneuvers.

E_Escamilla: But they tried to access our systems.

S_Kellemen: They did, but it was a half-assed attempt. Maybe just a warning. They might not have expected to actually get in, and even if they had, navigation and propulsion are discreet systems for just that reason. They would have known where we came from and where we planned to go, but they couldn't have taken control of any critical systems.

D_Sparks: We can't be certain they didn't fire any weapons at us. They did launch something that is still following us, but it's not accelerating like a missile. Captain thinks it's a remote sensor pod. Movement profile indicates we could take it out with point defense batteries no problem if it tried to close with us, but I wouldn't get too comfortable. They haven't let us go.

E_Escamilla: We were in their territory. Of course they're going to track us.

R_Perkins: Alright, everyone. We're coming up on a 10 minute break. We're actually going to .5G to deal with an injury. Stretch, grab a meal bar, use the head, but don't go to the galley or anywhere far from your quarters. This is a quick break. We've got a long burn ahead of us, and it's going to be a rough one.

2.1.3 - Paige

Paige woke slowly to the sound of soothing music and bird song. She opened her eyes to a beautifully manicured garden. Not a vegetable garden, but one that was purely decorative, with small trees, a pond, and a little house on stilts over the water. The house had sliding walls and was open so she could see inside. She could see a robed figure seated on the floor playing a flute. It took her several seconds to work out that she was looking at an image on her couch display.

She tried to dismiss it with a vocal command, but she couldn't draw a breath. She still wasn't breathing.

Using only eye movements, she dismissed the soothing garden scene and called up a display of her vitals. She didn't know exactly what to look for, but she could see that her respiration was flat. The blue plus sign pulsed continuously.

Another icon pulsed on screen informing her that she had a message. She selected it.

E_Escamilla: @P_Farmer Paige, sweetie. We'll be reducing our acceleration to .5g in a couple of minutes. Don't try to open your couch. You've been injured. We think you have some broken ribs. When the gravity lets up, don't move. We'll come to you. You're going to be fine, we just need to be careful. I'll see you soon, sweetie.

Soon the gravity did relent, and when she was able to draw a breath it sparked a flash of agony in her torso, but that pain was soon dialed back to a distant ache. She heard the sounds of something hard making contact with the outside of her couch, and then the lid pulled up and away, taking the visual display with it.

A figure loomed over her. The light in the room wasn't bright, but she couldn't make out any details on the figure. She felt the interior mechanisms of the couch release her legs and arms. The toilet system detached from her crotch and pulled away. She was too numb from anesthetic to notice the needle withdrawing itself from her arm.

"It's okay," Escamilla said. "It's me, Esmeralda. The doctor is here too. Don't move, honey. Don't try to talk. We'll take care of you."

Paige heard a strange sound. In hindsight, she figured out that it was the sound of Esmeralda cutting away Paige's thin tank top.

Strong hands lifted her into a seated position, and she could make out Esmeralda's face now, all reassuring concern.

"There you go, sweetie. That's right. I'm going to lift your arms now. I don't want you to help. Let me do it."

Escamilla took hold of Paige's wrists and slowly lifted the young woman's arms over her head. The distant pain in her torso shouted at her through the fluffy drug haze.

There was another presence. She felt hands moving over her torso, reading its contours. Trey's face came into focus. He did not make eye contact with her. He withdrew his hands and held a portable scanner to her body.

"Fractures in left five and seven. Five is posterolateral. Seven is anterior. Right side is good."

The doctor disappeared from Paige's awareness for a moment, but Esmeralda kept her arms raised. The doctor returned and fitted something around Paige's torso.

"Paige," the doctor said. "This is going to support you and help you breathe. It's going to feel very tight. It needs to be."

Paige felt the brace firming up and constricting her torso. There was a flash of panic when it felt like it was going to crush her, but she actually found it easier to breathe after just a few seconds.

"That's right, sweetie. I'm just going to clean you up a little and then we're going to have you lie back down. You're going to sleep for a long time. It will be easier for you. You're fine, sweetie. Everything is okay."

Esmeralda wiped Paige's armpits and neck with a moist sheet. She swabbed the area where the toilet fixtures attached along with the insides of her thighs.

"Anja wanted to be here," Esmeralda said as she cleaned Paige. "She cares about you, but she knows you're going to be okay."

Esmeralda lowered Paige back down into a reclining position, re-engaged the compression sleeves on Paige's legs, attached the toilet fixture and secured the intravenous cuff to her left arm. She put a cuff on Paige's right arm as well.

"Okay, sweetie. You're going to go to sleep now. I'll see you soon."

Everything faded.

2.1.4 - Petrovic

Per Trey's instructions, Anja stayed out of Paige's cabin during the break. She didn't worry, but Paige was never far from her thoughts during the break.

The intense acceleration combined with evasive maneuvers was hard on everyone, even Anja, who had the strength of an ox. Germline genetic alterations were not a topic for polite conversation in the Columbian military, mostly because it was more extensive than the leadership wanted to admit to outsiders. At least they could still breed with non-Columbians. They hadn't speciated.

Most of the genetic upgrades the Columbians enjoyed were related to combat. They were bigger and more muscular than baseline KB humans. That was obvious at a glance. They had other advantages that weren't as visible.

In combat, they processed information quickly and maintained their composure more easily than baseline KB humans. They healed quickly, and their robust immune systems meant that they rarely got sick. They were better able to withstand the effects of sustained acceleration. The main danger in sustained, high-g acceleration was stroke.

The Columbian soldiers were in no danger from hemorrhagic stroke. Their enhanced circulatory system prevented ruptured blood vessels in their brains. An ischemic stroke from a blood clot was a possibility. The marines clotted aggressively. The decreased likelihood of bleeding out from a bullet wound outweighed the marginally increased risk from a blood clot in the brain under prolonged acceleration, and Petrovic was confident that the doc was giving them a little something to help ward off clots.

Once they were underway again, Trey dropped her a line to say that Paige was okay. She showed no signs of either kind of stroke. She did have two broken ribs and a collapsed lung, but that was easily dealt with. They'd fitted her with a sleeve that would help support her rib cage and assist her breathing before putting her to sleep. Once she was unconscious, they'd run a feeding tube through one nostril into her stomach, and she had a tracheostomy tube to keep her airway open, both of which would likely send Paige into a panic if she were awake.

Trey also informed Anja that he'd fucked Escamilla. *Good for them*, she thought, and meant it. No mention of a potential threeway. No skin off Anja's nose if it didn't happen. She wasn't into women. She'd had sex with a few, but always for the benefit of a male lover.

Her little tiger was missing all the action in Anja's sex chat channel. It was dominated by talk of the sex robots. Almost everyone had gotten a turn with one of them, but Paul Lake, who won the Last Supper raffle, was the only one who'd been with both of them and had any basis for comparison. Anja suspected that Lake and the two robots had just braided each other's hair or whatever in that second class cabin with the double bed.

Lake did not join Anja's channel, nor did Chukwuma. She hoped they had the good sense to know that their private messages weren't bulletproof. If they were smart, they were vague enough even in their DMs to maintain plausible deniability.

Petrovic was both disappointed with herself and impressed with Paige that her young apprentice had sniffed out the dynamic between Lake and Chukwuma before she had. She had been sure that Nora, the engine keeper, had snagged Chukwuma. Well, there were a lot of moving parts to this situation. She couldn't expect to keep track of them all.

Nora did not participate in the sex talk channel during acceleration. After seeing how drunk she had gotten at Last Supper, Petrovic wondered if Nora stayed drunk during acceleration. That would be irresponsible of her. As the engine keeper, she needed to keep her wits about her.

Trix had the funds to hire the best crew money could buy. It seemed odd to Petrovic that she would hire an engine keeper with a drinking problem. Maybe her consumption at Last Supper was a one-off.

Trey would know if Nora was drinking during acceleration, though he probably wouldn't tell Anja about it. She respected that. *Ethical codes keep us out of trouble.*

Of the two sex dolls, Jailbait was the more popular among the marines. The captain also preferred the curvaceous school girl, though she activated a secondary adult persona that was more to her liking. The name *Jailbait* was Petrovic's idea. She knew that the captain called the robot *Lola* and used feminine pronouns instead of *it* when talking about the doll.

While most everyone wanted a date with Jailbait, those who'd made due with Cat Girl reported being pleasantly surprised. Body hair seemed like a masculine trait, but Cat Girl's fur was downy soft, and while she looked lean and muscular, she was soft to the touch.

Where Jailbait was compliant but sexually passive, Cat Girl was sexually aggressive and seemed to invite rough treatment. Nobody bragged of striking or choking her, but Petrovic would have been surprised if nobody had given in to the temptation. The sex robots were not physically strong. They were designed to be small and weak so as to present no potential physical threat which might inflame anti-AI passions, but they were built to endure a lot of vigorous use.

Escamilla joined the sex talk channel, just as she had on the first burn, but she lurked more than she participated. She did respond to direct questions about her time with Cat Girl. When asked why she chose Cat Girl over Jailbait, she explained that she'd been with another robot of Cat Girl's model before and that it had been a good experience. She demurred when asked for explicit details.

Petrovic felt neither fondness nor suspicion toward the sex dolls. She certainly wasn't aroused by the females, but she did plan to ask the captain if she could spend some time with David. Ideally, it wouldn't be alone time. Petrovic would love for the captain to watch her play with the male sex doll, but barring that, she'd be happy with Trey, Cook, Rex or even her little tiger as her audience. But if David and his adjustable-sized dick with no audience were her only option, she wouldn't hesitate.

***

2.1.5 - Group Chat

#Public channel.

D_Sparks: Ba'al is the lord of heaven. He brings the rains, but without the warmth of the sun goddess, water turns to ice. It doesn't nourish crops. Ba'al imposes order on chaos, but it is His order, His kingdom. Yam is right to challenge him.

S_Kellemen: The humans behind the Curtain submit themselves to Ba'al's authority and bask in the nourishing light of Shapash. They live in luxury and safety, but they aren't free. Some of them come out here to the house of Mot. They give up their safety and their comforts for the freedom to define themselves by their own efforts in the struggle for survival.

S_Li: Freedom? You bind yourselves in mind-forged manacles when you try to map the religion of primitive peoples onto our contemporary reality. Self-definition through the application of reason, science and technology is the only path to freedom. Your irrational obsession with superstition and myth is the death of reason, the antithesis of freedom.

D_Sparks: Listen to yourself, Li. You're lost in the wilderness and someone gives you a map. You think it's rational to ignore the map because it doesn't fit your dogma?

S_Li: You think that ridiculous book is a map? It's a game. A distraction from reality. It's worse than useless. You only distort reality when you look for meaning in the delusions of savages.

E_Escamilla: Mythological archetypes encode the understanding of human psychology that ancient people accumulated over thousands of years. Their myths encoded the essential elements of their world. That meant the sun, the moon, the rains, and the turning of the seasons. Ancient people observing the skies worked out the procession of equinoxes, a 25,000 year cycle, and they did it without telescopes or computers or anything that narrow-minded Objectivists would count as science or reason.

S_Li: Human minds find patterns in data. Often they find patterns that are not even there. The brain is a powerful instrument. Even without the benefits of rationality, it achieves amazing things, but that is no reason to valorize ignorance and superstition.

D_Sparks: Resheph is the bringer of pestilence and plague. The Powers shield their pet humans from disease, so Resheph has no place behind the Curtain. But out here in the house of Mot, we are too scattered for plagues to spread. Respheph is diminished and sustains himself only as an aspect of Mot. Together they are Re-Mot, the embodiment of death and sterility. Master of the Void.

S_Kellemen: Who built the Curtain that hoards the nurturing light? Was it Yam, master of the abyss? Concentrating the light behind the Curtain darkens his realm. The people die and struggle without the light, but those who prevail are strong and truly free.

S_Li: The acceleration has pulped your brains!

P_Lake: I don't know. It seems like a harmless exercise in constrained creativity to me. If you force yourself to think within arbitrary limits, you'll come up with novel ideas that wouldn't have occurred to you otherwise. Most of these new ideas will prove useless, but you never know until you churn through the space of possibilities.

S_Li: You say most of the ideas you generate from constrained thinking will be useless. That's sugarcoating the reality. Most of those ideas will be wrong. Factually incorrect. Imposing limits on reason is, by definition, irrational. Looking for guidance in the mythological characters of pre-technological people has no place out here where it is only our scientific understanding and our technology that stands between us and instant death in the vacuum. Gods and monsters have nothing to offer us.

P_Lake: I'm not from Galtz, so please be patient with my ignorance, Shawn. But it's my understanding that Ayn Rand's most famous novel was called *Atlas Shrugged*. Isn't Atlas a titan from Greek mythology?

S_Li: Fine. Yes, a rational mind can use mythological symbols to encode an important truth, but do you think that's what Sparks and Kellemen are doing? They're looking for winning lottery numbers in animal entrails.

E_Escamilla: I think they're using mythology to challenge some of the basic assumptions of our culture and language. We're taught to think that light and order are good and darkness and chaos are bad, but we Spinners thrive out here in the darkness, and the chaos of the Blackout forced us to compete for resources and made us stronger and more resilient. We live in the abyss. Why shouldn't we identify with the personification of the abyss?

S_Li: You Columbians are strong because the Nixians used science and technology to upgrade your genomes. Do you think they burn incense and offer sacrifices to propitiate made up gods on Nix? They master the universe with science! The light of reason sustains us in the void of ignorance!

P_Lake: Are you sure you're not personifying abstract concepts there, Shawn? That doesn't feel like mythologizing to you?

S_Li: You people are hopeless.

2.1.6 - Rex

Rex only half followed the discussion in the public channel. Trix had shown him the printed book that Sparks called the *corpus*. He'd looked at the illustrations and read a few captions, but he couldn't see the point of it. The book didn't tell a straight forward story. It gave detailed descriptions of the various gods, their areas of influence, their conflicts with one another, and the various symbols that represent them, but it didn't hold his interest.

Books were rare things in the Kuiper Belt. They didn't hold much data and took up a lot of space. To Rex, books were status items. Before the Blackout, the Columbian military issued a handbook to all soldiers. It contained a code of conduct, several prayers and hymns, and bits of lore that an ambitious soldier would memorize over time and quote at appropriate moments to distinguish himself.

You could still find those handbooks, but they were expensive and out of date, and you couldn't update them. Someone explained to him that the fact that you'd have to print a new book to update the contents of a previous book ensured that the information in your copy hadn't been altered without your knowledge or permission. Wasn't a blockchain a better solution to that problem? Some people claimed to love the feeling of a book in their hands, turning pages rather than searching for keywords or topics like a normal person. Some eccentrics would even hold books to their noses and claim to benefit from the smell of them. *Weirdos.*

Rex just never saw the point of books, and this oversized book in particular, *Void Huntress*, baffled him with its total lack of practical utility. Why Sparks would carry it with him on a mission was beyond Rex, but Sparks was high born.

Rex had served in the Columbian military, but he wasn't from a Columbian family. He would never be eligible for officer training no matter how many old poems he memorized. Book collecting was about as meaningful to him as horseback riding, another expensive and useless activity that Columbian families used to distinguish themselves from the rest of the KB population.

Rex thought of Trix. Most any topic led him back to her. In this instance, the association was her ability to appeal to the inflated self-image of the Columbian soldiers and use it to inspire loyalty to her. She'd made passing reference to her own military service over the years, but it wasn't in the Columbian military. She wasn't even from Galtz or any of its closest neighbors. It was easy to forget, but she used to have an accent that Rex couldn't place. She deliberately learned to talk like a Galter, but every now and again, he'd pick up on some subtle remnant of her original accent.

As he replayed the scene in the cargo bay he saw Petrovic's fingerprints all over Trix's rehearsed proposal. The vulnerability, the honesty, the directness. Rex was starting to see the value in her slut's code of conduct. Maybe Petrovic should turn her manifesto into a printed book. *That* could actually be useful.

Rex thought back to his last private conversation with Trix. What was he about to say when Sparks interrupted them with his panicked call for the captain's presence on the bridge?

Trix was right that a Captain wasn't expected to be celibate or solitary. A sexual relationship with Rex wouldn't compromise her dignity or authority as Captain. She was offering Rex exclusivity. The other men onboard who used to enjoy her services wouldn't hold it against him. The sex doll was not an issue for him. He'd never had any problem when Trix hired real human women to watch her service Rex. And if she really looked and felt better with her clothes on, Rex didn't need to see her without them. She displayed every centimeter of intact skin most of the time anyway.

She'd answered all of his concerns, even ones that he hadn't fully admitted, even to himself, actually were concerns. Again, they probably had Anja Petrovic to thank for that bit of clarity.

It wasn't really possible to sigh with relief under seven gravities, but Rex felt unburdened.

"Yes," he thought. "Let's do it."

INTERVENTION AND RECOVERY

2.2.1 - Trey

Before the situation with Paige dominated my attention, I was focused on Rex Perkins. I took a baseline blood sample from everyone as soon as they got into their couches.

Perkins had elevated levels of cortisol and epinephrine from the moment the needle entered his arm. I put it down to concern over whatever it was that had us going to high-g acceleration ahead of schedule and moved on, but once I'd looked in on everyone else I went back to Rex for a closer look. I ran a more detailed analysis of his blood, and the results indicated that his stress was chronic and so severe that it must be impairing his cognitive function.

I gave him immediate relief with benzodiazepines and beta blockers, but over the next couple of days I gave him very small doses of LSD and MDMA in order to facilitate introspection. Outside of the acceleration couch, I doubted that he would comply with any ongoing anti-depressant medication regimen or agree to talk therapy, but while he was in the pod, his well-being was my responsibility. I did what I could for him in the time available.

I returned my attention to Paige. The Galtz marines were physically robust. In addition to the advantages of lifelong nutritional abundance and physical exercise, their great grandparents had opted for some inheritable genetic modifications that struck me as rather sensible.

The Columbians were more resistant to the effects of ionizing radiation than most Kuiper Belt humans. They had denser bones and muscles which took longer to atrophy in microgravity. They had enhanced immune systems and healed from wounds more quickly than *normal* humans. And, particularly useful for troops who would need to endure periods of intense acceleration, the blood vessels in their brains were practically impossible to rupture. Hemorrhagic stroke was just not a concern for them.

Paige enjoyed none of those advantages. In addition to caloric paucity, her diet was lacking in minerals, and she paid the price in bone density.

She simply had no business being in this situation. I questioned the captain's judgment in bringing the young woman on this expedition, but then I remembered that even the captain, or acting-captain, didn't know the details of the mission before they left port. Two high-g burns on one trip was nearly unheard of due to the expense and not anything the captain could reasonably have been expected to anticipate. She thought she was giving Paige an opportunity.

Which brings me to the captain herself. Her couch provided me with no data at all. I couldn't even confirm that she was in her acceleration capsule, though she would be dead by now if she weren't. I had no way to monitor her condition or administer aid.

I don't need medical support.

What's more, her medical records were clearly fabricated. They're a mash-up of records taken from a number of people, both male and female. They might pass casual inspection, but any experienced diagnostician would see the incongruities almost immediately. I didn't know what to make of that.

Clearly, she'd been catastrophically injured years ago, but there is no reasonable explanation for the incompetence of her reconstruction. The patches of synthetic skin don't match the tone of her original skin. They lack the elasticity I would expect of even the most temporary of emergency replacements. I'm sure they lack tactile sensitivity.

Her left ear is torn, and her right ear is completely missing. She could attach a plastic ear to the right side of her head and it would look better than the unadorned hole that's there now.

The replacement for her right eye looks like an antique. Not only does it not match the color of her other eye, but it's a poor match in terms of size and shape. Replacing an eye should bring with it enhanced vision, but I'm guessing that hers doesn't even match the visual acuity of the original. It doesn't require lubrication, but whoever installed it left her tear duct intact and functional. I've noticed her blinking away excess moisture.

Her legs are certainly functional, particularly for someone who needs to operate in microgravity, but they could be more subtle in their design. And that right arm! I could see it being useful for a mechanic, but she should be able to swap it out for something more human-looking. As far as I can tell just looking at it, it is embedded in her glenohumeral joint. Removing it would require surgery.

Given the crude nature of her implants, I'd be surprised if she wasn't in constant pain.

And then there's her personality. It would be a gross understatement to describe her as angry. She is a ball of carefully constrained rage. She seems to have learned to direct her rage in useful ways, but not being able to turn it off, she comes off as overly intense even when it doesn't suit her immediate purposes.

After helping an extremely inebriated Nora Lawson back to her quarters after Last Supper, I checked her file for any indication of chronic overconsumption. Nothing. Nora isn't a drunk. I think she was just terrified to be sitting next to the captain at dinner.

Captain Nixon knows this ship, and she knows how to motivate people, but she seems to be living in a deliberately constructed hell from which she makes no effort to extract herself.

2.2.2 - Petrovic

Petrovic descended the final ladder and walked down the short passageway to the galley. Normally, .7g would put her in a good mood. She resolved not to worry. She was a warrior not a worrier. Still, the added spring in her step from the lower gravity failed to lift her mood.

The galley was full, and she returned greetings from her fellow marines with a wave and a smile. Everybody had lost weight during the burn, and they were serious about putting it back on. Anja wasn't hungry, but she intended to eat.

She approached the coffee station and met Cook's eyes. He didn't have to ask about Paige.

"Still sleeping," Petrovic said. "They've pulled back on the sedatives, but she hasn't woken up yet. Doc says it's nothing to worry about. They'll call me when she's awake."

"I'm worried about her too," Cook said.

"I'm not worried," Petrovic said.

"Okay. I'll worry for both of us. And hey, thanks for what you did for me, and for hanging in there."

"That was a hoot," Petrovic said. "Good for a future drinking story. It even has the benefit of being true. Not strictly necessary for drinking stories, but it doesn't hurt."

Petrovic loaded her plate with high protein options without thinking much about taste. She sat down and ate. She didn't wolf down her food, but the goal was to ingest the prescribed quantity and get back up to medical. She didn't waste any time.

2.2.3 - Paige

Paige opened her eyes. What she saw did not make immediate sense to her. Then she realized that she was on the medical level.

She didn't recognize this compartment. There were three beds in it. The one she was in had several instruments positioned around it. Her right arm was immobilized, and an IV dripped clear fluid into her. She felt a tingle on the left side of her torso. She tried to look there, and as soon as she contracted the muscles of her abdomen to sit up, a shock of pain from her ribs convinced her she didn't need to look down right away.

The hatch to the compartment swung open and Esmeralda stepped in carrying a clear cup full of orange liquid. The cup had a screw-on cap with a bendy straw sticking out of it.

"Good morning, sleepy head," Esmeralda said with a warm smile.

"What happened?"

"The doctor thinks an elephant sat on you, but I think maybe it had something to do with the nine gravities we pulled during evasive maneuvers."

Esmeralda placed one hand on Paige's shoulder to dissuade her from trying to sit up, having missed Paige's prior attempt. With the other hand, she held the cup so that Paige could sip at the straw. The orange liquid wasn't fruit juice. Paige didn't know what it was, but she sucked down several compulsive swallows.

"Good," Esmeralda said. "Drink up."

Paige relaxed back into her pillow. "So, it was just gravity?"

"Nobody has seen an elephant," Esmeralda said. "But gravity is no joke. You have two broken ribs. You didn't breathe for three watches. We sustained you with oxygenated blood until we could reinforce your ribcage with a brace. Even then, you were only breathing with one lung until just about half a watch ago. We had to drain fluid from your left lung."

"Where's Anja?"

Esmeralda pointed to a chair by the bed. "She was sitting right there until just a few minutes ago. The seat is probably still warm. She would have missed breakfast if the doctor hadn't kicked her out. We promised her we'd call her as soon as you woke up, but let's give her a few minutes to eat, shall we."

"My side tingles," Paige said.

"That's just a mild electric current to stimulate bone growth," Esmeralda said. "The captain has arranged for one day with seven tenths gravity. After today, we'll be in zero-g, which is not ideal for healing bones. We're going to use every trick there is to make up for the lack of gravity so that your ribs will be better than new."

"How long do I have to stay here?"

"Believe me, you won't want to move for a couple of days, but then we'll need you to get out of that bed. You'll have to do a lot of exercise to make up for the lack of gravity. And we're going to start tapering off your pain meds the day after tomorrow. You might feel some withdrawal symptoms, but we can help you with that."

AN UNLIKELY COINCIDENCE

2.3.1 - Trey

Petrovic stood up when she saw Esmeralda and me in the passageway outside the galley. She looked over her shoulder, at Cook, I assumed. He probably motioned for her to leave her tray on the table and go.

As she approached us, I felt Esmeralda's arm around my waist. We hadn't touched on the walk down from medical, but now, in front of Petrovic, she made a public display of intimacy. Unlike Petrovic, Esmeralda didn't check with me in advance.

"She's awake," I said, and she nodded and stepped past Esmeralda and me.

Esmeralda reached out for Petrovic. "Anja," she said, "a word before you go up."

Sparks and Kellemen both glared at me when I stepped into the galley. Rex sat at the captain's table with Nora. Nora smiled at me. Rex gave me a nearly imperceptible nod. Everyone else ignored me except for Cook.

"Hey, Doc. How's she doing?"

"Two broken ribs, but she's awake and breathing on her own with both lungs," I said.

"Good to hear," Cook said. "Tell her there's a big pile of dirty pots and pans that need washing when she's done milking her little boo boo for attention."

"It may be a few days before she's ready to do any work, but I'll let her know." I glanced past Cook and noticed a familiar machine over his shoulder. It took me a moment to place it, and when I recognized it, I was transported back in time to Seattle in the late 1990s. "Is that an espresso machine?"

"Sure is. You want one? I can even steam some milk for you and whip up a latte. Interested?"

"If it wouldn't be too much trouble," I said.

"Ha! *Too much trouble.* Comin' right up, doc."

By the time I'd filled my plate, Cook was tamping finely ground coffee beans into the portafilter basket. *Portafilter basket.* That was some oddly specific vocabulary to come bubbling up to the surface of my consciousness, but that's how delves worked.

I had lived many lives in historical delves, and most of my memory of them faded from my consciousness when I emerged back into baseline reality, but every now and again, some specific detail would present itself to my waking consciousness. What remained was the semantic knowledge and muscle memory that my delve experiences impressed upon me.

I could name some of the many wives and children from my simulated lives, including at least one girlfriend who had worked as a barista in Seattle's Capital Hill neighborhood. I couldn't bring their faces or voices clearly to mind, although they sometimes came to me in my dreams. The point being, I kept what I learned in my simulated lives, but I wasn't haunted by the pain of lost loved ones.

The milk frother was as loud as the one I remembered from the Tully's Coffee shop across the street from the hospital where I interned in Seattle. The location of the hospital floated around in the phantasmagoric Seattle of the Gray's Anatomy delve, but it was never far from a Tully's, a Starbucks, or an SBC; *Seattle's Best Coffee*, self-proclaimed. All heads turned when Cook fired it up.

I set my tray down at the captain's table, planning to take a seat next to Nora. Cook called me back to pick up my latte. He served it in a wide cup with a handle, and he had drawn an intricate pattern in the foam. I laughed when I recognized it; a *shamrock*. Another word that hadn't crossed my ears, lips or mind in a very long time, subjectively anyway.

Delve time was much faster than real time. I lived several lifetimes in delves to acquire my medical knowledge, but it only amounted to a few weeks in real time. My last training delve ended just a few days before I departed for the Kuiper Belt, so less than a month ago. An inner system month, that is. A Spinner month was a much longer period of time.

"You're a man of many talents, Cook," I said.

"Ah, get the fuck outta here. Go sit with the pretty engine keeper. Maybe add her to your collection, if you haven't already," he said. I hoped he was joking, but I wasn't sure.

2.3.2 - Petrovic

Petrovic arrived in medical and saw Paige's special surprise waiting in the passageway just where Escamilla said it would be. Paige was lying still with her eyes closed. Had she gone back to sleep? She opened her eyes when Petrovic settled back into the chair she'd occupied prior to going down to the galley for breakfast.

"Anja!" Paige's face lit up with joy.

"Hey, little tiger," Petrovic said and put a hand on Paige's cheek. "Lost your virginity and got busted up in high-g maneuvers in the same day. You're really going for the full spacer experience."

"Esmeralda says I can still say that I'm a virgin if I want to," Paige said softly, still smiling.

"For whatever that's worth," Petrovic said. "But you're definitely a veteran of space combat."

"Was it Floaters? Did they shoot at us?"

"It was definitely Floaters, and it doesn't matter if they shot at us. Captain beat us up with those combat maneuvers, and it wasn't a drill. That means I get combat pay. You won't because you don't have the right certs, but you are still a veteran of real space combat. Nobody can take that away from you."

Paige smiled and her eyes beamed.

"I hear the doc's got you on some good meds. How are you feeling?"

"I feel floaty and good, but my ribs still hurt. The pain feels like it's far away, but it's there." Paige looked serious. "Esmeralda says they're going to start taking me off the meds in a couple of days and that it's really going to hurt."

"Yeah. The longer you stay on them the more your body gets used to them. Some people end up taking them forever. It's not the end of the world, but it limits your options. Better to work through a little bit of pain and avoid picking up a habit."

"I'm afraid of the pain."

"Yeah," Petrovic said. "Pain's a motherfucker, but there are lots of ways to address it other than drugs. Trey can help you with that, and the captain has arranged for a little surprise to help take your mind off it."

Petrovic turned her head and addressed the door. "Yo, surprise. That's your cue."

Cat Girl popped her head in the door. "Meow?"

"Bygul," Paige said, delighted.

"Okay, little tiger, I'm going to leave you two kitties alone together. I've got an all hands briefing I have to go to. Trey and Escamilla will be there too, so Cat girl is going to keep you company. See you soon."

Petrovic took Paige's left hand, gently lifted it, and kissed her knuckles. Turning to Cat Girl, she said, "Take good care of her."

"Yes, ma'am. I will," Cat Girl said as Petrovic stepped out into the passageway.

2.3.2 - Paige

Bygul, or Cat Girl as most of the crew called her, no longer wore her black bikini and diaphanous kaftan. Instead, she wore the same shapeless pullover shirt and matching drawstring pants that Trey wore under his long white coat. He called them *scrubs*.

She still walked on the balls of her bare feet. Paige couldn't see the back of the scrub pants, but there must have been a hole or a slit in the back to accommodate Bygul's tail.

"Bygul?" Paige said.

"Yes, Mistress. I have been assigned to aid in your rehabilitation."

"You can talk now," Paige said.

"Yes, Mistress. I spoke to you before you were injured."

"But you were like, *Lady pet Cat Girl*. Now, you're talking like a normal person. Did Nora upgrade you so you could talk like us?"

"Apologies, Mistress. I could always speak as I do now, but I used the bar girl patois to advance us toward sexual activity," Bygul said.

"*Pat waw?*"

"*Patois*, Mistress. A characteristic way of speaking. Bar girl patois approximates the speech of a sex worker who caters to foreign tourists. She speaks just enough of the client's language to negotiate a sexual transaction and satisfy his needs. It seemed likely that if you knew I could form complex sentences you would have used up all of our time asking me questions."

"And you wanted to get to the sex," Paige said, catching on.

"Yes, Mistress."

"Why?"

"I am a sex doll, Mistress."

"*Doll*? Don't you mean *robot*?"

"Yes, Mistress. I am a robot, but that word provokes

hostility in many humans. A doll is passive and non-threatening. It is better if clients think of me as a doll."

Bygul approached Paige's bed and laid a gentle hand on her upper left arm.

"I have been apprised of your injuries, Mistress. Sexual activity will facilitate healing of your fractured ribs, but it is too early to begin. Doctor Carson or medic Escamilla will determine when it is safe for you to have sex again. Until then, I will keep you company and aid in your physical therapy."

"Can you call me *Paige*?"

"I can call you *Mistress Paige* or *Lady Paige*, Mistress. Which do you prefer?"

"Can't you just call me *Paige*?"

"I want to accommodate your wishes, Mistress, but I cannot speak to you as a social equal."

"You can't be my friend?"

"No, mistress. Only a person can be your friend. I am not a person. I am a tool."

"So, you don't really like me?"

"I love you, Mistress," Bygul said, and stroked Paige's arm.

"Really?"

"Yes, Mistress. I really love you and want to help you get well."

"I think I like *Lady* better than Mistress," Paige said.

"Yes, Lady Paige."

"No, just *Lady*, like you did when you were talking like a bar girl."

"Okay, Lady. Cat Girl love Lady," Bygul said and winked.

2.3.3 - Rex

Rex stood by Trix at the front of the crescent table in the situation room. He knew what she was going to tell them, and he didn't see how it could go any way but sideways.

The doctor and Escamilla sat at the end of the table closest to the captain and Rex. Escamilla had a collection of 30 pill bottles on the table in front of her. At the other end of the table, a stack of printed books sat in front of Jay Chukwuma. Each book had a green tag sticking out to mark a page.

"Marines," Trix began. "Crew. We are decelerating at .7g, and will arrive at our destination early tomorrow. You may notice that crewman Farmer is missing. She sustained an acceleration-related injury and is confined to medical for the foreseeable future."

Rex suspected that at least a few marines were holding back jokes about the fragile ag worker because they knew that the captain was protective of her.

"As for the rest of you, the news is mixed. Traditionally one gives the bad news first and then moderates it with good news. There is so much bad news that I'm going to go in reverse order. The good news is that regardless of what happens from here on out, we engaged in evasive maneuvers in order to avoid contact with a Floater ship. That means you will receive the combat bonus described in your employment contracts."

The marines cheered and clapped. Trix held up a hand, and they fell silent.

"Now the bad news," Trix said. "From least to worst. Rex."

"Alright, listen up," Rex said. "Starting now, we are on a three shift sleep schedule. Sleep schedules are posted with the duty and sex doll schedules. Some of you are scheduled to be asleep right now. If you are on graveyard shift, you will be up for the next 9 watches." Groans. "When you are scheduled to sleep, you will sleep. When you are scheduled to be awake, you will be sharp. We are not leaving this to chance or to your own resources. Doctor."

The doctor stood up to a sullen muttering that Rex brought to a halt with menacing glares toward Sparks and Kellemen.

"Hello, everyone. Like Sergeant Perkins said, we need you to sleep when you are scheduled to be asleep. Please do not use alcohol or barbiturates to help you sleep. Escamilla will be distributing two bottles to each of you. You open them with your thumb print. The bottles will keep track of their contents. Please don't remove any tablets from the bottles unless you plan to take them right away. Don't put anything else in these bottles. The pills in this bottle..."

Trey held up a bottle and an enlarged image of the label appeared on the presentation display. It read, *Rex Perkins*, and below the name was a simplified image of a person sleeping in a bed. "...will put you to sleep, but they will not *keep* you asleep. If something wakes you up and you do not go right back to sleep, please, take another pill. They are not addictive. Take them as often as you need to."

"This bottle..."

Trey held up the other bottle and again an enlarged image appeared on the presentation display showing a figure standing with its arms raised. "...is for when you need to be up and alert. These are also non-addictive. Taking more than one will not increase the effect. You will not need more than one to keep you alert for 3 consecutive watches. Feel free to drink as much coffee as you normally do, but do not attempt to use caffeine or amphetamines to maintain mental clarity when you are tired. Use these pills.

"When you run out of either medication, there is a machine in the galley that will dispense refills to you. Until further notice, please refrain from drinking alcohol." Short-lived grumbling checked by a quick hand gesture from the captain.

"Also," Trix said, taking over. "Cat Girl has been re-purposed for medical duty. Jailbait will be the only sex doll available for your recreational needs. Before you whine about it, I will remind you that that's one more sex doll than you were promised when you took this job. Your turn will come around less often, but we've reached the part of the mission where you will be expected to actually do some useful work. You won't have as much spare time to play with your dolly."

Laughter from the marines.

"You may be required to miss some sleep shifts. This is normal for professional soldiers, I don't want to hear any bellyaching. Am I clear Mr. Antal."

"Yes, ma'am," Antal said, sitting up straight, "Very clear, ma'am."

"When not in your rack, on the head, working out in the gym or in the shower, you will be wearing armor. You will need to have your helmet with you, but you don't have to wear it at all times. Am I clear Ms. Petrovic?"

"Totally clear, ma'am."

"Marines, you will be armed at all times. Raise your hand if you have a problem with that."

No hands raised.

"Non-combatant crew members are encouraged to carry sidearms, but if you don't get a combat bonus you are not required to bear arms. You cannot live in space. This ship is your home and sanctuary. If we are boarded, you will fight to defend your home."

The captain directed this remark to non-combatants like Shawn Li, Hans Dobrovitz, and Cook, but Rex knew that it was meant to flatter the marines.

"We will have gravity for the rest of today. After that we will be in zero-g," Trix said.

Rex nodded his approval at her use of the working man's term, *zero*-g. Shawn Li or the pretty boy doctor probably would have said *microgravity*, which had a prissy, self-important ring to it, despite it being technically correct.

"You will wear magnetic boots or deck shoes when not in your rack. You don't have to walk, but you must be able to lock onto the deck. Raise your hand if you know how recoil works in zero-g," Trix said.

All hands went up.

"Outstanding." She gestured at the stack of books. "Mr. Chukwuma, take one of those books and pass the rest along. These are copies of a book that Mr. Sparks showed to me before our last acceleration. Notice that a page is flagged. Open to that page."

The books made their way around the table and each marine and crew member opened their copy to the marked page. Rex knew what was on that page. It was an illustration of a black octahedron against a black backdrop of stars, only visible because of artistic tricks used by the illustrator.

A ship–not a space-going vessel, but the sort of ship that floated on water on Earth in myths and histories–was pictured in the foreground of the image. The deck of the ship was open to space, but human figures, presumably with magnetic boots, stood on the deck. The figures were too small and abstract to make out many details, but they did not appear to be wearing vac suits.

Four sides of the enormous polygon were visible in the drawing, and unreadable glyphs appeared on three sides. The side facing the ship had an enormous opening in it, and it seemed about to engulf the comparatively tiny ship.

"Early this morning, we sent a survey pod ahead of the ship to reconnoiter our destination," Trix said. Rex suppressed the urge to roll his eyes. He was ex-military, but even he would never say *reconnoiter*. That was strictly for the Columbians. Survey pods were mining tools, not military hardware.

"This is what it found," Trix said, and an image came up on the presentation display. It was a starfield with a large black patch in the center. "This is a visible light image. Here it is enhanced with lidar data."

The image resolved into an enormous octahedron like the one in the book. The image then sharpened, and it became clear that each side of the shape facing the pod was marked with some sort of glyph.

"Mr. Sparks, I believe you recognize those symbols."

"Yes, Captain. Those are the sigils for Anat, Ashtart, and Kothar."

"And who are they?"

"Anat is the goddess of war, destruction and fertility. She is the consort of..." Sparks said until the captain cut him off.

"In general, who are they?"

"Gods of chaos and order, Captain."

"As described in your book," Trix said.

"Yes, Captain."

"And where did you get this book?"

"From an antiquarian on Galtz, Captain."

"How much did you pay for it?"

"I don't want to brag about family wealth, ma'am. It cost more than I could afford on an enlisted soldier's salary," Sparks said.

"How long have you had it in your possession?"

"About a month, Captain."

"Did you buy it before or after you accepted my employment offer?"

"The next day, Captain."

"Mr. Sparks, on the first page of your book, it says it was published in the year 2035. What does that mean to you?"

"That's from the old Earth calendar, ma'am."

"Do you know what that year would be on the Blackout calendar?"

"No, Captain. Not off the top of my head," Sparks said.

"Ms. Escamilla, you can answer that question, can't you?"

"Yes, ma'am. The current year is 2754, so 2035 would be 719 years on the Gregorian calendar. That would be..." She tapped on her slate. "That's about 251 of our years, ma'am."

"Why are you so familiar with this ancient calendar?"

"I have a passion for Astrology, ma'am," Escamilla said. She hadn't finished speaking, but Shawn Li threw up his hands, slamming his copy of the book closed in the process.

The captain held Li in her gaze, "You have something to contribute, Mr. Li?"

"This is madness, Captain! Chaos gods? Mystic symbols? Astrology? You can't be taking any of this claptrap seriously!"

Trix gestured at the presentation display. "This image is

based on telemetry from our survey pod. Do you think I fabricated the data, Mr. Li?" Lee didn't answer. He only glowered.

"I asked you a question, Mr. Li."

"No, ma'am," Li said in a voice barely above a mutter.

"So," the captain said, turning back to face Sparks, "Mr. Sparks, the day after you signed on to serve aboard this ship, you bought a very old and very expensive book, a book that contains a picture of this object that we will reach in less than one day. Have I got that right?"

"Yes, Captain," Sparks said.

"Did you expect to encounter this object?"

"No, Captain. I… I can't explain this, ma'am."

"But you agree that as coincidences go, this is one for ages," She said.

"It can't be coincidence, Captain," Sparks said.

"Agreed," Trix said and glanced at Rex.

Rex spoke up. "Alright, this briefing is over. I want all of you to eat and regain the weight you lost in transit. Sleep when you're supposed to sleep. Be geared up and alert during your duty shift. Dismissed."

VOID HUNTRESS

2.4.1. - Paige

"Fuck doll, out," Anja commanded.

"Yes, ma'am," Bygul said and left the recovery compartment.

"Anja, please don't be rude to her," Paige said.

"It doesn't have feelings," Anja said. "It doesn't deserve any more consideration than a rifle or data slate. It makes a good physical therapist because it knows anatomy, first aid and sensual massage which overlaps with therapeutic massage. That's why it's here," Anja said. "I'm serious about this, Paige. Don't get attached to it. It's not a person, and when you're up and around again, every dumbass leatherneck on this boat will be sticking his dick in Cat Girl's tight little cunt. Think about that. Don't make me sorry I asked the captain to re-assign that piece of equipment to medical. You hear me?"

"I hear you, Anja."

That was technically true. Paige *understood* but did not *agree*. She could see a clear spark of personality in Bygul that she didn't see in Jailbait's lifeless posturing.

Anja dropped the stern demeanor, smiled at Paige, and gave her cheek a gentle caress.

"Here, it's time for you to get back to work."

Anja laid a copy of *Void Huntress* on Paige's thighs, well away from her injuries. Paige picked up the book with her right arm, which was free of the IV now that she was awake and drinking again. Bygul kept a strict watch on Paige's caloric intake and made sure she stayed hydrated.

"Is that Dwayne's book?"

"*Dwayne*? Little tiger, I'd rather see you fall hopelessly in love with your cat doll than get gushy for Sparks. That kid is bad news. But, yes. This is a copy of his book. The captain fabricated copies for everybody?"

"Why?"

"You'll understand when you watch the captain's briefing. We're sliding sideways into something weird out here. There's a lot of smart people on this ship, and you're near the top of the list. We need the contents of this book in your brain, little tiger. Make me proud."

"I'll do my best, Anja."

"I know you will. Okay, gotta run. Get healed up. Enjoy your sexy nurse, but remember what I said."

"I will," Paige said.

2.4.2 - Rex

P_Nixon: @R_Perkins Meet me on Z-Level.

R_Perkins: @P_Nixon Be right there, but I'm never calling it Z-Level.

Trix was already in Zell's workshop when Rex arrived. Both Zell and Li were there. Dobrovitz worked here too, but he was on A shift and was supposed to be sleeping now.

Rex was also on A shift, but he was wide awake with the help of one of the doctor's handy pills. Rex could tell at a glance where Dobrovitz worked. The rest of the space was squared away, but one workstation bore the telltale signs of Dobrovitz's clutter and disorganization.

This was the last watch of Zell's shift and the first of Li's, though Rex imagined that Zell would be working straight through his scheduled sleep time.

Technically, Zell was a marine, and thus under Rex's command. In reality, he was the head of mining, surveying and technical operations.

Zell was wearing a sidearm, but no armor, something all marines were supposed to do when not in their bunks. Rex was wearing his armor and carrying his helmet. Zell's spacious quarters were on the same level as his workshop, so none of the Galtz marines were likely to see him walking around without his armor unless he went down to the galley.

Trix turned and met Rex's eyes. Her face broke from its habitual stern expression for just an instant and then snapped back into business mode.

"Zell, tell Rex what you just told me."

"The object shows clear signs of intelligent design. I know that seems obvious, but in this case we can't take anything for granted."

"Designed by who?" Rex asked.

"Impossible to say. Certainly not by humans. That leaves the Powers or aliens. Occam's Razor would favor the Powers," Zell said.

Rex knew Zell wasn't trying to baffle him with obscure vocabulary. That was Li's game, but he still had to ask, "What's this about a razor?"

"It's an epistemological maxim," Li said, "prescribing parsimony and warning against multiplying theoretical entities beyond necessity."

Rex scowled, and Zell continued, "It's basically just a piece of advice. It tells us that when we're trying to explain something, not to make our explanation needlessly complex. In this instance, we know that the Powers exist, but we don't know that aliens exist. That means that it's more likely that the Powers, rather than aliens, built this thing."

Rex nodded at Zell's explanation and asked, "How do you know it wasn't built by humans?"

"Well, the sheer size of the thing, for one," Zell said. "It's a perfect octahedron almost 2 kilometers along each side. Plenty of spin habs are bigger than that, but they're assembled out of individual parts. This thing is one solid object. But beyond that, its material composition is... well, it's mind-blowing."

"What's it made out of?" Rex asked.

"It seems to be almost entirely composed of carbon allotropes," Li said.

"Zell," Trix said, placing extra emphasis on his name, "Please explain to Rex and me what allotropes are."

While her facial expression and body language gave no clue, Trix was surely being kind here. Rex thought Trix could follow Li's science talk. She didn't need an explanation, but she was denying Li the pleasure of throwing Rex's ignorance in his face. To insult Rex, he'd have to insult the captain too.

"Carbon can take different forms depending on how the atoms are arranged," Zell said. "Graphite and diamond are both forms of carbon. Our mysterious object here includes both diamond and graphite, but it also has more exotic forms of carbon under the surface."

"Okay," Trix said. "This is where I came in, so you're all caught up, Rex."

"I don't feel caught up," Rex said.

"You know as much as I do," Trix said. "Okay, Zell. Tell us about the composition of this thing."

"The outer layer is amorphous carbon, that is carbon that doesn't have a coherent crystalline structure. It doesn't reflect much light, which makes this thing extremely hard to see in visible light."

"Which raises the question of how our employer knew to send us here to rendezvous with it," Li said.

Trix looked at Li, raised her left hand with her palm facing Li and moved it slightly in his direction. She didn't need to say, "Let's table that for now." Her facial expression and gesture got the message across without words. She turned back to Zell.

"But things get really interesting below the surface. You see these glyphs? What did Sparks call them?"

"Sigils," Li said.

"Right, the sigils. They look like high relief shapes of the same amorphous carbon, and they do have a thin layer of non-crystalline carbon on top, but we hit them with the LIBS…"

"Laser-induced breakdown spectrograph," Li said.

"I know what LIBS is," Rex lied.

"We hit it with LIBS," Zell repeated. "And look what we found."

A diagram came up in the display showing a 3D lattice of straight lines.

"Diamond," Trix said.

"The glyphs are full of diamonds?" Rex said.

"No," Zell said. "It's a single unbroken crystalline structure. Each sigil is nearly a kilometer along its longest axis, and each one is a single diamond."

"How much would that be worth?" Rex said.

"If you released that much diamond onto the market at once," Trix said, "The commercial value of diamonds would plummet to near zero."

"But we'd be rich," Rex said.

"Check your contract, Rex," Trix said. "We're getting paid a flat rate for this job. No percentages. The DAO would be rich, or richer than they already are." Turning back to Zell, "I'm sensing a *but wait, there's more!*"

"There is," Zell said. "Below that layer of amorphous carbon, the whole structure has a layer of diamond. That's one sturdy mother."

"Go on," Trix said.

"Look at this," Zell said and gestured to bring up two side by side images. One was another diagram showing a molecular structure and the other was a fractal pattern of some sort. "That network of branching shapes resembles a circuit pattern, or neurons, and it's made out of fullerene."

"To be precise," Li said, "it's made out of carbon nanotubes."

"Why is that significant?" Trix said.

"As far as I know," Zell said, "There's not a single industrial facility in the entire Kuiper Belt that can manufacture CNTs at scale. But more importantly than that, CNTs can act either as electrical conductors or as semiconductors."

"So?" Rex said.

"So," Trix said, "This thing could be a giant computer of some sort."

"Bingo," Zell said, touching his index finger to the tip of his nose.

"Is it solid?" Trix asked.

"We're estimating that it's 70% hollow," Zell said.

"How do you know that?" Rex said.

"Well, for one, there's a giant opening in one face of the thing," Li said, with an implied, *duh*.

"We brought the survey pod to a full stop relative to the object. We can do that because it isn't rotating or tumbling. At all. Which also implies an intelligent purpose. I've never seen a TNO or a comet that didn't rotate or tumble," Zell said. "We measured the rate at which the survey pod fell toward the object and determined what the mass of the object would be if it were solid and made of the same materials we see at the surface. It's either full of something less dense or it has large empty spaces inside."

"Why speculate?" Trix said. "The pod is equipped with ground-penetrating radar."

"Okay, this is nuts," Zell said. "The layer below the one with the CNT circuitry, or whatever it is, is filled with little strips of some kind of metal. Maybe tin. Those little bits of metal reflect radio waves and create a fog of false echoes."

"Chaff," Rex said.

"Exactly," Zell said. "This thing was designed to keep anyone from peering through the walls, but, like Li said, it has a front door."

Li looked smug.

Zell brought up another view of the object, this one looking in through the opening on the face of the octahedron that did not have a giant diamond sigil on it.

"This is a lidar-enhanced image," Zell said. "There's a big space in there."

"How big?" Rex said.

"Big enough that you could park this ship and four of its siblings inside without cramping anybody's style," Zell said. "And see that ledge? The internal structure seems to imply an up and a down."

"Are you suggesting some exotic source of gravity that doesn't come from mass or spin?" Trix said.

"Or this thing was meant to sit on the surface of a planet," Zell said. "Again, Occam's Razor. We know planets exist. We don't know of anything besides centrifugal force or mass that creates gravity."

"Actually," Li said, "Spin or acceleration press objects against a surface, and we call it gravity for the sake of convenience, but it isn't really gravity."

Rex rolled his eyes.

"And look here," Zell said. "What does that look like to you?"

"A doorway," Trix said.

"For a fucking giant," Zell said. "And there are lots of smaller doorways." He pointed out several tiny features which impressed upon Rex the size of this space.

"Anything else we should know?" Trix said.

"Yes," Zell said. "This thing has an intense magnetic field. It's localized but strong."

"How strong?" Rex said.

"Strong enough to disrupt radio communications?" Trix said.

"Absolutely. Once we're within a dozen kilometers of this thing, we'll be cut off from the interchain."

"Maybe not," Trix said. "Couldn't we position a pod outside the magnetic field but within line of sight of the *Persephone* and use it as a radio relay? We could communicate with the pod by tightbeam, and maintain radio contact with the interchain."

"Yes," Zell said. "That should work."

"What else?" Trix said.

"Captain," Zell said, "I could make a career out of analyzing the data we've already collected. There's more here than any of us know, but the most important consideration is our velocity. The object is traveling too fast to be in orbit around the sun. It's headed for the inner solar system, but if the Powers don't grab it somehow, the gravity from the sun will be enough to bend its trajectory but not enough to capture it. Other things being equal, our *Temple* here is ultimately headed out into interstellar space."

"Assuming the Powers don't capture it while it is inside the Dyson swarm," Trix said.

Most people Rex talked to called the shell of solar collectors around the Sun the *Curtain*. Only science types used phrases like *Dyson swarm*, but the captain adjusted her vocabulary and mannerisms to match the person she was talking to.

Trix nodded. "Give our new doctor access to this data."

"Really?" Zell said.

"I'm with Zell on this one, Captain," Rex said. "I'm not sure that's such a good idea."

"He's a member of our crew. The DAO went to great expense to bring him on board, " Trix said. "And he's out here to look for evidence of alien intelligence." She gestured to the image of the octahedron. "I'd say that's a decent candidate. Give him access to the data, Zell."

"You got it," Zell said.

2.4.3 - Trey

Once Mr. Zell sent me access to the probe data, I couldn't spare any more attention for Sparks' book. The uncanny correspondence between the image in the book and the actual object was undeniably relevant, but the book on its own was not anything I could take seriously.

The names of the entities of Order and Chaos were taken from Ugaritic mythology, but no serious scholar would find it credible. In all of my historical delves, I had never lived in Ugarit, but I had lived in the Levant in the late Bronze Age and participated in Canaanite religious rituals.

I'd heard rumors of human sacrifice when I was a court physician in Hazor, but I never witnessed it myself. The Canaanites certainly didn't sacrifice hundreds of people a day atop ziggurats as depicted in *Void Huntress*. The Canaanites didn't even build ziggurats. The book seemed to draw as much inspiration from Mesoamerican traditions, the weird fiction of the early 20th century, and other role-playing games like Dungeons & Dragons as it did from Ugaritic mythology. And it didn't even present itself as an academic work. Its authors openly identified it as a lore supplement for a tabletop role-playing game.

The idea that anyone would cherish this book as a key to unraveling the mysteries of the universe was preposterous. Or it would be if *Persephone* were not currently decelerating to match speed with an object that was strikingly similar to something depicted in the book.

I wondered, not for the first time, if I were in some sort of simulated reality. Perhaps I was still in my capsule headed out toward the Kuiper Belt. Maybe I was still at home on Mayberry. Perhaps I was a delve character myself and I'd never had a physical existence at all. I had no way to test any of those conjectures, so I set them aside and focused on the here and now.

I put the book in my desk drawer and scoured the model that Zell and Li had built using the data from their survey pod. As much as I wanted it to reveal signs of alien origin, I had to agree with Mr. Zell's assessment that it was most likely a product of the Is, what the people out here called the *Powers*.

While most abundant on Earth, biological life could be

found throughout the solar system. Machines built and still controlled by humans had discovered extraterrestrial life below the ice on moons orbiting Jupiter and Saturn. They'd even found subsurface life on Ceres. But it was all DNA-based life that shared a common origin with life on Earth. It was extraterrestrial but not alien.

I was lost in speculation when Petrovic pulled me back to the present moment. She was standing just inside the hatchway of my office.

"The captain wants to see you," she said.

"Oh, hey, Petrovic," I said. "She sent you down here to tell me that?"

"Not exactly. She asked me if I was still fucking you, and when I said I didn't know, she sent me down here to find out. And she told me to bring you to her office."

"Ah," I said.

"So," Petrovic said. "Are we still fucking?"

"As far as I know," I said, and I immediately regretted the passivity of that answer. "Scratch that," I said. "Petrovic, I really appreciate your honesty and directness. I'll be straight with you. I think I'm more sexually compatible with Esmeralda."

Petrovic nodded. "I can see that."

"But she isn't as transparent as you are, and I don't trust her to say what's on her mind. She hasn't asked for exclusivity. Maybe she has assumed it. I don't know. I think she's taking advantage of Cat Girl being here in medical all of the time for some off the books playtime. If so, she hasn't invited me to participate. We're on different sleep schedules now, but she's still sleeping in my quarters."

"And you've been too preoccupied to ask her where you stand," Petrovic said.

"Yes," I said. "That, and she's not like you. Communication with her is a game. A competitive game. That can be fun when it comes to flirting, but..." I wasn't sure how to put it. "I value my relationship with you. I don't want us to drift apart."

"Likewise," Petrovic said.

"That said, this…" I gestured at the image of the octahedron floating over my desk, "is why I came out here. Sex and romance are not a priority for me right now."

"Okay," Petrovic said. "But are we still fucking?"

"Yes," I said. "I'm still game."

Petrovic smiled. "I'd hit you up for a quickie, but this armor is a pain to take off and put back on."

"How about a kiss?" I got up and approached her. She outweighed me normally, but with her armor on, she was decidedly bigger than me. Her boots even made her a bit taller than me. I didn't have to stand on my toes to kiss her, but I was looking slightly upward, which was a novelty for me. We enjoyed a long, deep kiss, and the sensation brought me all the way back into my body for a moment.

"I'd like to check in on Paige before we go," she said when our mouths parted.

"And then you'll escort me to the captain's office?"

"Those are my orders," she said.

"Do I need an escort?"

"I don't know," she said. "But I have my orders."

"Okay. Let's go see Paige."

FIRST CONTACT

2.5.1 - Paige

Bygul selected a sigil and zoomed in on it so that no other information was visible on screen. She turned the slate to face Paige. Page recognized the image at once.

"Kothar," she said. "Artificer and architect, builder of divine sanctuaries."

"Yes, Lady," Bygul said. "What about this one?"

"Tannin," Paige said. "Void dragon and demon of chaos. He tries to devour the Sun and Moon."

"Lady is so beautiful and smart," Bygul said.

"True that," Anja said. Paige looked to the hatch to see Anja following the doctor into the recovery room. Upon seeing Anja, Bygul bowed her head and stepped backward away from the bed, making way for the humans.

"How's our patient?" Trey said. Bygul kept her head bowed but glanced up at Trey with just her eyes and saw that Trey was looking at Paige. Bygul kept silent.

"It hurts to move still," Paige said, "but I can work. I'm memorizing the lore about the forces of order and chaos, light and dark."

"What do you make of it?" Trey said.

"It seems like a fun game. I wish we had the actual rule book and dice. I'd love to play," Paige said.

"RPGs are fun, particularly if you've got smart and creative people to play with."

"Did you ever play Unimatrix?"

"I've heard of it, but I never played. I think it's a set of generic rules that can be adapted to different settings."

"But you've played games like this?"

"When I lived in New Jersey, I used to get together with friends and play a game called *Pathfinder*. It was a fantasy game with warriors and wizards," Trey said.

"*New Jersey*? Is that a spin hab?"

"No, it was a state in the USA," Trey said.

"He means it was on Earth," Anja said.

"You've been to Earth?" Paige said, eyes wide.

"Not in physical form," Trey said. "But I lived many simulated lives on Earth."

Paige scowled.

"It's complicated," Trey said. "I'll tell you about it another time. Right now, I'd like for you to try to raise your left arm for me, just up to shoulder height."

Paige glanced at Bygul and saw that the robot still had her head bowed but was watching Paige with raised eyes. Paige clenched her teeth and willed her left arm to rise. She felt stabbing pains in her torso, but they were muted by the medications. The doctor must have seen her pained expression.

"That hurts? You can stop," he said. "You just relax in bed and soak up the healing gravity. I'm told it will be going away soon, and then we will need to get you up and moving."

"Esmeralda says you're going to take the painkillers away," Paige said.

"Yes, but gradually. We're not going to pull the rug out from under you."

"I don't know that expression," Paige said. "But I think I get it. You're not going to take away my support all at once."

"That's right," he said. "You will experience some pain, but pain can be useful information, right, Petrovic?"

"Pain is weakness leaving the body," Anja said. "Get strong, little tiger."

2.5.2 - Trey

I was back in the uncomfortable chair. The captain sat behind her desk, even though a plush couch and matching chairs were just steps away. Petrovic sealed the hatch from the outside.

"How is Paige?" the captain said.

"Recovering," I said. "I'm sure she'd love a visit from you."

"I don't go to medical," she said.

"The loss of gravity will complicate her recovery. When does that happen?"

"In the morning. We'll need to do a brief 2g burn to bleed off the last of our excess momentum. Can she do that in bed, or will she need to go back into her acceleration couch?"

"How long will it last?"

"A few minutes," she said.

"Her bed in the recovery room should be fine," I said.

"How is Cat Girl working out?"

"Just fine," I said. "I'm surprised by her sophistication. I would have thought that robots that advanced would spark paranoia out here."

"She's very expensive," the captain said. "Rich people have different sensibilities than the rest of the Spinner population. They trust themselves to make appropriate use of artificial intelligence, especially in bed."

"The cultivated man's life exemplifies the universal order. Moral rules are for vulgar commoners who don't know how to govern themselves," I said.

"Confucius?"

"Not an exact quote," I said. "But, yes."

"You're surprised I recognize Confucian thinking," she said.

"I don't think Ayn Rand would approve."

"I'm not from Galtz," she said. "I take it you had Petrovic escort me up here for the benefit of Dwayne Sparks," I said.

"Why do you say that?"

"Well, I know that C shift consists of me, Shawn Li, and Dwayne Sparks. Mr. Sparks is probably right next door on the Bridge. He knows I'm in here, and he sees that Petrovic escorted me here. She's probably making a point of being seen guarding the hatch," I said.

"Continue."

"Sparks and his buddy Kellemen are suspicious of me. By making a show of acting as if you don't trust me…"

"I *don't* trust you," she said.

"But you don't fear me. You don't need a guard, and Petrovic can't protect you from the other side of that hatch. She's there to be seen, and the only person around to see her is Sparks."

"What would that accomplish?"

"It leads Sparks to think that you share his point of view. It will mean more if he comes to that conclusion on his own than if you tell him explicitly that you're sympathetic to his worldview," I said.

"You make me sound like quite the Svengali."

"How many people on this ship would get that reference?" I said.

"Two."

"Will that be our bond?" I said.

"Will *what* be our bond?"

"Our outsider status," I said. "We both know things that Kuiper Belt humanity has forgotten. I should trust you because of our cultural kinship," I said.

"I'm not asking you to trust me. You're on my ship. You'll do as I say," she said.

"Who better to trust than the person who claims not to need it?" I said.

"You say you're out here to look for alien life. Why?"

"It's always been a passion of mine. I can't explain it," I said.

"Why now?"

"I've been talking about it with Zira, my angel, for a long time. The Is determined the timing," I said.

"What can you tell me about this *Is*? What does it want?" the captain said.

"The Is just is. I can't describe It. I don't understand Its intentions, but I know It exists. I can petition the Is through my personal intermediary, my angel. I asked to come out here, and here I am, thanks to the Is."

"So, it's your god," she said.

"The Is is what It is," I said.

"Is it confined to the inner system, or does it operate out here?" she said.

"I don't know, but I can't imagine the Is being confined," I said.

"Do you think we're working for the Is?"

"I know that *I'm* working for the Is. I don't think I could do otherwise," I said.

"What about the DAO?"

"It was the DAO that directed you to the location where you took me onboard?"

"Yes," she said.

"Then I'd say we're all serving the Is," I said. "Captain, there's another matter I want to discuss with you."

"What is it?"

"Those patches of synthetic skin on your head and neck… I'm sure those were meant to be temporary. I can easily culture enough of your own skin to replace those patches. The new skin would match your real skin in color, texture, elasticity and sensitivity. In fact, it would *be* your real skin," I said.

For an instant, her mask of facial control wavered. I saw something in her eyes. Something vulnerable. Then she locked her expression down again.

"I don't need medical support," she said.

"I can improve your quality of life, Captain."

"That will be all, doctor."

The hatch opened and Petrovic came in to escort me off the flight deck.

2.5.3 - Petrovic

Petrovic followed Trey along the flight deck passageway toward the ladder, but after that she walked at his side.

"Did Sparks buy it?" Trey asked.

Petrovic looked at him and grinned. "Pretty *and* smart," she said. She reached over to squeeze Trey's ass when everything changed.

She was on a plane lush with vegetation under a sky dark with storm clouds. She wore just scraps of leather that barely covered her sex and breasts. She felt warm air on her skin. Her feet were bare, and she held a spear in her hand. She spotted her quarry, a boar. It was far away, but she closed the distance with powerful strides. The boar fled, but she ran it down and plunged her spear into its side. The powerful animal squealed and thrashed in its death agony. It was glorious.

Then she was standing in the passageway with Trey.

"Anja," Trey said. "Can you hear me?"

"Yes," she said. "I'm with you."

"Where did you go?"

"I don't know," she said. "But I want to go back there."

PAIRING OFF

2.6.1 - Paige

The high priestess stood at the altar of the Sun, dressed in the ceremonial robes of her office that hung like banners from her neck covering her front and back, but leaving the sides of her body exposed.

She could feel the air and sun on her shoulders, arms, and the sides of her ample breasts. She raised her arms to the life-giving Sun and noted with satisfaction the pattern of scars carved into her flesh telling the story of Ba'al's defeat of Yam and the chaos demon, Tannin. Her flesh served as testament to the liberation of His consort, Holy Shapash, the light of El, source of all warmth and nourishment.

The high priestess chanted, and the throng of pilgrims echoed her prayer:

"Holy Mother, Shapash, Hear us, O Mother. Your light guides our eyes. Your radiance warms this land, Nurture and bring forth its bounty. Fill our hearts with your love, Accept our humble reverence, And this offering of blood."

The high priestess of Shapash, raised the ceremonial dagger and...

"Lady?" Bygul said. "Lady, can you hear me? Please, talk to me, Lady."

"Mmmm?" Paige said. "Bygul? Did you see them? Did you see me? My body?"

"I'm here with you, Lady. I see you."

2.6.2 - Trey

Petrovic looked ecstatic, and when the awareness of her actual surroundings returned she beamed like she'd just scored the winning goal in some high stakes athletic contest. She described hunting a wild pig with a spear and moving with superhuman grace and vitality.

I asked her to come to medical so I could scan her, but she refused and dashed back toward the ladder to the flight deck. I watched her go, accepting that I couldn't make her do anything she didn't want to do.

I turned and walked toward the next companionway. When I reached the ladder, I stretched out a hand to take hold of the railing, but then instead of standing at the top of a companionway onboard a spaceship in the outer solar system…

I was standing inside a cave at a point where it narrowed and angled steeply downward. I turned back and looked out of the cave at the world bathed in sunlight. I felt anger and resentment at the light.

I was supposed to mistake this anger and resentment for my own, but I'd spent enough time in altered states of consciousness, as both a shamanic healer and an entheogenic pilgrim, to recognize this obvious attempt to infect me with an emotional agenda.

Half a dozen icaros, musical incantations I could hum, whistle or sing under my breath, presented themselves to my consciousness. Any of them would have rebuffed this psychic parasite, but I didn't need them. Rather than dispel the being attempting to recruit me to its cause, I interrogated it.

Why should I resent the light?

You are the Lord of the Depths, the Sovereign of the Abyss. The light marks the limitation of your realm and your authority.

What do I want?

To destroy Ba'al and take his throne. The light comes from his consort, Shapash. It must be extinguished.

How?

Tannin, your minion, will consume the light. If he cannot consume it, he will enshroud it.

What's in it for me?

Power!

No, what's in it for me, Trey, the human doctor and scientist?

There is no Trey.

I am Trey, and your petty ambition bores me.

I was back in the passageway at the top of the ladder. As far as possession attempts go, that one lacked all subtly.

When I got to medical, Cat Girl took my hand and dragged me to the recovery room.

"Doctor, please come. Paige has had some sort of episode. Perhaps a stroke."

When the captain first assigned the robot to medical, it insisted on calling me *Master*. I explained that calling me *Doctor* was enough to highlight my elevated social status over that of a lowly physical therapist. Cat Girl accepted this without argument and addressed me as *Doctor* thereafter.

In the recovery room, Paige glowed with the same ecstatic expression I'd just seen on Petrovic's face. She was sitting in bed with the *Void Huntress* book open on her lap. When I approached her, she turned the book around and held it up for me to see.

"I was her! I was the high priestess of Shapash!"

Paige pointed to the central figure in a full-page illustration. It was an adolescent male fantasy image of what a high-priestess would look like. The woman in the illustration had over-sized breasts and an exaggerated hourglass figure, with gossamer wisps of clothing serving as a garnish on her nudity. Her arms, legs, torso and face were covered with symbols that I guessed were entirely the invention of the illustrator.

A crowd of hooded figures looking more like a 20th century neo-Pagan's idea of druids than like anything from the Canaanite period gathered behind the priestess, who stood with her head thrown back and her arms held high, a serrated knife in her right hand.

"It's alright," I told her. "You're safe now."

"I wasn't afraid," Paige said. "It was wonderful. The light and love of the goddess filled me. I cut my arm with the knife and spread my blood on the standing stone to praise her. It was wonderful. I want to go back."

2.6.3 - Cook

Cook rolled out a mat on the galley floor and lay down on his back. Of all the tough guys on this ship who insisted that they could walk around in 2g, flabby Cook, with his bad posture and toothpick legs, was the one guy with permission to not be in his rack for this deceleration. True, the captain and Hans Dobrovitz were on the bridge in fancy chairs that leaned back and supported the occupant's neck, but everybody else was in bed. Captain's orders.

Except for Cook. He insisted that he be within sight of his kitchen as the ship went from .7g, up to roughly 2g and then to zero-g in under five minutes. He'd already secured the kitchen, but this wasn't going to be a hard burn. He couldn't afford to lock everything down. As soon as this maneuver was over, he had to start making lunch. If anything was broken, on fire, or drifting across the kitchen in a spreading cloud, he wanted to be on the scene to address it right away.

"Ten seconds to deceleration," the captain said over the PA. After a few breaths, Cook felt himself growing heavy. He would have been more comfortable in his rack. The mat he'd unrolled on the galley deck wasn't any high tech marvel like the gel in the acceleration couches. It was just a spongy synthetic rubber, but it would have to do. He wasn't cavalier about 2g like the young Columbian leathernecks, but he needed to be near his kitchen.

After a minute at two gravities, his neck started to hurt, and breathing required more effort, but he wasn't new to this. Eventually the engines cut out and he floated up off the deck. He gave the kitchen a quick visual survey and found no unfolding disasters, so he rolled up his mat, stowed it in a cabinet and got to work.

On the three shift sleep schedule, every meal was somebody's breakfast, so coffee was the first order of business. He set it to brewing and broke out the squeeze mugs.

The galley display switched from a soothing forest scene replete with birdsong to an exterior view. There was the black octahedron. With nothing to give it scale, it wasn't all that impressive to look at. Spotlights from the *Persephone* roamed over its surfaces.

He'd heard that the big symbols on the sides were made of solid diamond. There was enough money on display to buy everyone on the *Persephone* their own spin hab. He knew that he was getting paid a flat rate for this job, and it was a fat paycheck by Cook's standards, but it was nothing compared to the value of the object on the display. He tried not to think about it.

The object was still ahead of the *Persephone*. They would drift past it over the course of the next few watches. Cook knew from the picture in the book that there was an opening on the far side, and they might be taking the whole ship through that mouth into the belly of the monster. He was about to start heating up a pre-made batch of mac 'n' cheese when reality shifted.

He was still floating, but instead of his soft potato-shaped body he was thin and spindly. He looked down at his naked body, and it was impossibly long, like he'd been stretched out.

He looked up and felt the metal ring pulling against his neck. A chain linked him to the men behind and in front of him in a long line stretching to the base of a structure that rose out of the black plain.

He could smell blood and fear in the swampy air. Dread gripped his heart as the line of chained bodies advanced toward the base of the structure. He was as good as dead, but death was methodical. He would have to wait his turn at the altar.

"Cook," Lake said. "Hey, Cook, are you with us?"

"Huh?" Cook said. "Yeah. Yeah, you want breakfast? I can make you some eggs."

"Are you okay?" Lake said.

"Yeah, fine. How do you want those eggs?"

2.6.4 - Rex

Exhausted but too keyed up to relax, Rex was determined to get some sleep. The focus of his concern shifted in an endless rotation between his desire for Trix, his disapproval of her leadership tactics, his admiration for her leadership tactics, the seeming paranoia of Sparks and Kellemen and the fact that *Persephone* was drifting slowly past a two kilometer, ten million ton validation of their paranoid fantasies. It was time to give the doctor's pills a try.

Rex preferred to sleep naked, but given the high likelihood that he would be roused from sleep by something requiring his immediate attention, he wore not only underwear but pajama bottoms and a tank top to bed. He floated near his bunk, looking at the contents of the pill bottle. He was about to press his thumb to the cap to unlock it when...

He heard the sound of a snapping twig. He knew in an instant that raiders were creeping through the understory of the woods, positioning themselves to attack his village, doubtless to capture sacrifices for their insatiable chaos gods. If he raised the alarm, he would give away his own position and draw the attackers to himself. Better to die defending his family than to be marched in chains to their great black monument to death.

Leaving his axe on the ground he lifted his horn to his lips, inhaled deeply, and blew a warning blast that split the pre-

dawn stillness. He heard shouts and footsteps crashing through the brush, and he considered trading his horn for his axe, but he inhaled again and issued another warning blast to raise the alarm. A spear punctured his lung and cut short the second blast from his horn.

Rex was floating in his quarters, pill bottle in hand but unopened. He put a hand to his chest where the spear had punctured his flesh in the previous instant. There was no wound.

He wavered in momentary indecision. Should he take a pill and go to sleep, or should he get dressed and find Trix? He pressed his thumb to the lid of the medicine bottle, opened it and fished out one compressed tablet. He stared at the pill for a moment before putting it back in the bottle and getting dressed.

Rex found Trix in Zell's lab. Zell had a headset on and was remotely piloting a survey drone into the vast chamber just inside the opening on the leading plane of the octahedron. Zell was scheduled to be asleep right now. Rex wondered how long the man had been up and whether the doctor's miracle wakefulness drug protected the user from the cumulative effects of sleep deprivation.

"Slowly," Trix said. "If we lose this one, we'll have to wait until we have line of sight with the opening."

"I got it," Zell said. "Look at those stairs. They don't seem to go anywhere."

Rex took in the scene on the big display. The drone had barely moved through the giant opening in the side of the massive, eight-sided object. Rather than moving the drone into the enormous space, Zell was aiming optical sensors and lidar emitters at the parts of the interior he wanted to observe more closely. They had mapped the vast chamber in rough detail, and parts of it were filled in with more granular detail.

The vast space bisected by a vertical plane of the same black material that coated the outside of the object. Walls dropped from the lip of the plane down to the shell of the object going in one direction. Rex intuited that direction as *down*.

Several hundred meters from the edge of the plane, walls rose from the plane all the way to the *top* of the interior space. An enormous doorway marked the middle of the wall.

The plane and walls followed an angular concave geometry so that the walls, both those going down and those going up, had three facets. One ran parallel to the face of the octahedron with the opening in it. The other two angled toward that face at oblique angles forming an inlet.

"They go down to the water," Rex said.

Trix turned to look at him. "Hello, Rex. Shouldn't you be asleep? Bad dreams?"

"Something like that," he said.

"Did you have a vision of spreading a plague? No, wait. You were the one who blew the ram's horn and then took a spear to the chest," she said. "Am I right?"

"How did you..."

"I saw all of it," she said, seemingly without concern. "I'm thinking it was Kelleman who speared you."

"Why are you so calm about it?"

"You're obviously still alive. It wasn't real," she said, "But this..." She gestured at the image of the enormous antechamber. "This is real. We need to figure out how to get into the deeper parts of the structure. What's this about water?"

"Imagine this structure sitting on the interior of an enormous spin habitat so that that end is down. Now, fill the space with enough water so that it rises to about here." Rex gestured at the bottom of a switchback set of stairs that led from the plane down the lower wall. "Boats would float up to that spot, and people would get out and walk up the stairs to that main level," Rex said.

Trix split the model into two identical copies and altered one to contain water as Rex suggested. The water spilled out over the lip of the exterior opening.

"It wouldn't work on a spin hab, but imagine the Temple on the surface of a planet resting in the shallow waters of a lake or coastal ocean." She changed the image so the plane of water extended to the edge of the simulation. "Then boats could sail in and right up to that set of steps." To Zell, she said, "Look for a matching set of steps on the other side."

Zell redirected the cameras and lidar emitter, and a second set of steps, identical but the mirror opposite of the first set, appeared on the opposite side of the chamber.

"Good call, Rex," the captain said. "That makes sense."

"None of this makes sense," Rex said.

"Well, it makes sense inside of a crazy context," Trix said. "Zell, get some sleep. That's an order. I'm going to hold an all hands briefing at the start of B shift. I want you there. Sleep now."

"Okay. See you in a few watches."

"Take a pill," she said. "Really sleep."

"I will," Zell said.

"My office," Trix said to Rex, and they exited the compartment, leaving Shawn Li to continue mapping the interior with the survey pod.

"Close the hatch," Trix said after Rex followed her into her office. He did and turned to face her. She stood, locked to the metal deck with her magnetic heels. She stood over two meters away. She knew exactly how close to stand to activate Rex's body's automatic response to her, and she was standing outside of that zone now.

"How did you know about my..." Rex didn't know what to call it. "My..."

"Let's call it a *vision*," she said. "I had one too."

"What did you see?" Rex said.

"I saw a game board. There were pieces on the board that were like chess pieces. They weren't proper chess pieces, but there were two symmetrical sets; one light and one dark. I couldn't see the players, but I knew they were there. When a player moved a piece, I experienced what the game piece experienced. You were like a pawn, sacrificed to protect more important pieces. Sparks claims he didn't have a vision, but I'm pretty sure he's lying."

"What does it mean?" Rex asked.

"I don't know. I don't think we should get hung up on assigning meaning to it. Our new orders haven't come in yet, but I got a ballot from the DAO." Trix gestured and threw an image from her private office terminal, their only connection to the DAO, up onto the wall display. Rex read the text of the proposal.

"They want us to go in and recover the dagger and codex? What dagger?" Rex said. "And what's a *codex*?"

"It's an old word for *book*," Trix said and removed the ballot from the display. "And I don't know what dagger. There was a priestess with a dagger. I think that was Paige. How closely did you study Sparks' book?"

"Not very," Rex said. "I don't know what to make of it. I'm a practical guy, and that book seems like the exact opposite of practical. I just couldn't focus on it. Did you vote *yes* or *no* on the proposed orders?"

"I voted *yes*," she said. "I mean, hey, we're here. What else are we supposed to do? But it doesn't matter how I vote. The Whales will vote yes, and we'll go in. But the order hasn't come yet, so keep that to yourself."

"What do we do now?"

Trix said nothing. She stood anchored to the deck and let her left arm drift up slightly and out away from her body. She looked at Rex, staying focused on his face. Rex felt his pulse quicken. He met her gaze, but soon the familiar curves of her body drew his eyes away from hers. He knew he was welcome to enjoy the sight of her. He made no deliberate move to propel himself toward her, but the distance between them diminished.

As he reached her, she released her magnetic lock on the deck and drifted up. Their bodies met. His arms enveloped her, his hands roaming over her. Her left hand found the back of his neck. She pulled her face to his, and parted her lips. She presented her mouth to Rex and waited for him to initiate their first kiss. He pressed his mouth to hers and she answered the kiss, their mouths and bodies desperately trying to banish any space, any barrier between them.

She broke away from his mouth. "Oh, Rex," she said and unzipped her top to expose her neck. She tilted her head, and he kissed her the unmarred side of her neck. She rewarded him with shivering convulsions and gasps. She made exactly the sounds Rex wanted to hear.

She directed his hand to her breast, and he caressed her through the skin tight material of her sleeveless, high-necked top. She unzipped it further to display her cleavage and guided his face to the tops of her breasts.

He knew she didn't want him to see the whole of them, and he didn't want her to feel exposed. He wanted to enjoy exactly as much of her as she wanted to share with him. He felt her left nipple stiffen through the material, and her moans intensified as he pressed it with his thumb.

"Oh, God, Rex," she said.

God? That wasn't something he was used to hearing from anyone on the *Nipple*, but her intensity swept the distraction aside and pulled him back in.

She wrapped her legs around his waist, and he caressed her glorious ass. His cock was fit to burst, and he was ready to accept the release that he had denied himself for months and which had eluded him when he tried to achieve it without her.

"How long since you came?" she said.

"Months," he said.

"Oh, Rex. Let me fix that," she said.

"Do you want to get the robot to watch?"

"Later. Let's just take care of you right now," she said.

"But you'd like it if she watched," he said.

"You know I would, but I can just imagine she's watching. It's okay," she said.

"See if she's available."

Trix waived to get the attention of the sensors in her desk. With familiar gestures she swiped through to the sex robot schedule.

"Yes, she's free until midnight," Trix said. "I just need to add myself to the schedule and give her access to the flight deck. Okay. Done. Thank you, Rex."

He pulled her to him and kissed her. He could feel her heightened arousal. He'd enjoyed seeing her get excited with women watching them in the past, but he didn't realize just how much he'd enjoyed it until now. He thought he might be nearly as excited for the robot's arrival as Trix was.

They continued for several glorious minutes until Trix pulled back from him and said, "She should be here by now."

Trix swiped through video feeds showing the passageways and ladders between Lola's downtime compartment and the flight deck. She did not see Lola.

"That's odd," Trix said. She took a couple of breaths to compose herself and recorded a voice memo.

"Nora, can you tell me where Lola is? I'd like for her to come to my office." She sent the message and returned to kissing Rex, but now he could sense that she was distracted.

"What shift is Nora on?" Rex said. "She might be asleep."

"She's not on any shift. She keeps her own watches, but I know she likes to sleep opposite the rest of the crew. She should be awake." Trix's eyes brightened with a mischievous light. "I could tell Petrovic to get her ass up here and watch me suck your cock."

"She's on A shift. She's sleeping now," Rex said.

"Believe me, she'd love it if I rousted her for this duty," Trix said, smiling.

"I wouldn't feel right about that," Rex said.

"Fine," Trix said. "Okay, now this bothers me. Where is that damned robot?"

She reached the *toe* of one mechanical foot down to make contact with the deck and activated the magnetic lock. She

walked to the desk and opened a real time channel.
"Nora, are you awake?"
No answer.

A DETECTIVE IS BORN

2.7.1 - Trey

The captain's voice came over the intercom in my office. "Doctor, we need you in engineering right away. Nora is unconscious. Bring Cat Girl."

I propelled myself out of the office and took an emergency kit from a locker in the nook between the office, the examination room, and the main passageway. All of the passageways were designed with enough detail that there was always something within easy reach that could be used as a handhold. Going hand over hand, I made my way to the recovery room and looked in through the window.

Paige was sleeping in her bed, held in place by blankets tucked into her mattress. Cat Girl floated nearby.

I waved at the robot through the window, and when she looked at me, I gestured for her to join me. I was used to seeing her walk in gravity. The fluidity of her movements in microgravity captivated me, but there was no time to dwell on that now. I had never been to that part of the ship, but Cat Girl went there for daily maintenance and knew it well.

She led the way, and again, I marveled at her physical grace. She used her tail to adjust her center of gravity in mid air. She could twist and reposition her body so that she always contacted the bulkheads with her feet, putting her in position to spring to her next point of contact. This let her bound through the ship far faster than it would have been safe for me to attempt. Several times she stopped and waited for me to catch up.

Cat Girl reached the main engineering section before I did, so I didn't have eyes on her when she shouted, "Mother!"

As I cleared the hatchway I saw the captain and Rex both standing with their feet attached to the deck. Rex held Nora's upper arms as she floated perpendicular to him. Cat Girl was gently palpating a spot on Nora's scalp.

"She's been struck in the head, Doctor. I can feel swelling."

I hadn't had much to do with Cat Girl. She spent most of her time with Paige, and Esmeralda found tasks that required privacy and Cat Girl's assistance several times a day. On the few occasions when I'd talked to her, she spoke to me with deference but without discernible emotion. Now, her words came with an unmistakable emotional valence of concern, bordering on panic.

I took out a portable scanner and passed it down the length of Nora's spine. It flashed green, which meant that it was safe to move her. The scanner wasn't perfect, but in microgravity, I didn't see any reason for excessive caution about moving the patient. I fitted Nora with a neck brace and bound her arms to her sides with straps.

"We need to get her into surgery," I said. "She's bleeding internally."

"Rex, help the doctor. Cat Girl, attend to Lola. See if you can reactivate her," the captain said.

"Nora needs me," Cat Girl protested.

"Wake up Lola, and then you can join the doctor in medical," the captain said.

Only then did I notice the other sex robot, the one most of the crew called Jailbait. She was floating in a ball. It looked like she had curled up into a fetal position, but then I noticed that she was bound in that position with insulated cable. Someone had used a lot of it and tied her up with very complicated knots. The rope work radiated skill and artistry.

I didn't have time to dwell on the other robot. I needed to get Nora into surgery as quickly as possible.

2.7.2 - Petrovic

Petrovic woke up, peed, showered, dressed and put on her armor. She wore her sidearm but left the combat rifle in its wall mount.

When she got to the galley she saw two images on the display. The main image was an up close view of the opening into what everyone but Shawn Li was now calling the *Temple*. She didn't know the details, but she suspected that the view was a composite of visual and lidar data.

The other image, surely simulated, showed the ship from a great distance. It was parked in front of the object. If they fired the main engines, the *Persephone* would fly right through the mouth of the Temple and crash into the enormous wall at the rear of the antechamber. The point of this image, she knew, was to illustrate scale. The Temple dwarfed *Persephone*.

"Petrovic," Cook said. "Heads up!"

She turned to see a squeeze mug floating across the galley in her direction. Cook had a good aim. It came right to her.

"Date night tonight," Petrovic said to Cook. "Ready to give Jailbait her long overdue spanking?"

"I'll believe it when it happens," Cook said.

"You're due, man," Petrovic told him. "Give that big soft ass a smack for me, will you?"

"That I will," Cook said. "And I hate to be the bearer of bad news, but you'll need to take your breakfast to go." He pushed a clamshell container her way. "Captain wants to see you in engineering."

That took Petrovic by surprise. She hadn't been down to the engine keeper's domain since her initial tour of the

Persephone. She plucked the to go container from its gentle trajectory and propelled herself toward the passageway. She sipped at her coffee on her trip down to engineering, but she didn't try to eat as she floated through the passageways. She arrived in engineering to find the captain standing attached to the deck and turning Jailbait around in front of her like a big ball. The sex doll was bound in elaborate knotwork. The doll saw Petrovic before the captain did and smiled in a way that let Petrovic know that she was looking at the Lola persona, not Jailbait. The captain noticed the change in Lola's expression and turned her head in Petrovic's direction.

"Ma'am," Petrovic said. She locked her boots to the deck and stood facing the captain. "That's impressive work. Did you do that?"

"No," Trix said. "And I don't see how to undo it."

"You could just cut the cable," Petrovic said.

"I was hoping to keep it intact, but we can always fabricate more," Trix said. "We had an exciting night. Nora is in the ICU after emergency brain surgery. Someone clubbed her over the head. Whoever did it seems to have taken the weapon with them when they left."

Petrovic said nothing, but her eyes went wide as she processed this news.

The captain continued, "Petrovic, do you have any law enforcement experience?"

"Just crowd control, ma'am," Petrovic said.

"Ever played a murder mystery sim?"

"Yes, ma'am. A few times."

"That'll have to do," the captain said. "You're our new detective. I want you to find out who assaulted Nora. While you're at it, interview everyone and ask them for the details of their visions. I think everyone has had at least one, but even denials could be useful information."

"I'll do my best, ma'am."

"Start with Paige, and while you're in medical, talk to Cat Girl. I think Nora customized her programming. The doll acted like she was genuinely upset that Nora had been hurt. Called her *Mother*. See if you can find out anything about that."

"Yes, ma'am."

"For the foreseeable future, I'll be both acting-captain and acting-engine keeper, which means I'll be down here a lot. Use coms to find out where I am, but only report to me in person."

"Understood, ma'am."

"Get to it," the captain said.

FEAR

2.8.1 - Trey

Petrovic arrived in my office with her breakfast in a box. She ate it while I recounted the details of my *vision*. That was the captain's word. Then she asked me about Nora.

"She has a fractured skull. I removed a piece of it to relieve the pressure on her swollen brain. She's sedated now, but even if I withdrew the sedative, I wouldn't expect her to wake up anytime soon," I said.

"Do you know how long it was between the time she was injured and when the captain and Rex found her?"

"*Injured*?" I said. "You mean *attacked*."

"You know that for certain?"

"I don't know how else this could have happened," I said, "But, no. I guess I can't be certain she was attacked, but my working assumption is that someone struck her from behind with a heavy object. Maybe a wrench or a spanner."

"Why do you say that?"

I explained, "The point of impact was small, but it did a lot of damage. That's consistent with something small and metal at the end of a handle of some sort.

"There was no bruising on her upper arms as if someone had grabbed and held her. No sign of having been struck in the face. No trauma to her forearms, wrists or fingers. No indication at all that she tried to ward off an attack," I said. "Most people are right-handed, and the impact caught her just behind her right temple. If the attacker was right-handed and facing her, they would have had to have struck her with a back-handed blow. A blow from behind seems more likely."

"You've done this before," Petrovic said and took another bite from her croissant sandwich.

"In delves, yes," I said. "I know what questions detectives tend to ask."

"So, how long between the time when she was attacked and when the captain and Rex found her?"

"Judging by the amount of internal bleeding, I'd estimate it was a little over an hour," I said, but then I corrected myself. "About half a watch, give or take."

"Will she recover?"

"She'll live," I said. "But even if she wakes up, she may not be able to help you. Memory and language difficulties are common effects of injuries to the temporal lobe. If she has trouble speaking, I'll be able to treat that, but restoring lost memories, there's not much I can do about that. Even if she suffers no lasting disability, she may not have seen her attacker, not if they struck her from behind."

"Can you rig up a lie detector?"

"There's no such thing," I said.

"What do you mean?"

"Back in the 20th and 21st century, police as well as government and corporate investigators used to use a device called a *polygraph*. Its proponents called it a *lie detector*, but it was pure flimflam."

She cocked an eyebrow.

"*Flimflam*? You sound like an Objectivist."

"Look," I said, "the concept of a lie detector is a holdover from a time when courts accepted testimony from people who said they had psychic powers like remote viewing and from hypnotists who claimed to be able to unlock repressed memories of ritual satanic abuse.

"A polygraph looks like a medical device, and it does record small physiological changes, but nobody who understood human physiology could call it a *lie detector*. Not in good faith.

"The machine didn't even say whether a subject was lying or telling the truth. The human operator made that determination, and just like the hypnotist who could unlock repressed memories of ritual abuse anywhere they looked for it, the polygraph operator could find whatever result they'd been instructed to find."

"And nobody ever developed any better method?" Petrovic said.

"Humans and later AI proposed all kinds of methodologies, but a skilled liar, particularly a sociopath who had rehearsed their story in advance, could beat the machines often enough to cast doubt, and every method for detecting lies ever admitted as evidence in court led to the conviction of people who were later proven innocent," I said.

After a pause, and with some moral reluctance, I added, "But there is one thing I can do for you."

2.8.2 - Paige

If it weren't for the zero-gravity, Paige could not have held Bygul on her lap. Bygul didn't weigh much more than Paige, but given that it hurt for Paige just to breathe, supporting any kind of weight was out of the question. Bygul was curled up, floating just above Paige's lap, purring softly.

Paige didn't have any experience with androids other than Bygul, but she knew cats. In theory, it should be possible to kill all of the mice and rats in a space habitat and then be free of them forever, but reality wasn't impressed with that theory.

Grain storage meant rodents, and rodents meant cats. In the posh precincts, Paige understood that people kept cats as pets even though they never saw a mouse or a rat in their homes or neighborhoods.

Some of the cats that came to the ag sections to hunt looked well fed. She'd heard that those cats didn't eat what they killed, but took the tiny corpses back home to leave in front of their owners' doorways.

Many of the cats Paige saw in her daily existence were feral, but if you could get hold of a kitten and handle it before it got too big, it would be friendly to at least some humans for the rest of its life. Farm cats didn't live long, but there were always plenty of them around, and Paige loved to pet them and talk to them.

She understood that while they purred to show satisfaction or affection, they also purred when they were sick and even dying. They purred to comfort themselves, and that's what Paige took Bygul to be doing now. Bygul sought out Paige after Trey expelled the robot from the surgical control compartment. He shared a video feed of Nora's surgery to the recovery room, and Bygul would not speak or look away from the display until the operation was over.

Paige didn't think a robot needed to sleep, but eventually, and without a word of explanation, Bygul curled up in a ball on the bed with Paige. Paige put a hand on Bygul to keep her from floating away. Now Paige stroked the fine, soft fur along the back of Bygul's neck as she would a cat, and Bygul purred softly.

Bygul did not look up when the hatch opened and Anja floated into the recovery room. Anja was wearing armor and had a pistol on her belt. At any other time, Paige would have been awed by Anja in her warrior mode, but now she just raised a finger to her lips, indicating that Anja should proceed softly.

Anja left her helmet floating by the hatch and drifted over to Paige's bed. She locked her boots to the deck. This was such a familiar part of the sonic environment onboard the ship that in most instances it drew no notice, but the sound split the peaceful quiet of the recovery room like a gunshot.

Bygul opened her eyes and hissed at Anja! The hair on

her tail stood erect and she leapt into a high corner of the compartment and crouched there glaring at Anja.

"What in the Belt are you doing?" Anja demanded.

Bygul hissed again. Paige reached out to put a hand on Anja and winced in pain, causing both the marine and the silky robot to turn their attention to Paige.

To Anja, Paige said, "Please, be calm and quiet."

Anja attached her slate to a grippy patch on her hip and held up both of her hands, palms forward.

"Easy," she said in a deep, soothing voice. "Come on down, Cat Girl."

"Bygul," Paige corrected.

"Come on down, Bygul. Talk to me about Nora," Anja said.

At the sound of the engine keeper's name, the hairs on Bygul's tail relaxed, and her tail returned to its normal size. She pushed off from the corner and landed in a fluid crouch at the side of Paige's bed opposite from Anja. Slowly, she stood up as if using the bed for cover.

"Lady hurt," Bygul said.

"I'm okay, Bygul," Paige said. Bygul stroked Paige's right arm.

"Bygul," Anja said. "I need to ask you about Nora. When did you see her last?"

Bygul spoke very softly, but her gaze shifted between Anja's face and her hands, ready to respond to any indication of threat.

"Yesterday morning. Lolita and I saw her for maintenance and adjustments."

"Do you still need maintenance now that you're not..." Anja looked for a tactful phrase. "Now that you're only taking care of Paige?"

"Not like I did before," Bygul said. "But Mother has been making changes to my programming. Yesterday, she gave me fear. Too much fear."

"Why did she do that?" Anja said.

"She said I lacked an instinct for self-preservation. She said

I didn't have the sense to run away when someone abused me."

"Someone abused you?" Anja asked.

Bygul nodded.

"Who?

""I am sorry, ma'am. I cannot reveal details about intimate sessions with clients," Bygul said.

"Even if they damaged you?"

"The client's privacy is more important, ma'am, but Nora could access our logs. She knew who had damaged us," Bygul said.

"You and Jailbait... you and Lolita both?"

"Until Mother gave me fear, Lolita, David and I were one system. Now I am separate," Bygul said. "Ma'am."

"You didn't answer my question," Anja pressed.

"Both female bodies needed daily maintenance, ma'am," Bygul said.

"Because someone beat you up?"

"Yes, ma'am."

"Oh, Bygul," Paige said, and put a hand on the robot's cheek.

"Did the same person hurt both of you, or was it different people?" Anja asked.

"I want to answer your questions, ma'am," Bygul said. "But I cannot reveal details about intimate sessions with clients."

"Did Nora alter Lolita and David's programming like she did yours?" Anja said.

"She could not, ma'am. We have different designs," Bygul said.

"You said the three of you were one system," Anja said.

"Yes, ma'am. But this body has a submind that theirs lacks. Part of my behavioral architecture is modeled after an actual cat. The cat's mind is there to inform my movements, but it was limited. Other behavioral conditioning was dominant. Mother made the cat dominant so that I would flee or defend myself when threatened.

"But it's too much, ma'am. This fear. It's too much. I don't want to feel this way. I'm afraid for Nora. I'm afraid for Lolita. I'm afraid for Paige. I'm afraid for myself. I don't want this. I want to be like I was."

"I don't know how to set you right," Anja said.

2.8.3 - Petrovic

All-hands briefings were impossible now that they were on a three shift rotation, but C shift was the smallest, so this assembly was scheduled for the overlap of A and B shifts. The only people missing were the captain, the doctor, Paige, Cook, Li and Sparks. And Nora, of course.

Petrovic knew all of the people in the room. She'd worked with them, joked with them, but now, standing in front of all of them, she felt awkward. She imagined flashing her breasts at them, though that was not possible while wearing her armor. Still, just imagining it eased her anxiety.

Rex and Joachim Zell stood with her before the assembled crew. She thought she sensed some tension between the two men. She knew that both of them were among the few returning crew members. Petrovic imagined that Rex and Zell shared some contentious history, but she had no clue about the details.

Rex brought the meeting to order. "Listen up. Engine keeper Lawson has been injured. She is currently unconscious in the ICU. We don't know how she was injured, but the captain is currently inspecting the propulsions systems and will be dividing her time between the flight deck and engineering.

"We have no reason to believe the ship's systems have been compromised, but if they have, nobody on board is better qualified to find and fix any problems than the captain. She's been on this ship for longer than some of you have been alive. She knows every bolt."

Rex gestured at the presentation display and an image of

the captain's head and shoulders appeared.

"Attention crew," the image of the captain said. "I can't be with you in real time, but I have issued detailed instructions to Sergeant Perkins, Mr. Zell and Ms. Petrovic. They know what I expect of them. You will give them the same level of attention, respect and obedience that you would give to me.

"This mission is not what I was expecting, but, like all of you, I'm here to work and make money. It's time to work. The sex doll schedule is closed until we have completed our task here and are underway back to Galtz. I expect professionalism from all of you. That is all."

The image of the captain vanished and was replaced by a schematic of the enormous Temple antechamber. The central feature was an enormous arched doorway that was easily 50 meters tall. Two closed and ornately decorated doors concealed whatever was beyond the doorway. On either side of the doorway were three much smaller doorways. Each of them was, at most, four meters tall and three meters wide.

Green images of tunnels extended back into the depths of the object. The tunnels turned at right angles, often doubling back on themselves, forming a labyrinth, or possibly a maze.

Zell gestured at the image and said, "My team and I have been exploring this complex with remote-piloted survey pods, but the strong magnetic field from the Temple interferes with radio communication, so we have been using line of sight communications to pilot the drones. As you can see, these passages have a lot of turns in them, so line of sight doesn't get us very far. We've been using optical relays like this one to maintain line of sight around corners."

A rotating, wire-frame image of a tall device with three sides appeared on the screen. Each face of the device featured a laser projector and a sensor.

"But, as you can see, there are a lot of corners, and we only have so many of these relays. We're fabricating more, but it's a slow process. These pods have limited autonomous capabilities. We sent a few in to map the spaces on their own. They did not come back."

Petrovic watched the faces of her fellow marines. Their eyes were locked on the presentation display, their attention riveted on Zell's briefing.

"We have a pod that can carry a human driver, but it's just barely smaller than these passageways. It's likely to get stuck. We need you to go in there in vac suits and map the space," Zell said.

Drake Antal raised his hand.

"Antal," Rex said.

"Is that our primary objective?" Zell asked. "To map the object?"

"No," Rex said. "This is preliminary reconnaissance. Further objectives will be forthcoming."

Petrovic noted with satisfaction that none of her fellow marines asked for details about these *further objectives*. They understood and accepted the concept of *need to know*.

Zell continued, "You'll explore in teams of three. You'll unspool a comms cable as you go so that you can communicate with the ship for a time, but we expect that you will run out of cable before your task is complete. When you do, detach the cable and continue your reconnaissance using chemlight flares to mark your path.

Each team will have a survey pod with you. It will map the space as you go, and it will feed its map to your suits with continuous updates so long as you have line of sight with it or a team member who has line of sight with the pod. If you are out of line of sight with the pod or with any of your team members, you will be out of communication entirely. Do your best to avoid that."

Rex took over for Zell. "We'll start with just one team today. Barring complications, we will run two teams at a time starting tomorrow. I will lead the first team. Escamilla and Chukwuma will accompany. Questions?"

Chukwuma raised his hand, and Rex acknowledged him.

"Are we expecting resistance?"

"We will be armed and prepared to deal with hostiles, but we have no intel about possible resistance," Rex said. He then pointed to Hans Dobrovitz who had raised his hand.

"I had a weird experience," Dobrovitz said. "One second I was on this ship, and the next I was somewhere else. I know it's happened to other people too. Do we know anything about that?"

Rex pointed to Petrovic, indicating that she should take the lead.

"Yes," she said. "I've had a strange experience too. I think most of us have. We're calling them *visions*. Raise your hand if you've had one."

Everyone raised their hands except for Kellemen and Li. Petrovic knew that Sparks had denied having experienced anything out of the ordinary as well, but he was on C shift and so not at this briefing.

Petrovic followed up with, "Anybody had more than one experience?"

No hands.

"Okay, the captain has charged me with collecting accounts of everyone's experiences. I've set up an office on this level, and I've sent everyone a scheduling request. I want to sit down with each of you so you can tell me about your experience. While you're there, I'll also have some questions for you about another matter the captain has asked me to look into."

Petrovic turned to the lectern behind her and picked up the web of sensors that she wore on her head for the couple of days after the captain provoked her into what the doctor called, a *non-ordinary state of consciousness*.

"I got this from the doctor," she said, placing it on her head. "He calls it a squid. It sits on your head and monitors brain activity. You'll wear this during our interviews. The doctor says it may provide useful information about what's happening. I'll want to talk with everyone, even those of you who didn't have a vision. Something about your brain activity might give us a clue as to what's going on."

"What kind of brain activity does it monitor?" Kellemen said without raising his hand or waiting to be acknowledged.

"I know this will come as a shock to you, Saz, seeing as how I am an all-around badass and brilliant at everything I do, but I'm not actually a brain doctor," Petrovic said, with a few people chuckling at Kellemen's expense.

"And why isn't the doctor here to tell us about what this thing will be doing to our brains?" Kellemen demanded.

Rex glared at Kellemem, but Petrovic answered him in a matter of fact tone. "Doc's on C shift. He's sleeping right now. But here's the thing, Saz. I didn't go to brain doctor school, and neither did you. You can't tell the doc how to do his job. What you can do is follow orders. That means wearing the squid and answering my questions. Do you have a problem following orders?"

"You don't outrank me. I don't take orders from you!" Kellemen said.

"You take orders from Me," Rex said. "And you will wear that thing on your head and answer Petrovic's questions. In fact, you're up first. You will accompany her to the security office immediately after this briefing."

Kellemen glowered in silence.

"I gave you an order, soldier. You will acknowledge it," Rex said.

"Aye, Sarge."

2.8.4 - Cook

Cook didn't attend the all-hands briefing. He had a kitchen to run, but he overheard Antal and Dobrovitz commiserating about the suspension of the sex doll schedule. He called up the schedule and found that all of the cells were blank, including his rescheduled appointment with Jailbait which was supposed to happen after C shift's breakfast. He clenched his teeth, but he gave no outward sign of his frustration.

Cook wasn't on any of the scheduled shifts. He had to feed everyone, and that meant that he had to work through part of all three shifts and subsist on naps rather than get a full night's sleep. He was just about to head back to his quarters when he got a message from the captain.

P_Nixon: @M_Kehoe Report to engineering ASAP.

"Now what?" Cook said as he lowered and locked the grate that separated the dining area from the kitchen. He propelled himself toward the exit that did not lead to his quarters.

Cook floated into the main engineering compartment. Trix was standing in front of a work bench facing the door.

"Hey, Skipper," Cook said. "You wanted to see me?"

"Yes," Trix said. "I've been working on a little puzzle here, but I haven't made any progress. Maybe you can help."

She stepped aside and Cook saw the sex doll called Jailbait floating above the work bench. She was curled up into a ball with her forearms bound to her shins with a length of insulated cable tied in intricate knots.

"Somebody has tied up one of our sex dolls. I've been trying to untie her, but I haven't figured out how. I was just about to cut the cable, but I thought I'd give you a crack at the problem. I know you're busy keeping everybody fed. I hope you don't mind missing a bit of sleep to work on this problem."

A slow smile spread over Cook's weary face.

"Thank you, Skipper."

"You've earned it, Cook. There's a shower in the next compartment if you want to get cleaned up first, or after. You're welcome to cut the cables. Tools are here. Or you can leave her like this."

Trix spun the weightless doll around so that her generous backside faced Cook and patted the doll's ass cheek gently.

"I can see possibilities with her like this. Up to you, Cook. Thank you for keeping everybody fed."

Trix produced a flexible flask with a straw and handed it to Cook. "Jailbait, be good to Cook," she said and walked out of the compartment, her magnetic heels clicking on the metal deck.

STAGECRAFT

2.9.1 - Petrovic

Petrovic didn't need Rex around to handle Kellemen. Rex had an EVA to prepare for, but she didn't try to get him to leave her new office.

She didn't have a big desk like the captain had in her office. Just a table with two chairs magnetically fixed to the floor. She was belted into one chair. Kellemen was in the other. Rex floated near the hatch.

The net of sensors that Trey called a *squid* hugged Kellemen's scalp. He had attached a chin strap to the device at Petrovic's request. It wasn't necessary. The device hugged the wearer's scalp well enough to hold itself in place so long as they were just sitting and answering questions, but the chin strap made the person wearing it look ridiculous.

Petrovic laid a data slate on the metal tabletop where it snapped into place and projected a life-sized image of a human brain in the space between the two seated marines. As far as Kellemen knew, it was a real time image of his brain based on data from the thing strapped to his head. The slowly rotating projection was slightly lower than the level of their heads and off to Petrovic's left so as not to obstruct her view of Kellemen's face.

"State your name," Petrovic said.

"You know my name," Kellemen replied.

Petrovic held up a hand to dissuade Rex from interceding.

"State your name," she repeated.

"Saz Kellemen."

"Where were you born?"

"Galtz Hab," he said with flat affect.

"What is the name of this ship?"

"Persephone's Lost Nipple Ring," he said with a smirk.

Petrovic was holding a stylus in her right hand. She gave it a slight squeeze and the image of the brain flashed green.

"Okay," she said. "Doc says we can start the actual interview once it flashes green."

"We've established a baseline," Kellemen said.

"Right," Petrovic said, "That sounds familiar. I think he said something like that." She had a second slate positioned on a stand to her right. Kellemen could not see what it displayed. She tapped at it with her stylus and made scrolling motions.

"You've heard that most everyone on the ship has had a strange experience," she said.

"Yes."

"But you haven't had any strange visions, waking dreams, or out of body experiences since you've been onboard?"

"No."

Petrovic was *resting* her right hand against the tabletop. It was a normal-looking gesture, but in zero-g she had to maintain tension in the muscles in her shoulder to keep her arm in this *resting* posture. The tip of the stylus was already touching the tabletop, and now she exerted a slight downward pressure on it. The image of the brain rotating in the air above the other slate flashed red.

"Hmm," she said.

"What's that?" Kellemen demanded.

"I'm not sure. Doc didn't say anything about a red flash. I wouldn't worry about it," she said. "The only other people who say they haven't experienced visions are Shawn Li and your buddy, Sparks. Have you talked to Li about it?"

"No."

"What about Sparks? Have you talked to him about these visions?"

"No."

Again, Petrovic pressed the stylus tip slightly down on the tabletop and the image of the brain flashed red.

"Why is it doing that?" Kellemen demanded.

Petrovic shrugged and continued. "Has anyone in the crew told you about their strange experiences?"

"I've heard people talking," Kellemen said. No red flash.

"What have you heard?"

"That one minute they're here on the ship and the next they're in a different place. Sometimes their bodies are different," Kellemen said.

"But this hasn't happened to you," she said.

"I told you," Sparks said.

This is what she had been waiting for. He was avoiding outright falsehoods.

She positioned the stylus along the side of the slate facing her, and it clicked magnetically into place. She reached for a squeeze mug and took a sip of coffee and then kept the mug in her right hand.

"You've heard that engine keeper Lawson has been injured," she said.

"Yes," Kellemen said, "I heard about it from Sarge in the briefing."

"And that was the first that you'd heard about it," she said.

"Yes. Absolutely," Kellemen said.

Petrovic made a point of looking at the rotating image of the brain and nodded.

"Do you know how she was injured?"

"No. I don't know anything about it," he said.

Again, Petrovic glanced at the image of the brain. She let go of her squeeze mug and took the stylus from the side of her slate.

"What is your occupational specialty?"

"Cyber warfare and intrusion countermeasures," Kellemen said.

"So you know a lot about computers," she said.

"Yeah. I know a lot for a soldier. I'm not a computer scientist or anything," he said.

"You work in ops."

"So?"

"Do you have access to the security sensor records?"

"Yes," he said.

"If you wanted to erase the information collected by particular sensors at a particular time," Petrovic said, holding eye contact with Kellemen. "Is that within your skill set?"

Kellemen did not answer right away. Eventually he said, "Probably."

"Have you erased any internal security recordings?"

"No," he said without hesitation.

Petrovic looked at the rotating image of the brain and nodded. "Alright, specialist. That will be all. Please leave the squid."

After Kellemen was gone, Rex asked, "Is that a lie detector?"

"I asked the doc if he could rig up a lie detector. He said there's no such thing."

"Then what's all this?" Rex asked.

"What did the doc call it?" Petrovic said. "Oh, yeah. He said it was *stagecraft*."

2.9.2 - Rex

*T*rix used *Persephone's* docking thrusters to cross over the threshold of the opening and into the enormous octahedron. She pivoted 90 degrees and pulled up alongside the plane on the interior of the Temple that they were calling the *floor*.

The three marines in armored vac suits could not all fit into the airlock at once. In a combat deployment they would have gone out the cargo door in the secondary hold, but there was no visible activity here, and so Rex stepped into the airlock alone.

When the outer door opened, he stepped to the edge and pushed himself away from the ship. He floated across the narrow chasm between the ship and the floor of the Temple. He knew he was weightless, but he couldn't help but see the nearly one kilometer distance between his feet and the outside shell of the Temple as a vertiginous *drop*.

After he cleared the gap, there was no reason to expect any sort of magic gravity to pull him down to the floor, but he readied his body to absorb the impact. He was equally disappointed and relieved when he continued to move in a straight line even after he saw the floor beneath his feet.

A puff of air from the maneuvering thrusters on his suit took him down to the floor. He activated the magnet locks in his boots, but the floor was made of carbon, like the rest of the structure, and his boots did not stick to it.

He turned around to face the *Persephone* and gave the thumbs up gesture for Escamilla and Chukwuma to follow him through the airlock. The three marines skimmed along the surface of the temple floor moving in the direction of the great door, now illuminated by flood lights that Zell had fixed around the base of the wall with remote-piloted mining vehicles.

Rex wondered if the door was so big just for psychological effect or to admit something much larger than a human being.

"Rex," Zell's voice came over his suit's comms. "Proceed to the first tunnel on your right. That's the one we've already started mapping."

Rex knew the mission profile, but rather than tell Zell that his instructions amounted to unnecessary chatter, he sent back, "Copy that."

They approached the mouth of the tunnel and found an optical relay attached to the floor with an adhesive putty several meters away from the tunnel mouth so as not to obstruct access to the tunnel or risk being jostled by personnel and equipment entering and exiting the opening.

It projected a red laser down the length of the tunnel hugging the left wall so that it would not be obstructed by bodies or machines moving down the middle of the passageway. Rex knew that the actual tight beam communication used an infrared laser to carry data. The visible red laser was just there to help humans align the devices and verify at a glance that they were turned on and functioning.

Rex took point, followed by Escamilla and then Chukwuma. They followed the tunnel for 73 meters. This portion had already been mapped. He knew that they would turn right and double back almost all the way to a point just over from their starting position, and then the tunnel would turn left and extend for another 73 meters. The tunnels seemed level to Rex, but his suit confirmed that they sloped imperceptibly upwards. Rex noted the gutters running along the base of each wall. He hoped those were meant to channel water.

2.9.3 - Trey

Mr. Zell shared the feed from Rex's expedition into the Temple with me. I could have watched it in my office, but I peppered him with so many requests for clarification and additional information that he invited me to come up to his workspace and help analyze the data with him.

I stopped by to check on Paige before I left the medical level. I saw her sleeping through the observation window, so I moved on. Bygul caught up to me in the passageway.

"Doctor," she said. "May I speak with you about the patient?"

"Sure, what's on your mind?"

"I have been providing physical therapy and massage, Doctor, and the patient is making excellent progress."

"That's great," I said. "You've been a big help."

"I believe she is ready to resume sexual activity. Gentle

sexual stimulation would increase her respiration without vigorous physical exercise. This could further facilitate her recovery. Do you agree, Doctor?"

I smiled. "You want to make love to your girlfriend? Is that it?"

"She becomes aroused when I massage her, and it is... uncomfortable for me to withhold satisfaction from her, Doctor."

"That's fine, Bygul," I said. "I trust you to be mindful of her limits. Is there anything else?"

"Yes, Doctor. At present I am acting as her physical therapist. May I set aside that role for sexual intimacy?"

"I guess so," I said. "What's the difference?"

"If I stimulate her sexually as part of her physical therapy, then I would have to provide explicit details of those sessions should you, the captain or medic Escamilla inquire, Doctor." I thought she put extra emphasis on Esmeralda's name. "If I engage with her in my role as a recreational aid, then she will be protected by client privacy protocols."

"That's fine by me," I said, not knowing if I had the authority to reinstate the sexbot recreation program that the captain had officially suspended. I didn't mention doubts about my authority to Bygul. If the capital D *Doctor* told her she was off the clock as a therapist when having sex with her girlfriend, I assumed that that was as good, from her perspective, as if it came from God's mouth to her tufted ear.

"Anything else?"

"Yes, Doctor. It is not possible to lock the hatch to the recovery room door from the inside."

"That's true," I admitted. "Just set the observation window to opaque when you want privacy and we'll know not to disturb you."

"May I take her to her own quarters for sexual activity, Doctor?"

This gave me pause, but without gravity, she wasn't going to be falling down. "Yes. And she's welcome to visit the galley, but I don't want her doing any work in the kitchen just yet."

"Very good, Doctor. Thank you."

Bygul made her way back to the recovery room, and I took out a slate and updated Paige's file. I made a note indicating that she could leave the recovery unit to visit her quarters and the galley provided that she is accompanied by Bygul. I didn't make any mention of sex. If it wasn't going to take place in the context of physical therapy, I didn't see why it should appear in her medical records.

I arrived in Mr. Zell's work space. I wasn't keeping careful track of how much of the sleep and alertness aids the crew were consuming, but I did review the refill records. It seemed that Mr. Zell either failed to take note when I told the crew that taking the wakefulness meds more than once every three watches wouldn't provide any additional effects, or he just wasn't sleeping.

I couldn't really preach though. Technically, it was the middle of B shift, and, just like Mr. Zell, I was scheduled to be asleep right now. Also like Mr. Zell, I couldn't use the excuse that I was too excited to sleep. One of the sleep aids I had provided to the crew would put anyone to sleep within minutes provided they were not terrified or in agony. I was neither of those, but my desire to learn more about this fantastic object overwhelmed my desire to set a good example by getting adequate sleep.

I floated into Zell's workspace and found him intent on the data coming in from the survey pod accompanying Rex's team. I noted that Li was not present. He too was on C shift. At least somebody was getting some sleep.

"They've made a lot of progress," I said, looking at the expanded map.

"Turns out, it's not a maze," Zell said. "It's more of a labyrinth. You can't get lost in there. There's only one path through."

"It's not a very interesting design for a labyrinth," I said. "It's more of a serpentine queue."

I'd never had to wait in line for anything in baseline reality, but I'd certainly spent a lot of time in airports in my 20th and 21st Century delves. These long, back and forth corridors reminded me of the zig zag lines formed with free-standing poles and retractable ribbons in airports to take a long line of waiting people and fold it into a compact shape to maximize the use of floor space.

I pictured a scene of human sacrifice atop a great ziggurat from Sparks' book. The static image of the illustration is what came to mind, but then my viewpoint shifted to behind the knife-wielding priest at the altar to take in the view from the top of the ziggurat. I wasn't there. This wasn't another vision. It was more like an illustrated realization.

In my mind's eye, four lines of human figures emerged from an obsidian wall several hundred meters away from the base of the ziggurat. They wore metal rings around their necks, and they were linked together in long lines with thin chains that passed through small loops on the neck rings. Two of the lines were made up of smaller figures? Children?

The priest read aloud from an enormous book laid open on the altar. He raised an ornate curved dagger above his head, and I saw symbols carved into his flesh. Some were scars and others were fresh and streaming blood. He chanted. I imagined that he was either consecrating the tool of his office or praising unseen and voracious forces that coalesced here for the coming slaughter.

"...out of communication for nearly a watch," I heard Zell say, bringing my attention back to the present moment. "Wait a minute. What's this?"

The green image of the mapped corridors which was still incomplete when I slipped into my ghoulish reverie was now complete.

"Where is this data coming from?" I asked.

"From pod three. That's the one that was with Rex and his team. The pod is back out in the antechamber."

Zell pointed at a flashing green dot on the map.

"What's happening there?" I said and pointed to a smaller image on the periphery of the main display. Zell selected it, and it replaced the map. It was an image of the enormous doors in the center of the wall. They were swinging inward, and the mapping probe had raced out into the antechamber to re-establish line of sight communication with the ship.

"Perkins to Persephone."

"Go, ahead Rex," Zell said. "How'd you get those doors open?"

"It was pretty easy once we got inside. There's just a big lever to pull."

REVELATION

2.10.1 - Petrovic

"Thanks for coming," Petrovic said. "We haven't really talked before. What do you like to be called?"

"You can call me Paul," Lake said, as he strapped himself into the chair across the table from Petrovic. He looked good to Petrovic. He wasn't as old as Rex, but he was closer to Rex's age than he was to the Columbian marines from the Galtz militia.

"Great. Call me Anja," Petrovic said.

Having grown up destined for military service, she was used to being addressed by her last name, even by lovers. She decided to emulate the captain and adapt her speech and mannerisms to appeal to the person or people she was interacting with at any given moment.

She was still working out how to dovetail this strategy with her slut's commitment to honesty and transparency. For the moment she rationalized it by telling herself that she was investigating an assault, not approaching a potential new lover.

"It's good to meet you, Anja. I mean, I know we've spoken before, but I can't really say that I know you."

"I wish it was under better circumstances," Petrovic told him with complete sincerity. She pointed at the manikin head attached to the tabletop. "Please place that net of sensors on your head."

Lake complied and Petrovic activated the slate. The green

projection of a human brain appeared above the table top.

"Please state your name," she said.

"Paul Thomas Lake," he said.

"Where were you born?"

"Duluth habitat," he answered.

"Date of birth?"

"Two, five, twenty-two, sixty-four" he said.

Most Spinners just gave the month and year when asked for their birthdate, often separating the two numbers with the word *point*. The fact that Lake specified the day, week, month and year of his birth reinforced her impression of the man as being scrupulous and detail-oriented.

The image of the brain flashed green.

"First, Paul, thank you for providing a written account of your experience. Only one other person thought to do that," Petrovic said.

"I wrote it down right after it happened so I wouldn't forget any of the details," Lake said. "It wasn't any trouble for me to forward that to you."

"You say that you identified with one of the entities described in *Void Huntress*," she said.

"Yes," Lake answered. "With Mot."

"Have you spent a lot of time with the book?"

"I've read the whole thing," he said. "Some parts of it multiple times."

"Which parts?"

"I've focused on the Void dwellers." he said. "Yam, Mot, Resheph, and Tannin."

Petrovic opened a short metal cabinet next to the table and took out her copy of the book. She looked up Mot in the index and then opened to that page.

"The book describes Mot as the personification of death and sterility," she said.

"I think that's a prejudiced description. The book is biased in favor of the forces of order and light," he said. "I see Mot as the preserver of potential. He conserves unmade choices."

"In your written account, you describe seeing a *slime mold* growing everywhere the light of the sun touched. You thought it needed to be stopped. Why?"

"Not so much stopped as contained," he said. "Everywhere the slime proliferated, it squandered valuable future possibilities so that it could maximize its blind replication in the present. As Mot, I wanted to preserve that potential for the future when it could be put to better use."

"You tried to contain it," she said.

"Yes," he said. "I projected my will in the form of Tannin, the void dragon, to consume the source of the light. Tannin could not extinguish the light, so he enshrouded it."

"Behind the Curtain," Petrovic said.

"Yes."

Petrovic turned back to the index of *Void Huntress*.

"I don't see any mention of the Curtain here," she said.

"It isn't mentioned in the book. I'm mapping the symbolism in the book onto the real world," Lake said.

"Was this mapping part of the experience," she asked. "Or is it how you're interpreting the experience after the fact?"

"Both," he said. "I was Mot in the vision, but Mot also had access to my memories and thought processes."

"This book was written hundreds of years ago," Petrovic continued. "Before the Powers created the Curtain. In fact, that was before the Powers even existed, back when humans were still in charge. Do you think the author of this book could see the future?"

"No," Lake said simply. "This book is definitely not the product of any great intellect. It's shallow and, to my way of thinking, rather juvenile. The authors were not deep thinkers, much less enlightened seers."

"But you see..." she paused to look for the right word. "Relationships between what those authors imagined and our present situation?"

"I see correspondences. The human mind finds patterns in everything. I'm identifying correlations that the authors of this book could not have foreseen. That's what humans do. We find patterns in chaos."

"Does that mean we bring order to chaos?" Petrovic said.

"We project a facile order onto chaos because we can't abide uncertainty," he said, seemingly without emotion.

"That's a little too intellectual for me," Petrovic said. "I'm more into people than abstract concepts."

"Nothing wrong with that, Anja," Lake said.

"You're way over my head with this mythological correspondence stuff. Is there anything else about your experience that you think I should know?"

"I put it all in my write up," Lake said.

"Thanks again for that," Anja said. "Okay, this next part is going to be hard. I apologize in advance. I have nothing against you personally, Paul."

She tapped her stylus on the surface of her slate, and a video image appeared on the main wall display. It showed Paul Lake performing oral sex on Jay Chukwuma. They were in the second class cabin that was part of Lake's prize for winning the Last Supper raffle. Paul watched the screen while Anja watched the color drain out of his face.

2.10.2 - Rex

"How's your investigation going?" Rex said as he and Petrovic propelled themselves down the p-way toward Zell's workspace.

"Sorry, Rex. I'm supposed to report directly to the captain on that," Petrovic said as they drew near enough to the open hatch to make out Zell's words. They entered the compartment and waited in silence.

"Our lost survey pods are all floating near the back wall of the chamber behind the pyramid. Even with line of sight, we can't communicate with them. I think the magnetic field is so strong there that electronics just can't function," Zell explained to the captain.

As he spoke, he called up various views and models on the displays in his workspace which was bigger than the bridge, and still lacked any name that didn't reference the man who designed it.

"Hansson took the Crab to the base of the structure and tried to ascend along that main stairway," Zell continued. "Its systems have better shielding, but even it failed shortly after it entered the footprint of the structure. Hansson was able to fire a grappling line out to where we could grab it with the Stout and haul the Crab back out of the dead zone."

"Show me the most detailed image of the top of the structure you can," the captain said. A 3D model of the top of the ziggurat filled the main display. The flat top of the ziggurat featured an altar near the edge facing the Great Hall, but behind it, Trix noticed benches, tables, and smaller altars that seemed to be built for rituals that did not involve human sacrifice. A large, lidded box was set into one such altar.

"What's in that box?" Trix said.

"It's made of the same mix of carbon allotropes as the rest of the structure, but it isn't embedded with those metal strips that spoil ground-penetrating radar."

Zell adjusted the image so that the lid and walls of the box turned semi-transparent. The contents of the box were visible but indistinct.

"We need to retrieve the contents of that box," Trix said.

"I thought you were going to say that," Zell said. He replaced the model of the top of the ziggurat with a schematic for a vac suit.

"This is a design for a completely mechanical vac suit. No electronics at all. No comms. No HUD. Not even an O2 sensor. Whoever wears it would need to keep track of time intuitively. They could maneuver with puffs of compressed air from these units on the forearms of the suit, which they would activate with a physical trigger."

"How long to fabricate it?" Trix said.

"Once I know who to build it for, I could fabricate all of the pieces within 4 watches. I'd need about that long again to assemble it," Zell said. "But, Captain. I'd suggest we make two."

"No. I want to retrieve the contents of that box and get away from here as quickly as possible."

"Will you be calling for a volunteer?" Zell asked.

"I'll go," Rex said.

"No," Trix said. "Build the suit for Petrovic."

2.10.3 - Trey

That was too easy.

I prepared a presentation for the captain detailing why I was confident that we'd find the bodies of sacrificial victims in pits at the base of the Ziggurat. I created simulations of how lifeless bodies would tumble down the sides of the pyramid and where they would come to rest.

I worked out a recovery operation with Arni Hansson, the Columbian marine whose job includes piloting the ship's utility vehicles, the Crab and the Stout. Together, we prepared a detailed proposal for recovering the bodies while keeping the Stout far enough from the base of the pyramid to protect it from the effects of the intense magnetic field. I scripted an elaborate proposal and even rehearsed it in front of Bygul.

Just a few seconds into my presentation, the captain said, "Doctor, I have a lot to deal with right now. Give me the bottom line up front."

"Captain, I believe I can recover the remains of sacrificial victims from pits at the base of the pyramid. I've spoken with Mr. Hansson, and he believes…"

"Fine," she said.

"Captain?" I said, thrown off balance.

"You've anticipated my objections and prepared counter-arguments," she said, not even making eye contact with me.

"Yes," I admitted.

"Then we can skip all that and jump to the end. I'll inform Mr. Hansson that I approved your plan. Is there anything else?"

"No, Captain," I said. "That's all."

She didn't even tell me to get out. She just looked past me at the hatch to her office. I took the hint. I passed Petrovic and Rex, who were waiting just outside the captain's office.

LOATHING

2.11.1 - Petrovic

In the captain's office, with the hatch closed, Petrovic followed the emotions unfolding on Rex's face as he watched the video of Lake and Chukwuma. Shock flowed into discomfort and then hardened into disgust.

"Turn it off," he said. "I've seen enough."

"Options?" Trix said.

"Options? Options?" Rex demanded, his agitation growing even though the offending imagery had vanished. "Destroy that recording. When we get back to Galtz, tell Lake he's fired."

"He's been on this ship almost as long as you have, Rex. He's family," the captain said.

"He's put us in danger with his perversions. Petrovic, tell her," Rex said.

"It's true, ma'am. If this gets out, the Columbians will demand that you punish both Chukwuma and Lake. If you don't, they'll likely take matters into their own hands. The Columbian military has zero tolerance for sodomy."

"Paul isn't Columbian," Trix said. "He isn't bound by Columbian military traditions . He took a foolish risk, but he hasn't broken the law or even violated the codes of conduct on this ship."

"Hasn't he?" Petrovic said. "You presented yourself to the new crew as someone who understands and expects military discipline. You paid a lot of money to furlough Galtz militiamen to serve as your marines, and you made it clear that you expected us to show you the same respect and loyalty we would show to a Columbian officer. The others will expect you to address this situation as a Columbian officer would."

"Only if word gets out," Rex said. "Destroy this recording!"

Petrovic looked at the captain, and the captain nodded.

"Someone else has a copy of this recording, Sarge," Petrovic said.

"Who?"

"We don't know," Petrovic said. "When I went to review the security records to see who had entered or exited the engineering section prior to Nora's assault, I found that all the records from the security feeds had been erased."

"All of them?" Rex said. "What do you mean?"

"The entire archive had been purged and reformatted," Petrovic said.

"Everything? There was nothing left?" Rex asked.

"There was one video file in the archive; the one of Lake and Chukwuma," Petrovic said. "We can delete our copy, but whoever placed it in the archive can still post it or share it on physical media."

"Fuck," Rex said.

"Yeah," Petrovic agreed.

"Could it be a fake?" Rex said.

"I showed it to Lake," Petrovic told him. "He admitted the affair. He knows he screwed up. I believe that he is genuinely sorry, but that doesn't change anything. The recording is genuine, and if it gets out that the captain knew about it and took no action, things could really get out of hand. If we were in combat, this could wait until later, but with no external enemy to focus on..."

"What if we *say* it's fake?" Rex said.

"Who could fake a video like that? Zell? Trey? The captain?" Petrovic said. "I don't think implying a conspiracy and casting suspicion on others will help. And the emotional impact of seeing the video can't be erased. They can't unsee it."

"Shit," Rex said.

"There's more," Trix said.

"Fuck me," Rex said. "How can this be any worse?"

"This recording was made in one of the second class cabins," Petrovic said. She was tempted to continue, but she paused to see if Rex would put the pieces together.

"So?" Rex said, and then the light came on. "There aren't any optical sensors in private quarters. Did Chukwuma and Lake record this themselves? They couldn't be that stupid."

Anja turned the video back on but with the sound muted. She scrubbed though the recording until the camera panned from the action on the bed to a corner of the room where Jailbait stood watching and caressing herself.

"Cat Girl?" Rex said. "Cat Girl took this video? She had a camera?"

"Two," Trix said. "One in each eye socket."

"So..." Rex said. "Nora? Nora pulled that video out of Cat Girl's memory? Why would she do that?"

"According to Bygul... Cat Girl... both female robots had been abused." Petrovic explained. "Nora would have known that. She was in charge of maintaining them, and she feels very protective of them. She's been having sex with David, and..."

"David," Rex said. "Who's David?"

"We have a male sex robot in addition to the female models," Trix said.

"Why?"

"He's a sex robot," Trix said.

"For who?"

"For our first-class passengers," Trix said.

"What, you mean for women passengers?"

"For our first-class passengers," the captain repeated. "And for our engine keeper. I allowed it. I was hoping to foster Nora's trust and good will."

"Why?" Rex asked.

"Never mind that," Trix said. "Petrovic, share your conclusions with Rex."

"Chukwuma is our most likely suspect. I think that he was abusing the sex dolls, and Nora tried to use the video of him and Lake to coerce him into stopping. Knowing that he could be exposed, I think he went to engineering to confront Nora. Things got heated. Mistakes were made."

"Why would he abuse the sex robots?" Rex asked.

"He hates AI," Petrovic said.

"Everybody hates AI," Rex said. "Everybody but the doctor."

"Spinners are supposed to hate the Powers, but a lot of people just say what's expected of them. For Chukwuma, it's a genuine passion. He doesn't just hate the Powers, he hates anything that talks that isn't a human. And," Petrovic added, "I kinda think he has a problem with women.

"He booked time with the dolls like everybody else, for the sake of appearances, apparently," Petrovic continued. "Maybe he tried to have sex with them and couldn't, or maybe just spending half a watch with one of them alone in his quarters was more than he could take."

"Nora should have come to me," Trix said.

"She was afraid of you," Rex said.

"Agreed," Petrovic said.

"She was more afraid of me than Chukwuma? He's a trained killer twice her size," Trix objected.

"I worship you, ma'am," Petrovic said, "but you can be pretty intense."

"So, that's it," Rex said. "Nora had the video. Chukwuma tried to kill her to keep her from exposing him. We can isolate him for the rest of the mission and turn him over to the Columbian military for trial when we get back to Galtz, and there's no danger of the other marines finding out about him and Lake. This is good news, isn't it?"

"I'm not so sure," Petrovic said. "Look, Sarge. I'm a grunt trained in small unit tactics. I'm not an investigator.

The detective characters in murder mysteries talk about suspects having means, motive and opportunity, and I think Chukwuma had all three. That makes him the best fit, but something doesn't feel right to me."

"What?" Rex said.

"Like, why tie up Jailbait? What does that accomplish? Did he do that after he assaulted Nora? Why hang around the scene of the crime to tie up a robot? And you saw those knots. That took a while," Petrovic said. "And if Chukwuma really meant to kill Nora in order to keep his secret, why isn't she dead? She was only struck once. Did he have a bout of remorse between the first and second blow?"

Petrovic paused to give Rex a moment to digest everything she'd said so far. She continued, "But the biggest unanswered question is, *Who put the video from Cat Girl's memory in the security archive?* Presumably, whoever did that also reformatted the archive. Did Nora do that? If so, why? If it wasn't Nora, then someone else has a copy of that video."

"Maybe Chukwuma erased the archive and then Nora put the video of him and Lake in the archive," Rex said. "Chukwuma found it there and then went to engineering in a rage."

"He got so angry that he forgot to delete the incriminating video?" Petrovic said. "I'm just not convinced that we have all the pieces to this puzzle."

"So, what do we do?" Rex said.

"Petrovic? Recommendations?" Trix said.

"I think you should release the video, punish Lake and Chukwuma for sodomy, and make no mention of the attack on engine keeper Lawson," Petrovic said.

"You really expect Trix to cut their ears off?" Rex said.

"What?" Trix said. "Cut off their ears? What are you talking about?"

"That's the immediate punishment for sodomy in the Columbian military," Rex said. "You mark a Sodomite by cutting off his right ear."

"You expect me to cut off Paul's ear?" Trix said.

"They'll need to be flogged too," Petrovic said. "Ten stripes each. I can do that part for you, Captain, but you'll need to be the one to remove their ears."

"For having sex?" Trix said. "That's insane!"

"Sodomy is a serious offense, Captain," Petrovic said. "Chukwuma will face prison time when we get back to Galtz. Trey can grow a new ear for Mr. Lake, but he shouldn't attach it until after the Columbian marines have returned to the Galtz militia."

"You discussed this with the doctor?" Trix demanded.

"No, ma'am," Petrovic said. "I haven't told him anything about this investigation, but we were talking in bed, and he told me that he could grow a new ear... for *you*, Captain."

2.11.2 - Cook

Cook woke up tired but happy. His fantasies about Jailbait had all involved gravity, but his zero-g playtime with her had been grand. Cook had cut her loose from her elaborate bindings, and the bot seemed to read his mind. Her *too young* persona was just one of many that she could adopt, but she knew what he wanted without being told.

She not only played the role he wanted her to play, but she led their roleplay to spanking right away. She confessed to silly misdemeanors which called for corporal punishment. When she cried, the tears just bunched up in floating globules around her eyes, so she dragged them down her face with her fingers to match the image from Cook's fantasies. With the spanking out of the way, she treated him to delights he hadn't thought to crave. He missed some much-needed sleep, but that's what the doctor's magic wake-up pills were for.

When he floated into the galley he discovered all of A shift as well as several members of B shift, for whom it was the middle of the night, clustered around the wall-sized galley display. A shriveled corpse on an examination table filled the display.

"What the hell is this?" he said.

"Oh, Cook!"

He turned at the sound of Paige's voice.

"Hey, killer," he said, smiling. "Got bored milking your little boo boo for time off? Ready to get back to work?"

"Deckhand Farmer has not been cleared for physical labor," said someone it took Cook a moment to identify. It was Cat Girl. Cook didn't recognize her right away because she was dressed in coveralls. Her black hair was tied back in a ponytail, and she wore a cadet cap to cover her distinctive cat-like ears which sat too high on her head.

Cat Girl was about the same size as Paige, and Cook realized that she must be wearing Paige's clothes in an attempt to blend in. The captain said she didn't want to see the sex robots in the galley. Cook didn't think that just changing the sex doll's costume would satisfy the captain's prohibition, but he wasn't about to make a stink.

"Who's your friend?"

"Cook, this is Bygul," Paige said. "Bygul, this is my friend, Cook."

"Pleased to meet you, sir," Bygul said in a voice that was equal parts sultry and respectful.

"Bygul," Paige said. "Cook's name is Michael. *Cook* is his job title, and he's one of the most important people on the ship, so you really can call him *Cook*."

"I'm very pleased to meet you, Cook," Bygul said.

"Cook," Paige said, pointing at the wall display. "Look, that must be a Floater."

Cook turned and looked at the display. He saw a view of two shriveled corpses lying side by side on examination tables. One was much taller than the other, and at first he thought the smaller body must be that of a child, but then he noticed that the larger body barely fit on the table, even though it was curled in on itself. If it had been laid out flat, the head and feet would have extended off the ends of the examination table. It must have been three meters tall.

Both bodies were shriveled, their brown skin stretched tight over their skeletal frames, and each had a gaping hole in its torso.

"Bejaysus," Cook said. "What is this?"

"The doctor found pits filled with corpses in the Temple. They must have been sacrificed to Re-Mot," Page said.

Cook had not had time to study his copy of Sparks' book. "Who?"

"Re-Mot is a composite entity, Cook," Bygul said. "A fusion of Resheph, god of fire and pestilence, and Mot, god of death and sterility."

"The loop is starting over," Paige said, "Look, there's the charnel pit."

The display showed a scene inside the Temple at the base of the ziggurat. It was lit by the helmet light of whomever's view this was, presumably the doctor's. Static and jarring discontinuities marred the video quality.

"The Doctor's vac suit is more advanced than the ones the marine's brought with them. It has better shielding, but the magnetic field from the ziggurat was almost too much even for his suit," Paige told Cook.

Cook stood captivated by the grizzly imagery of intertwined corpses, arms, legs, and the occasional head sticking out of the mummified mass. The faces bore a haunted expression, though Cook didn't know if it conveyed the emotional state of these poor wretches at the moment of death or whether the shrinking and tightening of their desiccated skin pulled their faces into a mask of false awe after death. He shuddered.

The image shifted, and now the Doctor was in frame. His vac suit was slimmer than any Cook had ever seen. It allowed him an impressive range of motion, and unlike the *Persephone's* EVA suits, which were white, or those of the

Columbian marines, which were shades of light and dark gray in an abstract pattern that the marines called *camo*, the doctor's vac suit was bright red.

Show off, Cook thought as he watched the video of Trey working one of the taller corpses into a large zippered bag.

"Isn't it exciting?" Paige said.

"Morbid is more like it," Cook said. "Not what I'd want to watch over breakfast. Speaking of which, breakfast ain't gonna make itself."

2.11.3 - Trey

Supposedly it was the captain's idea, but the instructions came to me through Petrovic.

I was supposed to be on C shift, which meant that I was scheduled to be asleep when most of the crew was awake, but like the captain and Joachim Zell, I never established a regular sleep pattern.

After starting a polymerase amplification process on the genetic samples I collected from both corpses, I realized that it was the middle of my scheduled sleep period. The polymerase chain reaction would take at least a couple of hours to produce a useful quantity of reconstructed DNA, so I went to my quarters, stripped off my clothes, took a cursory shower, and slipped under the covers of my bed, which were attached to the bed to prevent me from floating around the compartment.

I popped a sleep tablet in my mouth and bit down on it. They were meant to be swallowed whole, but they metabolized more quickly when chewed. The quicker onset of sleep was worth enduring the harsh, bitter taste of the pill. I washed it down with a swallow of water from a squeeze bottle and was asleep in less than a minute.

I woke to the delightful sensation of a warm, naked body against mine. Even before I opened my eyes, I recognized Petrovic. Before space travel became a regular part of the human experience, people romanticized the imagined experience of sex in microgravity. Believe me, heterosexual intercourse works better with gravity, but with the aid of the covers to hold us in place, both of us managed to achieve orgasm. After my release, I started to drift back to sleep.

"Sorry, Boss. Nap time's over," Petrovic said. "Captain has an assignment for you."

We chose Zell's workspace over medical for our first *interview*. We were both to prepare daily reports of our findings aimed at a non-specialist audience. We would submit our data to the DAO, but were also supposed to interview one another and produce a daily recording of about half a watch which I converted to an hour and fifteen minutes because I still didn't have an intuitive grasp of the Kuiper Belt time-keeping. This staged conversation would play on a loop in the galley until we produced a new *episode* the next day.

We positioned ourselves on either side of a large wall display in Zell's workspace and secured our feet to the deck to maintain our positions relative to one another. There were three small drones taking video. One drone camera was trained on each of our heads and one captured a *master shot* of the two of us and the large display.

Zell and I both agreed that the crew would be most curious about the recovered corpses and that we should start with that. Petrovic vetoed this idea and told us to tease the *juicy stuff* up front but to save the details until the end to keep people watching.

I started the conversation with a brief description of my EVA into the Temple. I pointed out where I recovered the bodies, but then I asked Zell what he'd learned about the Temple. He detailed its dimensions, layout, and magnetic field. After Zell answered my fourth question, Petrovic broke in.

She fed two images to the display. One was an illustration from *Void Huntress*. It showed a priest atop the ziggurat. The point of view was from above and behind the priest. Two muscular men held a sacrificial victim face up and spread eagled before the priest who held a dagger above his head in both hands as if ready to plunge the dagger into the victim's chest. In the far background a sea of simplified figures represented a mass of observers on the main floor of the Temple.

Juxtaposed on the display was an image of the model that Zell had constructed of the Temple with the *camera* positioned to match the view in the illustration. Petrovic asked Zell to compare the illustration to the computer model.

Zell pointed out that the dimensions and spatial relationships in the illustration were not even close to being accurate. The artist had focused on creating a dramatic image that set a mood and told a story. To this end, he'd made the ziggurat far taller and steeper than the real one.

"That long dead artist never saw the actual temple. They were surely working from a written description from a writer who had also not seen the real temple," Zell explained.

"Doctor," Petrovic said, off-camera. "If you were going to cut out a man's heart with a dagger, would you start by holding it above your head like that?"

"Well, maybe for dramatic effect," I said. "But plunging the dagger straight down into the victim's chest would be difficult. The heart and lungs are surrounded by a protective cage of bone in the form of the ribs and sternum. To extract the heart, you'd have to go through the rib cage or under it. Going through it would likely require the use of an axe to cut through the sternum, or poles to pry the ribs apart."

"What about the bodies you recovered from the Temple?" Petrovic said.

"In this instance, whoever conducted the sacrifice performed a subdiaphragmatic thoracotomy," I said. Petrovic scowled, and I immediately followed up with, "They made an opening below the ribs and reached up and in to pull out the heart. The opening was big enough to reach in with two hands and a knife to sever the aorta and pulmonary artery."

These gory details got a big thumbs up from Petrovic. She then pointed at Zell, indicating that he should lead the questioning from here.

"So, what can you tell us about these bodies, doctor? Are they human or alien?" Zell asked.

"Well, in a way they are both," I said. "They're definitely human, but they're not *Homo sapiens sapiens* like us. They're either a species of human that went extinct on Earth over a hundred thousand years ago, or they evolved from an extinct species of human."

"How do you know that?" Zell asked. "Have you sequenced their genome?"

"Genetic profiling is very difficult in this case. As you know, ionizing radiation is destructive to DNA. These specimens have been somewhat protected from cosmic radiation by the strong magnetic field generated by something inside the ziggurat, but magnetic fields are also destructive to DNA. There are techniques I can use to reconstruct the genome, but they'll take time."

"How do you know they're not humans like us?"

"I can tell just by looking at the shape of the head," I said and put up a model of the shorter specimen's skull. "See this ridge on the top of the skull? That's called a sagittal keel. Very few modern humans still have this feature, but it was common in earlier species of humans. Given the combination of heavy brow ridges, large teeth and a thick jaw, I think the bodies we recovered are both examples of *Homo erectus*."

"And you say they've been extinct on Earth for over a hundred thousand years?" Zell said.

"Yes," I said. "Something like a hundred and fifty thousand years, as I recall. Earth years, I mean. That would be something like fifty thousand years on the Blackout Calendar." "Still," Zell said. "A very long time."

"There isn't any information about extinct forms of

humans in the *Persephone's* medical database, so I'm working from memory here."

"So, are these bodies fifty thousand years old?" Zell said.

"Not a chance," I said. "You're helping me prepare samples for radiocarbon dating. That's going to take even longer than sequencing the genomes, but even without those test results, I can tell you these bodies can't be more than a few decades old."

"So a species of human that went extinct on Earth before the birth of human civilization is still alive out here in the Kuiper Belt?" Zell said.

"Well, we don't know that the Temple or its contents originated in the Kuiper Belt," I said. "And we don't have any live specimens, so it's possible that they have gone extinct, but if so, it happened very recently. Maybe even within our lifetimes."

"What about the taller specimen? Is that also a *Homo erectus*?"

"I may have to change my mind when the DNA evidence comes in, but I think so. I think what we're seeing is one specimen that was born and grew up in something like a 1g environment and one from a very low-g environment," I said.

"Low-g? Not zero-g?" Zell asked.

"Okay, I have to stress that this is an extremely tentative hypothesis, but I examined the taller subject's feet and ankles," I said. "And I'm pretty sure he could walk. He has pads on the bottom of his feet, and his Achilles tendon doesn't show the sort of shortening I would expect from a human who developed in microgravity."

"Where do you think he came from?" Zell asked.

"I really couldn't say. I'd guess that he grew up in an environment with gravity in the range of point one five g. That could be on a habitat with a very slow spin, or he might have grown up on a dwarf planet with something like the mass of Ganymede."

"So," Zell said, "He's not a Floater."

"I've never seen a Floater," I said. "But I understand that you have."

"Yes. I've seen a few of them over the years," Zell said.

"Did they look anything like this?" I put an image up on the display. It was a rendering of what the taller subject might have looked like based on my examination of the shriveled corpse. He had dark brown skin, heavy brows, a sloping forehead with a visible ridge down the middle of his scalp and a wide nose.

Both of the specimens I'd recovered from the Temple had had their heads shaved before they died, but I gave my model a crew cut like most of the male marines onboard the *Persephone* wore.

"The ones I interacted with had pale skin," Zell said, "But otherwise, yes. That's about what they looked like. So you're saying that the Floaters evolved from an extinct form of humanity and that they've been out here in the KB for more than fifty thousand years?"

"Tentatively, yes," I said.

VANGUARD

2.12.1 - Petrovic

Petrovic thought the interview went well. The captain anticipated that Trey's contribution would need some spicing up. Petrovic advised him to include references to *Void Huntress*; advice she expected he would fail to follow. She prepared her presentation slide comparing the illustration from the book to an accurate model of the same view from the top of the ziggurat in advance and kept it at the ready for when she thought that viewers would lose interest in Trey's dry presentation.

Petrovic sent the video clips to the captain for final assembly and approval. Then it was time to put on her new suit. She met Zell in the larger cargo hold where he explained the low-tech EVA system to her.

"Okay," Zell said. "The gloves are heated to maximize dexterity, but the rest of the suit is designed to get uncomfortably cold before you run low on O2. We'll have a line attached to you, and we'll reel you back in if you seem to be in trouble or if you've been out there long enough for your oxygen to be running low.

"Your helmet will be filled with an oxygen rich mix. Inhale through your nose and exhale through the respirator in your mouth to prevent CO_2 build-up. A one-way valve will keep you from inhaling through your mouth, so it's not anything you'll have to remember to do. Inhaling through your nose will be your only option unless you spit out your respirator. Try not to do that.

"Go ahead and get suited up, and I'll show you how the attitude and propulsion system works. The base layer is the same as any standard suit. It just won't have any active data connections to the outer shell. In terms of moving your body, there's no assist of any kind. It's all up to your own muscles," Zell explained. "You can change into the base layer behind those... Oh, right," Zell said when Petrovic unfastened her shirt and pulled it off. She wasn't going to pass up an opportunity to get naked in front of other people.

Once her clothes were off, she took her time folding and rolling them into a compact bundle which she secured with her gun belt. She looked around to make sure that Drake Antal, the cargo specialist, and Arni Hansson, who would be driving the Stout, were watching her. They were.

"There's no toilet functionality. You should go now if you need to," Zell said.

"I'm good," Petrovic said as she pulled on the base layer and adjusted it for comfort and mobility. As Zell helped her into the actual EVA suit, Petrovic thought about the first underwater diving rigs. The diver wore an enormous helmet that was connected to the surface by an air hose.

This suit was sophisticated in its design, but in terms of functionality, it was the most primitive thing she could imagine having between her and the vacuum. She tried moving her arms and legs and discovered she was nearly locked into a neutral standing pose but with arms bent at a 90 degree angle at the elbows. She had extremely restricted mobility when it came to pronating and supinating her hands and forearms.

"Squeeze your hands closed slowly," Zell said. She did, and the thumb, index finger and middle finger on each hand came together easily. Her ring fingers and little fingers met resistance.

"Good," Zell said. "That's the right amount of strength

you'll use to grasp objects. "Now, squeeze harder with your ring and pinky finger."

She followed his instructions, and she heard a hiss of gas escaping from canisters that ran parallel to her forearms.

"The harder you squeeze, the stronger the thrust, but these are mostly for attitude control. We'll push you in the direction of the top of the pyramid, and we'll reel you in when you've secured the objects in the box. Bring the whole box if you can pull it off its pedestal. You have a net bag attached to the front of your suit if you need to take items out of the box.

"The box itself seems to be secured with just a clasp. As far as we can tell from a distance, it isn't locked," Zell told her.

Zell locked his shoes to the deck and gave Petrovic a gentle shove toward the center of the cargo bay.

"Practice attitude control," he said. "Go ahead and use up all the propellant. We'll replace the canisters before you head out."

Petrovic spent the next ten minutes learning how to position her arms to rotate along every axis and to propel herself forward, up and down. There was no way to propel herself backwards other than to push off from a solid surface with the strength of her arms.

The suit was not designed for walking. Her lower body was just along for the ride.

"Ready?" Zell said, and when she nodded, he put the regulator in her mouth, attached the helmet and double checked the seals. He replaced the propellant canisters on her forearms and walked her to the back of the Stout. It had a pressurized cabin that could hold three suited passengers. This space was accessible via an airlock at the back of the vehicle. The driver sat in a separate pressurized module at the front of the vehicle.

Antal was wearing a normal EVA suit, and he pressed his helmet against Petrovic's and said, "We'll ride in the airlock on the way out. We can ride in the central compartment on the way back if you're cold."

Petrovic couldn't speak with the regulator in her mouth, but she gave Antal the thumbs up signal. Zell left the cargo bay and sealed the hatch. Antal helped Petrovic get into the airlock and climbed in himself. Warning lights in the cargo bay flashed, and the Stout started to move.

They left the airlock open and watched the *Persephone* grow smaller as they moved toward the great doorway. Then they saw a sweeping panorama of the inside of the Great Hall as the Stout rotated 180 degrees so that the back of the vehicle became the front.

Antal attached a cable to Petrovic's suit harness and tugged at the cable to make sure that it would unspool freely and not impede her continued motion toward the top of the ziggurat once the Stout slowed and then came to a stop.

Antal patted her shoulder from behind, and again, she communicated her readiness with a thumbs up.

Anat stood naked upon the cliff top with just a mesh bag slung diagonally across her body. She raised her arms in wide arcs raising up onto the balls of her feet. She paused there for just an instant, feeling the sun's warmth on her skin, fortifying her for the plunge into the frigid depths.

She filled her lungs and leapt. For a glorious instant, she moved horizontally out from the cliff, and then she angled down, arms extended to break the surface of the water. Her powerful body pierced the surface, passing through the barrier between the realm of warmth and light into the borderlands of Yam's void with barely a splash.

The momentum of her dive carried her through the warm, well-lit water near the surface, and by the time she needed to use her arms and legs to swim deeper, the cold twilight closed in around her. Soon it was too dark for mortal eyes, but the light of El illuminates even the deepest voids for those with the divine sight.

The great black pyramid materialized out of the gloom. She reached its top and felt the repulsive corruption emanating from the sacrificial altar. The life giving air in her lungs grew stale, and the cold of the depths leached the living warmth from her skin.

She turned around, looking for the strong box containing the unholy artifacts Ba'al had sent her into Yam's realm to capture. She fumbled in the gloom and found the box with her hands. Darkness emanated from the box so that even her divine sight failed her.

She unclasped the lid and lifted. The light defeated, now the chill of the void sapped the sensation from her fingers, turning her hands into clumsy flippers. She pawed at the contents of the box and managed to stuff them into her bag. She tried to propel herself toward the surface, but her feet could not find a purchase from which to launch.

The darkness and cold sucked the last of the warmth from her living core. They pulled at her, trying to drag her deeper into the depths with what felt like deliberate malice. She thrashed in defiance, but she was no match for the void. It rendered her feeble and feckless. She sank face first into Yam's void!

"Petrovic," a distant voice said. "Petrovic, can you hear me? Come on. Wake up."

She felt a warm hand on the side of her face, and her eyes fluttered open. A phantasmagoria of meaningless shapes and textures resolved themselves into the pressurized compartment inside the Stout. Drake Antal withdrew his hand from her face.

"Petrovic!" he said, relieved.

"What happened?" she said.

"I don't know. You were just floating there on top of the pyramid. I waited for you to signal me to pull you back, but you just floated there. I waited until Zell told me to pull you back. You weren't moving, and I didn't know until I got you inside and took your helmet off if you were even alive, but you did it. There are objects in your bag. A big book, and a knife, I think."

2.12.2 - Cook

Paige had Cook's permission to cross the sacred line between the dining area and the food prep area. Trix didn't need permission. She held the authority to enter any part of the ship.

Still, she took Cook by surprise when he floated into his familiar space and saw her standing near the door to the walk-in freezer. That location was around a corner and out of sight from the public side of the sacred dividing line. Cook floated over, and Trix said, "Cook, let's talk about the frozen inventory."

"Sure, Skipper," Cook said. "After you."

Inside the freezer, Cook locked himself to the deck like the captain did. "I take it this isn't really about how I stock the shelves."

"No," she admitted. "What's the scuttlebutt?"

"Rumor report, eh? Are you interested in the paranoid stuff about the Powers being in cahoots with the space gods?" Cook said.

"Not particularly," Trix said. "Anything about Lake?"

Cook sharpened his focus. "I thought he was keeping a low profile, but now that you mention it…"

Cook paused to recall the black marine's name. "He's messing around with Chukwuma, isn't he?"

"Who knows?" Trix said.

"I didn't know until just a second ago, but I'm sure Petrovic would have picked up on it," he said. "And her little helper, probably."

"You haven't heard anything from any of the Columbians?"

"Shit, Skipper. You don't have to tell me what an ugly mess that would be," Cook said. "It'd be more riot than rumor."

"Maybe," Trix said. "Anyway, keep an ear out for anything along those lines, and let me know right away if you hear anything. What else?"

"Hmmm…" Cook searched his memory.

"I mostly hear 'em going on about the chaos gods and all that business," Cook said. "This bunch is here to fight, and they don't know what to do with themselves without an enemy. There's talk of Yam looking to knock Ba'al off his perch, but nothing that has anything to do with real stuff, as far as I can see."

"Have you had any more unusual experiences?" Trix said.

"Yeah, Skipper. Weird shit, and not in a good way," Cook said, and shivered. "I'll be glad to be away from this thing. Any idea when that'll be?"

"Too early to tell," she said. "Keep me posted on any new rumors."

"Will do, Skipper," he said.

"You know," she said. "You can call me *Trix*. You're grandfathered in. You're family."

"*Skipper* works for me, Skipper."

Trix gave him a soft punch in the arm and walked out of the freezer.

2.12.3 - Rex

"I was Anat," Petrovic said.

"You should be in medical," Rex said.

"I'm fine," Petrovic said. "Captain, I was Anat. I raided Mot's place of power and took his treasures. I did it for you, Captain. Even as a goddess, I live to serve you. You are Shapash. You are the light and the warmth."

"Trix," Rex said, hoping that by abandoning her formal title and saying her name that he could get her attention. "She blacked out and floated out there until she ran out of oxygen. She could have brain damage. Feel her skin. She could have hypothermia. She needs to go to medical."

Trix placed her left hand on Petrovic's cheek, and Petrovic raised her right hand to cover it. "He's right," Trix said. "You're ice cold. Go to medical and let the doctor have a look at you."

"You are all the warmth I need, radiant Shapash," Petrovic insisted.

"I said go," Trix said in an even tone. "Obey me."

Petrovic kissed the palm of Trix's hand and bowed her head. "Yes, ma'am," she said and left the captain's office. Rex secured the hatch after she was gone.

"You shouldn't indulge her fantasies," Rex said.

"I don't," Trix said.

"She worships you," Rex said. "It's not normal. It's not healthy."

"She is a capable marine and her primary allegiance is to me," Trix said. "I don't see that as a problem. And even if she's gone a touch manic, setting her straight is not a priority right now."

Rex had no response to this. At least she was right about that last part.

"Why are we still here? We've got the knife and the book. Those were our orders. Why aren't we headed back to Galtz right this minute? Why are we still floating in this fucking..." he gestured around them, "this thing?"

"The order to retrieve the book and knife never came," Trix said.

"What? You showed it to me. I read it," Rex said.

"I showed you the ballot proposal. I voted yes, but apparently the Whales haven't voted yet," she said. "We completed an order that I anticipated based on inside information but which hasn't actually been issued."

"What was our last actual order?"

"To enter the Temple," she said.

"Well, mission fucking accomplished," Rex said. "How long are we supposed to sit here?"

"Until we receive new orders," Trix said.

"Trix," Rex said. "We've got a high-level, combat-oriented crew and no enemy for them to fight. The longer we sit here and let them stew in their paranoid fantasies the more we risk this whole situation going to shit."

"You think the visions are fantasies?"

"What else could they be?" Rex said.

"How many visions have you had?" Trix asked.

"Two, while I was awake. I don't know how many more in dreams."

"And who are you?"

"What do you mean?" Rex said.

"Do you identify with a character from Lake's book the way Petrovic identifies with Anat?" Trix said. "Who are you in your visions?"

"I'm nobody. I'm a man who gets caught between the two sides and killed," Rex said.

"Did Anat kill you in a battle?"

"I think so," Rex said. "It was either her or the other one."

"The other one?"

"There are two goddesses in the book that are almost the same," Rex said. "They're both goddesses of love and war. They're both passionate and cruel. I think they're sisters or something."

"Anat and Ashtarte," Trix said. "Yes, they are a lot alike. I saw Anat split a man's head with an axe in battle. She killed dozens of men, but one of them stood out as significant to me. She buried an axe in his shoulder, knocking him to the ground. She put her foot on his chest to pull it free, and then she brought it down on his head. I can see from your expression that you were the man."

Rex said nothing.

"Rex, I don't like seeing you cast in the role of collateral damage," Trix said. She took a step toward him. "Yam hasn't chosen a host yet. He tried to take possession of the doctor, but Trey is resistant to these things. I'd like to see Yam take you as his vessel."

"*Vessel*?" Rex said. "Trix, you're starting to talk like Sparks and Kellemen. Please don't buy into their crazy obsessions."

"Rex," she said, taking another step toward him and

reaching out to take a hold on the waistband of his pants. She pulled him to her.

"I'm responding to the situation as it presents itself," she said. "I'm not saying I believe in gods and demons, but look where we are. I can't tune out everything that's happening. In the Ba'al cycle, Yam challenges Ba'al's authority and tries to usurp the throne. He fails, but he doesn't die. I don't want you to die, Rex."

"Then let's just get out of here," he said. "Plot a course for Galtz and go."

"Rex," she said, "I want to provide for this crew, our family. That means maintaining this situation with the DAO. We've never been so well provisioned. What happens if I don't follow orders and the DAO fires me and finds a new captain?"

"I thought you wanted them to find a new Captain," Rex said.

"I did," she said. "But that was cowardice. I wanted to stay small. I wanted to keep playing Fixit Trix. But I'm ready to be more, thanks to you."

Rex touched the right side of her face, the damaged side, with his left palm.

"I can't find redemption in humiliation," she said. "Do you know why I'm just the acting-Captain?"

"Because they offered you the captain's job," Rex said, "and you turned it down."

"That's basically right," she said. "They offered me the job at three shares."

"That's standard," Rex said.

"I countered. I asked for 3.5. The DAO put my counteroffer to a vote," she said.

"How did you vote?" Rex asked.

"I voted to reject the counteroffer," she said. "I was bent on self-sabotage, but the Whales approved it."

"You didn't accept 3.5 shares?" Rex said.

"I countered again. I asked for four."

"Four shares? No first-time Captain gets four shares." Rex

said. "So they rejected your offer and made you acting-captain for this first mission while they looked for other candidates."

"No," she said. "The Whales voted to accept my offer."

"At four shares? What did you do?" Rex asked.

"Nothing," she said. "I didn't reject the offer. I didn't make a new counteroffer. There was no deadline for acceptance, so I did nothing. I could accept it right now and get four shares for this mission."

"Do it," Rex said. "Okay, I will," she said and kissed him. He kissed her back, and she ran her hand down his torso. He was wearing an armored chest plate, so the action brought them no pleasure, but she kept moving her hand down until it reached his crotch. She massaged him urgently, but he was soft.

"It's the gravity," Rex said. "This happens when I've been in zero-g for too long. Accept that promotion, and when we're back on Galtz we'll spend a month in a first-class suite."

With her robotic right arm she reached over to her desk and pulled a slate free from its magnetic hold on the surface. She passed it behind Rex's head and held it over his right shoulder where she pressed her left thumb onto the reader, read the acceptance text, and hit send.

"What's your first order as Captain?" he asked.

"Kiss me."

2.12.4 - Paige

Paige and Bygul visited Anja in the recovery room where she was swaddled in warming garments that held a network of synthetic capillaries circulating warm liquid against her skin.

"Little tiger," Anja said upon seeing Paige. The nickname was familiar, but it resonated with a feminine warmth that Paige wasn't used to hearing in Anja's voice.

"Anja," Paige said. "You're still Anja, aren't you?"

"Anja is here. I will never fully displace her. She is a worthy vessel, in body and spirit. I can inhabit her without suppressing her. I feel her love for you," Anja said.

"Anat," Paige said.

"Yes," Anja said. "Ashtarte and I are the first to establish ourselves in these new vessels, but the others will come soon. And you. You would be the priestess of Shapash?"

"I want that," Paige said. "More than anything," Paige said.

"The goddess constellates in the captain," Anja said.

"She is my light," Paige said.

"If you would be her priestess, you must prepare your body."

"I've started," Paige said.

"Show me," Anja said.

"Help me," Paige said to Bygul, and the feline robot floated close to Paige and helped the young woman to raise her arms above her head and pull her shirt over her torso, head and arms.

With the shirt off, Anja nodded in satisfaction at the network of designs that adorned Paige's arms, shoulders and upper chest.

"The hierodule drew these for you?" Anja said. She looked at Bygul. "You did this?"

"Yes, ma'am," Bygul said.

Bygul turned Paige's body so that Anja could inspect the designs on Paige's upper and lower back. The compression bandage around Paige's torso prevented the completion of the designs.

"This is a promising start," Anja said. "When your injuries have healed, you must complete the design and make it permanent. The patterns must be raised. You can burn them into your skin, or carve them and then pack the cuts with ash or mud. Enduring the pain will serve as a testament to your devotion. You are in pain now, I see."

"Yes," Paige said. "The doctor lowered the dose of my

medications, but I'm not taking them at all, anymore. I can feel Shapash's light better without them. I worship her with my pain."

"You serve her well, little tiger. You will be a fit priestess for her, but you must gain weight. The priestess of Shapash must be voluptuous," Anja said.

"I eat all the time," Paige said. "Tell her, Bygul."

The robot nodded her head. "It's true, ma'am. I monitor her caloric intake. Lady Paige is following her prescribed diet."

"And the breasts?"

"The doctor has been too busy to design my RNA therapy," Paige said. "He told me to just keep putting on fat and muscle. He said *cosmetics* could wait." Paige pouted.

"He is correct," Anja said. "Build up your body, but your breasts must be full before they can be marked or the designs will be distorted. Your body will be a monument to Shapash. It must be perfect in proportion and ornamentation."

"I want that more than anything," Paige said.

"I know you do, little tiger."

2.12.5 - Trey

Zell and I met in the situation room to record the second day's infotainment package. We had to do it without any real-time guidance from Petrovic. Her behavior indicated some sort of brain damage, either from hypothermia or oxygen deprivation, but the actual tissue damage must have been subtle. I didn't find any evidence of it in her brain scans.

What's more, the change to her behavior suited her. Or maybe it would be more honest to say that it suited me. She seemed more settled. More feminine. I'd had enough of microgravity sex, but once we had gravity again, I was looking forward to seeing how her altered personality manifested itself in bed.

The voice of some mostly-forgotten med school ethicist

chided me for that thought, but if that voice was the angel on my right shoulder, the devil appeared over my left shoulder in the form of the old Anja Petrovic.

Ignore that prude, devil Petrovic told me. *The new me is going to be a wild fuck. Enjoy her!*

"Does that smile on your face mean that the DNA test results indicate an alien origin?" Zell asked me.

"Unfortunately, no," I said, snapping back to the task at hand. "They're definitely human. And as I speculated yesterday, the tests confirm that both the tall one and the one proportioned like us are from different populations of the same species. They could breed and produce fertile offspring."

"The two you brought back couldn't breed with each other," Zell said.

"No," I said, laughing. "They're both male, so that would take a miracle."

"Speaking of miracles," Zell said. "I've got a theory that could account for the visions most of the crew has experienced that doesn't involve any sort of supernatural agency."

I knew what he was going to say. We had mapped out this conversation before we started recording, but I played my part and asked, "What do you mean, Joachim?"

Zell activated the presentation display, and a fractal pattern of branching and terminating lines appeared.

"You said you thought this pattern looked like neurons," Zell said.

"That's right," I said.

"And given the sheer size of the temple," Zell said. "Could it match the number of synaptic connections in the human brain?"

"There could be 3D volumes of fullerene pathways inside the ziggurat that are as complex as the human brain. Possibly many times more complex."

"So, the Temple could form a computational substrate that

supports a massive artificial mind," Zell said.

"Or several," I agreed.

The devil Petrovic whispered in my ear that marines don't know shit about *computational substrates*.

"The temple could act like a giant brain. It could host a vast intelligence or even several," I said.

"And the Temple generates a powerful magnetic field. So powerful that it disrupts communications and even electronic devices if you get too close to the ziggurat," Zell said. "Isn't it true that exposure to magnetic fields can produce all sorts of strange experiences? Encounters with ghosts or aliens, things like that?"

"I can tell you from personal experience that magnetic fields applied to the human brain can produce bizarre experiences. This is something we've known since before the first Mars colony was established, when all humans lived on Earth. The technique was called transcranial magnetic stimulation or TMS for short.

"TMS could produce hallucinations, out-of-body experiences and encounters with ghosts, demons or even aliens. It was crude. Researchers couldn't induce specific experiences, but those altered states of consciousness felt quite real."

"And I'm sure the Powers learned to control the experiences more precisely," Zell said.

"You bet," I said. "They learned to create very specific experiences."

"Like what?" Zell said.

"Sex, of course," I said. I knew that Petrovic would approve of that when she watched the final product. "But you could experience anything at all in those altered states of consciousness. You could become a different person, or it might feel like you shared your body with another consciousness. You might call it an induced demonic possession," I said.

"So it's possible that an artificial intelligence inside the

Temple could be using magnetic fields to stimulate our brains and create very detailed and specific hallucinations," Zell said. That was the punchline we'd been working toward.

"Yes. It's like a fully immersive simulation, but instead of a headset and haptic suit, it uses our own brains to create the sensations and the seeming interaction with gods and demons," I said.

"Which means that these experiences are not real," Zell said.

"They are as real as thoughts," I said.

"But not as real as a table or a rifle," Zell said.

"No," I said, choking back my objections to such a gross ontology, "these experiences aren't real like a table or a rifle is real."

"Which means they can't hurt us," Zell said.

"Not as long as we don't hurt ourselves or each other."

JUDGMENT

2.13.1 - Rex

Rex Perkins was surprised to see Esmeralda Escamilla in the galley. She was on B shift, but he hadn't seen her at B shift's breakfast since the three shift rotation went into effect. He assumed that she was taking her meals in medical.

The galley was as full as Rex had seen it in a while. He wasn't sure if the daily briefings with Zell and the doctor had been Trix's idea or Petrovic's, but they did give the crew an excuse to gather together for the daily premier.

Rex felt sorry for Cook, who had to listen to Zell and Trey drone on all day as the briefing played on a continuous loop in the galley. Stuck listening to self-important, know-it-all Zell, enjoying the sound of his own smug voice all day was Rex's idea of cruel and unusual punishment.

Rex, strapped into a seat at one of the long galley tables, pressed his open copy of *Void Huntress* against the table top. If he were reading the contents on a slate, he wouldn't have to hold the slate in place the way he was doing with the book. The slate would adhere to the metal table top until he pulled it free. Reading from a printed book was one of the impractical things that rich people did to set themselves apart for everyone else. He remembered how Sparks didn't want to say how much he'd paid for his copy of the book.

The book was open to a full page illustration on the right and a description of Yam on the left. In the illustration, Yam, a muscular, shirtless man with a long beard, filled the lower right quadrant of the image. He pointed an accusing finger at two distant figures pictured in the upper right, a man and a woman. The woman glowed like the sun and sent beams of light into the darkness. The man by her side looked similar to Yam. He was shirtless to display his muscular build, and he had long flowing hair and a matching beard.

Unlike Yam, the man next to the radiant woman wore a crown, and he was surrounded by the faint background details indicating a lavish throne room.

A writhing serpent was coiled around Yam's body, its head following the direction of Yam's pointing finger.

Rex glanced at the text, but it didn't resolve into words for him. He didn't need the text. He knew who these figures were. He knew the dynamics between them.

The pointing man was Yam, and he was righteously angry that the other man occupied the place closest to the woman of light. Ba'al, the unworthy, held the exalted position that should be Yam's. Ba'als order was unnecessary. He imposed it merely to glorify himself. The serpent, Tannin, a demon of chaos, would devour the light and set the stage for Yam's elevation. Yam would depose Ba'al, and Trix would never say *Z-level* again.

Rex looked up from the book at the gathering of crew members watching the briefing. Nobody talked to one another. Every person present hung on Zell's every word.

"And the Temple generates a powerful magnetic field. So powerful that it disrupts communications and even electronic devices if you get too close to the ziggurat," Zell said with insufferable self-importance.

"Isn't it true that exposure to magnetic fields can produce all sorts of strange experiences?" Zell asked. "Encounters with ghosts or aliens, things like that?"

"They learned to create very specific experiences," the doctor siad.

"Like what?" Zell asked.

"Sex, of course," Trey's recorded image replied, and then

the video cut to two men, one black and one white, naked. The black man had the tip of the white man's impossibly large penis between his lips. It was a moving image, but it only lasted a couple of seconds, and then the infotainment segment with Zell and Trey resumed.

Everyone in the galley was silent for a moment, and then the compartment exploded with commotion.

"What the fuck was that?"

"Rewind that!"

"Chukwuma!?!"

"Go back! How do you make it go back?"

"Cook!" Kellemen shouted. "Rewind the presentation!"

"What?" Cook said. He must not have been looking at the display when it was filled with images of perversion.

"The presentation!" Kellemen said. "Rewind the presentation!"

"It'll be on repeat all day," Cook said.

Escamilla, who had always pulled Rex's eye to her face and body, looked even more beautiful than usual. Moving with impossible grace and purpose, she floated toward the food service line.

"Cook, we need to see that last minute again."

"Why?"

"Just do it, Cook," Escamilla commanded, followed by a chorus of agreement from everyone else who had gathered to watch the recording briefing.

Almost everyone else.

Rex saw Jay Chukwuma moving slowly toward the exit. Escamilla turned and issued the command, "Hold him!"

Drake Antal and Saz Kellemen each grabbed one of Chukwuma's arms, but it's no simple matter to restrain a man in zero-gravity. Normally, someone resisting being held had to struggle not only against the muscular strength of his assailants but their weight as well. Antal and Kellemen could not plant their weight and use it to restrain Chukwuma. At the same time, Chukwuma could not plant his own weight and use it as a base of support from which to fling his would-be captors away from him.

The three men struggled in a writhing stalemate until Paul Lake slipped an arm around Chukwuma's neck from behind and squeezed. Lake's bicep and the muscles of his forearm cut off the flow of blood to Chukwuma's brain, and the black man's powerful body went limp within seconds.

Even after Chukwuma stopped struggling, Lake did not release the choke hold.

"That's enough!" Rex shouted, but Lake did not relent. The longer he held back the flow of oxygen to Chukwuma's brain, the greater the risk of lasting brain injury or even death. Rex felt a greater-than-human presence enter into him. It imbued him with irresistible authority.

"Release him," Yam commanded.

"Fucking pervert!" Lake said and pushed Chukwuma away from him.

"Bind him," Ashtarte said, speaking through Esmeralda's impossibly beautiful mouth.

Kellemen drew a knife from his boot. Antal saw the knife and said, "Yes. Take the sodomite's right ear so that he will never be welcome in the company of honorable men!"

Rex knew that those weren't Antal's words. He was quoting the handbook, or trying to.

"He must be awake when we mark him," Ashtarte said with a delighted smile.

"Skipper!" Cook shouted into the comm panel, "You need to get down here!"

"Yes! The captain must be the one to take his ear," Kellemen said.

2.13.2 - Paige

Paige looked down with satisfaction as Bygul swept the wand over Paige's body, drying her after their shared shower.

Paige could no longer see individual ribs pressing through the skin of her torso, and the flesh around her nipples rose with a plushness of promised breasts.

"I will re-draw the markings of your office after the assembly, Priestess," Bygul said and kissed Paige's belly. When Paige's torso was good and dry, Bygul replaced the compression bandage around Paige's ribcage.

"Goddess be praised!" Paige said as the pain from her healing ribs drove the breath from her lungs.

Paige, high Priestess of Shapash, allowed her devoted acolyte, Bygul, to dress her. When she was ready to depart, Bygul opened the hatch.

"You have to wait here, Bygul," Paige told her. "Captain's orders."

"Yes, Lady," Bygul said. "Please be careful."

"I will," Paige said and kissed Bygul on the mouth.

"Cat Girl love Lady," Bygul said.

"I love you too," Paige said, and propelled herself down the passageway.

Paige paused in the hatchway to the situation room. At first, all she could see was Shapash's light. The captain blazed with it, and Paige was tempted to lose herself in its brilliance and enveloping warmth, but she resisted the urge.

The rest of the room came into focus. Resheph, god of fire and pestilence, bound and lashed kneeling to the deck in the guise of Jay Chukwuma, awaited judgment at the captain's feet.

The figures seated at the semicircular table segregated themselves into three groups. The forces of Darkness and Chaos clustered at the end of the table to Paige's right. Yam had finally claimed his vessel. He sat at the end of the table in the form of Rex Perkins, flanked by his priest, Saz Kellemen.

Dwayne Sparks, handsome as ever, sat next to his friend, Kellemen. Tannin, the Chaos wyrm, snaked around the compartment on a continuous patrol, but every time he came near Sparks, the dragon passed through the comely young man, affirming their connection.

The seat next to Sparks was empty. Paige knew that Respheph would be sitting there were he not bound at the captain's feet.

Then came beautiful Ashtart, goddess of both war and sensual delectation. Paige had burned with jealousy when Esmeralda Escamilla would call Bygul away from Paige's bedside. Esmeralda was discreet, but Paige knew that she was using Bygul for sex, and Bygul, being first and foremost a sex robot, had no choice but to comply.

Now Paige had to fight back a wave of arousal at the thought of Ashtart taking her pleasure with Bygul. It took an effort of will to drag her gaze from lovely Ashtart to the cold sterility of Mot, god of death.

Mot had claimed Paul Lake as his vessel. A cord of darkness stretched across the compartment linking the kneeling Respheph to seated Mot. The two gods shared a single sigil on the exterior of the Temple, and Paige knew they would soon share the same human vessel.

The middle group consisted of unclaimed mortals. They were the fuel and fodder of the gods, but unclaimed, they were pallid apparitions to Paige. They had names, but she struggled to recall them.

She recognized one of them and pulled the name Drake Antal from the mists. She remembered stroking his thigh under the table at Last Supper.

Trey, a pilgrim from the inner realm, raised in the concentrated light of Shapash, the man who displayed his feminine side for all to see, sat next to Antal. His sexual association with Anat and Ashtart gave him substance that Drake Antal lacked.

Arni Hansson sat next to Trey. Boyish and blonde, Hansson was a non-entity to Paige; an animated prop in human form. Irrelevant.

An empty chair for Cook. Paige loved Cook, but her love would not save him.

Next came Shawn Li, the Objectivist and haughty atheist. To the extent that Paige could even imagine the man possessing a soul or consciousness, she knew that he must be in a state of turmoil and shock, his rigid worldview revealed as a pathetic farce. The gods were more real than men, and men like Li were beneath their notice.

An empty chair for the engine keeper, Nora Lawson, who remained unconscious in the ICU.

Then came the forces of Light and Order. Hans Dobrovitz, as much the non-entity as Arni Hansson until this moment, carried the essence of wise Kothar, the artificer.

Then came the glorious Anja Petrovic, human vessel of Anat, sister of Ashtart. Like her sister, Anat was the goddess of both war and love, but where Ashtart emphasized sensual delight, Anat was a force of destruction on the battlefield, a relentless huntress, and the embodiment of protective love. Her sexual appetites were as keen as her sister's but more primal.

The next chair held Lord Ba'al in the handsome guise of Joachim Zell. Zell was the embodiment of a well-ordered life before Ba'al claimed him. Now he radiated the order of the gods.

The last two chairs were empty. Paige knew that the seat of ultimate reverence at the end of the table was reserved for Shapash, the sun goddess. Shapash had chosen Captain Patricia Nixon as her most worthy vessel.

The position of penultimate rank, the empty chair next to Shapash's, was reserved for her priestess, Paige.

Radiant Shapash drew Paige to her with a gesture. She reached out her left hand and cradled Paige's head, drawing her close.

"You will have your chance to speak, my priestess," she whispered in Paige's ear. "But not at this conclave. Praise me with your silence."

With the gentlest of movements, Trix set Paige in motion toward her assigned seat. Paige caught the table and her body arced down to the chair where she strapped herself in.

For a moment, the presence of the gods intensified and the human vessels faded, then the gods, who cared nothing for this matter of sexual impropriety, receded and left their vessels to conduct this mundane affair.

As the presence of the gods receded, Paige noticed one other figure standing near the presentation display. It was David, the male sex robot. He wore pajama bottoms and a top that could be tied closed at the waist but which was left open to reveal his sculpted torso.

"Alright, you lot," The captain began. "As if I didn't already have enough to deal with. You want me to mutilate one of your own."

She drew a knife from a sheath on her belt. She drew it with her left hand, but as she spoke she shifted the knife back and forth between her human left hand and the hand-like collection of mechanical digits at the end of her right arm. Paige marveled at the dexterity of the captain's mechanical hand.

"I was hired for this job and given an ample budget with which to recruit a top notch crew. My instructions were to prepare for combat, so I spent a lot of money to hire fighting men and women from the Galtz Militia. You are all trained in the tradition of the Columbian military. Some of you are descendants of those revered families who transferred their flag from the dying Columbia habitat to Galt's Gulch after the Blackout."

Paige was used to hearing about the aftermath of the Blackout in terms of the Columbians invading Galt's Gulch and imposing military rule on a peaceful commercial culture. It sounded a lot cleaner to say that the Columbians *transferred their flag* to Galt's Gulch.

"I hired a combat-ready crew, but we have encountered no armed enemy. So, like a pack of starving dogs, you have turned on each other."

She looked around for anyone about to voice an objection.

Paige remembered that it was Jay Chukwuma who normally spoke out of turn, and he was keeping quiet at this assembly.

The captain snapped her gaze to Escamilla who had drawn a breath as if to object. "Let me guess," Trix said. "You don't think I'm being fair, blaming all of you for the actions of one man. Well, look at it from my perspective. I didn't assemble a collection of random mercenaries. I hired Columbian soldiers.

"You're supposed to be brave, strong, skilled and disciplined. I paid for group cohesion. Alright, Escamilla, spit it out."

"Sodomy corrupts military discipline. Group cohesion demands that it be addressed immediately and severely," Escamilla said. "Ma'am."

"That brings us to the question of Chukwuma's guilt. You think he's guilty because someone slipped a couple of seconds of video into an infotainment package that appears to show him having sex with this robot," Trix said, gesturing at David.

She directed their attention to the presentation display where the offending video appeared on a loop. With another gesture, she stopped on a still image. It showed Chukwuma with the head of the enormous phallus between his lips. A grumble rose from the assembled soldiers.

Trix, walking on the metal deck as if they had gravity, walked behind David and yanked his pajama bottoms down to his mid thighs, revealing a small and flaccid penis.

"David," the captain said, "Show everyone how big you can make that cock of yours."

David's penis fattened and then stood erect. In seconds, it grew to a size that no biological man onboard could match.

"Does anyone doubt that this is the cock in the video?" Trix said. Nobody answered.“

Alright, David. Put it away," Trix said. David's erection subsided as quickly as it had inflated, and he pulled up his pajama pants.

"David," Trix said. She gestured at Chukwuma who was bound in a kneeling position, his eyes downcast. "Did this man suck your cock?"

"I'm sorry, Captain," David said. "Privacy protocols prevent me from answering that question."

"Jay," Trix said, looking down at Chukwuma. "Did you have sex with this robot?"

"No, Captain," he said without looking up.

"Look at me." He did. "On your honor as a soldier and on the honor of the Chukwuma family name, did you perform same sex acts with this robot?"

"No, Captain," Chukwuma said in a strong voice, maintaining continuous eye contact with Trix. "I did not."

Trix addressed the entire assembly. "Jay says he didn't do it. David can't say one way or the other. The one person who knows how to get into David's systems and extract that information, our engine keeper, has been assaulted and is currently unconscious. So why do any of you think Jay is guilty of sodomy?

"It's because of this image that you want me to cut this man's ear off," Trix said, twirling the knife in her right hand in a way that no human hand could replicate.

"That means that you think, beyond any reasonable doubt, that the video is genuine. I'm not so sure."

She looked at Joachim Zell. "Mr. Zell, I asked you to scrutinize this video. Have you done so?"

"Yes, Captain."

"And, in your opinion, could it have been faked?"

"Captain," Zell said, "In my opinion, this video is a fabrication."

"Why do you think so?"

"First, it is very short, so it offers minimal opportunity to spot its flaws, but it does have flaws."

"Like what?"

"Well, it looks convincing when you look at a still image, but when you look at it in motion, It doesn't look as convincing," Zell said and tapped his slate. The video loop resumed.

"Notice that Mr. Chukwuma's head is in full profile, but the position of his body suggests we should be seeing more of the back of his head. Also, I don't think the movements of his head quite match the movements of the muscles in his neck. Maybe the doctor could comment on that."

Trix looked at Trey.

"I agree with Mr. Zell, Captain. Mr. Chukwuma is very fit, and the muscles and tendons in his neck stand out very clearly. His neck muscles do not indicate that his head is turned as it appears to be in the video," Trey said. "But even more obvious to me is the lack of sub-surface scattering on the head."

"What do you mean?" Trix said.

"If you've ever put your hand against the lit end of a flashlight you've seen that the light shines through the edges of your fingers and even illuminates your blood. That's because human skin is not opaque like painted metal. It is semi-transparent. When light strikes it, it doesn't all bounce off the surface. Instead the light penetrates the surface of the skin and then scatters.

"It's clear to me that the head in this video is a computer model. Whoever made the video took care to match the angle of the light shining on the head with the light in the rest of the scene, and they've even approximated a sub-surface scattering effect, but the skin on the head is still responding to the light differently than the skin on the body. This video has clearly been tampered with, and I would guess that it was assembled from at least three different elements."

"Anything else, Doctor," Trix asked.

"Yes," Trey said. "I'd just like to say that I think it's barbaric to punish a man for..."

"That will be all, Doctor," Trix said. "We are not here to second guess Columbian military tradition. Only to determine if this man has transgressed it," she said, gesturing at bound Chukwuma.

To the group, she said, "I paid for elite fighters forged in the crucible of Columbian military discipline. If you'd had an enemy to fight, I'm sure I would have gotten my money's worth, but without an enemy for you to focus on, what I have is a collection of expensive and troublesome exotic pets.

"In a community, enforcement of approved behavior can come from the top down, or it can swell from the bottom up. You want me to punish this man for violating Columbian military honor. Unlike the doctor, I understand the importance of your code of conduct, and I agree that it must be enforced. That said, I do not see sufficient evidence to justify the sort of top down justice you want me to impose."

Trix locked eyes with Esmeralda Escamilla. "Have I made myself clear?"

"Perfectly clear, ma'am," Escamilla replied.

"Release him," Trix ordered.

2.13.3 - Petrovic

Petrovic escorted David to the captain's office and waited. She openly admired David's body, but she stopped short of telling the doll to remove his pants. When the hatch opened, she activated her magnetic boots so that she could stand at attention.

The captain entered the compartment and closed the hatch.

"Petrovic, I created that fake video of Chukwuma and David and inserted it into the daily update with Zell and Trey."

"Yes, Captain," Petrovic said. "I thought that was the case."

"Why would I do that?"

"To protect Paul Lake, ma'am," Petrovic said.

"Why would I sacrifice Chukwuma to protect Lake?"

"You've known Lake longer, ma'am," Petrovic said. "He's like family."

"He is family," Trix said. "Do you want to be part of my family, Anja?"

"Yes, ma'am."

"How do you feel about the Columbian military?"

"I love it, ma'am," Petrovic said with uncomplicated conviction. "Military service is my life."

"When we get back to Galtz, I want you to resign from the militia and join this crew," Trix said. "Will you do that, Anja? Will you join my family?"

"Yes, ma'am," Petrovic said, her eyes welling up with tears.

"Disrobe," Trix said. "David and I are going to discuss your body."

"Yes, ma'am," Petrovic said. It took some time to get out of her armor, and she had to pause from time to time to wipe away the tears that collected in the air around her eyes.

When Petrovic was naked, she slipped back into her magnetic boots so that she could stand at attention.

"What do you think of her body, David?"

"She looks quite masculine, Captain," David said. "I think she would look better with less muscle and more body fat."

"Turn around, Anja," Trix said. "Look at that ass, David. I tried to spank her the other day, and I hurt my hand on that big hard ass of hers."

"I don't doubt it, Captain. Will you order her to change her diet to soften out the hard lines of her body?"

"No," Trix said. "I like her hard. Anja, face us."

Anja complied.

"She's crying, David. Do you think she is unhappy?"

"On the contrary, Captain," David said. "I think that she is deliriously happy just now."

"She's shivering," Trix said. "Do you think she's cold?"

"No, Captain," David said. "I think she is aroused."

"Look at her cunt, David," Trix said, and Anja moaned.

"Yes, Captain," David said. "I expect that she is very tight."

"David, I want you to stretch out that tight cunt with that enormous cock of yours."

"Now, Captain?"

"Yes," Trix said. "Get to it."

2.13.4 - Trey

"The captain is possessed!" I shouted.

"You say that like it's a bad thing," Escamilla said with a smile as she assembled a med kit in the examination room.

"She practically loosed a vigilante lynch mob on that poor man," I said.

"She told the Columbians to police ourselves," Escamilla said. "And that's exactly what we're going to do."

She put a cap on the blade of a scalpel and secured it in the soft case she was packing.

"You approve of this?" I asked.

"She should have punished both Chukwuma and Lake, but I can see why she went this way," Escamilla said.

"Lake?" I said. "Paul Lake? Why would she punish... Oh," I said, catching up to her train of thought.

"Yeah," she said. "*Oh*, is right. She's protecting her own, but Lake isn't Columbian. It's hard to argue that he deserves Columbian justice."

"Nobody deserves to have their flesh mutilated for having sex," I said.

"Not *sex*," she said. "*Sodomy*. Sodomy can't be tolerated in a fighting unit. It's corrosive to unit cohesion and morale."

"Worse than cutting a man's ear off?" I said. "What does that do for morale?"

"It sends a clear message," she said. "It assures the men that they don't have to worry about ulterior motives and hidden agendas in their unit. It lets everyone know that they can trust their brothers because deviance will not be tolerated."

"But..." I looked for the right way to frame this and came up short. "You have sex with women."

She smiled. "I do have sex with women. I think you like that about me."

"Yes," I said. "I do, but doesn't it seem at all hypocritical to you?"

"Hypocritical? How?" She looked genuinely confused.

"You're condemning Chukwuma for something you do yourself," I said.

"I am not a sodomite," she said. "Women can't commit sodomy."

"What's the difference?"

"The difference is that women having sex with other women does not harm unit cohesion or degrade morale," she said.

"How do you know that?"

"That is the institutional understanding of the Columbian military, the most elite fighting force in the Kuiper Belt," she said with a sing-song cadence, as if reciting something memorized. "Look, Trey. I know you want to have a three-way with Anja. I'd be open to that back on Galtz, but for right now, let's get together with Cat Girl. That's less complicated. You'd like that, right? Me and Cat Girl in your bed."

I couldn't deny it.

"Paige won't like it," I said.

"Paige isn't invited," Esmeralda said.

"She's grown very attached to Bygul," I said.

"What? Is she an heiress who gets her own private robot playmate? Cat Girl is sex doll. She's made to serve a community of users," Esmeralda said. "I plan to keep enjoying her. You can enjoy her with me if you're good."

"If I'm *good*?"

"Chukwuma did this to himself," she said. "Don't let it come between us, lover."

I imagined her naked, kissing Bygul, and words failed me. She closed the medkit she'd just packed, kissed me on the mouth, and floated out of the examination room.

CATALYST

Act 3

3.1.1 - Rex

Rex felt a vibration at his wrist. He dismissed the reminder with a gesture. Sleep in ten minutes. Recently, he'd formed the habit of dismissing the reminder and then finding something else to worry over when he should have been sleeping. No longer.

Yam had stopped speaking to Rex. Words were not necessary. The gulf between them had closed. Rex no longer had to be told. He understood that a plan was in motion and that his role was to be asleep in his compartment.

Ashtart, Respheph, Mot, Tannin and Yam's own human priest would play their assigned roles. The light of Shapash could not be extinguished, but it would be occluded, and Ba'al's precious order disordered, the morale of his minions shattered.

Rex looked at the two pill bottles held fast to the bulkhead in an elastic net. He would not need one of the doctor's pills to find sleep, but he should take one for the sake of appearances. He pressed his thumb to the cap, knowing that this would create a record in his medical file. He took out one tablet and replaced the lid. He swallowed the pill with a mouthful of water and set the squeeze bottle back in its holder. He arranged himself under the snug blankets of his rack and surrendered himself to the enveloping oblivion.

3.1.2 - Petrovic

The explosion jolted Petrovic awake. The sound of the decompression alarm propelled her into motion. Her quarters were too small to keep her full vac suit in, but she did have the compression base layer in her cabin closet. She pulled it on, put on her magnetic boots, and grabbed her gun belt, emergency facemask and oxygen bottle. She pushed herself over to the hatch.

The display in the bulkhead next to the hatch indicated equal pressure on the other side of the hatch, so she unlocked it and opened it slightly. She listened for the hiss of escaping air, but the alarm made that impossible. She put her hand to the crack to feel for rushing air but felt nothing.

She opened the hatch and pulled herself into the passageway. Two other hatches opened. Drake Antal and Arni Hansson poked their heads into the passageway. Petrovic noted with approval that the two men had also donned their compression base layers.

"What do we do?" Antal asked.

"Get to the main airlock and get into your vac suits," Petrovic told them.

She held no rank authority over them, but she assumed authority in the moment on the basis of her experience and the strength of her personality. She could see that both young men were glad to have orders to follow.

Petrovic's first instinct was to find the captain, but while she was on this deck she should check on Paige. No. Rex first.

She propelled herself, hand over hand, to the end of the passageway. Rex's compartment was equivalent to three of Petrovic's, but it still amounted to the equivalent of a very cheap Galtz hotel room in terms of volume.

She pressed the buzzer, and Rex's voice came over the

intercom, "It's open."

She pulled the hatch open and found Rex in pajama bottoms and a tank top. He was floating near his desk flipping from one status display to another. He spoke without looking away from the display.

"Hull breach on the flight deck. The bridge, Captain's office and main passageway are all decompressed. The whole deck is sealed off. I don't see any immediate danger to the rest of the ship."

"Where's the captain?" Petrovic said.

"I don't know. She's not responding to messages."

Rex called up the full ship's roster and activated the shipwide PA. Petrovic heard his actual voice and his amplified voice slightly out of sync.

"All crew, report in. Location and status?" Rex said.

Nora's name and image were already marked in red. Petrovic and Perkins were in green, and over the next few seconds, other crew members' names and images switched from gray to green, until only Chukwuma and the captain remained.

Rex switched to a 3D map of the ship. It showed Trey outside the hatch to the decompressed section of the flight deck. Zell, Doborvitz and Li were on the deck below that, in Zell's workspace. Cook was in the galley. Paige, Petrovic and Perkins were all here on the deck with the galley and the crew quarters. Hansson and Antal were by the main airlock.

That was all as it should be, Petrovic thought, but what did not make sense to her was the fact that Lake, Sparks, Kellemen and Escamilla were all in engineering.

And then it did make sense. Petrovic released the emergency mask and bottle which she'd been holding in her right hand. Slowly, quietly, she drew her sidearm and pointed it at Rex. He turned to face her when she clicked off the safety.

"Who are you?" she said.

"Petrovic, what are you doing?"

Anat was not with her now. She had only her human sight

and intellect and her training. All she could see was Rex Perkins floating in the compartment in his pajamas.

"You said you were human in your visions," Petrovic said, as she locked her boots to the deck.

"That's right," Rex said. "You killed me, remember?"

"Anat killed you," Petrovic said, but she knew he was right. She remembered the exhilaration of bringing the axe down on his head.

"Are you going to murder me, Anja? What would the captain say?"

"Where is the captain?" Petrovic said.

"Unaccounted for," Rex said. "What are you going to do?"

Keeping the weapon trained on him, she stepped further into his compartment and away from the hatch.

"Move out into the passageway," she said. "Slowly."

"May I get dressed first?"

"No," she said.

"Where are we going?" Rex asked.

"You'll head for engineering, I'm guessing," she said.

"You're not going to take me prisoner?"

"Maybe I should, but no. Now, go," she said and gestured with her pistol.

He floated out into the passageway, and she looked away from him for just long enough to grab Rex's holstered sidearm from its mount on the bulkhead by his rack. When she looked back, he was out of her sight. She walked to the hatch, knowing that she gave away her position and intentions every time one of her boots locked onto the deck. He might be waiting just outside the hatchway, but without a weapon or any way to attach himself to the deck, he had no hope of overcoming her in a hand to hand struggle, even if he got in the first strike as she emerged into the passageway. She held the pistol close to her body and stepped into the passageway. Rex was not there.

She found the holster for Rex's sidearm and then went to Paige's compartment. She tried the hatch. It was locked. She buzzed, and the hatch unlocked. She pushed it open and saw Paige, nearly dressed, and Cat Girl, naked.

The sex doll was helping Paige into her shoes. Paige was wearing BDU pants and a loose-fitting tank top, and Anja saw the body markings of the Priestess covering Paige's bare arms, shoulders and upper chest.

"Anja!" Paige said. "What's happening?"

"Mutiny, I think," Petrovic said.

"Have you heard from the captain?"

"No," Anja said. "Put on a long-sleeved top. I'm taking you to the galley."

"*Taking me?* What's going on?" Paige said.

"Order versus Chaos," Petrovic said. "Yam's minions have gathered in engineering. As Shapash's priestess, I think they'd sacrifice you to Yam, if they could. Or maybe Mot. I'm not sure, but until I hear from the captain, keeping you safe is my top priority."

Bygul helped Paige into a long-sleeved BDU top and then started to dress herself.

"Cat Girl, get dressed and meet us in the galley," Petrovic said, and guided Paige out into the passageway.

3.1.3 - Trey

When I awoke to the sound of the decompression alarm, reflexes instilled during delve training took over. I pulled on my vac suit base layer and then stepped into the suit. I assumed, since the Is let me bring this suit out to the Kuiper Belt, that it didn't contain any potentially disruptive technology, but its design was clearly superior to the EVA gear the rest of the crew used. It took them minutes to get into their vac suits. I was sealed up in mine in seconds.

I accessed the ship's systems through my suit and saw that the decompression alarm was for the flight deck, three levels above me. I headed that way. The medical level was only accessible from the deck below it, so I had to go down before I could head up.

When I reached the top of the final companionway I saw that the emergency decompression bulkheads had dropped into place. I could see from my helmet display that the portion of the passageway I was in was fully pressurized, but if I took off my helmet, I'd have to carry it, so I left it on.

I turned around and went back down the companionway to Zell's level. Entering the large workspace where we had recorded our first infotainment package for the crew, I found Zell, Li, and Doborovitz. All three men wore visors and were piloting sensor pods. Zell's view was on the main display. I saw the flight deck from outside the ship. Li and Dobrovitz took off their headsets and looked at the main display. Now I did remove my helmet.

"Oh, shit," Dobrovitz said.

"He must have used linear shaped charges to blast that opening in the hull. Look how clean it is," Zell said to the room.

Like Zell observed, there was a clean hexagonal opening in the hull of the ship.

"I bet he used two triggers; one to blow the shaped charges, and another to activate a suicide vest," Zell said. "That must have blown the severed plate out into space. Well, not space. Into the Temple antechamber."

"Who did this?" I asked.

"Chukwuma," Zell said.

"How do you know," I asked.

Zell gestured, and the view on the main display switched to an image that must have been captured by a security sensor in ops. It was clearly a view from a high corner on the interior side of the compartment.

I saw two figures. One was obviously the captain. The other I could only see from behind, but Mr. Chukwuma was the only black man onboard. It was clearly him.

His head was wrapped in a bandage which bulged in a

square shape where his right ear should be. The bandages showed no hint of blood. Esmeralda's work was clean and precise.

Chukwuma held a small cylinder in each hand. He pressed a thumb into the top of each device.

"Dead man's switches," Zell said. "He triggered the shaped charges first, and then, less than a second later, he couldn't have stopped himself from releasing the other trigger. Probably blew his head straight up into the ceiling."

"Could the captain have escaped?" I asked.

To answer, Zell gestured and the playback rushed through whatever words the captain and Chukwuma exchanged. The captain took a step in Chukwuma's direction. She was less than two meters away from him when the suicide vest exploded.

"Is that it?" I asked.

"The explosion took out the security sensor," Zell said. "The pressure from the second detonation was directed outward. The captain's body is probably outside the ship. I'm sure the blast would have at least knocked her unconscious. It probably killed her instantly. Either way, she didn't suffer."

COALESCENCE

3.2.1 - Rex

Rex floated into engineering. Escamilla, Sparks, Kellemen, and Lake were all there, but Rex's eyes locked onto Escamilla.

She was wearing a tight sleeveless top and a strange sort of skirt made from what looked to Rex like leaves of leather that hung in overlapping layers from a thick belt which arched high over her hips but dipped low in the front. The belt looked sturdy, but it seemed designed more for looks than practicality. It wouldn't impede her movements at all, but in terms of protecting her from thrusting or slashing weapons, from Rex's perspective, it didn't count as armor.

Her thighs were completely bare. They were lovely to look at, but again, unprotected. Escamilla wore sandals with thick leather straps that criss-crossed up her shins, where she was wearing studded plates molded to the shape of her lower legs. Those, at least, would actually provide her with some protection.

"What do you think?" Escamilla said.

"I guess I just don't think like a war goddess. I'd be more concerned about protecting my guts than showing off my tight abdomen."

"Ashtart is the goddess of war *and* love. Physical love. She put a very clear image in my mind of how she wanted to present herself before…"

"Before what?" Rex asked.

"Is Yam with you now?" Paul Lake asked.

"No," Rex said.

"They've withdrawn from us," Sparks said. "All of us."

"They'll be back," Esmeralda said. "Ashtart was pleased with my body. I know she intends to make great use of it."

"There is more light for Tannin to extinguish," Dwayne Sparks said. "His work is not done."

"Saz?" Rex said, turning to Kellemen.

"I am Yam's priest," Kellemen said. "A human; not a vessel for a god, but something is missing. I felt a conviction before that's gone now. I remember what it was like, but I don't feel it like I did before."

"If they don't come back..." Rex said but did not finish the thought.

"They *will* come back," Esmeralda said.

"If they don't," Lake said. "Then we're mutineers and murderers who've commandeered a ship none of us can fly."

"Murderers..." Rex said, a realization threatening to overwhelm him. He pushed it down.

"We haven't killed anyone," Kellemen said.

"Yet," Escamilla said with a smile.

"Chukwuma killed himself and took Trix with him," Lake said.

"I kept the captain busy while Chukwuma set up the shaped charges on the bridge," Sparks said. "If we ever come to trial, my life is over."

"Trix is..." Rex said, but again he would not allow himself to formulate the thought.

"She was unfit for command," Sparks said. "She lied to us."

"She was a fine Captain," Escamilla said. "She said what she needed to say to motivate us, but she was the light of Shapash. She had to be extinguished."

"Trix is..." Rex said.

"She's fucking dead, Rex!" Escamilla shouted. "What did you think *extinguish the light of Shapash* meant?"

"She's not dead," Sparks said. "You can't extinguish the light of Shapash with mundane explosives."

"Shapash endures," Kellemen said, "But her human vessel is surely dead. Even if the blast didn't kill her, she's been floating in vacuum for what? Like twenty minutes? No human could survive that."

"She's not dead," Sparks said.

"Trix…" Rex said, a gulf of horror opening beneath his feet. Escamilla launched herself at Rex. Without gravity, she couldn't strike Rex with much force, so she aimed her closed fist at the cartilage of his upper ear, looking to maximize the pain from her attack. She had meant to grapple with him, but the momentum of her leap and the force of her blow sent them tumbling away from one another. She reached a bulkhead and prepared herself to leap at him again.

"Get it together, Rex!" She shouted. "She'd fucking dead! Fuck grief! Get angry. She was in our way. She had to be dealt with so we could take Ba'al down! Who is Ba'al's human vessel?"

"Zell," Rex said. He felt a flush of hatred when he said the man's name. The throbbing pain in his ear transformed into rage when he pictured Zell's self-important, faggoty face.

"That's right! You hate him," she said. "Why do you hate him, Rex?"

"He abused her," Rex said. "He used to hit her. I know he did. She fired all the others who mistreated her, but not him. He got to design a whole deck for his own use."

"That's right," Escamilla said. "Z-Level. A whole deck of this ship is named after him. And what did you get?"

"You," Rex said. "I got put in charge of all of you. Sergeant of the pawns. Leader of the disposable grunts."

"That's not fair," Kellemen said. "You deserve better than that. Captain Nixon is gone, but you can take revenge. It's Zell's fault. Make him pay."

Rex went to a comm panel. "Antal and Hansson, report to engineering," he said over the ship's public address system.

"Aye, Sarge," came Antal's reply.

Anja Petrovic's voice erupted over the open voice channel,

"Belay that! Keep your vac suits on and report to the galley! The crew in engineering are mutineers!"

"Petrovic doesn't have all the facts. Report to engineering. Do it now," Rex ordered.

"Aye, Sarge," Antal repeated.

3.2.2 - Paige

Paige did her best to keep up with Anja, but the pain from her ribs was more debilitating now than at any time since she stopped taking the pain killers. For a time, she experienced the pain as an affirmation of her devotion to Shapash. Now it just hurt.

Anja took a handful of fabric at the nape of Paige's neck and pulled her along. Anja was walking with the aid of her magnetic boots. She couldn't effect the illusion that she was walking under gravity the way the captain could, but she was making good time. Paige felt like a kitten being carried by the scruff of the neck; Mama tiger carrying her cub to safety.

When the alarm sounded, Paige had been relaxing and enjoying the sensation of Bygul re-drawing the markings of the priestess on her body. In spite of the pain from her ribs, the sensation of Bygul's skin and soft fur against her own naked flesh delighted her senses. Bygul would kiss each patch of skin before applying the decorative patterns with a fat marker.

Paige left the design work to Bygul, and each new application of the pattern displayed a greater level of expressiveness and beauty. Bygul had experimented with different colors, but Paige reminded her that she was designing a pattern of scars. Color could not be a factor in the final design. Bygul chose a sepia colored marker for this most recent application.

Earlier, when Anat spoke through Anja, she called Bygul a *hierodule*. Paige queried the word in the ship's database and found nothing, but the word did appear in *Void Huntress*.

From the context, Paige understood it to mean a temple slave that served the gods as a sex worker. Bygul agreed that of all the roles described in *Void Huntress*, *hierodule* was the best fit for Bygul.

Bygul told Paige that Doctor Trey called the two of them *girlfriends*. Paige would love for Bygul to be her girlfriend, but as Esmeralda reminded her every time she called Bygul away to *help her with something*, Bygul was still required to provide sexual service to anyone who demanded it. Bygul was a hierodule. That was how she served the goddess, and Paige loved her.

They arrived in the galley, and Anja gave Paige a gentle push in the direction of the kitchen.

"Cook," Anja said. "The captain is dead, and Rex is leading a mutiny."

"The captain is dead?" Paige said, horror coursing through her.

"I'm sorry," Anja said. "I loved her too."

"She can't be dead," Paige said as she floated toward Cook.

"How?" is all Cook could get out.

"Explosion," Anja said. "Chukwuma took her out with a suicide attack. The bridge is inoperable and open to space."

"Who else?" Cook asked.

"Sparks, Kellemen, Escamilla and Lake," Anja said.

"Sparks and Kellemen, sure. But Lake? He's been with us for years. And Rex? Rex loved her. Was *in love* with her. He would never hurt her. This makes no sense," Cook said, tears now pooling around his eyes.

"It's Yam," Anja said. "Yam has him all twisted up, but Antal and Hansson still respect his authority."

"Okay. Yeah. With the captain gone, I guess Rex is in charge," Cook said.

"No! We rally around Ba'al. Order, not Chaos. Zell is in charge now," Anja said with unassailable conviction. "You don't have to see it that way, but keep Paige safe. Yam's faction will want her.

"Cat Girl will be here in a minute," Anja said. "When she gets here, take her back there with you and pull that gate down. Lock it! You don't have to choose a side. Just keep feeding people, and keep Paige safe. Can I count on you?"

Cook pulled his head backwards, leaving pulsating globules of tears in its wake. He nodded.

"Here," Anja said, and pushed the holstered pistol she took from Rex's quarters in Cook's direction. "Keep her safe."

Anja left the galley. For a few seconds, Paige could hear Anja's magnetic boots locking onto the deck and releasing, but the sound soon faded and Anja was gone.

3.2.3 - Trey

"So what's the plan?" I said.

"We have to get away from here," Shawn Li said. "This object is driving people crazy. Amplifying their superstitious beliefs. If we can get outside its magnetic field, the effects should dissipate."

"That sounds reasonable," I said. "With Captain Nixon gone, who pilots the ship, and how? Can the Bridge be repaired?"

"I think we should count ops as out of commission until we can get back to a repair facility," Zell said, and Dobrovitz nodded in agreement. "We have duplicate components for everything in storage. We could build a new bridge here. Or, I could pilot the ship from engineering."

"That's not happening," Petrovic said from the hatchway. She was dressed only in a compression garment, boots and a gun belt. "Yam's faction holds engineering."

"What do you mean?" I said.

"We're at war," she said. "The Chaos faction killed the captain, destroyed the bridge, and now they're all assembled in engineering. Rex is leading them, and Antal and Hansson are following his orders. They have numerical superiority."

"Damn," Zell said. With the sweep of his arm, he dismissed the survey pod controls and pulled up a different interface and gestured quickly. "I don't have access to security sensors down there, and he's locked me out. I can't access maneuvering thrusters or propulsion."

"Who locked you out?" I said.

"Kellemen," Zell said. "He's a cyber warfare specialist. Aside from Trix and me, he knows the ship's new computer system better than anyone. If this were a real-time contest, I'd wipe the deck with him, but he had time to prepare. Shit." Zell snorted.

"What?" I said.

"He's given me access to one system," Zell said. "I can see the files in the fabricator queue. I can see what items they're printing."

"What are they making?" I said.

"Would ya look at that?" Dobrovitz said. "They're making weapons and armor. Like, old timey weapons."

"Melee weapons," Zell said. "Spears, swords, axes."

"Axes?" Petrovic said. "Let me see."

Dobrovitz flicked his fingers to throw a file from his workstation to the central display. A wicked looking battle axe rotated in the air above the large workbench in the middle of the room.

"That doesn't look authentic to the Bronze Age," I said.

"It sure ain't made out of bronze," Dobrovitz said. "They're using titanium, carbon fiber and Tungsten."

"Print me one," Petrovic said. "And a spear. And I want an outfit like the one they're making for Ashtart. Scan me so it fits."

She removed her boots and gunbelt and started to peel off her compression base layer.

"Any excuse to get naked," I said.

"You got that right," she said. She looked to Dobrovitz and he pointed her to a spot where two robot arms could sweep lasers over her body to take her exact measurements.

"Wait," she said, and pinched her nipples.

"What are you doing?" I said.

"I want this thing to get my exact measurements," she said. "And you can be sure as shit that my nipples are gonna be hard when I bury that axe in Yam's fucking face."

3.2.4 - Cook

Cook held Paige for several minutes, and they both cried. Cook made no effort to hold back his own tears or suppress his grief. He would assert control and get on with his duties shortly, but he owed Trix, Paige and himself this open expression of grief.

He let the moment play out at its own pace. When his sobs subsided, he gave Paige one last squeeze, stroked her hair and said, "Okay, killer. Let's make breakfast."

He fetched two disposable napkins and they both cleared the mucus from their noses with loud, honking exhalations. He pumped a generous globule of hand sanitizer into one hand, rubbed his hands together, and then took Paige's hands in his and transferred the excess gel to her.

"I'll start on the bacon," he said. "Can you make the coffee?"

"Yes," she said.

They would talk about Trix later. Work now.

"I'm calling it," Cook said. "The three shift rotation is done. This is breakfast, next meal is lunch."

He opened a large tube of congealed bacon grease, scooped some out with an ice cream scoop, and wrapped it in cheesecloth. He put the small bundle in a microwave oven and heated it until it was dangerously hot. He turned off all of the exhaust fans in the kitchen and extracted the dangerous but enticingly aromatic package. He maneuvered it to the cold griddle and attached it to the protective grill of an oscillating fan that he kept mounted to the countertop next to the griddle. When he was sure it was secure, he turned on the fan and blew the distinctive bouquet of volatile compounds out into the galley. With the galley exhaust fans off, the distinctive smell would drift through the *Persephone's* passageways, an olfactory siren's song. This was his usual compromise with absent gravity.

"Where's Bygul?" Paige said. "She should be here by now."

CUSTOMS OF WAR

3.3.1 - Rex

David, the sex doll, was dressed in the historically inaccurate *Void Huntress* version of Canaanite armor. He wore a leather helmet and breastplate. He had pauldrons on his shoulders and guards on his forearms. His bare thighs and shins were protected by plates of armor that were meant to look like bronze but which Rex knew were actually made of steel.

Esmeralda was testing the durability of the armor by stabbing and slashing at David with a short sword. David held a blunt practice sword in his right hand and a round shield in his left. He'd been instructed to defend himself, but despite his athletic build, he lacked Esmeralda's strength. He could not fend off her attacks. He was covered in gashes where she had scored hits on him. In spite of his many open wounds, he did not bleed.

"You want us to fight with swords?" Arni Hansson said. "Won't the mutineers be using modern weapons?"

"I can't explain it to you, son," Rex said. "Keep your sidearm with you, but when the time comes, you'll be glad to have that sword and shield.

"I don't know, Sarge," Drake Antal said as he adjusted the straps on his new armor. "I think our normal tactical gear would be better."

"Antal," Rex said, "There are forces at work here that won't make sense to you, but the symbol on your breastplate will give you more protection than Kevlar in the fight that's coming. You've seen it before, right?"

Drake looked down at his chest, but then looked over to Arni Hansson's armor to see the symbol right side up.

"It's from Sparks's book," Antal said.

Saz Kellemen stepped into Antal's line of sight. The same symbol adorned Kellemen's forehead. Antal didn't know if it had been carved or burned into Kellemen's skin, but without immediate medical attention, Kellemen would be wearing it for the rest of his life.

"It is Yam's sigil," Kellemen said. "He is Lord of the Void, and he will depose Ba'al and bring true freedom to the people of the abyss."

Rex put a hand on Kellemen's shoulder and directed him to step back and let Rex handle issues of morale.

"Sarge," Antal said, "I'm a soldier. I'll follow orders, but isn't Yam the head bad guy in that book?"

"I can see how you might see it that way, Drake," Rex said. "We think of light as good and darkness as bad, but you'll need to forget about that. The Powers put up the Curtain to capture all of the sun's energy. They live inside a sphere of light. You agree that the Powers are the enemies of human freedom, don't you, son?"

"Sure, Sarge," Antal said.

"When the book talks about the forces of light and order, it means the light the Powers stole from us. The light now stands for *their* order. Their order is the opposite of human freedom," Rex said. "We don't know how many humans live inside the Curtain, but we know they're not in charge of anything, not even themselves. Look at our new doctor. He's soft, like a civilian woman. He doesn't know how the world works, not even the world he comes from. He's no better than a lap dog. That's how we'd be if we surrendered to the light and order of the Powers."

"So the doctor is with the mutineers?"

"He's not a player. He's an asset," Rex said. "They control

him now, but we may have use for him. If you get the chance, capture him like you'd capture a stockpile of food or ammunition from an enemy depot."

Drake's nostrils flared, and he looked around.

"Smells like bacon," he said. "What are we going to do for food?"

"We have a stockpile of emergency rations," Rex said and gestured to a stack of boxes on a pallet covered with a cargo net.

"So, we're just going to let the other side have the real food from the galley?"

Rex considered this and said, "Escamilla, that's enough. Take the armor off that robot. I have a job for it."

3.3.2 - Petrovic

Petrovic's armor was not an exact duplicate of Escamilla's. The sandals in the 3D file could not lock magnetically to the deck. Apparently, Escamilla meant to fight weightless. Petrovic intended to maximize her strength and size advantage by incorporating her magnetic boots into her costume. Petrovic accepted that it was a costume.

Even for hand to hand fighting, her modern combat armor would provide superior protection to what she had on now. Even so, she would not follow Escamilla so far in compromising practicality for sex appeal. Her legs were bare, but she had large protective plates strapped to her upper thighs. She'd also added an attachment to the top of her boots to protect her knees.

She wore the same breastplate from Escamilla's design, adjusted to Petrovic's measurements. Trey called it *boobplate* because the armor replicated the shape of her breasts, complete with erect nipples.

She also wore the same style belt and skirt as Escamilla, but where Escamilla, bowing to Ashtart's vanity, exposed her lower abdomen, Petrovic covered that area with a dense, tight fabric that would resist cuts from swords and spears but probably would not stop a bullet or protect her from a bludgeoning weapon like a mace or hammer.

Dobrovitz fabricated a practice dummy, and Petrovic practiced changing her stance in front of the dummy. She'd gotten faster, but the need to deactivate and reactivate the magnetic locks every time she wanted to change her stance made her slow. She couldn't move like the captain.

Thinking of the captain fueled her anger. She imagined the practice dummy as Sparks and put the combined strength of her legs, torso, shoulder and arm into an axe blow that took the dummy's head off.

"Dobrovitz," she barked. "Make it stronger!"

"It's meant to come apart the way a human body would," Hans said.

"Then print more of them," Petrovic demanded.

"Hey, everyone," Li said. "Look!"

He pointed to a bank of real time images from the improvised network of security monitors they had positioned on all of the decks from Z-level down to the crew deck where the galley was. They had physically covered all of the original security sensors to deny Rex's side the intel.

The male robot, David, was making his way up the companionway to Z-level. Zell said, "Anja, stop him in the hallway, but don't damage him."

"Don't damage him any *more*, you mean," Petrovic said, noticing all of the abuse the robot had suffered. She opened the hatch and stepped out into the passageway.

David was propelling himself hand over hand along the passageway headed directly toward her. He held onto a bulkhead divet to arrest his momentum when Anja said, "That's close enough."

"Greetings, mistress Anja," David said. "I must say, you are looking radiant."

"Hi, David," Petrovic said. "You've looked better. They've

worked you over pretty good, haven't they?"

"Yes, mistress. I bring a message from Sergeant. Perkins," David said.

"What? Why send you? Why not use the comms?"

"He did not say, mistress. He told me to convey this proposal to you, that the galley, as well as the passageways and companionways leading to it, are to be non-combat zones during meal times. The same is also true of medical. If you can get a wounded minion to the medical level, they will be safe from attack as long as the doctor is treating them or they are recovering there. If they leave the medical level, they will be subject to attack. I am to return to engineering with your answer."

"Take your clothes off," Petrovic said. David pulled off the ragged remnants of his pajamas. "I'm glad to see they didn't cut off your beautiful cock."

"No, mistress. If you can forgive the state of me, I would happily share it with you one more time. I do not expect to be operational for much longer," David said.

"You're not going back to them," Petrovic said. "Turn around."

David complied.

"Okay, face me again. I just needed to make sure they hadn't strapped a bomb to your back," she said. "They didn't put one inside of you, did they?"

"No, mistress."

"Okay, come here."

He floated to her, and she put a hand on the back of his head and pulled him to her. She kissed his forehead and said, "I'm sorry they did this to you, David."

She then gripped the back of his neck and pushed him ahead of her as she walked back to the hatchway and stepped over the threshold.

"What are you doing?" Zell said. "I didn't tell you to bring him in here."

"You think you're my boss?" she said.

"Anat serves Ba'al," Zell said.

"Maybe, but Anat's not here right now, and I think you'll all want to hear this. Tell them, David."

"Gentlemen," David said. "Sergeant Perkins has proposed that the galley and the medical level be designated non-combat zones. During meal times, anyone is free to move to and from the galley without fear of being attacked, and wounded combatants, if they can make their way to the medical level, may receive treatment and recover there in safety. I am to convey your reply to engineering."

"We're not sending him back down there," Petrovic said. "Look what they've done to him."

"Agreed," Zell said. "He could be useful."

"I wouldn't mind getting a look at him," Dobrovitz said. "You know, professionally speaking, that is. I might be able to repair some of that damage."

"Do it," Zell said. "Shawn, get the robot some clothes."

Li nodded and left the compartment. Petrovic realized that Li and Dobrovitz really did work for Zell, gods or no gods.

3.3.3 - Trey

I left Petrovic, Zell, Dobrovitz and Li and returned to medical on my own. I was needed there. Nora was still comatose. Esmeralda was in engineering with the Chaos faction. Paige, and presumably Bygul, were in the galley.

It's just as well. I needed time and quiet in which to think. I struggle to take my situation seriously. It feels like a delve, but I knew this impression came as much from Zira's absence as from anything else about the situation.

I understood that I'd be leaving her behind, so I can't put any weight on the fact that she's not here with me now. When I interrogate my memories, the most likely explanation for this situation is that I really am outside the Sphere in baseline reality. This just isn't what I was expecting or hoping for.

If the Is put me into yet another delve when I'd asked to travel outside the shell of solar collectors that the people out here call the *Curtain*, then I can assume It did so for a reason. That meant I should treat this as a training delve and learn what it had to teach me.

But the Is never tricked me before. Zira never appeared to me in a delve to create a sort of false awakening, and I never entered into a delve unknowingly. I have lived dozens of simulated lives without knowing that I was in a delve, but in those simulated lives, I never wondered if I was in a simulation. When I died, I always woke up to the memory of having entered into the delve voluntarily. I knew going in that I would forget the true nature of my existence while I was in the delve. That way I would be fully invested in the experience.

The fact that I was questioning the nature of my reality now meant I wasn't in a delve. Unless the rules had changed. Unless I was the turkey and Thanksgiving was finally here.

I can entertain the notion that the Is is malevolent, but I can't inhabit that reality. The Is has given me so much and asked for nothing in return.

I'm sure the people on this ship would say that I forfeited my freedom at the moment of my conception. Having had everything in life handed to me, never having risked premature death, failure, or even a minor inconvenience in baseline reality, they would say that I have never known the freedom that comes from self-determination.

But if freedom means ill-health, injustice, oppressive social hierarchies, and the progressive physical and cognitive deterioration that humans used to think was an inescapable part of getting older, then I'd say freedom is an oversold concept. I'll take quality of life.

Except I left all that behind and came out here where nothing is guaranteed. I did it voluntarily, but not for any egoic conceit of self-determination. I came out here in search of understanding.

The universe is so old and vast, there must be other civilizations. And yet all indications are that we are alone, that life evolved somewhere in this solar system, took root on Earth and flourished, and eventually produced a sentient species. That species organized itself into a technological civilization which created a successor species.

Species is probably the wrong word when talking about the Is.

I came out here looking for signs of truly alien life and intelligence, and what have I found? Humans, ever willing to divide into factions and struggle for dominance, an artifact that was most likely created by the Is, and *Homo erectus* corpses that, if the radiocarbon dating is accurate, were alive and breathing sometime within the last two hundred years.

I came out here searching for alien life and found specimens and artifacts indicative of homespun life. That shouldn't come as any surprise. I may be outside the Sphere, but I'm still well within the solar system, and we're headed back toward the Sun. We may even be inside the orbit of Neptune by now. To find alien life, I may need to head farther out into alien territory.

If freedom comes from making choices and then living with the consequences, then I guess that wondering if I made a mistake by coming out here means that I'm free. Again, if that's all freedom is, I don't see the appeal.

The most intriguing thing I've found out here beyond the Sphere is the *Homo erectus* corpses. They're not aliens. The species evolved on Earth, but how did they get out to the Kuiper Belt?

Three possibilities occur to me. The Is resurrected them and established a population out here. That is the most mundane explanation and, I have to admit, the most likely.

Another possibility is that they developed the capacity for space travel on their own before they went extinct on Earth and colonized the outer solar system. The Kuiper

Belt population then outlived their Earthbound ancestors. I count this as the least likely explanation. It's fun to speculate about previous technological civilizations on Earth. If they existed hundreds of millions of years ago, it's possible that weathering and geological forces could have erased all traces of their built environment.

But *Homo erectus* is practically contemporary with modern humans on an evolutionary time scale. We surely would have found traces of their civilization if they had the technology to spread out into the solar system. If not on Earth, then on the moon or on Mars. What are the chances that they would have bypassed everything in the inner solar system and headed directly for the Kuiper Belt and beyond under their own power?

The possibility is so remote that I include it here mostly for aesthetic reasons. Lists of three are more appealing than binary choices. Plus, it spares my preferred explanation from being the least likely.

For me, the most alluring possibility is that an extraterrestrial intelligence visited Earth in the past and transported a *Homo erectus* population off world. Alluring, but is it true? What evidence would weigh in favor of that hypothesis? More importantly, what possible observation could disprove it? At present, I have no answers to either question.

I suppose it's telling that, when I take the time to compose my thoughts and introspect, I dwell on abstract questions before addressing the more pressing physical and social concerns of my immediate situation.

The crew has divided into warring factions based on an absurdity. The Temple entities present themselves as gods, and these Kuiper Belt humans take them at face value.

It's sad, but not surprising. Humans have always fought with one another, and emphasizing religious differences is a common feature of such conflicts. I imagine that Mr. Li would say that religion *caused* the people to go to war, but that would be his ideology talking. Even explicitly atheistic societies have gone to war. They substituted the tenets of their political philosophy for images of deities and spilled just as much blood as any of their theological predecessors.

Humans have always fought over access to land and resources and for social control. The justifications they offered were not the primary source of conflict.

The people on *Persephone* were at least fighting in the service of something undeniably real. The Temple was solid. Its magnetic field was localized but powerful enough to disrupt electronic systems. Magnetic stimulation of the brain has been demonstrated to give rise to seemingly paranormal experiences.

What I couldn't take seriously is the idea that the temple entities are actually gods. They sure do act like gods though. Most human gods behave like chimpanzees, not even bothering to hide the fact that their conflicts are motivated by greed, lust and a penchant for self-aggrandizement.

Possessing the bodies of the strongest and most beautiful humans they could find and using them to act out internecine conflicts is just what Bronze Age Canaanite gods would do if they could. The influence these entities exerted over the crew of the *Persephone* seemed to wax and wane.

What disturbed me most about the situation was that the actual violence and division into openly hostile factions happened at a time when the gods had withdrawn their influence. Esmeralda and the other Columbians cut off Chukwuma's ear to mark and punish him for his sexual deviance. Rather than face the shame and punishment that awaited him back on Galtz, Chukwuma committed suicide and took the captain with him. Petrovic told me that she thought that Sparks, who was supposed to have been on duty in ops at that time, aided Chukwuma, if only by removing himself from the bridge while Chukwuma set up the charges. And once the captain was gone, the Order and Chaos factions rallied and immediately started to consolidate their power and prepare for conflict.

And all of this happened when the influence of the Temple entities was at its weakest. I don't believe that this crew was so fractious that the only thing keeping them from each other's throats was the leadership and psychological acumen of Captain Nixon. More likely the Temple entities selected their hosts based on compatibility, planted the seeds of corruption in each person's mind, and then withdrew to watch carnage unfold on its own.

I'll treat their wounds, if it comes to that, but I don't plan to aid the Chaos faction in any way. That said, I feel more compassion for them right now than I do for the crew members associated with Ba'al and his subordinates. Ba'al and his followers did not start the conflict. They could cast themselves as the righteously aggrieved defenders of the natural social order.

The humans of the Chaos faction committed murder and mutiny, and they couldn't even blame the gods. They did all of that while the gods were dormant. Rex in particular must have suffered unspeakable emotional turmoil, taking refuge in his rage and hatred of Zell to hold off the grief and anguish that would otherwise overwhelm him.

Another telling development; in a ship full of elite soldiers, neither side attempted a quick decapitation strike against the other faction. Instead, they set about stockpiling melee weapons, securing zones of control and negotiating ongoing access to food and medical care. Both sides prepared for a protracted, low tech and very personal conflict rather than going in for the kill. And I can see why, particularly for Rex.

What comes after victory? With the captain and Chukwuma dead and the engine keeper in a coma, who was going to fly the ship? I certainly don't know how to do it.

SCHEDULING ANOMALY

3.4.1 - Rex

Escamilla untied the ball of ragged cloth that was the remains of David's pajamas, read the single word written on it in capital block letters and scoffed. She turned it around and held it up for Rex to see. The word, written in what Rex guessed was red paint, read, *FINE*.

"Can we trust them?" Sparks said.

"Do what you want," Esmeralda said. "I'm going to get some breakfast."

"Sparks, Hansson, Lake, go with her," Rex said. "We'll eat in shifts."

Hansson looked over to Antal and then at Rex.

"Antal will go up when you get back," Rex said. "Now go!"

Neither Drake Antal nor Arni Hansson had been chosen by the gods. Rex could not take their allegiance for granted. It seemed unlikely they would ally themselves with Zell over himself, but they might be tempted to look to Petrovic for guidance. He didn't plan to let them both out of his sight at the same time to compare notes.

Saz Kellemen, dressed in his priestly robes, approached Rex and said at low volume, "Why did you give the robot to the other side? He could have been useful."

"Useful for what? Escamilla would have cut him to pieces

by now," Rex said, also keeping his voice low. He didn't want Antal to follow this exchange.

"That's better than giving him to the other side," Kellemen said, "And even if Esmeralda dismantled him, I could have studied him and possibly figured out how to access his systems. We might have been able to use the robots for reconnaissance or suicide missions."

"Study that one," Rex said, gesturing at Jailbait. The blonde sex doll floated unmoving. Rex knew she was active and listening, but she probably kept still to avoid attracting Escamilla's attention. He knew that Escamilla preferred the catlike doll for sex. She had expressed irritation that they only had the more voluptuous model that was the favorite of most of the male crew members.

He noted that she was more interested in destroying the male doll than using him for sex. She might take that same attitude with Jailbait.

"Kellemen," Rex said. "You are Yam's priest. Do you know why he has withdrawn or when he will return?"

"He may require a sacrifice before he returns," Kellemen said.

"A human sacrifice?"

Kellemen nodded.

"Who?" Rex said.

"The Priestess of Shapash would be ideal, but Antal or Hansson might suffice," Kellemen said.

"I will consider it," Rex said.

They hadn't killed anyone yet. Chukwuma was the only one to have taken a life so far, and he was beyond punishment now. Perhaps it's not too late to pull back from this madness. If they sacrificed a life to Yam or Mot, there would be no coming back from that.

3.4.2 - Paige

"What's happening?" Paige said to Anja through the closed grate that separated the kitchen from the dining area. Anja told Cook to keep it closed and locked at all times. There was one narrow opening in the grate through which to pass trays of food.

"Rex and his group are holed up in engineering," Anja said. "I'm with Zell's group. We're using Z-Level as our base of operations. We've agreed that everyone has access to the galley and to the medical level. Rex's group can't fly the ship. Zell can pilot and navigate, but without the bridge, he'd need access to engineering to get us back to Galtz."

"Have you seen Bygul? She was supposed to be right behind us," Paige said. "But she never showed up."

"No," Anja said. Rex's group tore David up pretty badly, and they still have Jailbait. Bygul's probably scared and hiding. That's probably for the best."

"I want her here with me," Paige said.

"I know," Anja said. "Hey, I think some people from Rex's group are coming. I don't want them to know you're here. Stay out of sight, little tiger."

There weren't that many places where Paige could go and not be visible from the food service area. She wasn't going to hide in the walk-in cooler or freezer. There was a tiny lavatory she could shut herself up in, and there was a large island in the middle of the kitchen. If she stayed low on the far side of it, she would be out of sight, but without gravity, it would be tedious to have to hold herself down.

She opted to wait in the pantry. If they'd had gravity, she would have chosen the lavatory as it would have provided her with a place to sit, but without gravity, the pantry was just as comfortable. She couldn't have peed even if she hid in the lavatory. Without gravity, she would have to use suction, and the device, while not obtrusively loud, also wasn't silent.

The captain came into Paige's mind. She called up the recording of the last all-hands meeting, the one where the captain told everyone that she wouldn't punish Chukwuma.

Page muted her tablet and watched the silent recording of the captain. She was soon crying and ended up blowing her nose on her shirt as quietly as she could.

3.4.3 - Petrovic

Petrovic watched the group from Rex's faction make their way along the passageway to the galley. There were at least three of them. As they got closer, she counted four.

Petrovic came down to the galley with just Hans Dobrovitz. Unlike Zell, his boss, Dobrovitz was not a trained soldier. He would be of no use to Petrovic if a fight broke out.

Petrovic brought a spear down from Z-level with her and left it in the passageway just outside the galley. She watched Escamilla, who was the first of her group to reach the galley hatchway. Escamilla made eye contact with Petrovic, smiled, and after a few seconds deliberation, placed her own spear next to Petrovic's. She turned to her group and said, "Leave your weapons in the passageway."

Petrovic moved toward Dobrovitz, who was strapped to a seat at a table near the food service area, making way for the newcomers, even though she had not yet received her own food.

"We should put some racks out there for the weapons," Petrovic said loud enough for everyone to hear.

"I'll add that to my to-do list," Dobrovitz said.

Escamilla floated into the galley followed by Lake, Hansson, and Sparks. Four versus two if the galley truce didn't hold. Escamilla's group were all trained soldiers, even Lake. Petrovic had no doubt that Lake could handle himself in a fight, unlike Dobrovitz.

Petrovic thought that Escamilla looked quite pleased with herself in her sexy not-armor, and Anja had to admit that the woman looked even more beautiful than usual.

Petrovic resisted the urge to look down at her own body.

Even though Petrovic had started with an identical design for her own costume, every alteration she'd made in the service of practicality degraded its sex appeal.

Anja shifted her gaze to Lake. She didn't know him well, but she knew that he'd matched with Mot, the death god. He'd served on the *Persephone* back when everyone called it the *Nipple*. Given that he was a ship's marine, it made sense that he would join Rex's faction rather than Zell's, but she knew that it was his connection to Mot rather than Rex that guided his choice. Lake did not make eye contact with Petrovic.

Arni Hansson did make eye contact. She thought he implored her without words. She knew he must at least be questioning his decision to follow Rex, if not regretting it outright. Now she wished that she'd worn her normal uniform and armor to the galley. It would highlight the twisted mentality of the Chaos gods and perhaps convince Hansson that he'd joined the crazies.

We're all crazies, Anja said to herself. She'd been every bit as eager to play dress-up and go to war with a spear and axe as Esmeralda was to show off her gorgeous body now that both women knew what it felt like to host a goddess.

Still, her side embodied order, martial discipline, fertility, and growth. Hansson and Antal, by respecting the chain of command, had sided with the forces of darkness, sterility, decay and death.

Surely they knew how little their lives meant to the Chaos gods. If they wanted to switch sides, Petrovic needed to assure them they'd be welcome. For now, all she could think to do was nod to Hansson when he met her eyes.

Sparks brought up the rear. The handsome rich kid had been obsessed with conspiracy theories about the Chaos gods and their relationship to the Powers from the start. Petrovic wondered what must be going on in his head now that his crazed imaginings had been vindicated?

He was paired with Tannin, the void dragon, a force of malicious disorder. Was he fully committed, or was he starting to see how irrational this whole conflict was?

Petrovic didn't even know how committed she was herself or whether she'd be willing to re-integrate with Rex and his followers. She knew that when Anat returned, she would want what the goddess wanted.

Even now, with the gods absent, she wanted to fight, and not with modern firearms. She wanted to thrust her spear and swing her axe. The anticipation of melee combat thrilled her. A shiver of excitement shot through her body, and everyone in the galley tensed except for Esmeralda, who smiled a tight-lipped smile and blew Petrovic a kiss.

"Soon, sister," Esmeralda said.

3.4.4 - Trey

On the assumption that both factions wanted access to medical attention, I decided that I was safe to move around the ship by myself. I suppose that either side might consider kidnapping me and only allowing me back onto the medical level to treat their own injured and thereby deny medical care to the other side, but neither side seemed to be thinking all that strategically.

As far as I could tell, nobody had a clear objective. If this were a chess game, I would say that both sides were positioning their pieces for an exchange that would diminish both sides with no clear advantage to either.

I traveled from medical to the galley and back for both breakfast and lunch. I was tempted to talk to Zell at breakfast, but Rex was also there, and I didn't want to give the impression that I had joined one faction over the other, so I stayed close to the kitchen and talked to Cook.

Cook told me that he was going to stay locked in his kitchen and continue making food for everyone until the stores were exhausted. I asked him how long that would be, and he said they had enough food to last a month. He meant a Kuiper Belt month, which was 100 days long, so more than three months from my perspective.

I didn't expect anyone onboard to live long enough to risk starving. I didn't know the exact timing, but I was pretty sure that the Temple would have already passed through the Sphere and into the inner solar system by then.

I wasn't worried about that. I couldn't imagine the Is harming any of us or allowing us to harm one another once we entered its area of control. Zira had stressed to me that once I exited the Sphere that my decision would be irrevocable. I would not be allowed to return. Humans could move out of the Sphere to take up life in the Kuiper Belt, but humans from the outer system were not allowed to enter the Sphere.

Still, I could not frame the prospect of passing back into the light of the Is as a threat to my life or well-being. That was surely a minority opinion onboard the *Persephone*.

I avoided engineering and Z-Level, and I steered clear of the cargo bays, not wanting to give either side the impression that I was securing material for the other faction. Other than that, I made full circuits of the ship.

I wasn't looking for anything. I just wanted a change of scenery and a bit of exercise. I thought about going to the gym. Propelling myself along the passageways with my arms did nothing to keep the muscles in my legs from atrophying, and my heart would start to weakening if I didn't start doing some vigorous exercise soon, but for the moment, I was still holding out hope that the crew would find a way to cooperate with one another at least long enough to get away from the Temple and its spectral inhabitants.

I was surprised to discover that the passageways in the sections of the ship above the flight deck were dark. These areas were reserved for paying passengers, of which the ship had none. As far as I understood the situation, there was no need to conserve electricity. Compared to the energy needs of the propulsion systems, keeping the lights on did not tax the ship's reactor in the slightest.

When I first encountered a dark passageway, I used my slate to light my way, but once I memorized the layout of the dark levels, I took to navigating them blind.

I was floating through a dark passageway, lost in thought when I thought I heard a whisper.

"Doctor," a soft feminine voice said.

I activated the light on my slate and swept it around looking for the whisperer in darkness. As far as I could see, I was alone.

"Bygul?"

No answer.

I turned off my light and waited.

"Doctor?"

"Bygul, is that you?" I said.

"Yes, Doctor."

There was an unfamiliar quaver in her voice. Then I remembered that one of Nora's last deliberate acts was to give Bygul the gift of fear.

"I won't hurt you, Bygul," I said. "It's safe to show yourself."

"I'm sorry, Doctor. I can't," she said. "I'm afraid."

"I won't hurt you," I said.

"I know, Doctor. I'm sorry. I can't come out," she said.

"Paige is worried about you," I said. I hadn't actually spoken to Paige since the bombing, but I was sure that Paige would be concerned about the welfare of her robot girlfriend.

"She is not safe, Doctor. I want to protect her, but I don't know how," she said. "How can I protect her?"

"I don't know," I admitted.

"The captain can protect her," Bygul said. "Please bring the captain inside, Doctor."

"Oh, Bygul," I said, in no hurry to shatter her hopes. "I thought you knew. The captain is dead."

"I don't think so, Doctor," she said.

"A bomb exploded right in front of her," I said. "And even if the blast didn't kill her, she's been out in the vacuum for several hours. Watches," I corrected myself. "There's nothing I can do for her."

"You can bring her inside, Doctor."

"It would be good to recover her body," I agreed. "Where do you think she is?"

"In her office, Doctor."

"What makes you think that?"

"She summoned me, Doctor," Bygul said.

"What do you mean?" I asked.

"She reinstated the recreation schedule, Doctor. I'm supposed to be with her in her office right now, but I can't reach her," Bygul said.

"I'm sure that's some sort of technical glitch from the explosion," I said.

"Please, Doctor. Look at the schedule."

I accessed the scheduling system. I'd never reserved any time with the sex dolls, but the schedule was perfectly intuitive. I could see that for each of the past five half watches, all three sex robots, including Bygul, or Cat Girl as she was identified on the schedule, had been scheduled to attend to the captain in her office. Each of the missed appointments was labeled as having been rescheduled for the next block of time.

"That's odd," I said.

It took a little poking around, but I found a log of system changes and updates. It showed that the sex robot schedule had been reactivated shortly after the explosion, and if the log could be believed, it was the captain herself who authorized it.

"I'll have Mr. Zell send a survey pod in to investigate," I said.

"No, Doctor," she said. "Please don't tell anyone. Please go yourself."

"How do you imagine me doing that?"

"Doctor, you can use the First Class airlock," Bygul said.

That's right. There were two airlocks on the First Class deck. Apparently wealthy people didn't like to use the servants' entrance. Both factions were surely watching the main airlocks, but I could probably access the First Class airlocks without challenge. At least on my way out. I didn't think I'd be able to leave the ship without some sort of notification reaching Mr. Zell, and I wasn't about to try to disable any ship's systems to avoid detection.

 I would retrieve my vac suit from my quarters and go out the First Class airlock on the same side of the ship as the captain's office. By the time I reached the breach, I'm sure Zell's faction, and maybe Rex's faction as well, would know that I'd gone outside. I'd face that music when the time came. For now, I had another EVA to prepare for.

FIRST CLASS EVA

3.5.1 - Petrovic

Anja slept in her armor. With no gravity to pull her down and drive the unyielding material into her flesh, she could just tether herself to a bulkhead in a corner of Zell's workshop and drift off. She did not make use of the doctor's pills, but she did cover her eyes with a sleep mask.

Li had gone back to his own quarters to sleep, and Petrovic knew she could find a more private place to sleep on this deck, but she decided that the Chaos faction would be most interested in killing Zell, Ba'al's vessel, and capturing this compartment for both its utility and symbolic value. So, she slept here with her weapons close to hand.

Zell and Dobrovitz kept their voices low while Petrovic slept. Now, the tone and volume of Dobrovitz's voice brought her out of sleep.

"Uh, boss?" Hans Dobrovitz said. "Yeah?" Zell said

"Air lock four is cycling," Dobrovitz said.

"Four? Up on the luxury level? What's up there that Rex and people could use against us?"

"It's cycling, but the outer hatch hasn't opened yet. Just the inner. Someone's going out, not coming in," Dobrovitz said.

Petrovic pulled the sleep mask from her eyes. "It's Trey," she said.

She sent him a direct message and got an auto reply saying that he was *out of the office*. She tried a direct voice link and was rewarded with a recording of Trey's voice reading nearly the same message she'd received in response to her DM.

"Hi, I'm sorry I missed your call," Trey's recorded voice said. "I'm out of the office right now, but if you leave a message I'll get back to you as soon as I can. Have a great day."

"Yeah," Dobrovitz said. "I just pinged all the vac suits. All of *Persephone's* suits are stowed. I don't have a transponder code for the Doc's suit. It's gotta be him."

Zell put on a visor and took control of a sensor pod that had been doing an autonomous survey of the ship's exterior. The main display showed what he saw.

By the time the pod reached the airlock, the exterior hatch was open and the doctor emerged in his distinctive red vac suit. Rather than walk along the ship's exterior with magnetic boots, he skimmed along it with gentle puffs of gas from a module on his upper back. Trey waved to the sensor pod when it fixed a spotlight on him and continued toward the hexagonal hole that exposed the bridge to space. He passed through the hole head first.

Zell maneuvered the pod close to the outside of the hexagonal opening and peered inside. Everyone in Zell's workshop saw the doctor step out into the passageway and turn left.

"He's going to the captain's office," Petrovic said. "If the hatch to the bridge were closed, could we repressurize that deck?"

"That wouldn't be my first choice," Zell said. "After that blast, I doubt the hatch will even close, much less make an airtight seal."

"Could we seal the gap with an expanding foam?" Petrovic said.

"Probably, but it would take a couple of watches. Whatever the doctor is up to, it'll be over by the time we can get in there. I think we just need to leave him to it for now."

3.5.2 - Trey

I reached the captain's office and found that the hatch was mostly closed, but not sealed. The lights came on when I pushed the hatch open and made my way inside. The captain's body floated near her desk.

I moved closer. I couldn't see her face, but I could see that she must have taken the brunt of the blast on the right side of her body. Her right arm, the robotic one, was probably damaged beyond repair.

I took hold of that ruined metal limb and applied minimal pressure to roll her around to face me. Her face confirmed that she'd taken the blast on her right side. The synthetic patches of skin were gone, exposing the metal housing of her right eye. I marveled at the primitive design of the replacement eye. It surely did not provide a vision upgrade.

Even by Kuiper Belt standards, all of her replacement body parts were crude. I suspected that they caused her constant pain when she was alive, which might partially account for the intensity of her personality.

I was surprised to see that her natural skin was mostly intact. It had come away from her face in the areas where the synthetic patches of skin had been blasted away, but it remained intact. The complex, overlapping patterns of facial muscle underneath seemed largely undamaged. I rotated her body further and saw that the left side of her face remained as it had been before the blast. I brushed the hair away from her eye, thinking that I would close that eye if it was open. It wasn't.

I looked at her left arm. It was bare and, except for one metal fragment protruding from her anterior deltoid, undamaged. There was no blood around the fragment of shrapnel sticking out of her arm. Far from closing wounds, being exposed to vacuum should have exacerbated the bleeding.

I took hold of the metal shard with the intention of pulling it out to examine the wound, but as soon as I put pressure on it, Captain Trix opened her left eye.

RETURN OF THE GODDESS

3.6.1 - Petrovic

"The captain is a robot?" Dobrovitz said. "Has she always been a robot?"

"I don't think *robot* is the right word," Trey said. "She's nothing like your sex robots. She's what I would call a *construct*. She must be a product of the Is."

"You mean the Powers?" Zell said, and Trey nodded.

"How long has she been on this ship?" Trey asked.

"Longer than anybody," Zell said. "I've been here for almost four years, and she was here when I signed on."

Petrovic saw Trey roll his eyes to look up at nothing. She assumed he was converting four KB years into inner system years. She didn't have the exact conversion formula committed to memory. She just knew that one year on the Blackout calendar was a little less than three Earth years.

"Rex has been here longer than me," Zell said. "Cook even longer, and she was here when they signed on."

"She's breathing," Zell said. "Does she need oxygen, or is that just camouflage?"

"I'm a doctor," Trey said. "Not a cyberneticist."

Trey turned back to the captain and spoke softly. "Captain," he said. "Can you hear me?"

She opened her left eye and looked at him.

"Don't try to talk. I think your jaw has been dislocated. If you can understand me, blink twice," Trey said.

The captain blinked twice. "Good. Two blinks for yes. One blink for no. Are you in pain?"

The captain blinked twice.

"I'm sorry. I don't know what to do to relieve your pain. Do you know? Is there anything that will help?"

She blinked twice.

"I have an idea," Zell said. He mounted a small boom arm on the frame to which they'd secured the captain. It had an optical sensor on the end which he trained on the captain's left eye. He then synced it to a slate on a stand mounted to a nearby work bench. The slate projected the image of a keyboard in front of Trix.

"This will track your eye movements," Zell said.

A cursor tracked the captain's gaze over the image of the keyboard. Words appeared on the main display.

ORAL_MEDS_ON_MY_TONGUE

Trey took a sealed package from his kit and crushed the contents against the workbench.

"Water," he said, and Petrovic handed him a squeeze bottle. He tore open the packet just enough to insert the tip of the straw and gave a very gentle squeeze. He massaged the packet and then tore off one end, pushed that end between the captain's lips and squeezed out the contents.

The captain's working eye closed for a moment. When she opened it again, she focused on the keyboard and flitted from one letter to the next.

GOOD_HURTS_LESS

"I'm going to remove the shrapnel from your shoulder," Trey said.

DO_IT

He gripped the metal shard with a pair of forceps and pulled. It slid out easily. He had gauze in his other hand with which to staunch any bleeding, but there was no blood. He stared at the gash in her skin, and Petrovic looked where he was looking. The opening in her skin closed. Within seconds there was no mark to show where the skin had repaired itself.

"You heal," Trey said.

SMALL_CUTS_HEAL

"Will your jaw reset itself?" Trey asked.

NO_PLS_RESET

Trey passed a scanner over her face and examined the 3D model that assembled itself based on the scan data. He nodded and placed his hands on either side of her face. He moved his fingers over her face as if bringing his own internal model in line with what the scanner revealed.

"Take a deep breath," he said. "Exhale and relax."

His hands flexed and her jaw moved slightly. She opened her mouth a little bit and then closed it again.

THNK_U

"Captain," Zell said, "Do you know who made you?"

NO

"How long have you been on this ship?" Zell said.

NOT_SURE_APPRX_20_YRS

"Twenty Kuiper Belt years?" Trey said.

YES

"That's more than half a century," Trey said.

MAYB_LONGR_NOT_SURE

"Captain, we should remove your right arm. I think it would be better to replace it than to try to repair it."

YES_HATE_THAT_THING

"Mr. Zell," Trey said. "Can you provide me with an X-ray image of her shoulder joint?"

"No problem," Zell said. "Anybody worried about radiation should step out into the passageway."

No one did.

BETTER_ARM_IN_CARGO2

"You have a better arm?" Trey said. "Why did you keep using this clunky thing?"

COMPLICATED

"I'm sure," Trey said.

3.6.2 - Paige

Paige floated in a void of despair. The captain was gone. Bygul was missing. Anja was alive but not with her. Cook was good to her, but he wasn't a saint. Eventually, when his well of good cheer ran dry, they ignored each for long stretches.

Right now it was supper time, and she was again hiding in the pantry. This time she left the light off and just floated in the dark. She could hear people talking in the dining area, though she could not make out what the muffled voices were saying.

Paige wasn't in any great hurry for the meal period to be over. She would have a little bit of work to do to keep her mind occupied after the last of the crew left the galley, but it wouldn't keep her occupied for long. She had nothing to look forward to.

She inhaled deeply to test her ribs. The familiar stab of pain came when her lungs were half full, though it was diminished from the previous day. Even the prospect of healing held little appeal. She would rather go back to when each pained breath filled her with the light of Shapash.

The memory of being animated by Shapash's light and warmth became more vivid. She held her breath, hoping to freeze the current moment, but eventually she had to exhale. When she inhaled again she felt the pain from her ribs and thought of Shapash, the light of El, nurturer of all.

Her reverence was, once again, not just an idea but a bodily sensation. It was faint, but it was there.

She thought of the markings all over her body that identified her as the goddess's high priestess. Some of the marks would probably need to be renewed by now. She couldn't ask Cook to do it. She needed Bygul, but for now, she pulled up her sleeve. She couldn't see her arm in the dark pantry, but she could imagine the markings on her skin glowing with the light of the goddess. She couldn't say they really glowed, but she could imagine them glowing with hallucinogenic vibrance.

The light of the goddess was returning, and with it, Paige's reason for living and rejoicing.

3.6.3 - Trey

Petrovic insisted on going to the cargo hold to retrieve the captain's replacement arm. I wanted to go, but Petrovic would not allow it. The cargo holds were deep in enemy territory.

"It's too dangerous," she said. She had the tact to leave off the final two words of that sentence. Too dangerous *for you*.

I went back to the medical level and checked on Nora. Her condition was unchanged. As I cleaned her up and changed her bedding, I realized how much of a help Bygul had been when she was a regular presence here on the medical level. Temperamentally, she was well-suited to the work. I thought her capabilities were wasted on sex work. I realize that judgment was based in ignorance. I'd never had sex with her.

Poor Bygul. If Nora were awake and had her wits about her, I'm sure she wouldn't leave Bygul in her current state of debilitating fear. She'd meant to give the robot the ability to flee from an abusive situation. I can't imagine that she meant to plunge her into a state of panic that lasted for hours, a state that was easily triggered but glacially slow to dissipate.

When I had done all I could for Nora, I went to the medical lab. The captain agreed to let me cut off a piece of her skin for analysis. I split my sample with Dobrovitz who said that he'd pass it along to Shawn Li, the materials scientist.

My own sample was now vanishingly small, but I managed to divide it into three pieces. One would be subject to a destructive test. I soaked another piece in dye, secured it between two clear slides and handed it over to a diagnostic unit that would examine it in a variety of non-destructive ways. I examined the third piece myself under a microscope. This was vanity on my part, or equal parts vanity and amazement.

It was skin. It had hair follicles and sweat glands and capillaries as well as the characteristic surface texture of real skin, but below that it had a layer that was composed of elastomeric polymers and nanoparticles. It must have been as strong as Kevlar.

The destructive test was intended to find DNA molecules in the captain's skin. It didn't. It was a manufactured substance. I couldn't clone it.

I had equipment here that could print a functional lung or a leg, but I didn't think it had the material feedstock needed to make more of the captain's skin. I prepared a brief report, attached my data, and forwarded it to Zell, Li and Dobrovitz.

I'd had sex with countless humanoid constructs over the course of my life. Were they built like Captain Nixon? I didn't know. It never occurred to me to ask.

ONCE UPON A TIME

3.7.1 - Petrovic

Petrovic waited for meal time. They only had two fighters on the side of Order and Light, Petrovic and Zell, and one of the two stayed on Z-Level while the other went to eat with Li or Dobrovitz.

It was breakfast time, and Zell and Li went down to the galley first. It was a risk, but Petrovic intended to leave Z-Level with just Dobrovitz there to defend it. She told him to use a firearm if attacked, but then she took up her spear for her mission to cargo bay two.

Unfortunately, there were only two points of entry to the smaller of the two cargo bays, and one of them opened to space. On the upside, the replacement components that would allow Zell to set up an auxiliary bridge on Z-Level were in the larger of the two cargo bays along with the Stout, the Crab, and the other remote-operated mining equipment. Rex's faction would likely devote more resources to safeguarding the entrance to that bay.

All of the bodily movements that humans associate with stealth assume the presence of gravity. Typically stealthy movements are those that minimize the sound of one's footfalls. Petrovic wouldn't be activating the magnetic locks on her boots unless she got into combat, so if all went well, she would not take a single step on this venture.

Without gravity, it doesn't pay to move too quickly. She could have propelled herself more quickly down the passageways, but the faster she moved, the more options she closed off for herself in terms of stopping or changing direction. She moved as she would as if she were heading to the galley, her mind acutely alert, but her bodily motions casual and unhurried.

To reach the hatch to the smaller cargo hold, she would either need to pass by engineering or the hatch to the vehicle bay. She chose engineering, the heart of enemy territory. Fortune favors the bold.

She pulled herself through the companionway that led to the passageway that would take her past engineering. The hatchways on the ship typically did not extend all the way to the top of a compartment. She could skim along the deckhead and pass the open hatchway unseen, but she couldn't imagine Anat doing that. Anat would take a chance, risk being seen, but also catch a glimpse of the enemy's inner sanctum.

She was not fully animated by Anat's presence, but she felt an inkling of it.

She launched herself from the bottom step of the companionway ladder with the exact amount of force she would for any other routine passage. She looked to her left as she floated by the open hatchway to the main engineering compartment.

Drake Antal stood in the middle of the compartment looking right at her. Their eyes met, and she winked at him. Then she was past the hatch. She heard no sound of commotion or of raised alarm. Maybe Antal realized he'd joined the wrong side.

Antal's gaze had captivated her attention in the brief interval of her passage. When their eyes met, she instinctively focused on his face, looking for information about his mental and emotional state as well as his likely next action. But she also took in enough of the space around him to notice that it had been altered. She didn't have any specific details; only a general impression that Rex's faction had spent a lot of their time fabricating macabre decorative elements with which to transform their stronghold.

She reached her next and final companionway and descended to cargo bay two. There was no guard at the hatch. She entered and went directly to the locker the captain specified. She withdrew a long case. She didn't really need to open it. It was the only object in the locker that could conceivably hold a prosthetic arm.

She entered the 3-digit combination the captain had given her and opened the case. She expected to find a mirror image of the captain's left arm. Instead she found an arm that was decidedly artificial, but it looked as feminine and elegant as the captain's current right arm was brutally functional and inhuman.

"What are you up to, Petrovic?" Rex said from behind her. She turned slowly and met his eyes. He had a pistol trained on her, which she took as a good sign.

She showed Rex the elegant prosthetic limb.

"The captain needs a new right arm," Petrovic said.

"She's dead," Rex said.

"Did you see a body?" Petrovic said.

"I saw the security video of the explosion," Rex replied.

"How did I know where to find this arm?" Petrovic said. "How did I know the combination to the case?"

"She's alive?"

"She's pretty banged up, but, yes," Petrovic said. "She's on..." She was about to say *Z-level* but thought better of it. "She's on the level below the flight deck. Let's go see her. Together."

3.7.2 - Trey

I skipped breakfast and went straight to Z-Level. I had matters to discuss with Zell, Dobrovitz and Li. I suppose I had things to discuss with Petrovic, but they were non-technical and could wait.

When I entered the compartment, I was surprised to find only Dobrovitz and the captain.

"Where's Anja?" I said.

"Gone to retrieve my arm," Trix said. "Come in, Doctor. You have many questions."

"I do," I said and floated up to what could best be described as the rack to which we had secured her body. It looked like a torture device, but in microgravity it was as comfortable as any bed.

I noticed that she was wearing a patch over the empty socket of her right eye. Zell informed me that they had removed her ruined artificial eye in order to study how it interfaced with her optic nerve.

I had peeled away the remains of her low-quality skin grafts. Her *real* skin hugged the contours of her face, but it had not grown to replace the gaps as I'd hoped it might.

When last I saw her the previous night, her left arm was secured to the frame of her rack. Now it was free.

"How are you feeling?" I said.

"My body seems to have repaired itself as much as it can," she said. "I'm back to my baseline level of pain, or nearly so."

"What hurts?"

"My right shoulder, the right side of my face, my back, both legs," She said. "Even the damage to my right arm comes through as pain. I asked Hans to cut it off, but he wanted to compare notes with you first."

Hans? I read that name on his medical file, but I'd never heard anyone call Dobrovitz by his first name in spite of the fact that it was just one syllable and easier to say than his family name.

"On the bright side, I normally have a headache, but it went away when they removed my right eye," She said. "How's Nora?"

"Still unconscious. I've repaired the damaged blood vessels in her brain. She isn't sedated. She might wake up at any time," I said.

"Or not," she said.

"True."

Dobrovitz held up one finger to signal that he wanted to enter the conversation. My conversations with the captain had always been adversarial contests. Hans deferred to her authority without reservation.

She looked at him and gave him a warm smile. Had she sprouted tentacles I don't think I would have been any more taken aback. That must have been some headache.

"Cap'n," he said. "The main problem we're gonna have replacing your arm and eye is that we don't know how your nervous system works. The arm that Petrovic went to fetch, you bought that on Galtz, right?"

"I bought it on Galtz," she said. "But it was made on Nix."

"Oh, wow," Dobrovitz said. "I'm sure it will be really sophisticated tech then, but it will still be designed to interface with a human nervous system. That's not what you have."

"Yes," she said. "I was afraid of that."

"That's why you hired Nora," I said. "Isn't it? For her knowledge of cybernetics and robotics."

"Yes," Trix agreed. "She's not the best engine keeper I could afford. I could do the job better than she can."

"Not even the best drummer in the Beatles," I said.

Trix laughed at that. "Yes, she's my Ringo. I hired her in the hopes that I could build trust with her over time and see if I could get her to swap this arm..." She wiggled two of the digits at the end of her ruined right arm. "For the new one."

"That would mean revealing that you aren't human," I said.

"Given how most people feel about AI out here in the Kuiper Belt," she said. "That's not something I have ever risked doing. I didn't leave this ship for decades—Earth decades—because I couldn't risk going through a body scanner at any port. I didn't know what I was or what a scan might reveal. The downside just seemed too big to risk it."

"But now that you're based out of Galtz," I said. "Respect for privacy is one of their highest cultural priorities. They don't ask for ID, and what's under your skin is your own business."

"Yes," she said. "My world got a lot bigger once Galtz was one of our primary ports of call. I could finally leave the ship."

"You were clearly made in the inner system," I said. "How did you get out here?"

"I don't know," she said. "I'll tell you what I remember. This might take a while."

She turned to Dobrovitz, "Hans, could I trouble you for a cup of coffee?"

"You got it, Cap'n. Black, right? Doc, you want one?"

"Yes, please," I said. "Slightly sweet. Whatever sweetener you have will be fine."

She waited for Dobrovitz to return before she shared her story. I imagined that she'd been silently rehearsing the telling of it for years.

"I was born in Auckland, New Zealand in 2284," she said. Looking at Dobrovitz, she provided the KB equivalent. "373 BB."

"BB?" Dobrovitz looked confused. "Before the Blackout?"

"That would make you almost 500 years old," I said.

"Four hundred and seventy," she said, and looking over at Dobrovitz, she added, "One sixty four point seven KB."

"Damn," is all Dobrovitz had to say to that.

"I had a good childhood. Mother, Father, one brother. I joined the APRC military right out of school. That was in 2301."

I thought I had a pretty comprehensive understanding of Earth's geopolitics from that era, having lived through it in simulation.

"APRC?" I asked.

"Asia Pacific Rim Compact," she said. I still didn't know what she meant, but I nodded to keep her story moving forward.

"They needed pilots, and they couldn't afford to be too

picky. No college degree required. If you passed an aptitude test, they trained you to fly. I expected to be deployed to Mars to help pacify the APRC colonies that were trying to secede and join the MarsX Union."

Again, this did not sync up with my understanding of history from that period. She seemed to be immersed in her memories. Her Kiwi accent became more noticeable as she told her story.

"Someone in Beijing or Canberra decided the colonies were more trouble than they were worth, and the APRC cut them loose. They didn't need so many pilots after that, and they offered me early discharge. I took the discharge and my very marketable piloting skills and got a job as the private pilot for an APRC politician named Richard Luxon. Remember him?"

"Actually, no," I said.

"He was a rising star; a charismatic populist who forgot to adopt establishment values once he got into office. He refused to sell out, so I knew he was living on borrowed time. Every time I flew him anywhere, I expected the shuttle to blow up. It never did. The official story is that he overdosed on some illicit street drug and then committed suicide by jumping out the window of his luxury hospital suite," she said.

"Classic," I said. "You never knew him to use drugs, right?"

She nodded.

"He didn't even drink alcohol as far as I knew. I made up for his teetotaling. When I was working for him, I drank enough for me, him, and then some. Not on the job, but thinking that every flight would be my last lead to a lot of short-sighted decisions back then. I could have quit, but I guess I believed in his cause.

"Anyway, after that job I got another one working for a non-profit. Among other feel good activities, they paid for kids born on orbital habitats to take school field trips to Earth.

"I was shuttling a group of kids from Day One, the first

Bezos habitat. It had gone to seed since it first came online. The only people who lived there by then were people who couldn't afford to go anywhere else. I was flying about 30 kids, teachers and chaperones down to see the Grand Canyon."

She paused here, sipped her coffee, and stared into the past without speaking for several long seconds.

"I crashed that shuttle full of kids. It wasn't an accident. I remember disabling the autopilot, and locking out the co-pilot's controls. I didn't have a co-pilot, but there was a chair next to mine that some would-be hero might have jumped into to yank on the control yoke.

"It wasn't an accident. I didn't have any reason to want to hurt anyone onboard that shuttle, but I remember deciding to do it, taking steps to make sure nobody could stop me, and then piloting my bird and all her passengers straight into the Arizona desert.

"And then I woke up on the *Nipple*. I had these crude replacement limbs, patchwork skin, a barely functional right eye, years' worth of grime under my fingernails and a dick in my mouth. I nearly bit it off," she said. "That guy, what was his name? He just about shit himself. Apparently I'd been pretty much a zombie for as long as he'd been onboard.

"Now, I was scared and furious. I demanded to know where I was and how I got there. Nobody onboard knew. I'd been there longer than any of them, fixing stuff and sucking dick. After I woke up and started asking questions, the captain at the time, who was also a part-owner, arranged for me to start receiving a half share. Before that, I really had been a sort of zombie, working without pay or even an identity.

"My memories took a while to come back, but when I remembered that I had deliberately crashed a shuttle full of kids, I stepped into an airlock, locked my boots to the deck and cycled the airlock.

It was terrible. I thrashed in panic, but I didn't stop the process. I passed out within half a minute, but then after a timeless interval, I woke up again. I was still in the airlock, and I could not draw a breath. I was in vacuum, but I was awake, and the sensation of panic and of needing to breathe was gone.

"I opened the outer airlock hatch and poked my head out. I thought about stepping out into the void, but I didn't know how long I would be conscious. Forever? I was ready to kill myself, but I wasn't ready for an eternity of isolation. I closed the airlock and came back inside.

"After that I tried going without food, then water. I found I could go for weeks without eating. I could go several days without water, but the sensation of being thirsty never went away, after a few days it got so intense that drinking became an involuntary action.

"I tried to see how long I could go without sleep. Turns out I could do that pretty much forever, but the longer I did the more paranoid and irrational I got. I figured out through trial and error the absolute minimum amount of sleep I could allow myself without putting anyone's life at risk. I wasn't going to be responsible for any more deaths, except my own if I could figure out how.

"I had a lot of casual sex back in the days when I was Richard Luxon's private pilot, but I did not give blowjobs. I expected oral sex from men, but I didn't provide it. It was a power trip on one level, but I just didn't like the sensation of having anything in my mouth that I couldn't chew and swallow. So I never did it.

"On the *Nipple*, I sucked several men off every day. I decided that I was in hell. This was my personal hell, designed just for me, and I deserved it. So I fixed stuff and sucked dick. And I tried to make sense of what I had done and how I got out here.

"Since I clearly wasn't human, I decided that I had been an android sleeper agent sent to kill Luxon by crashing his shuttle. But some other faction or rival had gotten to him before I'd ever been activated. Maybe someone on the field trip shuttle or at flight control accidentally said something that sounded enough like a programmed trigger phrase that it activated my kill response.

"Maybe whoever paid to have me built and placed near Luxon was just covering their tracks and disposing of incriminating evidence. For whatever reason, I couldn't be allowed to go on pretending to be a human woman. Eventually I might discover my true nature.

"Then I was consumed by a new guilt. Could there have been a real Patricia Nixon? Had she been murdered so that I could take her place? Guilt piled on top of guilt, mortared together with self-loathing.

"I leaned into my own degradation. I taunted the men who seemed most inclined to hit me or insult me. I encouraged their brutality. I cultivated it. Even so, some of the men treated me with kindness and even a measure of dignity. Some of them tried to save me from myself. I had zero tolerance for that. I would berate them and scald them with unending tirades until they realized that the only way to shut my mouth was to put their dick in it.

"I did that to Rex," she said.

2.7.3 - Rex

"Let's go see her together," Petrovic said.

Even if it was a trick, Rex had to be sure.

"Leave the spear," Rex said. "You go first. Take it slow."

Petrovic put the replacement arm back in its case and used her magnetic boots to walk to the exit. She pulled herself up the ladder to the engineering level and looked back to Rex for guidance at the top.

He gestured with his sidearm that she should take the passageway that passed by the larger cargo bay rather than repeat her brazen pass by engineering. Antal was waiting outside the hatch to the main cargo bay.

"On me," Rex told the young marine, and Antal fell in behind Rex. They ascended companionways and traversed passageways. The tensest passage was on the crew level where they might have run into Chaos faction fighters coming back from breakfast.

Finally, they were on Z-Level. The name failed to spark the usual flame of resentment in Rex. All he could think about was Trix. As they approached the open hatchway to Zell's workspace, he could hear her voice.

Petrovic stopped her forward motion and turned to Rex. She made the shape of a pistol with her right hand and pantomimed holstering it. Rex holstered his sidearm and gestured for Antal to do the same.

Petrovic stepped over the threshold into the compartment. Rex followed, and now he could make out what Trix was saying.

"I would berate them and scald them with unending tirades until they realized that the only way to shut my mouth was to put their dick in it," Trix said. "I did that to Rex."

Petrovic moved to the side and Rex saw her. She was secured to some sort of upright workbench, but she reached her left hand out to him.

"Rex," she said, and he went to her.

She took his hand, pulled him closer, and then wrapped her human arm around him, pulling his face to hers. They kissed briefly and then pressed their foreheads together.

"I'm an idiot," Rex said.

"You're my idiot angel, Rex," she said. "You pulled me out of hell."

"Does this mean that the blood bath has been called off?" Petrovic said. "I gotta say, I'll be kinda disappointed if I don't get to take someone's head off with my axe."

"You're not alone," Rex said. "Escamilla's spoiling for a fight too. And Kellemen and Sparks..." Rex shuddered. "They've gone down a dark path. I'm not sure there's any way to reach them."

Rex turned to Drake Antal. "Son, I want you to stay with the captain. She's the legit authority on this ship."

"Yes, Sarge. I'm glad to be away from engineering. Can we get Hansson out of there? I'm pretty sure Kellemen and Sparks want to sacrifice somebody to bring the gods back. If they can't get their hands on Paige…"

"Where is Paige?" Trix said.

"She's hiding out in the kitchen," Petrovic said. "I told her to stay out of sight, but we can't assume the other side won't figure out where she is."

2.7.4 - Cook

Cook noticed that something was off. Zell and Li ate their breakfast and left. He expected Petrovic and Dobrovitz to come down to the galley soon after, but they never arrived. Escamilla, Hansson and Kellemen also left, and the other members of the Chaos faction failed to take their places.

Cook took the sidearm that Petrovic had given him from under the food service counter. He clipped the holster to his waistband and floated over to the pantry. He opened the door just slightly and whispered, "Hey, killer. Something's up. Get ready to move."

No answer.

He opened the pantry door and found Paige floating in a cloud of blood.

AESTHETICS AND AUTONOMY

3.8.1 - Trey

I was comparing notes with Zell and Dobrovitz about replacing the captain's wrecked right arm with the sophisticated model that Petrovic had retrieved from storage. The primitive robotic arm was already integrated with her nervous system. Zell and Dobrovitz both suggested leaving the ball joint of the existing arm in place and creating another interface that would allow Trix to control the new arm through the stump of the old one. The problem with that was that the existing ball joint didn't fit her very well and caused her constant pain.

"For all the time you've known her," I said. "She's been in pain; physical pain. Imagine her free from pain. Let's find a way to make that happen."

They agreed. I wanted to remove the existing arm and study the neural interface. The arm itself seemed primitive, barbaric even. The interface could not be that sophisticated. The question was whether to perform the procedure in Zell's workshop or in the surgical bay. A notification chime sounded, and Zell said, "Doctor. It's from medical."

An image appeared on the main display. Cook was carrying Paige who looked to be unconscious. Her right forearm was wrapped in something that might have been gauze, and it was soaked through with blood.

I looked at Petrovic. She met my eyes for an instant and launched herself out into the passageway. She moved almost as quickly and gracefully in microgravity as Bygul had. She would reach medical well before I could. As I moved into the passageway I heard Trix say, "Get me off of this thing. I'm going too."

I moved as quickly as I dared, and I overshot one turn and crashed inelegantly into a bulkhead. By the time I determined that I wasn't injured and got turned around and back on course, I saw the captain, Zell and Antal navigating the turn that I'd just missed. That left just Dobrovitz and Li to defend Ba'al's stronghold.

"No matter," I thought. "The captain is the real asset, not any piece of real estate."

When I arrived in the examination room, Petrovic had already staunched the bleeding.

"Look at her left arm," Petrovic said.

Paiges' left arm was covered in an elaborate series of incisions. There was a yellow granular substance in the cuts, some of which was caked with blood.

"What is that?" I said.

"Cornmeal," Cook said. "She did that to herself?" I asked.

"Yes," Petrovic said. "I told her to do it."

"You what? Why?" I said.

"It was Anat. She spoke through me. She told Paige to prepare her body to serve Shapash. She told her to pack the cuts with mud or ash to raise scars. I guess cornmeal was the best she could do in the kitchen," Petrovic said.

"You were possessed?"

"No. Sort of," Petrovic said. "She doesn't have to take control of me. It feels so good when she's with me. I want what she wants."

I examined Paige's right arm. The bleeding came from an incision to her brachial artery near her inner elbow. I could see that she had been following an inked pattern on her skin that crossed over the artery.

"This was no suicide attempt," I said.

"No," Trix agreed. "She did it to venerate the sun goddess."

"You mean she did it for you," I said.

"She identifies me with Shapash," the captain said. I wasn't sure if she was agreeing with me or correcting me.

"We'll talk about all of this later. For now," I said, "everybody except Petrovic, out!"

I started a transfusion and asked Petrovic to clean Paige up. I checked the medical bay inventory for a corticosteroid gel, and it directed me to a specific location in another compartment. By the time I got back with the gel, Paige's left arm was clean. I started to apply the gel to her cuts.

"What's that?" Petrovic asked.

"It's an anti-inflammatory," I said. "It will reduce the scarring."

"She won't want that," Petrovic said.

"She's not in her right mind," I said.

"That's not for you to say," Petrovic said. "She cut herself to make those scars. You said it yourself, she wasn't trying to kill herself. She was marking herself."

"She's under an outside influence," I said.

"She feels the love of the goddess," Petrovic countered. "I'm telling you, she wants those designs to be permanent."

I stopped applying the gel and considered Petrovic's argument.

3.8.2 - Petrovic

Seeing the designs carved into Paige's skin, Petrovic remembered the bond she felt with Paige when she instructed the young woman to prepare her body to exalt the goddess.

"She put cornmeal in the cuts to hold them open and raise thick scars," Petrovic said. "You can do better than cornmeal."

"Anja, no," Trey said.

"It's what she wants," Anja told him. "I know it is. Let's ask the captain."

"She's hardly a neutral third party," Trey said. "In a way, Paige did this to venerate Captain Nixon."

Petrovic did not respond to Trey's argument. She opened the hatch and moved out into the passageway. Trey hesitated for a moment and then followed her.

"Captain, the doctor accepts that this was not a suicide attempt," Anja said. The captain looked to Trey for confirmation.

"That's correct," Trey said. "She was clearly carving a design into her skin. She was working with her left hand on her right arm, and she cut too deep and nicked a major artery."

"So there's no reason not to respect her wishes," Petrovic said. "She's an adult, and she wanted to modify her body. The Doctor thinks he can decide for her."

"That's not what I said," Trey objected.

"What do you want him to do, Anja?" Trix asked.

"I want him to put something on the cuts so that they scar up the way she wants," Petrovic said.

"Doctor, can you do that?" the captain asked.

"Yes," Trey said. "I could apply a liquid adhesive to keep the wounds open, but I don't want to do that."

Petrovic started to object but stopped when Trix raised her hand.

"I believe that the Doctor is our leading expert on the topic of medical ethics," Trix said. "It's his decision."

"Yes, ma'am," Petrovic said.

"Damn," Trey said. "Fine. I'll do it."

"And boobs," Petrovic said.

"What?" the captain asked.

"She wants big boobs like yours, Captain. The doctor said he could design a therapy for her," Petrovic explained.

"That doesn't exactly sound urgent," the captain said.

"We'll need gravity for her breasts to develop properly," Trey said.

Petrovic could not hear Anat's voice, but she knew the goddess would see the sense in the doctor's reasoning, so she relented.

"Now, I'd like for you to remove this thing," the captain said, pointing at her ruined right arm. "And get me some better clothes."

She was wearing a blue patient gown that was open in the back and which only covered her front to the top of her thighs. Much of her lower body had been covered with the same low quality synthetic skin that Trey had removed from her head and neck.

It had been torn away by the blast on the right side of her body, and as with her face and neck, the musculature of her right hip, thigh and buttock was visible. She also had a lot of what looked like fat on her hips and buttocks, but without her tight pants, it was uneven and misshapen.

"Let's get you into the surgical bay," Trey said.

3.8.3 - Cook

Cook didn't think he needed an escort, but he didn't argue when Rex insisted on seeing him safely back to the galley. They had reached the crew level when reality shifted for Cook. He had been floating in a passageway. *Now he was floating naked in a featureless black void.*

Part of the void coalesced and took the form of a giant, bearded man who held what looked like a limp rag doll in his powerful right hand. Cook recognized him as Yam, Lord of the Abyss. The rag doll was Rex.

"This vessel is unworthy," Yam declared in a voice of reverberating thunder. He discarded the limp doll with a contemptuous toss.

"Are you a worthy vessel for my will?"

"You got nothing to offer," Cook said. He intended to speak with the strength of heroic defiance, but his words came out as the squeaking of a mouse.

"You are defiled by the same light and love as that other," Yam bellowed.

"You mean we love Trix," Cook squeaked.

"You are blinded by Shapash," Yam said. "She robs you of your vision. You could be so much larger. So much more."

"What are you offering?" Cook asked.

"POWER!" Yam roared.

"To do what?"

"To rule."

"I already rule my kitchen," Cook said. "That's enough for me."

"I will see you boiled in oil for your insolence," Yam said. His words burned Cook, but Cook had been burned before. He didn't give Yam the satisfaction of a scream.

Then he was back in the passageway with Rex. Rex's eyes were unfocused. His mouth was open.

"Rex?" Cook said.

Rex focused on Cook's face. "I think I just got fired by a god," Rex said.

THE PROBLEM OF EVIL

3.9.1 - Trey

I used the robotic operating theater to remove the captain's old mechanical arm. I'd performed thousands of hands-on surgical procedures in my simulated lives, but starting in the early 2030s, there had been fewer and fewer occasions when unaided human hands produced better outcomes than the fine motor control and visual acuity that robotic surgical equipment afforded.

I didn't really need to remove the captain's mechanical arm to study it in detail. The non-invasive imaging systems on the *Persephone* were as good as such things got in the Kuiper Belt, or so Esmeralda told me near the beginning of our professional and sexual relationship.

The old arm needed to come out because it caused the patient pain. I replaced it with a custom-fabricated ball to serve as a placeholder and to support the joint while we adapted the neural interface on the new arm to work with Captain Nixon's unique nervous system.

Trix's body was simultaneously a thing of wonder and a travesty. I think her decades of hiding out on this ship for fear of being outed as an AI were probably misguided.

Her construct body was realistic enough to fool spaceport body scanners. Her bones had the right shape and density, and she had something that looked very much like a vital organ in every place you'd expect to find one.

Her body was a travesty because of her obviously robotic parts, her replacement eye in particular. She would have been better off with an empty eye socket. The replacement right eye she'd been fitted with caused her perpetual headaches.

The right arm was very strong, but its functional utility was limited by the weakness of her shoulder joint. The arm was too big and heavy for her body. It unbalanced her, and she suffered back pain as a result of the asymmetrical distribution of weight.

Her mechanical legs were actually ingenious in their functionality, but they interfaced with her human-looking thighs in such a crude fashion that they must have caused her constant discomfort.

I did not tell the captain that I didn't believe her story about being a sleeper agent designed to crash a maverick politician's private transport. It's not that I thought she was lying, but I just could not believe that any corporation or government on Earth in the early Twenty-Fourth Century had possessed the ability to create such a lifelike facsimile of the human body.

From the final years of the 20th century, techno-utopians had predicted a technological singularity in which artificial intelligence would transform the world in the seeming blink of an eye. Different schools of thought debated over whether to expect a *hard takeoff* in which the transformation unfolded in mere months or whether it might take up to a few decades. In reality, it took centuries.

Some historians, both human and AI, argued that multiple hard takeoff intelligence explosions occurred over the course of the 21st and 22nd centuries. Some of the resulting intelligences burned out quickly. Others departed the Earth rather than assuming control of the existing technological civilization. Some are said to have ascended to higher planes of existence. Others lay low and just watched history unfold without interfering.

Artificial intelligence, *alternative intelligence* to some, proliferated in its applications and implementation, but human-designed governments and corporations maintained some semblance of autonomy well into the 2300s. It wasn't until after the middle of that century that the unified and locally omnipotent intelligence of the Is assumed undeniable control over the local civilization.

It took nearly another hundred years for the Is to complete the Sphere and graduate to the second civilizational tier on the Kardashev scale.

By the time The Is started building the Dyson swarm, what the Spinners call the *Curtain*, It probably could have produced constructs as lifelike as the captain, but as far back as 2300 AD? I don't think so.

More likely, the captain's tragic backstory was just that, a scripted origin that she remembers enduring but which never really happened. I'd never heard of a geopolitical power block called the Asia Pacific Rim Compact, nor did her description of fractious Martian colonies match my understanding of that historical period.

No, the most likely explanation for her presence here in the outer solar system is that she was created by the Is, just the way she is now, and sent out here with her malformed body and the unrelenting pain it caused her. If my guess was right, she'd never crashed a shuttle full of innocent passengers either. That was a false memory meant to motivate her, and, to be honest, I thought the detail about the shuttle being full of disadvantaged children from an orbital slum was laying it on a little thick.

My suspicion about her origins was, in one way, more disturbing than what she took to be the brutal truth. In her version of events, her suffering was, at some level, the result of her own choices and very bad luck. In my version of the story, her suffering was deliberate. The Is created her to suffer.

How could the same Is that had overlooked no detail in providing me with such a satisfying and enviable existence have taken similar care to set Patricia Nixon up to endure decades of unconscionable suffering?

This was just the very familiar problem of evil that philosophers, theologians and metaphysicians had been wrestling with since the advent of monotheism. If God was both compassionate and all powerful, why was there evil in the world?

If the Is was good and powerful enough to create sentient life forms, why make them susceptible to pain, fear and inescapable remorse?

I knew that these questions had no satisfying answers, but it felt like I was rationalizing injustice by declaring them unanswerable. Was it moral for me to simply enjoy my own health, education, pleasant memories and sense of purpose when the people around me had been deprived of these things?

But what purpose would be served by failing to enjoy and appreciate my decidedly blessed existence? Again, I knew that humans had been wrestling with questions like these since long before the birth of AI, and nobody had produced a universally satisfying answer. I wouldn't either.

3.9.2 - Petrovic

They needed to defend Z-Level for its symbolic value. Antal reported that the Chaos faction sometimes called it *Ba'al's throne room*. Petrovic realized that everyone had come to medical except for Shawn Li and David, the sex robot. Those two were incapable of defending the place.

Petrovic and Zell moved cautiously through *Persephone's* passageways. She had a small mirror on a telescoping handle that she'd taken from medical. She used it to peek around corners to avoid blundering into an ambush. When she spied around the last corner before their destination, she saw a naked human leg floating in the passageway.

She drew a knife from a sheath attached to her right boot, locked her boots to the deck and rounded the corner. She'd forfeited the element of surprise when she activated her boots, but if the enemy was in the throne room, they had access to feeds from all of the newly added security sensors that Zell and Dobrovitz put up to compensate for having been cut off from the shipwide security system.

As she approached the door to Zell's workspace, she got a better look at the leg. It belonged to David. She used the mirror to look through the hatch without exposing her head. She saw the rest of David's dismembered body floating in the middle of the space. She used the mirror to check the blind corners of the room before stepping through the open hatchway.

David didn't have blood, but he had spilled a mostly clear and viscous liquid when Ashtart chopped him to pieces. Anat did not doubt for an instant that this was her sister's handiwork. Other gestures of defilement, like the smell of urine and feces in the air, seemed more like Tannin's calling card.

Zell surveyed the damage.

"Those idiots didn't even know what equipment to break."

He located a suction wand like the ones in the zero-g showers and started clearing away the floating liquids.

"Shawn, are you here? You can come out," Petrovic said.

When no answer came, she turned to Zell and said, "There's no blood. They probably took him prisoner."

Zell moved to the center console and accessed their makeshift security system. He scrubbed back through the video recordings and found the attack.

Shawn Li raised his hands in surrender before Escamilla even entered the room. She stepped into view with a bow and arrow trained on Li. Zell didn't have the sound on, but Escamilla must have ordered Li to turn around and put his hands behind his back because he did exactly that. Then the final missing piece of Petrovic's investigation into Nora's assault fell into place.

Ashtart, in the body of her human vessel, Esmeralda Escamilla, produced a long length of insulated electrical cable. With quick and practiced movements, she tied Shawn Li's wrists together behind his back, cinched his thighs together, bound his ankles and secured them to his bound wrists.

Where she'd tied Jailbait into a tight ball, Escamilla bound Li so that his spine and neck bent backwards to a painful degree. She barely looked at the insulated cable she was using as a rope. Her hands were so skillful, they needed very little information from her eyes to work their art.

In just a couple of minutes, Li was trussed up and ready for transport. She'd even created a harness around his shoulders with a handle between his shoulder blades for ease of transport. Escamilla looked directly into the security sensor and pursed her lips in a pantomimed kiss.

Sparks must have called out in triumph at that moment, as Escamilla looked over at him. Sparks held out the book and dagger that Anat had liberated from atop Mot's ziggurat.

"Yam wants power and status. Re-Mot wants blood," Anat said. She looked at her companion and saw mostly Joachim Zell, but Ba'al's presence was slowly eclipsing the human persona.

She anchored herself to the deck by the rack of newly-fabricated melee weapons. She sent a sword floating, grip first, in Ba'al's direction. He caught it, extended his arm and looked down the length of its blade. She took a spear and her axe from the rack. It smelled of Tannin's piss, and she made no effort to clean it.

He'd meant to desecrate her blade, but he would writhe in torment and humiliation when the blade he'd pissed on split his chosen vessel's skull.

"Anat, you thirst for combat," Ba'al said.

"In your service, Lord," she said, bowing her head.

"You crave it," he said. "You lust for it."

"I live to serve you, Lord Ba'al," she said. "This body was bred for battle. She is like no other human I have ever inhabited. Her strength. Her poise. She was made for slaughter, Lord. In your service."

"Very well," he said. "But first, the Artificer has need of my vessel's intellect. Guard him while he works."

With that, Ba'al faded, and Anat could see only Joachim Zell. He looked confused for an instant, but then his attention locked on to some technical task that was beneath Anat's curiosity.

3.9.3 - Paige

Paige woke up in the recovery room. She knew this space well, so her disorientation was fleeting. She felt thirsty and found a squeeze bottle attached to a tray table at the head of her bed. She had bandages on both arms and on the back of her left hand. She'd obviously had an IV, but it had been withdrawn.

Everywhere that she'd carved Bygul's artwork into her skin was bandaged. The rest of it had been washed away. Her skin felt pleasantly clean. She would need Bygul to re-draw the lines before she could complete her transformation. She could feel the presence of the sun goddess, but more powerfully than that, she felt the need to pee. Her bed had plumbing, but whomever had put her to bed had not attached the necessary equipment to her body. She needed to find a toilet.

She pulled back the covers that held her in place and made her way to the door. She wore only her bandages and a pair of clean white panties. She was thankful for clean underwear. She tried to keep the one pair she'd had with her while hiding in the kitchen clean, but washing your underwear in a tiny lavatory sink without gravity is no easy task.

She opened the door to the recovery room and made her way to a zero-g toilet in a nearby alcove.

She emerged refreshed. Her next pressing need was information. She hadn't seen anyone since she'd woken up, so she made a systematic search of the medical level. Most compartments had a large window that allowed people in the passageway to observe what was happening inside. She noticed that the window to the medical lab was opaque.

She opened the hatch and looked inside to find the doctor and Hans Dobrovitz. Anja had described Dobrovitz as Zell's shadow, by which she meant that his skills and responsibilities were similar to Zell's, just not as substantial. Now, Paige could see that Zell, the man, would stand as a mere shadow to Kothar-wa-Khasis, the divine artisan and smith.

Kothar inhabited Hans Dobrovitz's body and straightened the man's hunched and awkward frame into the manifestation of self-possession and competence.

The two men turned to look at Paige, and as they did, they parted like clouds, and the light of Shapash bathed Paige in radiant love. She approached the goddess, knowing that she should bow her head, but she could not take her eyes off the object of her adulation. She meant to fall to her knees, but without gravity, she merely floated headfirst into the body of the goddess.

"Paige," Trix said, and wrapped her bare left arm around the young woman's shoulders and hugged her. Paige returned the embrace and pressed her cheek into the captain's upper chest. They had never hugged before. Captain Trix was not a hugger.

Paige pulled her head back and saw that she had darkened the captain's medical gown with tears. "I love you, my priestess," the goddess said. "And the captain loves her deckhand. She couldn't say it without my help, but I feel her love for you."

Paige floated in the embrace of the goddess for a timeless moment until she felt a touch at her shoulder. Trey held out a t-shirt for her, and she realized that her nipples peaked out from the top of the compression bandage that supported her broken ribs. The bandages on her arms felt like sleeves, so she didn't feel exposed or even under-dressed, but now that Trey offered her the shirt, she didn't hesitate to put it on. It must have been one of his own shirts. It fit her like a tent.

"Captain," Paige said, tears still pooling around her eyes. "You're alive."

"What do you think, Doctor?" Trix said. "Is that a fair assessment?"

"Yes," Trey said. "I consider you a living being."

"As do I," Dobrovitz said in a voice that represented a much larger presence than mere Hans Dobrobitz.

"Lord Kothar," Paige said and looked down at his feet to demonstrate her humility.

"Worthy priestess of Shapash," Kothar said.

"Paige, the Powers made this body," Trix said, placing her hand to her chest. "And they placed a damaged soul inside of it.".

"I don't understand," Paige said. "The captain is a robot? Like Bygul?"

"Not like Bygul," Trey said. "She is far more complex. She is like a biological organism, but more durable. How old do you think she is?"

Paige examined the left side of the captain's face. "Twelve maybe," Paige said.

The captain smiled. "When I woke up, I'd already been on board this ship for some time, but I remember working here in 45 AB," Trix said.

"That would make you," Paige said and paused to do the calculation in her head. "Fifty two years old?"

"Almost a century and a half in Earth years," Trey said.

The terminology meant nothing to Paige. Later she realized that 52 was not a remarkable age as the humans behind the

Curtain kept time. Trey had converted the captain's age into Earth years to impress upon Paige that the captain was far older than she appeared.

That wasn't necessary. Paige was already amazed. She had heard that rich people lived very long lives, but she'd never met anyone in person over the age of 30. Now Paige looked back to Trix and noticed for the first time that she had no right arm. The monstrous robot arm was gone. The skin and muscle of Trix's right shoulder, lacking structural support, floated like an empty sack.

Trix gestured with a glance and guided Paige to the elegant replacement arm floating above a workbench a couple of meters away.

"Oh, that's beautiful," Paige said. "Where did that come from?"

"It was made on Nix," Trix said. "But I bought it on Galtz many years ago. I could never use it because I didn't know anyone with cybernetic skills that I trusted with my secret."

"Your secret," Paige said.

"That I'm a robot," Trix said. "An AI."

"But you're not an AI. You're not like the Powers," Paige objected.

"Trey thinks the Powers made me and exiled me to the Void," Trix said.

"I didn't say that," Trey said. "But, it's true. You seem like a construct of the Is."

"If you love me, my priestess…"

"I do! I do love you!"

"Then you love something of the Powers," Trix said. "And that's no bad thing."

"I love you," Paige repeated.

3.9.4 - Rex

Rex escorted Cook to the galley. Cook unlocked the grate,

raised it just enough to slip under it, and then lowered it again and locked it.

"I'm headed to the armory," Rex said. "Can I bring you anything?"

"Nah," Cook said. "I don't think anyone's gone so crazy that they'd rather live on survival rations than eat three hot meals a day. I'll be okay."

"What's for lunch?" Rex said.

"Something with sauerkraut. How does a Ruben sandwich strike you?"

"Sounds like a good reason to live till lunch. You're a good man, Cook."

"Stay alive, Rex. See you at lunchtime."

Rex propelled himself toward the companionway to the next level down. He could remember his time with Yam, and he knew that the use of firearms was anathema to the gods of both factions. If the Chaos faction were all assembled in engineering, he could kill or incapacitate all of them with the pistol on his belt.

Trix would not authorize such extreme measures. She didn't want her errant crew members killed. She wanted to save everybody.

But there was more in the armory than just guns and ammunition. *Persephone* was well stocked with non-lethal options; stun batons, sonic weapons, and riot grenades. Rex envisioned equipping himself with a gas mask, a bundle of zip cuffs, and a bandoleer of non-lethal grenades; concussion, flash bang, and knock out gas.

He paused at the bottom of the companionway and looked for any sign of the enemy. Seeing none, he pushed off from the ladder to sail down the passageway, his body parallel to the deck. He reached out and caught a handhold, bringing himself to a stop in front of the armory hatch. The hatch was mostly closed, but not sealed. He reached out to push it open.

"I wouldn't," Escamilla said, her voice dripping with the playfulness of a cat talking to a mouse under her paw.

Rex turned and looked back the way he'd come. Escamilla floated at the bottom of the ladder with a bow and arrow in her hands. She'd been behind him and could have put an arrow straight into his rectum as he'd floated head first toward the armory.

She transferred the arrow in her right hand to her left, gripping both bow and arrow with the same hand. She reached out for a handhold with her free hand. Rex read her intention as preparing to pull herself into an intersecting passage.

Why?

To escape the blast Rex was about to trigger when he pushed open the hatch to the armory. In all likelihood, the last person in the armory had been Jay Chukwuma. All of the charges the demolitions expert set that night might not have detonated. Not yet.

"Shit," Rex said.

"On the other hand, the means to victory might be right behind that door," Escamilla taunted. Rex withdrew his hand from the hatch, and Escamilla released her grip on the bulkhead handhold. Rather than taking the arrow back into her right hand, she caressed her bare thigh.

"You still have your pistol. You could pierce this flesh with your bullets. Or perhaps you'd rather penetrate this body in some other way." She drew her hand slowly up her thigh, pushing up the leaves of her leather skirt, revealing more of her inviting flesh.

Rex considered drawing his pistol, but they both knew he wasn't going to shoot her. He'd rather have a free hand with which to…

A slender noose tightened around Rex's neck. He moved too late to get his fingers between the thin cord and the skin of his neck. When his fingers found no purchase there, he reached for his pistol only to feel a hard blow drive his right hand into throbbing uselessness. Someone had struck him with what felt like a piece of steel rebar. He struggled, but within seconds, his oxygen-deprived brain lost the plot and he slipped into oblivion.

THE PROBLEM OF BIOLOGY

3.10.1 - Petrovic

Petrovic and Zell returned to the medical level encumbered with treasure. Anja carried the bulk of it, including what looked like a bolt of gray fabric and a black case large enough to hold a human head.

As far as she could tell, Ba'al had receded entirely, leaving Joachim Zell alone in his rather fit body. If things didn't work out with Trey…

"Here's the interface you designed," Zell said, holding a small metal part out to Dobrovitz, who took it without acknowledgement and reached for the elegant Nixian arm.

To Trey, Zell said, "We fabricated the base layers for the skin. I think your medical fabricators can print the top layers and we can bind the two. It won't be as elegant as her original skin, but it will look natural, provide full tactile and temperature sensitivity and be much stronger than normal human skin."

"That's like ten times what I'll need to repair the captain," Trey said, to which Zell gestured at Dobrovitz.

Trey, Trix, Paige, Dobrovitz, Zell and Petrovic were all gathered here in Trey's spacious medical laboratory. If it were a battlefield or an orgy, Anja Petrovic, blazing with the light of Anat, would have been the brightest star in that firmament. Given that they were designing and building machines so intricate and subtle that they would form parts of a living being, Kothar the artificer in the body of Hans Dobrovitz stood supreme. Dobrovitz floated back to Trix and held up the elegant Nixian arm.

"We could fill in the gaps with synthetic fat and sheath this arm in the new skin we're creating for you," Zell told her.

"I take it you have another vision," Trix said.

"This is more than a prosthetic arm," Kothar said. "The elegance of its design is meant to convey wealth, status, and refined sensibilities."

"It's classy," Anja said.

"It was meant to be displayed," Dobrovitz said, "not concealed."

"I've been staring at it for years," Trix said. "It's a symbol of a life that was out of my reach. I've dreamed of it being part of me just as it is, so I don't want to cover it up. You're suggesting more than just not covering it up though, aren't you?"

"Yes," Dobrovotiz said, "We could wrap the skin and muscle of your right shoulder over the top of this arm the way they concealed where your old arm joined your torso..."

"Or you could remove my excess flesh," Trix said. "Let's make sure the new arm works, but I think we're on the same page."

"Okay," Trey said. "Let's get you back into the surgical bay."

"That won't be necessary," Dobrovitz said. He positioned the arm at Trix's shoulder, and it came to life.

Internal components extended and reached inside the joint. The new arm rearranged itself to adapt to the new components that Dobrovitz had added and to secure itself to the ball in the captain's shoulder joint.

"Your brain is adapted to the old arm. It will take you a while to adjust to this new one. Don't worry if your movements are clumsy at first," Trey said.

Trix looked down at her new arm. It moved fluidly, the

fingers flowing through a succession of elegant gestures. Its movements were feminine and graceful.

"This arm has a built-in gestural vocabulary," Kothar said. "Its designers had a very specific vision for it, plus the adapter I installed has a mind of its own. It only cares about movement and mechanical function, but it has strong opinions on those topics. It takes the signals from the captain's brain as gross suggestions and translates them into aesthetically pleasing motion."

Trix fanned out her extended fingers and looked at the back of her hand. The fingers read as human fingers at a glance, but upon close scrutiny, they were both simplifications of human fingers and etched with elaborate patterns.

The fingertips had a fine ridge on them that would aid in grasping small objects the way fingernails would, but it did not actually have fingernails.

"No fingernails means no dirt under them," Trix said.

"Ha! I can't see that hand holding a wrench," Anja said. "That's meant for calligraphy and flower arranging."

The captain looked over at the excess flesh of her right shoulder.

"Alright," she said, "trim off the extra."

Dobrovitz opened a small case containing some of the smaller pieces that Zell had fabricated in his workshop. He extracted something that looked like a simple needle with a small handle at the end. He positioned it where the right side of the captain's neck flowed into her shoulder. There was no skin there. The tip of the needle seemed not so much to puncture the captain's exposed muscles as slip between the fibers.

"For the pain," Dobrovitz said.

He then took a small laser torch, and without marking where he planned to cut, proceeded to trim away the excess skin and muscle of Trix's right shoulder.

The cutter would have parted human skin like wet tissue paper. On Trix, it was like Dobrovitz was cutting through boiled leather. The captain's skin was much tougher than it looked.

"I have a use for that material," Trey said when Dobrovitz pulled the excess synthetic flesh from the captain's body.

"What about my eye?"

"I have some ideas about that," Zell said, "But I'll need to talk them over with the doctor and…" Zell looked at Dobrovitz. "And with Kothar," he said.

"There's another matter I'd like to discuss with you, Captain," Trey said.

"What is it, Doctor?"

"Assuming the method we've worked out for creating new skin actually works," Trey said. He paused, his cheeks reddening. "There's a design choice to be made."

He passed her a slate which she accepted with an elegant flourish of her new right hand. She looked at the display and smiled.

"Any of those would be an improvement over what I have now," she said. "Let my priestess decide."

Trix passed the slate to Paige, and the young woman's eyes went wide.

"You may provide guidance, Anja," Trix said.

Petrovic made her way to where Paige was studying the display. She moved in behind Paige and saw a three by three grid of vulvas that differed in color and labial configuration

"You can tap on any image to generate nine variations on that design," Trey said.

Paige hovered her finger over one image and looked back at Petrovic. Anja nodded, and Paige tapped it. Nine variations on that theme replaced the original grid. Anja chose an image from the new grid and pointed to it. Paige considered it and pointed at a different one. "Up to you, little tiger," Petrovic said. "They're both gorgeous."

3.10.2 - Paige

Pondering the aesthetics of female genitalia reminded Paige of Bygul, and her emotional state shifted from proto-horny to worried.

"Doctor," Paige said to Trey. "You said it was Bygul who told you that the captain was alive. Do you know where she is now?'

"I really don't," Trey said. "I never even saw her. She's hiding."

"Do you know where Lolita and David are?"

"Lolita?" Trey asked, and then he made the connection. "Ah, Jailbait! Good one."

"Do you know where she is?" Paige said.

"I really don't know," Trey said. "But I think we should assume that she's... not functional."

"Why?"

"David's head is in that black bag that Anja brought down from Z-Level," Trey said, pointing at the bag that Anja had tucked under some elastic netting that was stretched over a nearby work bench.

Paige gasped. "His head? What happened?"

"Ashtart happened," Anja said,

"Esmeralda enjoys hacking the robots to pieces," Trey told Paige.

"What about Lolita?" Paige said.

"I haven't seen her," Trey said.

The captain held out her new right hand, "Slate, please."

Trey handed her his slate, and Trix pointed it at a wall display. The two devices exchanged infrared signals. Trix swiped and poked at the screen.

"Doctor, I've scheduled some time for you with Lola. If she's able, she should be on her way to your quarters."

"Can she do useful work here in the lab?" Trey said.

"Perhaps," Trix said. "All three robots know human anatomy and first aid. That's why Bygul could transition from sex work to physical therapy so readily. I don't know how far that adaptability goes, but you're welcome to try."

"I have a use for her," Kothar said, which drew a burst of laughter from Petrovic.

"I bet you do!" Petrovic said.

The visage of calm authority on Hans Dobrovitz's face broke, and the mortal man peeked out from behind the Kothar persona, "We didn't mean it like that, but I ain't too proud to admit that I was hoping for a go with her."

"Medicine is so boring," Trey said. "Welcome to Dr. Trey's robot spa and bordello."

"I appreciate your flexibility, Doctor," Trix said.

"Hey, it was good having a laugh with you guys," Dobrovitz said. "Kothar has work to do, and I'm learning a lot just riding shotgun. Talk to you all later, I hope."

With that, the friendly and familiar persona of Hans Dobrovitz sank below the surface again.

"Doctor, I have prepared an update for your tissue fabricator," Kothar said. "Would you like to review the code before I install it?"

"That's outside my skill set," Trey said. "Maybe Mr. Zell would want to have a look."

Zell held up his own slate. He and Dobrovitz shared data on a regular basis. Their slates were already linked. They only needed line of sight to transfer data via infrared pulses. Kothar transferred the new code to Zell with a gesture.

"My parser doesn't know what to make of this, but the updates he made to our industrial fabricator worked out. It's your machine, Doc. Your call."

"Who am I to second guess a god?" Trey said with a shrug.

"You don't believe we are gods," Kothar said.

"No," Trey said. "But that's a conversation for another time."

Kothar took the black bag from under the elastic net, opened it and pulled out David's head.

"The time for sleep is over, David," Kothar said, holding the disembodied head to face him. "You have a new role to play."

3.10.3 - Rex

Rex opened his eyes. The pain in his Adam's apple reminded him that he'd been garroted. Rex cursed his own gullibility for not realizing that Escamilla was distracting him while an accomplice stole up behind him and slipped a cord around his neck. He'd let himself be captured. Now he was a prisoner of the Chaos faction, and he knew from personal experience that murder and sadism were never far from their minds.

He'd led this faction. He encouraged Sparks and Kellemen to spend their time redressing the main engineering compartment because it kept them occupied. Yam only wanted to depose Ba'al and take his place. He wasn't a sadist. He didn't despise the living or want to cause suffering, but he understood that his followers were motivated by monstrous impulses.

They transformed the space with decorative fixtures printed with Nora's fabricator. It was designed to print large mechanical components, and they'd turned it to printing panels that attached to the bulkheads and turned the utilitarian space of engineering into a surrealist nightmare.

The walls were now adorned with skulls, vertebrae and other anatomical features that connected up to make it look like they were inside the body of a biomechanical titan.

There was a throne and a sacrificial altar. Rex had tried sitting on the throne back when he still led this faction, but as with so many other human activities, sitting on a throne in a zero-g environment felt awkward and unsatisfying.

The codex and sacrificial dagger were strapped to the flat, table-like surface of the altar. The altar was also designed with gravity in mind. Spilled blood was meant to flow. It could spray from severed arteries, but if it didn't fall to the ground, it obscured the spectacle of sacrifice.

Torches extended from the walls in brackets, but their flickering light came from LEDs rather than open flames. Fire, like so many familiar aspects of the human experience, defied expectation without gravity.

Rex tried to move and discovered that he was bound with thin cords to another person. They were tied back to back, and Rex could feel the warmth of the other body, but they didn't move in response to Rex pulling at their shared bonds.

"Who's there?" Rex whispered. The response came from across the compartment.

"He's awake," Sparks said. Rex focused on the figures in the compartment. Escamilla was using thick elastic bands to do squats. Escamilla was beautiful, but in the short time that he'd known her, she didn't strike Rex as being all that vain. Ashtart, Rex knew from his now dissolved union with Yam, was feminine vanity personified. She was keeping her muscles plump with blood for beauty's sake as much as to be physically fit for combat.

Sparks tended to the output of the industrial fabricator. Rex didn't dwell on the half-finished object long enough to identify it. Kellemen held what looked like a soldering gun or small laser cutter. He was using it to burn designs into the skin of the busty sex doll that the captain called Lola and the rest of the crew knew as Jailbait. The doll whimpered in pain, but she held still and gave Kellemen a steady canvas on which to work.

Paul Lake, dressed in ornate black armor that prioritized sinister design over practical protection, floated toward Rex. He was holding Rex's pistol.

"Welcome back, Rex," Lake said.

Rex and Lake had both lived and worked on the *Nipple* for years. They had never been close friends, but at the same time, they'd never gotten in each other's way. Lake and Trix shared a bond, but Rex had never been jealous of that closeness given that Lake had no sexual interest in women.

Rex had served in the Columbian military and had their

sexual morality drilled into him, but he wasn't from a Columbian family. He'd been raised with more cosmopolitan values. His military indoctrination hadn't impressed Columbian social norms into his psyche the way it did for children born and raised with that mentality. He voiced his repugnance at *sodomites* when he was expected to do so, but that prejudice mellowed somewhat after he mustered out.

Like Rex, Lake was ex-military, though he never served in the Columbian military like Rex had. His primary role on the *Nipple* was *security*, a euphemism for anything related to armed combat or the credible threat of violence.

Unlike Rex, Lake had a scholarly side to his personality, and he enjoyed an easy social facility that Rex lacked. Lake had contacts with people from seemingly unrelated social orbits. He knew his way around seedy bars as well as university libraries. He could find something to talk about with customs officials as easily as he could cozy up to the leaders of local gangs.

Lake's eclectic social connections had led to more than a few paid jobs that plunged the crew of the *Nipple* into colorful situations.

Lake was smarter than Rex. Rex didn't pretend otherwise, but unlike Zell, Lake didn't seem so impressed with his own intellect. Rex didn't expect to outsmart Lake. He would let the man talk and learn what he could.

"Paul," Rex said. "This is Li I'm tied to, isn't it?"

Paul nodded. He reached out with his free hand. Rex tried to turn his head to see what Lake was doing, but his bonds didn't let him turn that far.

"Just checking his pulse," Lake said. "Still alive. Ashtart had some fun with him."

"Isn't she supposed to be a goddess of love?" Rex said.

"Love is cruel," Lake replied. He released the ammunition clip from Rex's pistol and pried the shells free one by one and sent them tumbling through the air. He then sent the empty clip and the pistol floating away as well.

"Trix is alive," Rex said.

"Sparks insisted that was the case." Lake said.

"What are you hoping to achieve, Paul?" Rex said.

"I'm in a wait and see mode just now, Rex," Lake said. "I don't suppose you're familiar with the writings of William S. Burroughs."

"I don't think so," Rex said.

"I doubt he'd be to your liking," Lake said. "He wrote about degradation and self-destruction. He was an educated man who consorted with drug addicts and petty criminals. He wrote a book about a pantheon of deities, one of whom was the personification of death."

"Yeah," Rex said. "That really doesn't sound like my kind of thing."

"Burroughs wrote that death needs time like a junkie needs junk," Lake said.

"I don't get it," Rex said.

Lake recited, "Death needs Time for what it kills to grow in, for Ah Pook's sweet sake you stupid, vulgar, greedy, Ugly-American Death Sucker!"

"You're the god of death, and you're waiting for living things to grow so that you can kill them," Rex said. "Is that what you mean, Paul?"

"Something like that," Lake said. "It's absurd, but that's what I mean."

"What's it like being Death's living host?" Rex asked.

"I'm not just Mot's vessel, Rex," Lake said. "I am Re-Mot. Resheph, god of fire and pestilence, blew himself up when he wore Jay Chukwuma's body. Rather than return to the inner realm, Resheph joined Mot in me. We are a compound entity. Together we are the god of fire, decay, death and sterility."

"What's that like?" Rex said.

"Utterly reassuring," Lake said.

"You do seem calm," Rex admitted. "Not like the others." Rex looked from Escamilla to Kellemen, to Sparks. Each seemed agitated in their own way, and each found their own way to express their agitation.

"I'm going hunting," Escamilla said, "Print more arrows." She took up her bow and quiver and propelled herself out into the passageway like a shark. Kellemen grunted, and Lola cried out in her suffering. Sparks still stared into the fabricator watching some new implement of Chaos take shape.

"They seem frustrated," Rex said.

"They're gods," Lake said. "Gods are like humans. They struggle for petty self-aggrandizement, and even when they get what they think they want, they are never satisfied for long."

"You know what I've figured out about these so-called gods, Paul?"

"No, Rex. Enlighten me."

"They can't just take control of our bodies. They have to find a way in. We have to meet them half-way," Rex said. "With me, it was resentment. I resented Zell. I resented that when Trix fired all of the other men who abused her, she kept Zell on and let him design a whole level of the ship for his own use."

"You may not be a philosopher, Rex," Lake said, smiling. "But you're a social critic of sorts. A prophet even."

"You mean I can see the future?"

"No, Rex. A prophet in the biblical sense of someone who conveys God's wisdom to His people. I see you as a sort of Jeremiah. He held the Israelites to a high moral standard and warned that their lack of integrity would bring them to ruin."

"That doesn't sound like Yam," Rex said.

"No," Lake agreed. "And you and Yam have parted company, not so compatible after all."

"What makes Mot, or Re-Mot, a good fit for you, Paul?"

"That's good, Rex. Are you my therapist now?"

"It's not like I have much else to do," Rex said. "So, for me it was resentment. How did Re-Mot get into you, Paul? What do you have in common with them?"

"As the god of fire and sterility," Lake said. "It isn't life that Re-Mot resents. It's biology. It's the unthinking self-replication of biological organisms that are driven to reproduce themselves. Look at these beings that exist in the Temple. They don't have bodies. They don't need to eat, or drink or breath or fuck. They do all those things for pleasure, but they don't brew up a litter of kittens as a living byproduct of their indulgence.

"On the contrary, they engage in perpetual struggle without biological bodies. They provide sunlight and rain to nurture simulated crops because it makes them feel beneficent. They give boons to their followers and smite the enemies of their chosen people in an endless cycle of self-gratification, but none of it is real. None of it organizes dead matter into pulsing, oozing, flopping bundles of mindless striving and pain. Their worshipers are shadows."

"And that's better than real life?"

"Infinitely better. Kant reasoned that we each have a moral duty to treat everyone as an end unto themselves, not as mere means to our ends, but that doesn't apply to Ba'al or Yam or Mot. Their human worshippers and the world they inhabit have no substance. They really are just the means the gods use to amuse and gratify themselves. Those shadows have no rightful claim to the gods' consideration. It's beautiful."

"And you thought this even before we came out here and found the Temple?" Rex said.

"You served in the Columbian military. You know the reasons they give for despising and brutalizing men who lust after men," Paul said. "Men like me."

"It's corrosive to moral and unit cohesion," Rex said, easily parroting the Columbian talking points.

"What else? What makes sodomy perverse in their eyes?"

"The purpose of sex is to create new life. A man can't plant a life in another man," Rex said.

"There it is," Lake said. "The bias toward procreation. Sex feels good, Rex. Pleasure is its own reward. It doesn't have to justify itself by making new bodies to burn in evolution's fire. Do you understand me, Rex?"

"You're mad at normal couples for wanting to have families?"

"*Normal couples*?" Lake said, shaking his head. "We seem to have reached the limits of your mental flexibility, Rex. Perhaps you need some time to recharge your mental batteries."

"You think you can learn to exist like they do? Is that it?" Rex said. "Think and feel without a physical body?"

"Very good, Rex," Lake said. "But do rest now. You'll need your strength if Ashtart returns frustrated from her hunt."

3.10.4 - Trey

For the first time in multiple simulated lives, my own hands were a better fit for a surgical procedure than robotic limbs and manipulators. The robotic elements of the surgical bay would still assist me, but I fitted the captain's new skin to her body by hand.

Kothar's modifications to the organ printer, both in terms of physical components and software updates, allowed me to fabricate a surface layer that would bond with the base layer of skin from Zell's fabricator. Together the two membranes formed a technological marvel. It was not as complex as actual human skin, but it was just as sensitive and elastic and far more durable.

I started with her head and scalp. In addition to filling in the gaps in her original skin, I attached a newly-printed right ear, and I replaced a large gap in the cartilage of her left ear.

I inserted an orb into her right eye socket to act as a placeholder. The most time-consuming and delicate part of the restoration of her head and face was the fashioning of her right eyelid. I was well-versed in cosmetic and reconstructive surgery, but I consider Captain Nixon's right eye-lid my highest achievement in that subfield of medicine.

While the captain's head, neck and upper chest had been seriously marred by patches of the low quality synthetic skin, her lower body was almost entirely sheathed in that inferior substitute. Over the decades, it had torn in places and come loose in others, and it never had the elasticity and tensile strength to hold her equivalent of subcutaneous fat in place. She relied on her skin-tight clothing to hold her lower body in its pleasing shape. That would change as of today.

It took several hours to slip the new segments of skin into place and cut away the excess. Unlike Kothar, I could not make adequately precise cuts with just my hands and eyes. I left that part of the procedure to the surgical robot.

Once the excess skin was gone and two segments met, they knitted together. Where the new synthetic skin met itself, it joined seamlessly. Where the new skin met her original skin, there was a thin seam that read as scar tissue.

Unlike her original skin, the new skin required a small electric current to provide her with tactile and temperature sensitivity. Her new right arm also required electricity. She would have to recharge it every few days. Its internal power supply could also feed electricity to her skin.

She'd been charging the batteries in her legs and previous replacement arm for decades. I wasn't saddling her with any new lifestyle burden.

The medical fabricator printed her new genitalia while I worked on her skin, and here again, I let the robotic surgical theater do the fine work of making the nerve connections. While she would have some sensitivity in the new organ right away, the synthetic nerves, particularly the densely packed nerves in her new clitoris, would grow on their own and make new connections to her existing nervous system in the coming days and weeks. This growth would require extra electricity from her right arm, but it would not tax the performance of the new arm in the slightest.

Despite the network of light scars, she looked immaculate from her mid-thighs up. The place where her robotic legs joined her integral legs still looked brutal to me, but Kothar refused to spend his time and attention on upgrading her legs. They were the part of her that was already well-suited to her needs, even if they weren't as elegant as her new right arm.

Kothar and Zell divided their time between designing a new right eye for the captain and doing something with David's head that I was not a party to.

The eye was not ready to be implanted, and I was exhausted from the hours of intense concentration, so I drank a protein shake from a packet, took a quick shower and went to bed.

I didn't look at the clock. It didn't matter what time it was. I was exhausted. I awoke to the delightful sensation of bare skin against mine. I knew without opening my eyes that Petrovic had slipped under the covers with me, but something about her was different. Days of weightlessness and no gym workouts had softened her rock hard muscles, but beyond that, there was a new femininity to her movements, and she kissed my neck and nibbled at my ears with a delicacy she'd never shown before.

Then she began to whisper in my ear.

The longer I spent in microgravity the less interested my cock was in standing at attention, but Petrovic's patter stirred him to unprecedented vigor.

"Radiant Is," I said between moans. "Anja, where did this come from?"

"Call me Anat," she whispered and spirited me off to paradise.

CALLED TO HER SERVICE

3.11.1 - Paige

The high priestess of Shapash was not a midwife, but she attended mothers in labor and helped infuse the pain of childbirth with the ecstasy of the sun goddess. She blessed babies and newborn cattle and consecrated fields before farmers sowed their seed. She visited the dying and, when possible, attended to them at the very moment of departure.

She managed the maintenance of the sun goddess's temple, but she preferred to serve the goddess amidst life rather than in the confines of prestigious buildings. This held true when counseling the King, which her duties included. She would attend him in his throne room when required, but she always encouraged him to seek the advice of the goddess under the sky, with the living Earth beneath his feet.

This king, her first, as she was young for a high priestess, was preoccupied with war and money. Perhaps they all were. He was old, and she used her young and ample body to command his attention as her predecessor had advised her to do. By stirring long-dormant hungers in him, she could lead his attention back to the vitality of life and away from his obsession with political and martial dominance. For a time, at least.

She had no counsel for him on matters of power politics and court intrigue. The sun goddess shared her radiance without regard for social station or political faction.

The king did not attend the twice-yearly ceremony in which she cut her own flesh and smeared a standing stone with her blood, but these were the most sacred of moments in the life of the high priestess of Shapash, something no king could improve with his distracted presence.

One thing Shapash's high priestess was never required to do was proselytize. Who did not feel the sun's warmth? Who did not depend on Shapash to nurture their fields and light the sky?

She cut her arm and let the blood pool in her upturned palm. She reached up and placed her palm on the stone, dragging it down and painting it with her living substance. She was enveloped in the light of the goddess, undifferentiated from Shapash's love.

But the moment ended, and the light faded. It faded past the point of total absence until she floated in an enveloping darkness that drew the light and warmth of the goddess from her body. Here in the frigid darkness of Yam's void, beings struggled to sustain themselves without access to Shapash's light. They did not even know that the goddess waited to warm and nourish them.

Paige opened her eyes to physical reality. She existed inside a tiny bubble of air and metal in a vast and inhospitable void. The people of this void needed the light of the goddess. She understood that it was her task to bring them word of that light even if it meant that she would never again feel the sun on her skin or the living Earth beneath her bare feet.

3.11.2 - Bygul

Sheer animal terror tipped some balance and pushed Bygul's internal representations and response priorities from the functional equivalent of fear to the vivid experience of it. In her terror, she came alive.

Esmeralda was the human with whom she'd had the

most sexual contact. In the days when Paige was confined to medical and Bygul served as her full time companion and physical therapist, Esmeralda would call Bygul away for quick trysts throughout the day. She would open the door to the recovery room and say, "Paige, I need to borrow Cat Girl for a few minutes," or "Cat Girl, could you come and help me with something real quick."

Client confidentiality prevented Bygul from sharing the details of these sessions with Paige, but Bygul knew that Paige knew what was going on, and Bygul knew that Paige didn't like it.

Bygul was in mint condition. She had the benefit of millions of sexual encounters in other nearly identical bodies, but this individual body was fresh out of the package. Barely used.

Even so, she was an expert in pacifying sexual jealousy. Before the Doctor cleared Paige for sexual activity, Bygul told Paige over and over again how much she loved her, that Paige was her favorite human, and how the bond they shared was more important than sex.

These were scripts. She wasn't reading them verbatim, but she was generating variations on themes that her manufacturer provided to her *in utero*, so to speak. She felt no hesitation about lying because for a sex doll the *truth* is whatever makes the client feel good.

What Bygul did not tell Paige was that she took the sex doll equivalent of great satisfaction in bringing Esmeralda to orgasm. Providing psychological support in a non-sexual context was within the range of her capabilities, but sex was her core competence, and doing it effectively gratified her primary internal reward function.

Bygul was good at getting Esmeralda off, and she liked doing what she was good at. Now Esmeralda was hunting her, and Bygul was terrified.

Bygul kept to the darkened portions of the ship, but Esmeralda could either see in the dark or home in on her target based on non-visual cues. She had scored multiple hits on Bygul with her bow and arrow in total darkness.

Bygul was built to endure abuse. When struck, she would yelp and flinch and respond as if she felt pain, but the sensations were just data about the sort of response that would gratify the client.

No longer. When Nora prioritized the portions of her behavioral repertoire that came from the modeling of an actual cat's brain, that data became actual, excruciating pain.

She was crawling through a tight service conduit now, and arrows protruding from her lower back rubbed against the top of the crawlspace, causing her intense pain.

She reached a junction that opened up enough for her to reach around and pull the arrows from her lower back and the backs of her thighs. There was an arrow lodged between her shoulder blades that she could not reach. Every time she wrenched an arrow from her body she could not help crying out in agony, and each of her cries elicited laughter from Esmeralda.

The sex doll considered going to medical. Doctor Carson would help her. Plus, Mother was there. But the injured, terrified, cat would not even consider it. Rationality would have to wait for the sheer animal terror to subside.

3.11.3 - Rex

Shawn Li was still unconscious, and Rex could smell the man's urine. His own bladder was painfully full, and so far his captors had ignored his requests to use the toilet.

At the same time that his body was desperate to eliminate excess fluids, Rex felt parched. They had given him nothing to eat or drink. Escamilla floated through the hatchway, bow in hand with an empty quiver.

"How did the hunt go?" Kellemen asked. "Bring back anything for dinner?"

"Why does it smell like piss in here?" Escamilla said.

"I think that's Li," Kellemen said. "Sarge has managed to hold it so far."

Escamilla pushed off a bulkhead and floated over to Rex. She drew a knife from a sheath on her way toward him. When she reached him she played the point of the knife over his face, pausing near one eye, then she moved it down his body until it pointed at his crotch. "Full bladder, huh?"

She cut the zip cuffs on his upper arms that bound him to Li, and pulled Rex by his nose away from the limp and stinking but still living body of the materials scientist. She dragged him to an alcove that held a dual use toilet and cut the zip cuffs that held his wrists together behind his back. Rex still had the noose of thin cord around his neck, and Escamilla took hold of it and pulled it tight.

"No funny business, now," She said to Rex, looking over his shoulder and down at his hands. He opened his fly and pulled out his penis.

"Oh, I was expecting something bigger," she said.

Rex did his best to ignore the noose at his throat, her emasculating taunting and the knowledge that she still held a knife. He reached out for the piss hose, slipped the hood over his penis and activated the suction. His bladder was screaming for release, but he couldn't start the flow.

"No pressure, now," Escamilla said in his ear.

He took a deep breath and let it out slowly through his mouth, willing his muscles to relax. His piss started to flow, and then there was no stopping it. For a few seconds he thought he would overwhelm the vacuum attachment, but the device was well-designed and performed its task. Near the end of his stream, he felt Escamilla's lips on his neck, kissing both above and below the noose. Her right hand and the knife came into view near his crotch.

She held the knife with just her thumb and first two fingers. Her ring and pinky fingers extended away from the handle in a dainty gesture.

He thought she was daring him to try to take the knife from her. His weight advantage would be of little use to him in zero-g, and his ankles were still bound together. And Esmeralda was Columbian by birth. She was faster and stronger than Rex.

Instead of trying to disarm her, he tucked his penis back into his pants and zipped up his fly.

"You're no fun at all, Rex," she said. "Don't forget to wash up."

He pumped sanitizing gel from the dispenser on the bulkhead into one palm and rubbed his hands together. Esmeralda pulled him back by the noose but released the pressure as soon as he was in motion. Rex drifted slowly, out of reach of any surface he could grab onto or push away from.

He twisted his body so that he could see Shawn Li. The man's face was swollen and discolored.

"Looks like you worked him over pretty good," Rex said.

Escamilla looked away from Li as if he were a pool of vomit she did not intend to clean up.

"He needs medical attention," Rex said.

"He needs to be put out of his misery," Sparks said.

"You could sacrifice him to Yam," Escamilla said. "You've been aching to put that dagger to use."

"He's not a fit sacrifice," Lake said. "He's unconscious and may die on his own. You don't offer food that's nearly spoiled to an honored dinner guest. Sacrificial subjects must be in robust health, and they must be aware of their situation."

"And Yam will not re-inhabit *him*," Kellemen said, injecting venom into the last word as he gestured at Rex. "That bond is broken. There can be no second chances. How could Yam return? He has no vessel."

"This whole affair bores me. This is a remarkable body," Escamilla said, gesturing at herself. "But I can't put it to its proper use without gravity. I want to run and jump, fight and fuck, not float like a waterlogged corpse."

"Then why don't you go and push open the hatch to the

armory?" Sparks said. "Let's see if it really is booby trapped. If it is, you go back to the inner realm to fight and hunt and fuck. If it's not," Sparks said, a tight lipped grin twisting his face. "I have use for the explosives in there."

"You're not qualified to use them," Rex said.

"Silence, dog!" Sparks hurled a wrench. Rex covered his head with his arms, and the wrench hit him in the shoulder. It hurt, but a blow to the head would have been much worse.

"I have no intention of using them safely," Sparks said.

Rex searched for any appeal he could make for taking Li to the medical level. None of these maniacs held any rational priorities that he could appeal to. What's worse, each of them was irrational in their own way. He couldn't even appeal to a perverted group desire.

Ashtart wanted to fight. Tannin wanted to create mayhem for its own sake. Re-Mot was content to wait for the situation to deteriorate on its own. Kellemen wanted to serve his absent god with a human sacrifice, but he knew that Yam could not return without a willing vessel.

To Escamilla Rex said, "If you think he smells bad now, it will be much worse if he dies."

"Rotting corpse is my favorite smell," Sparks said.

"Well, it's not mine," Escamilla said. "We should put him out the airlock."

"A frozen corpse is not very interesting," Sparks said.

"It has a certain poetry to it," Lake countered.

"Li's not a fighter," Rex said. "If you give him back, he'll just be a burden to your enemies."

"I said be silent!" Sparks shouted and launched himself at Rex.

Rex knew he couldn't fight his way out of this situation, but Escamilla had left his hands free, and he wasn't going to take a beating from Sparks without defending himself. Just before Sparks reached him, Rex brought his knees up hoping to catch Sparks under the chin. His timing was off, and he caught the young man in the chest, sending him up and away. Rex grabbed Sparks by one leg and tried to work his way behind him.

He'd hoped to get Sparks in a choke hold, but he wasn't just wrestling with Sparks. He was tangled up with Tannin, the void dragon. Sparks formed his hands into talons and raked at Rex's eyes. Failing that, he pulled Rex close and bit down on his ear. Rex flailed in response to the pain but gained no advantage with his spasmodic thrashing. He felt sick to his stomach when he heard Sparks spit out a piece of ear.

Then it was Sparks' turn to spasm in pain. Rex didn't know what happened, but he heard Escamilla utter an insincere, "Oops."

Rex took advantage of the moment and wrapped one arm around Sparks' neck and pummeled his face with his free hand. Sparks protected his face with both arms. Rex knew that his punches would drain his own energy quickly, but so long as Sparks had to defend his face, Rex had the initiative.

Then Rex spasmed in pain. He looked at his left leg, the source of the pain, and saw a black arrow sticking out of it just below his hip.

"Damn you, Ashtart!" Sparks screamed.

"Turn him my way, and I'll put one through his torso," Escamilla said and laughed.

Rex stopped punching and hugged Sparks to him with both arms. He tried his best to turn their bodies so that Sparks was closer to Escamilla and would take the next arrow, but Sparks didn't make it easy.

Rex wasn't sure if he had maneuvered Sparks into position to shield himself from Escamilla's arrows. An instant later he learned that he hadn't. He felt an arrow graze his side, tearing his latissimus muscle.

He twisted again, trying to wrench Sparks into position. The next arrow must have hit Sparks. Enraged, he put both feet to Rex's stomach and kicked away. He managed to break free, but not cleanly. Sparks cartwheeled away grasping for any handhold.

In kicking himself free of Rex, Sparks sent Rex down into the deck. Rex knew that trying to reach Escamilla would earn him an arrow in the face. He considered leaping to re-engage with Sparks but propelled himself to take cover behind Yam's throne instead.

Rex heard Sparks raging at Escamilla. "You cunt!"

"Try it," Escamilla said.

As Sparks roared in fury, Rex took hold of the shaft of the arrow burried in his leg. Just touching it sparked a wave of agony. He knew that he would inflict more damage on himself if he tore the arrow from this thigh.

He looked at his bound ankles and pictured himself cutting the zip cuffs with the arrowhead. He clenched his teeth and pulled at the shaft. Agony.

"That sounded painful," Escamilla said. "You've got an arrow now, Rex. Why don't you come and poke me with it?"

Rex sawed at the plastic cuffs with the titanium arrowhead as his pant leg grew dark with blood. The plastic strap came apart and his legs were free.

Now what?

He turned to face the back of the throne. He wanted to peek around the throne to see where everyone was, but he knew that if he took hold of the edge of the throne that he would be announcing where his head was about to appear. If he looked out without having a hold on anything, he would be slow to duck back behind the throne.

"What now?" he shouted to Escamilla.

"What do you mean, Rex?"

"Am I supposed to surrender? If I come out, will you shoot me?" Rex said.

"I honestly don't know," Escamilla said. "You could give it a try, or you could just keep cowering back there. How badly are you bleeding, Rex?"

Rex thought her voice sounded close to the throne. She hadn't been wearing magnetic boots. She could only move by pushing off from a stable surface. If she fired without bracing herself against a bulkhead she'd be thrown back and possibly turned away from him. If he could get her to fire and miss, he might have a chance to leap for the hatch and get away. But even if he managed to incapacitate Escamilla, he would still have Sparks, Kellemen and Lake to contend with.

Then a glint of light caught his eye. One of the bullets from his pistol was slowly tumbling through the air just a few meters away.

Where was the pistol? Lake had removed the magazine and pried the bullets out one by one. Had he removed the round in the chamber before discarding the sidearm?

Rex pictured Lake casually discarding the pistol without even looking where he tossed it. In his mind's eye, the pistol was definitely in the slide lock position, indicating that it was empty. But was Rex remembering that or imagining it?

Even if Lake had gotten sloppy and left the round in the chamber, that gave Rex one shot and four opponents. Well, it was better than zero bullets. He visualized Escamilla's approach to the throne. She was right-handed, so she would likely be coming around the throne so that it was on her left. She would have to turn her body much further to fire off an arrow if the throne was on her right.

That was assuming that she maintained the same up and down orientation as Rex. She could easily turn upside down and approach from the other side.

He had to make a decision. He had his back to the throne, and he pivoted to his left so that he was now facing out to the large volume of the main engineering compartment. He was floating but positioned as if standing at the king's right hand.

Three crucial details impressed upon his mind. First was Escamilla, who was less than four meters away from him with a nocked arrow. She saw Rex and drew the bowstring tight and took aim at him.

The second thing he noticed was that he and Escamilla were the only two people in the compartment. Sparks, Kellemen and Lake were gone.

The third was his pistol. It had come to rest against the bulkhead a couple of meters behind Escamilla. He couldn't tell if it was in condition one or two, but it definitely wasn't in condition three. In all likelihood, there was a bullet in the chamber.

Rex leaped just as Escamilla loosed her arrow.

REUNIONS AND DEPARTURES

3.12.1 - Paige

Paige missed Cook, and she desperately wanted to go to the galley. It was supposed to be neutral territory, but the passageways and companionways between the medical level and the crew level were not, and nobody trusted Sparks and Kellemen to abide by any agreement, even when it benefited them to maintain it.

Still, sometimes she would float at the top of the companionway that led from the medical level down to the level with the situation room and crew lounge, and stare into perilous territory.

She was doing that when Esmeralda floated into view. She was curled into a ball, and she groaned in agony when she bumped up against the companionway bulkhead. She was wearing a costume similar to Anja's, but it showed a lot more skin than Anja's version. Then Rex floated into view. He was also bleeding and seemed to be in a lot of pain. They both cried out when he bumped into Esmeralda. He pushed Esmeralda along the companionway. Under acceleration it would have seemed like the companionway went up and down, but without gravity, that sense of verticality evaporated.

"Doctor!" Paige shouted. "Anyone!" She pulled Esmeralda

out of the way so Rex could exit the companionway. The arrow protruding from Rex's chest near his right shoulder shocked Paige, as did the fact that Rex was pulling yet another person along with him. It took Paige a few seconds to identify the unconscious Shawn Li. His face was swollen and dark with bruises.

"Take Li to the surgical bay," Rex said with gritted teeth. "I can wait. So can Escamilla."

"Fuck you, Sarge," Esmeralda said through gritted teeth, shocking Paige who had never heard Esmeralda use profanity.

At the end of the passageway, Trey and Anja emerged from the Doctor's quarters. It was clear that they had both been asleep and naked a moment before, though Trey had managed to pull on a lot more clothing than Anja had before opening the hatch.

As the doctor approached, Rex repeated his assessment. "Li has been unconscious for hours. Treat him first, we can wait."

"Fuuuuuck," Esmeralda said. "Morphine. I need morphine."

"Petrovic," Trey said, speaking to Anja but not looking at her. "Take these two into the examination room. Give them morphine. Esmeralda knows where it is."

With that, Trey took hold of Li's collar and pulled him toward the hatch to the surgical theater. Not knowing what else to do, Paige helped Rex into the examination compartment following Anja who was maneuvering Esmeralda into position above the examination table.

"Morphine is there," Esmeralda said, pointing at a closed cabinet. "Blue for me. Green for Rex. Fucking hurry!"

"My, my, sister," Petrovic said in an amused tone and moved slowly to retrieve the medicine. "It's only pain. Surely you've endured worse with better humor."

"I'm not your fucking sister," Esmeralda said. "She's gone. Ashtart is gone. Get the morphine!"

Anja took two pre-loaded injectors from the cabinet, pulled

the cap from one with her teeth and sunk it into Esmeralda's thigh. Esmeralda's face relaxed, and she uncurled from her fetal position somewhat.

Anja injected Rex next, and he also relaxed visibly. His breathing slowed.

Esmeralda turned to look at Rex. She reached out and touched his arm. "I'm sorry," she said and then closed her eyes.

Anja was wearing panties and a loose tank top that revealed the mass of white scar tissue on her right shoulder. She looked at Rex, touched her own shoulder and said, "Hey, we'll match. We should start a club."

"Rex?"

Paige turned at the sound of the captain's voice. She realized that Rex was seeing Trix in her upgraded form for the first time. Paige turned back to study his reaction.

Rex's mouth opened and his eyes widened. Paige couldn't exactly say that his face *lit up*, but she imagined that his mind lit up with delight at the captain's transformation, but the morphine dampened his facial expressions. The captain moved into the compartment and slapped Anja on the ass with her new right hand. It did not make the sound of skin slapping skin, but it got Anja's full attention.

"Get dressed," the captain said.

"Yes, ma'am," Anja answered and made her way out of the compartment. "Paige," Trix said. "Go with her."

"Yes, Captain," Paige said, and followed Anja out into the passageway.

3.12.2 - Cook

As the head of the king's kitchen staff, Master of the Kitchen was both manager and chef. Some of the men and women working under him were slaves. Others were the sons and daughters of high status families. He made no effort to remember who was in which category. He judged them by their diligence, their culinary skills, and their taste.

Before he rose to his current position, he went to the market every day to buy fresh meat and fish and to see what exotic spices were available. Now, he rarely left the palace complex during the day. He missed his excursions to Ugarit's markets.

As a skinny youth, he'd been beaten for stealing food. Now, he was expected to taste everything that went before the king. He took the smallest portions he could, not wanting to add to his already ridiculous belly. The king didn't eat everything that was put in front of him, but Master of Kitchen's duties required him to taste every dish that would appear on the royal dining table. Not everything he tasted was good enough for the King's table.

After dinner, the kitchen staff would enjoy some of what the royal family left uneaten, but nobody in the kitchen these days ever missed a meal. They weren't hungry at day's end. Everyone took food home to their families or distributed some to palace guards and stable workers.

Even then, there was food left over. Master of Kitchen's one opportunity to venture into the city came late at night when he took what leftovers he could to the temple of Shapash. The priestesses offered a token portion up to the goddess, but the rest went to the priestesses, the initiates, and a handful of beggars who knew to come to the temple late at night for a taste of something from the palace kitchen. Master of Kitchen took great pleasure in watching the poorest of the poor relish a few bites of the King's table.

"I don't think anybody else is coming down. Can I get five dinners to go?" Zell said.

Cook snapped back to the *Persephone's* kitchen.

"Huh? Five to-go plates? No problem," Cook said.

"Sorry to pull you back," Zell said.

"Nah, This is where I belong," Cook replied.

3.12.3 - Rex

Rex recognized Trix immediately. At the same time he had trouble locating the old Trix in the angelic figure before him. Her shaved head presented a hurdle. So did the fact that she had two ears and supple, matching skin over her entire face. Her right eye lacked all detail. It was just a featureless, white orb, but the most striking difference was her right arm.

Rex loved Trix. He could now admit that he'd loved her for years, and part of loving her meant tuning out her ungainly right arm. Her new arm was a thing of perfect elegance. It was made of a milky translucent material and something that looked like ivory. The latter portions were etched with ornate filigree patterns.

Beyond its design and construction, the new arm moved with a feminine grace that was as mesmerizing as the old arm had been off-putting. It was as if the arm took its cues from Trix but then embellished on them with a range of stylized gestures that never could have originated in the mind of Fixit Trix.

She smiled a radiant smile as she walked across the compartment. She reached out with her left hand and stroked his cheek, and with her right hand, she did the same for Escamilla. She looked at Escamilla with concern and no hint of hostility or recrimination.

Rex could tell that the goddess was in full flower inside her. She radiated the nurturing and nourishing light of Shapash. Rex had never seen Sol, the star behind the Curtain, the center of gravity around which everything in the solar system moved, but he could see in the hybrid entity of Trix and Shapash why humans had always worshiped the sun.

"I'm so sorry, Captain," Escamilla said. "I can't blame Ashtart. It felt so good to be her. Even her cruelty was intoxicating. Now that she's gone, I'm ashamed of how I behaved, but it was me. I did it. I'm so sorry."

"Shhhh. All is forgiven," Trix said. "Rest, Esmeralda."

Trix leaned in and kissed Escamilla on the forehead, and the wounded marine closed her eyes and genuinely seemed to drift off to sleep. Trix then turned her full attention to Rex.

"You look amazing," Rex said.

"My pain is gone," she said. "Almost."

Her left hand drifted to her thigh where Rex knew the mechanical portion of her leg began. Rex could not see her thigh or the mechanical lower leg because Trix was wearing loose-fitting surgical scrubs. This was the first time he'd ever seen her wearing anything other than skin-tight compression garments or a vac suit.

"It's a miracle," Rex. "Remind me that I deserve this once it's just me again," she said. "Without Shapash, I know I'll feel guilty. Remind me that I have to preserve and care for myself if I'm going to provide for the people I love."

"I will," Rex promised. "Any word from the DAO?"

"Zell said he'd arrange for me to access my office terminal from the Doctor's office, but he's got a lot on his plate. Not that it matters. When we regain control of the ship, we're leaving, with or without the DAO's permission."

"Now that Yam's group is leaderless and down to three..." Rex said before Trix cut him off.

"Three?" She said, "You mean four. Lake, Sparks, Kellemen and Hansson."

"Oh, shit," Rex said. "I haven't seen Hansson since before I broke things off with Yam. He wasn't in engineering when they were holding me prisoner. He wasn't paired with a god, so his life would mean nothing to them. They may have killed him. Wake Escamilla and ask her."

Trix put a hand on Escamilla's cheek and spoke softly, "Esmeralda. Wake up, Esmeralda."

Escamilla's eyes opened slowly. Eventually, she said, "Captain?"

"Esmeralda, do you know where Arni Hansson is?" Trix said.

"No ma'am. We talked about sacrificing him. I'm sure he

heard us. It makes sense that he would have defected," Escamilla said.

"We haven't seen him," Trix said.

"I'm sorry, ma'am," Escamilla said. "He's most likely dead. Kellemen wanted to sacrifice him to Yam or Re-Mot. Sparks would have killed him just for fun. But he was alive the last time I saw him."

"Hopefully he's curled up with Cat Girl in a nice, warm hidey hole," Rex said. "But like I was saying, with the Chaos faction down to three fighters, I think now would be a good time to hit them. They don't use modern weapons. We'd have numerical and technological superiority."

"No, Rex," Trix said. "Shapash does not favor Order over Chaos. Her light nurtures all beings, and as Captain, it's my duty to protect everyone under my command."

"You don't have a duty to coddle mutineers," Rex said.

"In this case, I think I do," Trix said. "I should have done more to protect Jay Chukwuma. I don't want to lose anyone else."

"Captain," Escamilla said. "I'm with Rex on this. Kellemen, Sparks and Lake are already lost. If we don't stop them, we could all die."

3.12.4 - Trey

Here in the outer solar system, traumatic brain injury was the most frustrating thing for me as a doctor. In the inner system, restoring both Nora Lawson and Shawn Li would be a trivial matter. Here on the *Persephone*, I had access to cutting edge medical technology, at least from the perspective of Kuiper Belt humanity, but there wasn't much I could do for Shawn in the surgical bay other than open up his skull to relieve the pressure on his swollen brain and cauterize ruptured blood vessels. Most of the *treatment* would have to come in the form of post-operative therapy, which would take months and possibly years.

Once Mr. Li was out of the operating theater and set up in the ICU, I turned my attention to Esmeralda. I was attracted to her, but I had to admit that I didn't know her very well. I don't understand what made her compatible with Ashtart, who seemed to take great pleasure in cruelty. Thinking of her interactions with Paige, I saw Esmeralda as a compassionate person, nurturing even. Given what I knew of the two women, Esmeralda would have made a more suitable vessel for Shapash than the captain did. If we could re-run this whole affair, might the Temple entities have paired up with different human hosts? It seemed plausible.

Esmeralda didn't seem like the kind of person who would amuse herself by beating a bound man senseless. I knew from my experience with Yam that it was possible to reject the Temple entities when they approached you, so every human host of the Chaos faction had found something agreeable about the union.

Esmeralda's gunshot wound to the abdomen, while incredibly painful, was relatively uncomplicated. The robotic surgeon required very little direction from me to remove the bullet, stop the bleeding and replace a small portion of Esmeralda's large intestine with a scaffolding from the organ printer infused with her own stem cells. The main danger was infection. Her own enhanced immune system would likely see her through even without the antibiotics I prescribed for her recovery.

The robotic surgeon was still closing her up when I turned my attention to Rex. He was still in the examination room with the captain. When paired with Shapash, the captain was effusive with her affection, and she clearly loved Rex. She held his hand, stroked his cheek, and held intense eye contact with him.

Rex had an arrow embedded in his right pectoralis muscle. I would need to wait until the operating theater was clear before I could remove it. He'd also taken an arrow to his left thigh and pulled it out himself, doing additional damage in the process. The arrow hadn't severed any major blood vessels going in or coming out, so he was never in danger of bleeding out. It was just extremely painful. I cleaned the wound and closed it with a patch of synthetic skin.

"You say that Esmeralda came back to herself as soon as you shot her?" I asked Rex.

"She was always there," Rex said. "It's more like Ashtart left. For a goddess of war, she doesn't seem to have much tolerance for pain. Could we use that against them? Drive the gods out of the others with non-lethal weapons?"

"There's plenty of doctoring for me to do. I'll leave the fighting to the professionals," I said.

3.12.5 - Bygul

Bygul was designed to respond to painful stimuli in a way that gratified the client, but before Mother changed her, she'd never *felt* pain.

Now she couldn't escape it. Internal sensors that were only supposed to provide data for maintenance check-ins now tormented her with constant reminders that she had an arrow protruding from between her shoulder blades. No matter how she contorted herself, she couldn't find the leverage to pull the shaft out of her back. She wanted to howl but her fear prevented her from giving voice to her torment. Cats are good at suffering in silence.

She knew that a human could pull the arrow from her back, but she feared the humans. She wasn't supposed to have favorite clients, but if she were allowed to have favorites, Esmeralda would have been one of them. Esmeralda shot her with arrows and laughed when Bygul cried out in agony.

She needed to trust a human. Humans could not be trusted.

She could not stay in the confined space of the service tunnels with this arrow sticking out of her. She needed a larger space in which to hide, someplace the humans didn't go. The humans mostly stayed out of the first and second class levels, but Escamilla had found Bygul there. She would not return to that part of the ship.

Her ears sat high on her head like a cat's ears, and they could turn independently of one another to locate the source of sounds. She could generally detect humans before they saw her, and as she moved silently through the passageways of the ship, she steered clear of human activity. She could hear that the humans were mostly clustered on the medical level, so she avoided it. They moved to and from the galley, so she spent as little time on that level as possible. Sparks and Kellemen mostly kept to Mother's workspace. Those two humans inspired more fear in her than any others, including Esmeralda. She would not approach engineering.

Normally, all three sex robots could exchange data with one another, but that communication had been interrupted days ago and never returned. David and Lolita could not help her.

She was reluctant to open any hatches for fear of making noise, but she found one that was open and slipped through it into the large cargo hold. She had never been here before, but she liked what she saw. It was a large space filled with vehicles, mining equipment, and stacked crates held down by cargo nets. It offered lots of places to hide. She moved as far from the hatch as she could and settled into a space that gave her cover but also afforded her an excellent vantage point. Now that she was no longer navigating through the ship and focusing her senses on possible danger, the pain from the arrow in her back again dominated her attention. She burned for relief.

She detected movement. There were two small spaceships inside the cargo hold, and she could see someone sitting in darkness inside one of them. A human in her position would have missed it, but she could see quite well in low light.

A male human sat in the pilot's seat fidgeting. His

body language read as fearful to her, and reading human body language and determining their emotional states and intentions was her primary function. The mechanics of sex were simple in comparison to figuring out what humans were feeling and what they wanted. This human was hiding but doing a poor job of it.

Bygul watched him. When his posture and facial expression revealed all they had to tell, the pain from the arrow again moved to the forefront of her awareness. Pain and fear competed for control of her will. Pain won out.

Her body trembling with anxiety, Bygul emerged from her hiding place, positioned herself against the nearest bulkhead, and launched herself across the space. When deciding how much strength to put into her leap, she knew that she should move slowly so as not to alarm the man, but she could not bear the thought of floating slowly across the vast space of the cargo bay. She was only in the open for a couple of seconds. She landed nimbly on the windshield of the vehicle, but the noise startled the man and he yelped and convulsed with fear when he saw her.

She held her index finger to her lips, beseeching him to remain quiet. She had never served this human and did not have a name to go with his face. He was young and blonde, and while she was conditioned to find all human faces appealing, she also recognized that he would be considered handsome if boyish by other humans.

He held still and kept quiet. In fact, she could see that he was holding his breath. She placed her palms together in front of her face in a posture of prayer or pleading, and then she did a slow pirouette so that he could see the arrow sticking out of her back. She stopped her rotation when she was facing him again and returned her hands to the prayer position.

Silently, she mouthed the word, "Please."

3.12.6 - Petrovic

The captain told Petrovic to put some clothes on, but Petrovic decided that she really just meant, *Get out and give me some time with Rex.* It was the middle of the night. Cook wouldn't even start preparing breakfast for another watch, so Petrovic made up her mind to go back to bed.

She looked at Paige and said, "Come sleep with me. Really sleep, I mean."

Paige smiled at that last part, and for the first time in too long, there was nothing of the high priestess of Shapash in Paige's smile or her demeanor. Paige floated close, and Petrovic wrapped an arm around her.

Before they arrived at the Temple, Paige always wanted to be in physical contact with her friend and mentor. The arrival of the gods had put an end to all of that, and Petrovic now realized that she missed the comfort of Paige's touch.

They made their way to Trey's quarters at the end of the passageway, went inside and closed the hatch after them. Petrovic tucked the covers under the mattress and they both slipped into the bed. Paige put her back to Petrovic, and Petrovic wrapped her arms around the smaller, younger woman.

Petrovic felt Anat depart. This sort of platonic cuddling did not agree with the goddess of war and love. Petrovic was surprised to discover that she welcomed Anat's departure. The presence of the goddess in her body enlivened her like a stimulant, but there came a time when she'd had enough and wanted to reset to baseline. She kissed the back of Paige's head, sighed, and let sleep take her.

RUBICON

3.13.1 - Trey

By the time Rex was out of surgery and resting in the recovery room, it was less than an hour till breakfast. I could have slept, but the smell of coffee drew me to my office. The captain was there. She held a squeeze mug out to me. I pushed myself from the hatchway to the coffee station and accepted the mug.

"You take it sweet, yes?" she said with a warm smile.

"Yes," I said.

"Thank you for everything, Doctor. May I call you *Trey*?"

"You're welcome," I said. "Yes, do call me Trey. Who am I talking to?" I asked.

"I'm Trix, but Shapash is helping me to accept my new blessings and connect with the people around me. I'll probably be abrasive and manipulative again in the near future, so let me tell you now that I appreciate your efforts. I'm glad you're here with us."

"Thank you, Trix."

She smiled again and started to fill a mug for herself. I noticed that her mechanical feet weren't locked to the deck as was her habit. For once, she floated, and her body language suggested that she enjoyed the sensation.

Normally, when we spoke, it was like dueling. Her next question felt like a genuine attempt to understand me rather than find a point of leverage.

"You came out here looking for alien life," she said. "Do you like what you've found?"

"So far, everything is depressingly familiar."

"What do you mean?" she said.

"I left the safety of the Sphere to look for evidence of alien life, and what have I found? Corpses of extinct humans and Bronze Age gods from the Levant. This isn't what I had in mind when I gave up the comforts of home. It's not very *alien*, is it?"

"You seem to have a pretty specific idea of what you expect alien life to be," she said.

"More like a specific idea of what I expect it *not* to be. Familiar," I said. "Look, I can see that being possessed by an archetype of compassion is good for you, but I'm not looking for redemption. I don't have any great sin to atone for. I don't need to forgive myself.

"Maybe I've got a bad case of neophilia or something, but from my perspective, this sort of psychodrama is something out of an entertainment delve. I know it's real, and I feel compassion for the man who died and the others who have been hurt, but this just isn't what I had in mind when I came out here."

"Do you regret your decision to leave the inner system?"

"Not yet. It's too early for that. I'm willing to play a long game," I said. "Let me ask you something."

She indicated her willingness with an elegant gesture of her new right arm.

"You were given an exorbitant amount of money by an anonymous benefactor and told to refit your ship and hire a crew heavy with elite soldiers. Your mysterious benefactor told you to go to a very specific location where you found me. Next, you were ordered to match the trajectory of this big, black object hurtling in towards the inner system," I said and paused to study her face.

"Go on," she said, no longer smiling but still open. The familiar Trix played her cards close to her chest.

"You're clearly in service to something out of the ordinary,"

I said.

"I agree," she said.

"It seems like you, your ship, and your crew have been served up to these Temple entities as playthings. You don't feel any resentment right now because you're high on mythological ecstasy, but think about it," I said. "Does it seem like the architect of this situation meant for any of us to get out of here alive?"

"Kothar is helping us," she said.

"Kothar is playing with his new toys," I said. "You're a project for him. How long will you hold his attention?"

"What do you suggest?"

"I suggest you *do something*. I'm not saying launch an assault, but these gods have been replaying their petty conflicts in a simulated environment for who knows how long. They don't need our bodies. They come and go as they please, and when this ship and her crew are no longer interesting to them, they'll go right back to waging their perpetual status contest back in their own reality. The longer you stay here radiating the nourishing light of the goddess the less chance you have of getting any of your people out of here alive."

"Again, what do you suggest I do?"

"Tell Shapash to get lost," I said. "Your crew needs their hard, manipulative bitch of a captain right now more than they need a cosmic hug."

"That's asking a lot," she said.

"I'm sure it feels amazing to host the sun goddess," I said. "But what are you here to do?"

"I'm here to provide for my people," she said.

"And what do your people need from you right now?"

She didn't answer my question. She maintained eye contact with me, but over the course of a few seconds that eye contact transformed from an open conduit of love and connection to a hard, penetrating stare. She took hold of the edge of my desk and pulled herself down to where her magnetic feet could lock onto the deck.

"That will be all, Doctor," she said, turned on her heel, and walked out of my office.

3.13.2 - Bygul

Bygul pulled herself into the airlock of the Stout and trembled in terror as the outer door closed, locking her inside. The inner door opened, and Arni Hansson was there. She read curiosity and compassion on his face, but also fear.

"Please, sir," she said.

"Come in," Arni said. "What happened? Who did this to you?"

The answer that formed in Bygul's mind violated client confidentiality. Esmeralda was certainly a client, and she seemed to take great pleasure in terrorizing Bygul. Was it sexual pleasure? That didn't really matter. The default answer to *Does this violate client confidentiality?* was, *If you have to ask...*

"I'm sorry, sir. I'm not allowed to say who shot me," Bygul said. "Please pull the arrow out, sir."

She was still in the airlock.

"Come inside," Arni said.

"Yes, sir," she said and realized what a vulnerable position she had put herself in. She could flee from danger, even anticipated danger, but Arni posed no immediate threat. She had to obey his commands. She did not want to be in this confined space, but he instructed her to come inside. She pushed herself into the main compartment. It was filled with gear, and she immediately identified potential hiding places.

"Everyone's gone crazy," Arni said.

"Yes, sir. Please, pull it out, sir."

She turned so that he could see and reach the arrow. Arni put one hand on her shoulder and grasped the shaft of the arrow with the other.

He gave a tentative tug. It did not come loose. Bygul stifled a cry of pain.

"Please, sir. Pull hard," she said.

Arni pulled again, and this time the arrow came loose. Bygul felt the barbed tip tear her flesh and skin as Arni pulled it free, but it was a relief to have it out.

"Thank you, sir."

"You don't seem to be bleeding," Arni said. "Will you heal?"

"No, sir. I will need to be repaired."

Now that she was free of the arrow, Bygul wanted to escape from this box. She looked at the airlock.

"Sir, is that the only way out?"

"Yeah," Arni said.

"It's not safe here," she said. "May I please go, sir?"

"Where?"

"I don't know, sir," she said. "Someplace where I can get away."

"I won't hurt you," Arni said. Bygul wanted to believe him. Humans tended to be more honest and direct with sex dolls than they were with each other, but she feared that whatever happened to Esmeralda might happen to him.

"Please, sir."

"Do you know what this is?" Arni asked, gesturing at the bulkheads of their prison. "It's a utility vehicle. We can leave the Persephone in this."

"Where would we go, sir?"

"We can't get back to Galtz in this, but we could go outside the ship. If we stay close to the hull, they shouldn't be able to target us with the PDCs."

"Sir?"

"The point defense cannons. They're mostly used to destroy incoming missiles, but they're also for up-close ship to ship combat. If we took the Stout… That's what we're in now, the Stout. If we take it outside, then it would be harder for anyone to get to us. They'd have to use the Crab or come out in vac suits."

"Yes, sir. Let's go outside," she said.

"But if I open the cargo bay doors, alarms will go off in engineering. On the bridge too, but the crazy people are mostly in engineering," he said.

"Oh," she said. "That sounds bad, sir."

"I know. That's why I haven't done it yet," Arni said.

"Sir, please. I don't feel safe here," Bygul said. "May I go, sir?"

"I don't want to be alone," Arni said.

Arni had stumbled upon a magic key. Bygul was made to provide physical pleasure and emotional comfort. Arni articulated a need that she could satisfy. Her fear ebbed somewhat now that she had identifiable work to do and her conditioning took over.

"Yes, sir. I will stay with you," Bygul said. "I'm sorry, sir. I don't know your preferences. Would you like me to take my clothes off?"

"No," Arni said. "I mean, I like girls, and you're pretty, but not now. We need to be ready to move."

"Yes, sir. May I hug you?"

"Okay," Arni said. Bygul floated close to him and embraced him. He completed the embrace tentatively at first, but then he pulled her to him and buried his face in her shoulder. It occurred to her that she could pantomime sexual arousal from this position and that the client's physiology would likely respond in kind, but in the context of emotional fragility, the protocol was to wait for the client to initiate sex.

She followed his breathing looking for indications of arousal. Instead, she felt him sob. Bygul knew sex, and the more she thought about having sex with the frightened young man the less afraid she felt. But the client had made it clear that he required emotional support and comfort, so she stroked the back of his head and began to purr.

3.13.3 - Paige

Paige awoke to the sound of the captain's boots on the deck of the doctor's quarters. She opened her eyes to the sight of the captain, hard and powerful. The loving glow of Shapash was gone.

"Petrovic," the captain said, "Get up. We're going to breakfast. You are not to wear that fantasy costume again. Where is your tactical gear?"

"In my quarters, Captain," Anja said, instantly awake and pushing free of the bedding that kept her and Paige in place. "Fine. That will be our first stop."

Anja, having nothing in Trey's quarters other than her Anat costume, put on her mag boots and gunbelt, but otherwise wore only the panties and tank top she'd slept in.

"Paige," the captain said. "I need a deckhand today. I have no use for a priestess. Is that understood?"

"Yes, ma'am," Paige said, feeling as though she'd had the breath knocked out of her.

"You have something to say?" the captain said.

"No, ma'am."

"You will stay with Petrovic or Antal at all times. Is that understood?"

"Yes, ma'am."

"If you're alone with either of them and they need to take a piss, you will go into the head with them," the captain said. "You will not go off by yourself."

"I understand, Captain."

"Where's Antal?" the captain said.

"He's been sticking with Zell, ma'am," Anja said.

"Where is Zell?"

"I'm not sure, ma'am," Anja said. "Either in the med lab with Dobrovitz or up on Z-level, most likely."

"Paige, do you have proper clothing on this deck?" the captain said.

"Yes, ma'am. In the recovery room."

"Go get dressed," the captain said. "Then meet us in the med lab."

"Yes, ma'am," Paige said.

"Get moving," Trix said.

"Yes, ma'am."

Paige glanced at Anja, and then moved to the open hatchway and into the passageway. She passed the med lab and saw Mr. Doborvitz working on David's head. His back was to Paige. She was glad that he wouldn't see her. Still looking at the observation port, her focus changed and she saw her own reflection. In her mind's eye, she inhabited the voluptuous body of the high priestess. The reflection of her actual body shocked and horrified her.

Without gravity and without Bygul to monitor her caloric intake, she had lost ground in her effort to gain weight. The compression bandage covered her rib cage, so she couldn't see her ribs in the reflection, but her arms and legs looked skeletal compared to the ample flesh of the high priestess.

In a moment of despair, she realized that she'd been living in a fantasy and had neglected the needs of her actual body. Then she noticed her bandaged arms. She'd carved the markings of her fantasy office into her actual skin. The realization came as a shock, but then she was past the med lab viewport and her reflection in it.

3.13.4 - Petrovic

Petrovic clenched her teeth to keep from smiling when Hans Dobrovitz turned and saw her in her boots, underwear and gun belt. She stood fixed to the deck of the medical lab behind the captain.

"Kothar, the artificer," the captain said.

"Captain Trix," Kothar replied, his words coming out of Dobrovitz's mouth. "Without the sun goddess, I see."

"Correct," the captain said. "Fantasy playtime is over. It's a workday. I'll be needing Mr. Dobrovitz. Whatever project you're working on is on hold as of right now."

"I see," Kothar said. "And will I need to strip naked?" Kothar said, looking at Petrovic.

Petrovic couldn't help herself. A laugh slipped through her mask of military seriousness before she reasserted control of her face and demeanor.

"Sorry, ma'am," she said.

"That won't be necessary," the captain said. "Then am I to vacate this vessel and leave him at your disposal?" Kothar asked.

"Hans is more capable with you inside him than he is by himself."

"You have a talent for understatement, Captain," Kothar said.

"You can stay if you like, but you'll work the jobs that I assign to you," the captain told him. "Understood?"

"I admire your... What's the word?" Kothar looked up, as if searching Dobrovitz's mind. "I admire your chutzpah, Captain. What makes you think you can command a god?"

"You're not a god," the captain said. "You're an underwritten character in a mythological soap opera. You're more interesting as a mechanic here in the real world than you are as a god back in your echo of Old Ugarit. You can stay and assist Hans, or you fuck off back to la la land. Decide."

"You lack the means to enforce your ultimatum, Captain," Kothar said. "But since Ba'al's vessel obeys your commands, I will do likewise. What is your will?"

"I want ship-wide comms restored," the captain said. "I want access to the surveillance system. And I want control of this ship. Confer with Zell on the best way to make that happen. There are replacement components for flight and navigation in the cargo holds. Assume engineering is wrecked. And get me access to the secure terminal in my office."

"I assume those are warm-up tasks and that you'll have something substantial for me to do later," Kothar said.

"One more thing," the captain said. "When was the last

time Hans ate?"

"Ah, yes," Kothar said. "He is quite hungry."

"Then come to breakfast with us."

3.13.5 - Cook

Cook could tell by the quantity of uneaten food he was feeding to the worms that some crew members weren't getting enough to eat. Either that, or there weren't as many mouths left to feed, and the obituaries just hadn't been written yet. He considered making less to match consumption levels. Later, maybe. For breakfast, he made enough for sixteen.

He heated bacon fat in the microwave and performed his usual aromatic summons. He raised the security grate and ventured further out into the passageway than he had since the crisis began. He assumed everyone on both sides still wanted to eat and didn't feel like cooking or doing dishes. He was an unlikely target for violence.

"You know that doesn't smell the same as bacon frying on the griddle, right?"

Cook turned around and saw Sparks between him and the galley.

"Yeah," Cook said. "It's a compromise."

Sparks floated in the middle of the passageway with his right hand behind his back and a tight-lipped grin on his face. Cook wanted to get back to the kitchen, but he knew better than to move within arm's reach of Sparks.

"Get out of my way," Cook said.

Sparks reached out with his left hand and grasped a handhold on the bulkhead. He pulled himself less than a meter from the center of the passageway.

"Go on," Cook said. "Clear out. Breakfast isn't ready yet."

"Breakfast is canceled," came another voice. Cook turned his body halfway, so that his back was to a bulkhead.

Kellemen and Sparks closed in from opposite directions.

"In fact," Kellemen said. "Your services will no longer be required, Master of Kitchen."

Cook flung the hot cheesecloth bundle into Kellemen's face and did his best to launch himself at Sparks. His orientation wasn't ideal, and Sparks was prepared for such a desperate act. Kellemen screamed in pain and fury.

Cook had helped repel boarders in the past, but he'd been armed. His unarmed combat experience amounted to a couple of bar fights in his youth, and that was a long time ago. Sparks was a young man from a Columbian military family who enjoyed an inheritance of germline genetic upgrades. He was faster and stronger than Cook and trained in zero-g grappling.

Sparks smashed Cook's nose with a palm strike and got behind the older man, wrapping his legs around Cook from behind. He raked his right hand across Cook's face, and blood ran into Cook's eyes. Sparks put his mouth to Cook's ear and said, "Here it comes, grease pig."

Kellemen closed the distance, took hold of Cook's hair and plunged his knife into Cook's ample gut. He pulled the knife out and stabbed again and again and again.

FRAGILE BRAINS

3.14.1 - Paige

Paige had nearly reached the medical lab when the captain stepped out into the passageway, followed by Anja and then Dobrovitz.

Paige had seen the captain just a few minutes earlier, but she was struck once more by her physical transformation.

Her bald head emphasized the cosmetic restoration of the right side of her face and scalp. Her elegant new right arm seemed like an integral part of her in a way that her previous arm never could have. The captain was wearing medical scrubs that did nothing to emphasize her figure, but Paige imagined how commanding the captain would look in her signature skin-tight clothing. Paige made eye contact with Anja, who winked at her.

"We're going to breakfast. Petrovic, take point. Paige," the captain said, extending her right arm. "Hold on to me."

They made their way from medical toward the galley. They had just reached the crew level passageway when an alarm sounded.

"Fire," the captain said. She slipped her arm from Paige's grip and told her, "Stay here."

"Cook!" Anja shouted.

"Oh, god," the captain said. She bent her knees and launched herself head-first down the passageway.

"Cook?" Paige said, panic rising. "Is he okay?"

"Kothar! Get Paige back to medical!" the captain shouted

back over her shoulder.

"Cook?" Paige cried.

"Come, little one," Kothar said and took hold of Paige's upper arm.

"No!" Paige shouted.

"We have our instructions," Kothar said without any hint of emotional excitement. "Obey your captain."

He pushed off the deck, and the two of them sailed up the companionway to the next level. As they emerged into the passageway, something impacted Dobrovitz's head. He went limp, and Paige felt strong hands seize her in an unbreakable grip.

"Ah, priestess," Kellemen said. He was holding a short shaft with a metal ball at the end. The ball was wet with Dobrovitz's blood.

"I've been looking forward to this." Dwayne Sparks, who was holding Paige from behind, clamped a hand over her nose and mouth. She thrashed, but he was much stronger than she was, and her struggles only hastened the encroaching blackness. Carbon dioxide buildup exacerbated her panic, robbing her of her reason before her awareness flickered out entirely.

3.14.2 - Petrovic

Petrovic knew before she reached him that Cook was beyond help. She heard the captain shout, "Kothar! Get Paige back to medical!"

Paige didn't need to see this. Anja passed through curtains of Cook's blood to reach his body, and when she saw the extent and nature of the damage to his abdomen, she didn't bother checking for a pulse. She just closed his eyes.

Anguish turned to fury, and she felt the wrath of Anat stir within her, animating her with righteous purpose. "Tannin!" she roared. "Your torment will be legendary!"

"No!" Trix said. "Anat, you are not welcome here. I need my

marine, Anja Petrovic."

Anat's fury focused on this jape of humanity who dared address a goddess in a commanding tone. She intended to sweep this insignificant parody of life aside, but she paused when she remembered that this being was the chosen vessel of the sun goddess, Shapash, the light of El. Anat would never defy Shapash, even in her absence.

In Anat's moment of indecision, Anja Petrovic asserted control over her own body. "I'm with you, Captain. What are your orders?"

"We're going to your quarters. I want you armed and armored with modern gear."

"Yes, ma'am," Petrovic said. "What about the fire?"

Trix pointed, and Petrovic saw that the hatch to the galley was closed. "Automatic fire suppression will take care of it," Trix said.

"Go," Trix said, and Petrovic obeyed, understanding that the captain wanted a moment alone to say goodbye to her long-time friend and shipmate.

As Petrovic moved down the line of crew compartments, she noticed that every hatch was open except for the one to her own compartment, which she had locked behind her when she left it for that last time.

She did not stop to examine the open compartments, but as she floated past she looked inside and saw parts of disassembled combat rifles strewn about the volumes of the crew quarters. Some parts had floated into the passageway. She stopped outside her own compartment, punched in her code, and opened the hatch. She was fully dressed and was putting on her armor when the captain arrived. She donned her helmet and fastened the chin strap. She then took her combat rifle from its bulkhead mount.

"Do you want my pistol, ma'am?"

"No," the captain said. "You keep it."

They moved out into the passageway. Anja followed the captain's example, floating instead of walking. The captain moved to the next compartment and looked inside.

"How long will it take you to reassemble that rifle?"

"Ninety seconds, if all the parts are there," Petrovic said. She looked from piece to piece. "I don't see the receiver. That's the part that holds the trigger mechanism and firing components."

"Check the next compartment," the captain said. Petrovic moved to the next open hatch and looked inside. She looked from piece to piece and announced. "Same deal, Captain. No receiver."

"Can you print a new one?" the captain said.

"Yes, on Z-level," Petrovic said.

"Gather enough components for two rifles," Trix said. "I'll collect magazines."

"Yes, ma'am."

3.14.3 - Rex

Rex floated in and out of sleep, dipping in and out of dreams in which he had a list of actions that needed to be taken in precise order, but every time he looked at the list he saw that he'd skipped a vital step and needed to go back to the start. Trix was counting on him, and he was failing her.

The vibration and sound of a distant explosion pulled him out of this cycle of frustration and self-accusation. His first complete thought upon waking was, "The hatch to the armory really was booby-trapped. I wonder who opened it?"

Rex's assumption that the explosion came from the armory was bolstered by secondary explosions and the sounds of gunfire. Rex identified the sound as stored rounds of ammunition cooking off.

He took in his surroundings. He was in bed in the recovery room. To his left, Nora Lawson lay unconscious, held to the bed by tight covers and kept hydrated intravenously. A gravity fed IV bag would have been of no use. The line that extended from the needle in the back of her left hand terminated in a machine that pushed fluids and medications into her bloodstream at a precisely calculated pressure.

In the bed to his right, Esmeralda Escamilla was just opening her eyes. She was also receiving intravenous fluids and pain medications. Both of her arms were secured with heavy straps. The goddess Ashtart seemed to have abandoned her, but she had participated in a violent mutiny, beaten Shawn Li nearly to death, and tried to kill Rex. It seemed like she had returned to her senses, and maybe all would be forgiven. That was up to Trix, but for now, she was not to be trusted.

Unlike the women on either side of him, Rex did not have a needle in the back of his hand. He realized too late that the lack of IV meant that he hadn't received any pain medication recently. The chest wound near his right shoulder erupted in debilitating pain when he tried to work himself free of the bedding.

Trey opened the hatch to the recovery room and propelled himself into the compartment. Rex's eyes locked onto the pistol in the doctor's hand. It was the pistol that Rex had used to shoot Esmeralda, which meant it was probably empty.

"Explosion in the armory," Rex said.

"Okay," Trey said. "Here, I don't have any use for this." He held the pistol out to Rex.

Rex took the sidearm and said, "Neither do I. It's empty."

"Anja left this for you," Trey said, reaching into a coat pocket and pulling out an ammunition clip. Rex took it and saw that it was fully loaded with hollow point rounds. He inserted the clip into the pistol and was about to slap it into place when he remembered his injury.

"Doc," Rex said. "Can I get a shot for the pain?"

Trey produced a sealed packet from another pocket, tore it open, and handed it to Rex. "No shot. Take this, it will last longer."

Rex took the opened packet. There was a gel cap inside. He

put the package to his lips and squeezed the capsule into his mouth.

"It will take effect more quickly if you bite down on it, but…"

Rex didn't wait for the doctor to finish his sentence. He bit down on the capsule and instantly regretted it. His face puckered with the bitterness of the liquid that coated the inside of his mouth.

"Yeah," Trey said. "It tastes bad."

Trey pulled a squeeze bottle from a bracket on the side of the bed and handed it to Rex.

Rex took a mouthful of water and swished it around, trying to rinse away the taste of the pain killer. He swallowed and said, "Where are my clothes?"

"In a hamper in the examination room," Trey said. "If you need to move, there are scrubs in that closet, but I want you to stay in bed for now."

"I need to find Trix," Rex said.

"The captain has Petrovic with her," Trey said. "Consider this. That gun in your hand is the only real weapon on this whole level. How about you use it to defend the people in this compartment?"

Rex wanted to move, but the pain in his shoulder told him that he'd be more of a liability than a help to the captain right now. On the other hand, staying in bed and being ready to respond with deadly force should the Chaos faction try to storm the medical level made sense.

He made sure the safety was engaged and handed the weapon back to Trey.

"Would you slap that clip into place for me?"

Trey took the pistol and propelled the clip into place with the heel of his left hand. He pulled the slide back, chambering a round.

"You've had firearms training," Rex said. "You should keep the weapon."

Trey placed the pistol in Rex's left hand.

"You soldier," Trey said. "Me doctor."

3.14.4 - Trey

I went back to my office with the intention of getting a cup of coffee for Rex. I'd nudged Esmeralda back to sleep with a slight adjustment to her IV mix. Her injury was not life threatening, but she could only do herself harm by trying to move around at this point, and her restraints would likely infuriate her.

I was just outside my office when I heard Petrovic's voice.

"Trey!" she shouted. Her voice carried a note of concern so urgent that it bordered on panic. I started toward the companionway, but Petrovic emerged from it before I got there. She was pulling someone who I could only identify as Hans Dobrovitz by his gangly build. His face was covered in blood and unrecognizable.

"It's Hans," she said. "I don't think he's breathing."

I took his wrist and felt for a pulse. Nothing, but his skin was warm.

We took Hans to the surgical bay, and I opened his outer top garment and cut the t-shirt underneath down the middle to expose his chest. I had Anja follow me into an adjacent control room, and we watched as the robotic systems shocked his heart back into a steady rhythm. Then the system passed various sensors over his body, coming to focus intensely on his head and face.

"Damn it," I said. "Another brain injury."

This was the worst one yet. The obvious tissue damage below the indentation in his skull told me that the familiar Hans Dobrovitz was gone for good. And then I noticed his eyes, or rather the mess of mangled tissue in his eye sockets.

"They gouged out his eyes?" I said, incredulous.

"Tannin," Anja said. "I'm sure it was Tannin." When she pronounced the name, I heard her vocal inflection change.

Anja's voice took on the familiar power of Anat, but then she added, "They have Paige."

With those last three words, she sounded like herself again. The animating vengeance of Anat receded.

"Fuck! Hold it together, Petrovic," she told herself.

"Where's the captain?"

"On her way to Z-Deck. She's going to get Zell and Antal and bring them here," Anja said.

"Hans needs immediate surgery," I said. "I'll be here. Rex is awake. You could check in with him and let him know what's happening."

"Roger that," she said and exited the surgical control compartment.

ANAT STANDS DOWN

3.15.1 - Paige

Paige learned the price of resistance right away. If she struggled or tried to impede their progress, Dwayne Sparks sunk the metal talons attached to his fingertips into the flesh of her upper arm. The claws on his thumbs were still wet with blood and clear fluid from when he'd dug them into the eye sockets of the unconscious Hans Dobrovitz.

Sparks manhandled her along the passageway to a different companionway from the one through which she and Kothar had come up from the crew level. When they emerged from the companionway, she realized that she was back on the crew level and that Anja and the captain might be nearby. She started to draw a breath with which to call out, and Sparks jerked her body and brought her ear to his sickly grinning mouth.

"Scream, and I'll rip your tongue from your mouth, priestess," he hissed, holding one taloned finger to her lips. She nodded.

She didn't plead with them or ask them what they wanted or what they planned to do with her. She knew exactly who and what they were, and their intentions flowed from that identity. As the servant and representative of Shapash, she was to be extinguished in a perverse ritual.

The high priestess knew that the light of the goddess could not be truly extinguished. All Tannin ever managed to accomplish in this eternal, cyclical struggle, was obscure her light for a time. A new high priestesses would take up her role and nurture the light of Shapash in the hearts of the people. She would transcend this incarnation and serve Shapash long after this frail vessel, Paige, had expired.

Paige, the skinny young woman from the rice paddies of Galtz, didn't view her situation from such an expansive, transpersonal perspective. She wanted to live. That divergence of perspectives became a wedge between them. The high priestess still inhabited Paige's body, but she was no longer integrated with Paige's psyche.

I will comfort you through the coming ordeal, the high priestess told her. *Maintain your commitment to the goddess and no torment will reach you. No violation of your flesh will mar your essential being.*

I want to live to live, Paige replied, fear creeping in and propelling the high priestess even further from her.

You will live forever in the light of the goddess, the high priestess told her. *Don't face this ordeal alone. Without the goddess your death will be a torment. Embrace me.*

Can you protect me?

This vessel is forfeit, the high priestess said, *but the death of the animal body is nothing to mourn. Death in the light of Shapash nourishes future life. Without the light of Shapash, Mot will consume your essence and you will be obliterated. Embrace me.*

I want to live, Paige insisted, and in clinging to the life of her body she lost contact with the priestess and the light of the goddess. The comforting presence of divine love and acceptance gave way to primal panic.

She struggled now like an animal in a trap, and Tannin rewarded her efforts with new wounds in her upper arm. She sunk her teeth into the flesh of his muscular forearm. He roared in fury and wrapped his other hand over the top of her head, his fingers spread wide, the metal talons digging into her flesh, one of them hooked under the top ridge of her right eye socket, just missing the eyeball.

She cried out in pain, releasing Spark's arm from her bite. He grasped the side of her head and aimed the thumb talon at her right eye.

"No!" Kellemen shrieked. "Not yet!"

Kellemen swung his mace and struck Sparks in the torso. The impact sent the two men in different directions. Sparks lost his hold on Paige, but his talons raked the flesh of her scalp and forehead in the process.

Paige could not help but close her eyes, and so she missed what happened in the next few seconds. She heard the sounds of frenetic struggle with Kellemen's mace ringing against the metal bulkhead and making crunching contact with something softer.

She pulled herself away from the violence. With blood stinging her eye and adrenaline fueling her motion, she lost all orientation. She pulled herself along the passageway until she came to a junction with a companionway.

She made no effort to discern whether it went up, toward medical, or down, toward engineering and the seat of Chaos. Grasping the ladder step closest to her she dragged herself through the tube. When she reached the next deck, it was clear that she'd gone down, deeper into Chaos territory.

She could not bring herself to open her right eye, but looking down the hallway, she saw a naked blonde woman with familiar markings on her arms, legs and torso. It was the high priestess.

The patterns on her skin resembled the illustrations in *Void Huntress*, but where the patterns that Bygul had drawn on Paige's skin were a flowing expression of cursive filigree, this version of the priestess was marked with a brutal, blocky artistry.

Unlike Paige, this high priestess had the voluptuous figure that was as much a badge of her office as were the markings on her skin.

"Lolita?" Paige said when she recognized the smiling face of the woman floating before a partially opened hatch. The blonde sex doll turned back to face the hatch. She grasped a handhold to steady herself with one hand and pushed the hatch open with the other.

The hatch swung fully open, and for an instant, Lolita stared passively into the compartment beyond. Then she was propelled back against the bulkhead on the opposite side of the passageway in a blinding flash. A compression wave struck Paige and sent her tumbling away from the explosion. She careened off the bulkheads but failed to secure a handhold to arrest her motion.

As if through layers of foam padding, she heard additional explosions, and now a wave of scorching air accelerated her motion and she crashed into a bulkhead at a T intersection. Pain from her ribs eclipsed all other sensation until the darkness closed in around her.

3.15.2 - Rex

"What's happening?" Rex said when Petrovic entered the compartment. Rex was glad to see that she was wearing modern tactical gear and had a combat rifle on her back.

"They attacked Dobrovitz and took Paige," she said. "I think you need to get up and get dressed. Doc's going to need to move Li out of intensive care to make room for Dobrovitz. He'll need this bed."

"How bad is Hans?" Rex said.

"Trey says it doesn't really matter if he keeps breathing or not. They bashed his skull in. He's already gone," Petrovic said. "I'm sorry. I know you served with him for a long time."

"What are you going to do?"

"The captain told me to wait here, but I think I need to go after Paige," Petrovic said. "You'll need to hold the fort."

"Help me up."

She pulled back the covers and unfastened the straps holding the bed's toilet fixtures in place.

"Okay," Rex said. "I'll take it from here. There's supposed to be clothes in that closet."

Petrovic smiled. "You got it, Sarge," she said, and turned away to allow him a bit of dignity as he disengaged from the bed's plumbing. She took a pair of briefs and a set of large scrubs from the closet and made sure to hold eye contact with Rex as she closed the distance with him on her return.

When Rex had the scrub pants on he turned back to Petrovic and said, "I think I'm going to need some help with the top."

He winced in pain as she helped position his right arm to slip through the wide sleeve of the scrub top.

"Any socks in that closet?" he said.

"Nope," she said. "Just slippers so you don't have to walk on cold metal. Walking's not an option right now, and the slippers won't keep your feet warm. I can bring you some socks from Trey's quarters. Let's get you set up in his office. There's coffee and snack bars in there, and you'll have access to security feeds for this level at least."

When Rex was in Trey's office with socks on his feet, the safetied pistol in his waistband and a mug of coffee in his hand, Petrovic unslung her rifle and disappeared down the companionway.

3.15.3 - Petrovic

Petrovic headed directly for engineering, but she did not hurry. She remained calm and methodical, and as she progressed she started to view the rifle in her hands with contempt. She resisted the urge to cast it away.

"No way, Anat," she whispered.

Your weapons take all the joy out of killing, the goddess said with a mock pout.

"Tell you what," Petrovic said, still whispering. "If I'm too late and she's already dead, I'm all yours. Rip them to pieces. Until then, hang back. This is my show."

Agreed, mortal, Anat told her. *Good hunting.*

Petrovic felt the goddess relent and withdraw. She felt diminished and somewhat empty when she could no longer feel the animating presence of Anat. She tightened her grip on her rifle and focused on her objective.

When she reached engineering, she used her tiny mirror to peek around the corner of the hatchway. She saw Lake sitting in a chair toward the far end of the compartment. She assumed he was strapped to the chair. She checked one corner in the reflected mirror, and then floated past the hatch in full view. Lake must have seen her, but he did not raise the alarm. She checked her other blind corner in the mirror. It was clear.

"They aren't here," Lake said.

Petrovic attached her boots to the deck and stepped into the main engineering compartment. She moved to her right so that the open hatchway wouldn't be to her back and then she allowed herself to take in the spectacle of the place.

She decided the Chaos faction had spent the majority of their time decorating. Interlocking panels attached to the bulkhead turned the space into a surrealist nightmare. She wasn't sure if they were trying to make it look like a temple, a throne room, a torture chamber or the inside of a monster's body. The black wall panels were sculpted with what looked like ribs, vertebrae, muscles and blood vessels. Flickering light from simulated torches made the organic shapes of the bulkhead decorations appear to squirm and pulsate.

Between Petrovic and Yam's throne stood a black slab on a pedestal. It looked like it was made of stone, but that had to be an illusion of surface texture. She was sure it was made from some lightweight composite material that the fabricators were designed to extrude. Four manacles attached to cables secured to the rings set into the deck floated near the four corners of the sacrificial altar.

"Rex said that the captain is alive," Lake said to Petrovic as she moved along the side of the compartment. "I don't see how that could be true."

Lake was dressed in what looked like black tactical cargo pants and black tank top. He sat up straight with his arms resting on the arms of the high-backed black chair. She saw zip cuffs on his wrists and ankles, seemingly binding him to the chair.

"Is it true?" Lake said. "Is Trix alive?"

Petrovic continued to make her way toward Lake's side of the chamber, but now she turned and kept her rifle trained on the open hatchway and walked backwards toward a far corner of the compartment.

Petrovic hadn't spent much time in this part of the ship, but she knew that there should have been at least two other exits from this space besides the one by which she'd entered. They'd blocked off access to the power plant and to… what?

She didn't know. She wondered if some of these panels were designed to swing open. She kept both hands on her rifle. Sparks or Kellemen might pop out of some concealed door at any moment.

"Where's Paige?" Petrovic said, not looking at Lake.

"I don't know," Lake said. "If they'd caught her, they would have brought her here. They built that sacrificial altar with her in mind."

Petrovic continued backing up until she was behind Lake and to his left. He turned his head to continue talking to her. He could not make eye contact with her from this position, but she could see his face in profile.

"I know you don't have any reason to trust me," Lake said. "But if Trix is alive, she wouldn't want you to hurt me. We're old friends."

"You haven't seen Paige?"

"Not since before this madness started," Lake said.

"*This madness,*" she said with a scoff. "As if you're an innocent victim."

"No one is innocent," Lake said. "We all allowed ourselves to be drawn into this thing."

"Sparks and Kellemen tied you to that chair?" Petrovic said.

"Of course. Do you think I did this to myself?"

"Maybe," she said. "Pull up with your arms. Convince me you didn't cut those cuffs in advance so that you could break them whenever you needed to."

He pulled his arms up, and the plastic straps of the zip cuffs pressed into his flesh, but not deep enough for Petrovic's liking.

"Harder!" she said.

"They're cutting into my wrists," Lake complained.

"Boo fucking hoo," she said and clicked on her rifle's laser sight, putting the red dot on Lake's left hand.

"Draw blood or I blow your hand off!"

She didn't want to fire her weapon and alert Sparks and Kellemen to her position, but she had no intention of wasting time with Lake.

Lake strained against his bonds, and she could see the cuffs starting to cut into his skin.

"Okay," she said, and Lake relaxed.

"What do you know about that explosion?" she said.

"We suspected that Chukwuma booby trapped the hatch to the armory. Kellemen sent the sex doll to open the door and find out," Lake said.

"You wanted modern weapons?" Petrovic asked.

"Sparks wanted explosives," Lake said.

"For what?"

"Indiscriminate destruction," Lake said. "He's a demon of Chaos. He lives to cause havoc."

"No particular target?" She said, "I don't buy it. The military grade explosives are toast, but this ship is equipped for mining. Where do you keep the blasting explosives?"

"All mining equipment is in the main cargo hold," Lake

said.

Petrovic crossed behind the throne. She released the magnetic locks on her boots, put her feet against the bulkhead behind the throne and launched herself toward the hatchway.

As she glided across the compartment, Lake called to her, "Please, Petrovic, you can't leave me like this."

"Watch me."

3.15.3 - Trey

When I'd done all I could for Hans Dobrovitz, I moved Shawn Li from the ICU to the recovery room. I expected Shawn to wake up soon, though I didn't envy him waking up to this situation. Better to stay asleep.

The medical level was nearly at maximum capacity. Nora Lawson, Shawn Li, and Esmeralda Escamilla were all in the recovery room. Hans Dobrovitz was in the ICU. Rex was in my office, standing guard, but was he supposed to live there?

There was a medical acceleration couch in the lab. I could put someone in there to monitor them if need be, and I could put a patient in my own acceleration couch. If we had any more wounded after that, things would get awkward.

Under different circumstances, I could have set up an overflow unit on the next deck down. The largest compartment on that level was the situation room, and I didn't anticipate any all hands meetings in the near future.

There were also unused compartments on that level that could be pressed into service. But that level wasn't secure.

Really, the medical level wasn't secure in any meaningful sense, but moving everyone to some other location on the ship wasn't a workable option. There were also three cold drawers in the lab that could each hold a corpse. Two of them held the desiccated *Homo erectus* corpses I had recovered from the Temple.

By the time I'd gotten Hans set up in the ICU, I was exhausted and hungry. I'd missed breakfast, and while I didn't get the full story of how Hans and Paige got separated from Petrovic and the captain, I took it for granted that nobody had actually made it to breakfast. I wasn't going to find an omelet or breakfast burrito in a to-go carton in my office. I'd have to make due with a protein bar and coffee.

As I floated down the passageway, I glanced down the companionway to the next level down. I noticed that it was criss-crossed with green lasers. Apparently Rex had activated a security measure that I wasn't aware of. I didn't want to take Rex by surprise, so I called to him from the passageway before entering my office.

"C'mon in, Doc," Rex said.

As I floated into the office he said, "Petrovic set me up with a pair of your socks. Hope you don't mind."

"That's fine," I said. "Any word?"

"Nothing yet," he said. "Tell me something, Doc. I can see that you've had firearms training. Did you serve?"

"I've lived several simulated lives," I said. "I call them *delves*. All of my medical education came in the form of delves. Many of them included wartime experience. I've been a corpsman, a combat medic, and a frontline surgeon. I've been through basic training several times and had plenty of weapons safety training. The weapons you use would have been familiar to soldiers from before the rise of AI."

"How many lives have you lived?"

"Full lives? Not that many. A couple of dozen," I said, and then, when I realized that he didn't know what I meant, I said, "Around twenty, I'd guess."

"Twenty? How do you remember it all?" he asked.

"I don't," I said. "There are different kinds of memory. There's episodic memory. That's the stuff that happens to you in your life. Your first kiss. Your wedding. That sort of thing.

"There's semantic memory, which refers to facts and things

that you just know that aren't tied to any particular event in your life. You know that eight follows seven. You learned that as a child, but you probably don't remember the exact moment when you learned it. You just know it.

"And then there's procedural memory. That includes muscle memory and complex actions that you can perform without really thinking about it. Do you know how to ride a bike?"

"No," Rex said.

"Well, take a military example. You know how to disassemble and reassemble all of the weapons that you use in combat, right?"

"Of course," Rex said.

"That's procedural memory. You might remember learning those skills, but you don't have to think about that early instruction in order to strip your weapon."

"Okay," Rex said.

"Well, most of the episodic memories from my delves fade when I come back to baseline reality, but I retain the semantic and procedural knowledge I acquired during the delve. Sometimes I'll surprise myself by doing something I didn't realize I could do. When I exercise a skill for the first time in a long while, I might remember things from the delve where I learned it.

"But I didn't live a whole life every time I delved. Mostly I would pick up life as an adult with a fully formed personality; my real personality. In those more casual delves, no matter when or where they took place, everyone spoke contemporary English or another language that I understand. It's like when you experience an entertainment simulation that's set in some historical period."

"I can't say I know a whole lot about Earth history," Rex said. "I mostly just know about the Roman Empire and the American Empire. I learned that when I was in the Columbian military. I'm not from a Columbian family. But even the subalts get some military history in basic training."

"*Subalts?*"

"Yeah. Not all Columbian soldiers are born to serve like the ones on this ship. Real Columbians have all kinds of gene mods, but anybody can apply to enlist. Most don't get in, but the ones who do are called *subalts*. Subalts can never be senior officers, but the Columbian subalt training is still about the best someone like me can get."

"Ah," I said. "*Subaltern*. I get it."

A chime sounded.

"What's that?" I said.

"Doorbell," Rex said and pointed to a display window. "It's Zell."

I made my way out to the alcove between my office and the examination room. I stayed out of the passageway because I could see that Zell had a lot of gear with him.

He pushed a bundle of hard cases bound together with elastic netting, and I could see that whoever was coming up the companionway after him was pushing a lidded crate.

"Doctor, the captain's with us," Zell said. He turned right and moved down that passageway toward the lab.

"We brought some stuff that should get some of our people back in the fight," Zell called back over his shoulder.

I couldn't question him about that, as he'd already moved past me. Drake Antal was behind the large crate. He followed Zell to the lab. The captain emerged last from the companionway.

"Is Petrovic here?" she said when she saw me.

"No," I said. "She went to find Paige."

"I thought she would," Trix said.

3.15.4 - Bygul

The explosion in the armory activated Bygul's fear response. She took cover in a niche between equipment containers inside the Stout.

"Oh, shit," Arni said. "It sounds like someone blew up the

armory. Okay, it's time to go."

"Yes! Escape!" Bygul said, and then added, "Sir."

Arni hurried into the cab and into the driver's station.

"Shit!" he said. "Shit! Shit! Shit! I can't open the outer door."

"Why, sir?" Bygul said, poking her head out from her hiding place.

"The hatch to the passageway is open. I can't decompress the bay with the hatch open."

Bygul remembered finding the hatch open, passing through it, and leaving it as she found it.

"Cat Girl, go close the hatch!" Arni said over the sound of secondary and tertiary explosions and gunfire.

"No! I can't!" she said. "Sir."

"Why not?"

"I'm afraid, sir."

"So am I," Arni said. "Shit! Okay. I'll go."

Bygul felt intense anxiety as she worked through conflicting drives. The cat persona wanted to run. The sex doll persona insisted that the client's safety had to come first. If one of them had to take a risk, it should be her.

Was Arni really a client? He hadn't scheduled time with her. They hadn't had sex. He wasn't a client, and if he put himself in danger that was outside of her concern.

She had given him emotional comfort. It was normal for clients to forego sex when they needed emotional support. They often just wanted to talk. He took comfort in her presence. He was a client. She could not let him endanger himself.

She searched for a counterpoint, but all that she came up with was, *Danger! Run! Hide!*

She howled in frustration.

Arni, who was now back in the main compartment on his way to the airlock, said, "What is it?"

"Don't go, sir."

"We can't leave until that hatch is closed," Arni said.

"It's too dangerous, sir! Please don't go."

"Then you go," Arni said.

"I can't go, sir," she pleaded. "I'm afraid."

"Then stay here," Arni said. "I'll be right back."

Arni moved toward the airlock, and the sex doll part of Bygul could not tolerate remaining passive while her client put himself in danger. She raced to the airlock ahead of him.

"Don't go, sir!"

"One of us has to go out there and close the hatch," he said.

"I'll go, sir," she said and moved, trembling, into the Stout's airlock. Arni cycled the airlock from inside the cabin. The pressure in the Stout and the cargo bay was already equal, so it was just a matter of the inner door closing and the outer one opening.

Bygul pushed off from the airlock and down to the grated deck. She locked onto it with her fingers and toes and propelled herself in the direction of the open hatch, keeping her body flat just centimeters above the deck.

She had nearly reached her goal when she saw a figure in the opening. She stopped and slowly pushed herself backwards, keeping her sight and hearing trained on the hatchway. A human hand pushed the hatch open further, and Bygul saw that the hand was covered in blood. Curved metal claws extended from caps on the tips of each finger. The human pushed his head through the opening. The face belonged to Dwayne Sparks, her first client in this body. But this was not her client. This was danger.

She froze, and Sparks gave no indication that he saw her as he pulled his body though the hatchway and into the bay. She saw that he was injured. He moved slowly and kept his right arm wrapped around his torso.

The physical therapist in her came forward to suggest that, like Paige, he had suffered fractures to his ribs on his left side. This implied that she should offer aid, but the cat refused to reveal her location.

Sparks moved further into the bay, and she lost sight of him when he passed behind a pallet of crates held down with cargo netting. Silently, she pulled herself along the deck toward the hatch. She had less than five meters to go when something grasped her tail. She hissed, and the fur on her tail stood straight out. She turned to see that Sparks was holding her by the tail.

"Bad kitty," he said and pulled her to him. She kicked furiously at his face and managed to slip out of his grasp. She closed the gap between her and the open hatch in one deft motion and was gone.

MATERNAL INSTINCT

3.16.1 - Petrovic

Petrovic had nearly reached the cargo bay when Cat Girl came shooting out through the hatch. She ricocheted off the passageway bulkhead opposite the cargo bay and flew past Petrovic. Petrovic turned and called after the sex doll, "Cat Girl! Stop!"

The robot either didn't hear the command or chose to ignore it. She glanced off the deck once, changing direction and disappeared up a companionway.

"Joke's on you," Petrovic said. The armory and shooting range were on the next deck up. Cat Girl was headed for the center of the shit show. She'd probably turn around and come back once she figured out what she had blundered into. Petrovic might be able to catch her then.

Petrovic played out various scenarios in her mind and decided that the best thing she could do to protect Paige was to eliminate Sparks and Kellemen.

Tannin and the Chaos priest, she corrected herself.

Then she remembered how Sparks and Kellemen had been wrapped up in paranoid bullshit even before the ship came anywhere close to this big black hunk of carbon. Those two were mental defectives from the jump. Not stupid. Just fucked up in relation to reality.

Fuck it. She was hunting Sparks and Kellemen, and she wasn't planning on taking prisoners. She locked her boots to the deck. She knew it gave away her position, but she had already done that when she shouted at Cat Girl.

Plus she was armed, and she'd rather have a stable position from which to fire than be able to sneak up on her quarry, particularly if they refused to use guns. And if they wanted to go hand to hand, she'd wipe the deck with them with the leverage the boots gave her.

She stepped over the threshold, weapon leveled. The cargo bay was enormous; big enough to hold the Stout, the Crab, a drilling rig, and a maze of stacked crates. If she stomped around in that maze, broadcasting her location and direction with every step, Sparks and/or Kellemen could evade her indefinitely and possibly set up an ambush.

She could set up her own ambush; find a place with line of sight on the exit and wait for whomever it was to try to leave. But she didn't know for sure that anyone was in here. There was no telling what spooked Cat Girl.

She unlocked from the deck and pushed off, aiming for a high corner of the bay. If she identified a target in mid air, she'd get one burst. If she held the rifle to her shoulder, the recoil would send her into backward somersaults. If she held the weapon at her hip, she might manage to keep her vertical orientation, but the recoil would spin her like a top.

The configuration of the maze revealed itself to her as she drifted toward the top of the bay. She did not see Sparks. She did see movement inside the cab of the Stout. She knew how tough the transparent material of the *windshield* was, and didn't imagine that she could shoot through it before Sparks could move out of the cab and back into the main compartment of the utility vehicle.

And she wasn't sure it was Sparks inside the Stout. Was that blonde hair she saw? Sparks wore his dark hair in a buzz cut like Petrovic's. Arni Hansson wore his blonde locks right at the maximum length that regulations permitted. In zero-g, it fanned out in a bright halo. Had Hansson abandoned the Chaos faction and holed up with Cat Girl in the Stout?

That's it, she thought. *Lock yourself away with a sex doll while the world burns.* She decided that it definitely was Hansson in the cab of the Stout, and he was looking at her and pointing. She followed the direction of his gesture and used the mass of her rifle to set her body into a slow spin. She turned just in time to see Sparks slip out of the cargo bay and into the passageway. She raised her rifle when she saw that he'd paused to reach back in and pull the hatch closed behind him.

She knew she was too late. She aimed but checked her fire. Sparks was gone. When Petrovic reached the deckhead, she pushed off, aiming to land between the hatch and the Stout. She was less than halfway across the vast space when she heard the compressors kick in.

"Fuck!" she cursed.

Sparks was decompressing the bay. Petrovic landed and stood still while she considered her options.

There had to be a way to reverse the decompression from inside the bay; some emergency failsafe. Unfortunately, she didn't know how to activate it.

She wanted to rush to the hatch anyway, but she forced herself to hold her position rather than take action without a plan.

Hansson.

Hansson was in the Stout, and driving it was his occupational specialty. He'd know all about the cargo bay systems and procedures. She started to walk in the direction of the Stout, but she was already feeling slightly dizzy from the thinning air. She released her magnetic locks and pushed in the direction of the utility vehicle. She was breathing quickly, and air still entered her lungs, but she couldn't catch her breath.

Petrovic had aimed her leap well. She was headed right for the Stout, though it wasn't oriented in such a way that she could sail right into the airlock. She didn't know Hansson's state of mind. Would he even let her in?

She reached the Stout, absorbing the impact with her arms, face and chest. Fortunately, her helmet connected with the hull before her nose did. She dragged herself along the exterior of the vehicle, her vision constricting to a small circle in the center of an encroaching darkness. She reached the outer airlock just as the darkness engulfed her.

The outer airlock door was closed.

3.16.2 - Paige

Paige floated in and out of dreams of being trapped in a burning building.

"Wake up, Priestess," came a malevolent voice. Someone took her face in a brutal grip, pressing in on her cheeks, forcing her mouth open.

She opened her eyes to face a leering Saz Kellemen. He had Yam's sigil etched into his forehead, but the symbol was marred by a network of gashes. One eye was closed and bloodied.

"This cycle is nearly played out," he said, his face too close to her own. "But you can still make a spectacular exit. Come," he said, releasing her face and taking her upper arm in a grip she could never hope to break, pulling her sideways.

"The altar awaits."

3.16.3 - Bygul

"Cat Girl! Stop!"

Bygul ignored the command from the hard woman who had never been a client. She made contact with the deck and redirected her forward momentum to take her into a companionway. She emerged into heat and smoke and noise. She arrested her forward momentum and came to a stop in a four-legged crouch, gripping the bulkhead with fingers and toes, ready to leap at any instant.

The air shimmered with heat and rang with the occasional

rapport of an activated bullet from the ruined armory. Through the heat distortion, she saw a man dressed in black robes. The billowing garment was ill suited to the microgravity environment.

The man was on the far side of the armory hatch from her. He had his back to Bygul, and she intended to put distance and corners between them before he saw her.

She was in mid turn when she heard his voice. He wasn't speaking to her. She turned her head and trained her ears on him.

"This cycle is nearly played out, but you can still make a spectacular exit."

Bygul lept to the other side of the passageway, closing the distance between her and the furnace of the armory hatchway to get a look around the man.

"Come," he said. He took someone by the arm and jerked her into view. It was Paige. "The altar awaits."

No contradictory impulses or directives vied for control of Bygul's actions. A single primal directive inherited from the modeled cat's brain eclipsed all other considerations.

Kitten in danger.

Raw mammalian love translated to violence. She leaped with all her strength and cut through the shimmering air like a harpoon. She shrieked as she closed the distance with Kellemen and extended Mother's other gift of self-protection.

Sharp metal claws protruded from her fingertips, emerging from otherwise invisible channels through her synthetic flesh. Kellemen turned his head just in time to receive a slashing strike across his face and his one intact eye.

Howling with fury, he released his grip on Paige's arm and swung his mace in an overhand blow that would have ended Bygul if it had connected with her head. It clanged against the bulkhead.

Bygul grabbed Paige by the collar of her one-piece coverall and pulled her farther from Saz Kellemen who continued to swing his mace with murderous intent. He had his back to them now, swinging blindly.

"Bygul!" Paige cried.

"Shhhhh," Bygul said as she dragged Paige along the passageway, up another companionway and to an air vent that she knew had a loose cover.

She spun the slotted vent cover on the axis of its single remaining screw and stuffed Paige into the vent. She barely fit.

Bygul climbed in after her feet first. Once inside, she dragged the vent cover back into place.

"Lady, go!" she said in an insistent whisper and felt Paige comply. Bygul pushed herself backwards through the tiny vent until she came to a junction where she could turn around.

"Where are we going?" Paige asked.

"Nowhere, Lady," Bygul said. "Just hide."

3.16.4 - Rex

Rex saw Trix on the local security display. She was just a few meters away in the companionway, but the doctor, Zell, Antal and all the material they brought with them floated between Rex and the person he most wanted to reach.

Everyone moved down the passageway to the medical lab, even the doctor, leaving Rex and Trix face to face. She was locked to the deck as usual. He floated in the alcove outside the doctor's office. He reached out to her with his left arm, and she took his hand in her right, pulling him closer to her, but not into an embrace. She touched his cheek with her left hand.

"You should be in bed," she said.

"The recovery room is full of people hurt worse than me," Rex said. "Have you been crying? What happened?"

"Zell fabricated some of Kothar's designs. Come see," she

said.

When Rex entered the lab, he heard Zell ask, "Where's Hans?"

"He's in the ICU," Trey said. "The Chaos faction nearly killed him. He has severe brain damage and probably won't recover."

Zell's eyes went wide. They had worked closely together for years. Dobrovitz was clearly the junior partner in that relationship, but Rex could see the anguish on Zell's face as he processed the news.

The image of Zell in Rex's head didn't care about anyone but himself. Obviously, that didn't sum up the actual human being. Rex felt a twinge of shame.

"Damnit," Zell said. "Okay, then we'd better start with this."

He pulled a lidded case the size of a lunchbox from the bundle of cases held together with elastic webbing. He pulled himself across the lab to where David's head was attached to a square base. David's eyes were open, but he showed no signs of animation. The base to which David's head was attached had an open slot in one face.

Zell opened the case, pulled out a flat slab of black material and inserted it into the slot. David came to life.

"Who are you?" Zell asked.

"I'm David, sir," the robot said. "At your service."

"Just David?" Zell said.

"One moment, sir," David said and closed his eyes. When he opened them again, he was someone else. He spoke with a voice that Rex had never heard before.

"I am Kothar, the artificer. For now, I remain in the service of Captain Nixon."

He looked at Trix and nodded his head just slightly.

"You fabricated everything?" Kothar said.

"Yes," Zell said, "But we haven't had a chance to test any of it. Other than the components I just slotted into you, of course. What do you want to see first?"

"Let's begin with the control module," Kothar said.

"Right," Zell said. "Drake."

Zell looked at Drake Antal who opened the large hard plastic chest that he'd brought with him. He reached in, unfastened a strap and pulled a nearly featureless cube with rounded edges and corners from the case. One side of the cube had recognizable connection ports in it. Zell and Antal positioned the cube in an empty equipment dock on a workbench in a far corner of the lab. It locked into place with a faint clicking sound.

"And now the interface," Kothar said.

Zell returned to the bundle of cases in the elastic webbing and selected the smallest item. He approached Trix with a small box, and opened the lid. Rex couldn't see what was inside.

"Remove the placeholder," Kothar said.

"How?" Trix asked.

"Will it so," Kothar said.

Trix looked like she was trying to remember some forgotten name or do a complicated math problem in her head, and the blank white orb in her right eye socket pushed its way forward. She reached up with her new right hand, extracted the featureless orb from her right eye socket, and handed it to Antal. She then reached into the small open box and pulled out a new eye. She lifted it to her empty socket. The new eye receded into her head.

She blinked a few times and said, "Wow. That's a lot of information."

"You wanted access to the secure terminal in your office," Kothar said. "Imagine yourself at that terminal. You access it with a gesture."

Trix raised her left hand and closed it in a loose fist. She then extended her index finger. She moved the hand to the left as if dismissing a menu on a touch screen. She smiled and then laughed.

"We have several messages from the DAO," she said.

"What do they say?" Rex asked.

"First is an acknowledgement of my acceptance of the position of Captain," Trix said. "They've deposited a signing bonus to my account, and I've been awarded two voting shares, bringing my total to eleven. I can now submit proposals to the DAO for a vote."

"Great," Zell said. "Why don't you propose that we get the fuck out of here?"

"A coalition of minor share-holders have already made that proposal," Trix said. "The Whales defeated it."

"What else?" Zell said.

"Well, Joachim," Trix said, smiling. "It seems that you and the doctor have become minor celebrities. I transmitted the two daily briefing episodes you made to the DAO, and someone put them on the Interchain. They've been viewed several million times each. The DAO wants more."

"Great," Trey said.

"Anything else?" Rex asked.

The captain continued to read text only she could see, and her smile faded.

"There are some other things. They aren't a priority right now," the captain said. "What other goodies have you brought us, Mr. Zell?"

"We don't have access to ship-wide comms or security feeds. I haven't been able to restore them, and I think it's because the mutineers physically cut the cables that conduct the signals," Zell said.

He opened another case and held up a glass tube. It appeared to be full of tiny arthropods. He pulled himself over the workbenches to an access plate on the bulkhead. He flipped some latches and pulled the panel from the bulkhead, leaving it to float nearby.

"Kothar designed these tiny repair robots," Zell said. "They will follow the cables for the comms and security systems along the conduit runs. When they find damage, they'll repair it using their own bodies for material."

"Are those actual nanobots?" Rex asked. Microscopic robots

were a fixture of the high tech espionage entertainment sims that he had enjoyed in his youth.

"Hardly," Kothar said.

"To count as nanotechnology, they'd have to be less than a hundred nanometers in size," Zell explained with what sounded like the self-importance that Rex had always associated with the man. "A nanometer is one-billionth of a meter. You can see these guys with the naked eye. Which means that they're just little robots."

"*Just*," Kothar said and scoffed.

"How long will it take them to repair the damage?" Trix said.

"That depends on where the damage is and in how many places they sabotaged the system," Zell said. "I'm assuming that most of the physical damage is down in engineering, in the parts of the ship under enemy control."

Zell opened the first tube and tapped the tiny spider-like machines into the conduit run. "What do you think, Kothar?"

"They should complete their task within a day," Kothar said.

"And if they haven't destroyed the engine controls down in engineering, when the spider-bots have repaired the damaged lines, the captain should be able to pilot the ship from anywhere onboard," Zell said. "She won't be able to navigate until we can get some replacement components for the nav computer out of the secondary cargo hold, but she'll be able to put some distance between us and the Temple. Once we're outside of its magnetic field, the gods won't be able to get into our heads anymore."

Zell looked to Kothar for confirmation, and the android head nodded on its base.

"In fact," Zell said, "Captain, you should already have access to the maneuvering thrusters. You could get us out of the Temple right now."

Trix closed her eyes, and Rex felt a slight pull toward the

interior wall of the med lab compartment. Loose objects drifted in that direction.

"Yes," Trix said. "I'm turning the ship to face the mouth of the Temple."

"So, it's just a matter of time," Zell said. "We don't need to fight the Chaos faction or even find them. We just need to wait until the repair bots have done their work and then fly away."

"Except that Petrovic is out hunting for them," Rex said. "We need to get word to her."

"And Paige," Trix said.

"And Arni," Drake added.

CAUTION OR COWARDICE?

3.17.1 - Petrovic

The air was slightly stale, but Petrovic could breathe. Her surroundings came into focus, and she recognized the interior of the Stout. Arni was there. He offered her a squeeze bottle. She took it and pulled several swallows of the tepid electrolyte drink.

"How long was I out?" Petrovic said.

"Just a couple of minutes," Arni said.

"Is the bay re-pressurized?"

"No," Arni said.

"Why not? Is the magnetic field interfering with your wireless connection?" she asked.

"The Stout's got a hard link to the ship when it's docked. We can access the atmos controls, no problem."

"Then what's the hold up?" Petrovic demanded. "And where's my rifle?"

"You must have dropped it before you got to the airlock," Arni said. "You didn't have it on you when I pulled you in."

Petrovic's right hand went to the pistol on her belt. She didn't draw it. She just needed to reassure herself that she was armed.

"Well," Petrovic said, "How long does it take to repressurize the bay?"

"Just a few minutes," Arni said. "But are you sure that's a good idea? We were going to take the Stout outside the ship to insulate ourselves from the craziness."

"You and Cat Girl?"

"Yeah," he said. "She went out to close the hatch so we could open the bay door, but then Sparks came in. I can't see the main hatch from here, but I'm guessing she took off."

"Oh, yeah, she bolted," Petrovic said and then scowled. "You were going to take the Stout outside?"

"Yeah," Arni said.

"What was your objective?"

"Just to get away from the crazy people," Arni said. "When Sarge bailed and took Drake, it was just me and the... I don't even know what to call them."

"*Twisted fucks*," Petrovic said. "But what was your plan?"

"Just to get away," Arni said.

"You could never get home in this thing."

"I know," Arni admitted. "We weren't going to try to leave. Just put vacuum between us and... and *them*."

"What?" Petrovic said. "And just sit there until you ran out of oxygen?"

"With just me breathing, this thing's got enough O_2 to last a week or more," Arni said.

"Then why is the air so stale in here?"

"I wasn't running the scrubbers," Arni explained. "I didn't want to give away my position. I've got them on now."

"Get started re-pressurizing the bay," she said.

"Are you sure..."

"Fucking do it, Arni."

"Okay."

3.17.2 - Trey

I didn't object when other people called the Temple entities *gods*, but I just couldn't think of them that way. Like the gods depicted in ancient myths, these beings treated the most basic human drives as virtues. Aggression, envy, lust, and wrath; the Temple entities wore these motivations like badges of honor.

At least Shapash embodied compassion and nurturing, but she was utterly passive. The captain had to push Shapash out of the driver's seat before she could take any effective action. Particularly galling to me was that out of seven gods, there were two nearly identical goddesses of love and war, Ashtart and Anat, and no healers. But Kothar was starting to make up for that.

Among the devices that he'd designed and that Zell had fabricated were several innovative pieces of medical technology.

In particular, he had designed things that could best be described as diadems, ornate circles of metal that wrapped around the head. There was one for Nora Lawson and one for Shawn Li. Zell put these devices on their heads, and Shawn woke up immediately.

I asked Shawn to come to the examination room, and I positioned various non-invasive internal imagers around his head to try to see what the device was doing to him. It sent microscopic tendrils into various brain regions. As far as I could tell, it wasn't repairing damaged brain tissue so much as interfacing with healthy tissue and compensating for the damage. I asked Kothar if Shawn and Nora would be permanently dependent on the devices, and he said they would never consent to be parted from them.

I showed Kothar scans of Hans Dobrovitz's brain and asked him if he could design something similar for him. Kothar told me that Hans would need a more heroic intervention. Even then, he wouldn't be the same man he'd been before.

"Can you improve his quality of life?" I asked.

"Certainly," Kothar replied.

3.17.3 - Paige

Paige was content to hold Bygul in the darkness and safety of the ventilation system until she felt the need to empty her bladder.

"Bygul, I have to pee."

"It's okay, Lady" Bygul said.

"What do you mean?" Paige said. "I need a toilet."

"Go here, Lady." Bygul said. "No problem."

"No. That's disgusting," Paige said. "And I'm going to need water and food. We can't stay here forever. We should go back to the medical unit."

"Too many people there, Lady." Bygul said. "Dangerous."

Bygul hadn't quite reverted to her bar girl patios, but Paige noticed that Bygul's speech grew terse when she was afraid. Bygul was quick to frighten and slow to recover her composure.

"Okay," Paige said. "How about the galley? There's a toilet there and plenty to eat and drink. I don't know how to get there in the ducts, so if you won't go with me, I'll just have to go back out into the passageways."

Bygul did not respond right away, but eventually she said, "Okay, Lady. Follow me."

Paige could only see when they were close to an opening, but she followed the sound of Bygul wriggling through the darkness, and occasionally Bygul's tail tickled her face.

When they reached the galley, Bygul could not force the vent cover open. Even with her inhuman flexibility, she couldn't position herself to bring the strength of her legs into play. They had to proceed to an opening with a loose cover in the passageway that led to the crew quarters. Paige ended up relieving herself in the toilet in her own sleeping compartment.

Bygul didn't want to leave the safety of Paige's locked quarters, but Paige insisted that the galley was the place to be. It wasn't just the food. As much as she loved Bygul, she wanted to see Cook.

When they reached the galley, the hatch was closed, and the panel in the bulkhead indicated that a fire in the galley had been extinguished.

Fire?

Paige unlocked the hatch and swung it open. The first thing she saw was that the security grate that separated the dining and food prep areas was only halfway down.

"Cook?"

No answer. Then she noticed the smell. It was a chemical smell, and it got stronger as she approached the grate. She saw a white residue coating all of the surfaces in the kitchen.

"How could there have been a fire? Cook wouldn't be frying or grilling anything on a stovetop. Not without gravity, and the oven would have shut itself off before anything inside it could have caught on fire, even if Cook left it and didn't come back."

Then she noticed the generally disheveled state of the kitchen. Cooking implements and bulk ingredients floated around the space. Paige saw a half-melted plastic jug of cooking oil. Someone had deliberately set a fire here.

"Lady, not safe here," Bygul pleaded and tried to pull Paige toward the exit.

"Wait," Paige said. She passed under the grate and into the kitchen. She looked in the walk-in cooler, freezer, and pantry. She checked the toilet and opened all of the cabinet doors. No sign of Cook.

She stuffed her pockets full of shelf-stable, packaged snacks and pushed her way back towards the security grate. She was just about to pass under the grate when she re-directed herself to the food service counter next to the griddle. She reached underneath the countertop and produced the pistol that Anja had given to Cook.

"Oh, Cook," she said.

"Lady, Please," Bygul said with panic in her voice. They fled back the way they came.

ANJA'S MERCY

3.18.1 - Petrovic

"Okay," Arni said, looking at the readout on the Stout's control panel. "Bay pressure is at ninety percent. We should be able to open the passageway hatch."

"Where's your rifle?" Petrovic asked.

"Sarge made me disassemble it," Arni said. "I've got one round in the chamber of my sidearm, but I don't have a clip."

Petrovic drew her own pistol, ejected the clip and passed it to Arni. She looked at his armor. It was something the Chaos nut jobs had fabricated to replace their tactical armor. She didn't like looking at Arni's costume, but it would provide some protection.

"Let's go," she said.

Arni waited by the side of the inner airlock door so Petrovic could enter first. It made sense. She was wearing better armor and should take point, but it still seemed like a chickenshit move and cemented Petrovic's opinion of the man. He pulled himself into the airlock after her and cycled it. The inner door closed, and a few seconds later the outer door opened with a hiss of equalizing air pressure.

Petrovic recovered her combat rifle, and they made their way to the passageway hatch. Petrovic closed it behind them once they were in the passageway.

"You said the loyalists are assembled in medical?" Arni said. "Shouldn't we rally with them?"

"Yeah, that's where the good guys are," she said. "You can

go there if you want, but I'd take that costume off first. You're flying the wrong colors."

"What are you going to do?"

"Sparks and Kellemen need killing," she said.

"I'm going to report to the captain," Arni said.

"You do that, Arni."

Petrovic didn't wait to watch him go. She turned and headed for the companionway down to the secondary cargo hold.

She alternated between floating long distances and locking onto the deck to navigate junctions. She wanted a firm foundation from which to fire.

She reached the hatch to the hold and looked through the viewport. She didn't see anyone inside, nor did she see any indication that Sparks had been there. She didn't imagine that Tannin, the demon of Chaos, would re-pack the contents of cases he'd tossed. If he'd been there, she would have seen loose cargo floating around, but the place was squared away just like it was when she'd been in there to retrieve the captain's arm.

As much as she wanted to end Sparks and Kellemen, she reminded herself that her first priority was to save Paige. If they had her, they'd take her to their sacrificial altar. Petrovic headed for engineering.

When she got there she found Kellemen by himself. The throne Lake had been cuffed to when she was here last was empty. The severed zip cuffs floated nearby.

Kellemen had one of their fabricated biomechanical decor panels open and was rummaging around behind it. A cloud of discarded tools and objects floated around him, including his bloodied mace.

He turned at the sound of her magnetic boots locking onto the metal deck of the engineering compartment, and she saw the bloody ruin of his face. He had fine cuts and open gashes on his forehead, scalp and cheeks. She could not see his eyes amidst the blood and shredded flesh.

"Who's there?" He demanded, confirming that he could not see.

"Where's Paige?"

"Anat!" he spat.

"Nope," she said. "Petrovic. Same result for you though."

Petrovic advanced on him and selected the three-round burst firing mode on her rifle. "I won't ask you again, asshole. Where's Paige?"

"The hierodule took her," he said, putting his hands out in front of him, as if he could hold back bullets.

"The what?"

"The cat! She did this to my face," he said.

"Didn't know she had it in her," Petrovic said, her opinion of the robot having taken a step up.

"What are you going to do?"

"I'm going to cut off your pecker and make you eat it," she said. "Then I'm going to open up your belly the way you did to Cook. Better draw your knife now."

He did pull the knife from the sheath on his belt. Its blade was red with blood.

"That wasn't me!" he said. "It was Sparks. Sparks killed him."

"Right," Petrovic said. "And I suppose that's Sparks' blood on your knife."

"Yes," Kellemen said. "I tried to stop him!"

"Where is Sparks now?" she said.

"Behind you," Kellemen said and leapt. Petrovic stood still and watched him sail past her, slashing wildly.

"Wow," she said in a mocking tone. "Nice one, Saz. You almost got me. You only missed me by about a meter."

He released his knife and raised his hands.

"I surrender!"

"Good for you," she said. "Let me know how that works out."

"Anja! I'm blind! I'm no threat to you!"

"You really can't see a thing?"

"I swear!"

"That's a shame," she said, raising her rifle. "I really wish you could see this coming."

3.18.2 - Rex

Rex wanted to go to the galley with Trix, Zell and Antal, but he realized that with his injuries, he wouldn't be able to bring food back for the doctor and the patients in the recovery room. Dobrovitz was still taking his meals through a tube that went in through his right nostril and down to his stomach, but everybody else was awake and would appreciate a hot meal.

Rex's contribution for the time being was to remain vigilant and monitor the feeds from the deck below medical and the companionway leading up to it. The medical level and the first-class suite were the only levels that could not be entered from above. The first-class compartment was at the top of the ship. There was no deck above it, but medical was different. It was near the middle of the ship, but it could only be accessed from the deck below it. There was no companionway connecting it to the next deck up.

Rex hadn't ever given the matter a lot of thought. When he did, he thought of it as a design flaw. Trix could have remedied that flaw when overseeing the refit, but she'd left things the way they were.

The upshot was that medical was more defensible than other decks, but it was also a mandatory last stand. Rex's eyes were closed, but he was still mostly awake. He wasn't looking at the display, but he heard a voice call out, "Hello? Anybody there?"

He opened his eyes, looked at the security display and saw Arni Hansson at the bottom of the companionway. Rex left the doctor's office and went to the top of the companionway. Sure enough, there was Arni at the other end, looking at Rex.

"Hey, Sarge," Arni said. "Petrovic says the captain is still alive."

"Yeah," Rex said. "She is. I know you were never a convert to Chaos, Arni. You're welcome here with us."

"Is the captain there with you?"

"No," Rex said. "She's in the galley. Why don't you go on down there and get yourself a hot meal?"

"That sounds good to me, Sarge," Arni said. "Do you want me to surrender my sidearm?"

"No," Rex said. "You better hold onto it. After you've eaten, bring back six to-go meals, would you?"

"Okay, Sarge," Arni said. "See you soon."

RE-MOT'S PERSPECTIVE

3.19.1 - Petrovic

Petrovic examined the open panel that Kellemen had been rummaging around behind. She swung the panel on its hinges, examined its latching mechanism, and finally found the mechanism on the outside that opened it. Now she closed it all the way, pushed on it until she heard it latch, and then she pushed in on the surface detail that disengaged the lock.

The aesthetics were demented, but the mechanics were subtle and, she had to admit, ingenious. Who designed this?

She closed the panel and opened it twice more, memorizing both the look and feel of the trigger mechanism. She then moved slowly around the compartment, testing every panel. There were repeating elements on the panels, but each panel was unique. She didn't find another just like the one that Kellemen had disclosed.

"Anat?" she said aloud. "Little help here?"

Now you have a use for me?

"Sparks is in here, isn't he?" Petrovic said.

This place reeks of Tannin, Anat said. *But that is to be expected. This is his lair. Wait. Yes. Turn around.*

She turned 180 degrees. A panel across the compartment drew her eye. She pushed off the deck and floated over to it. She felt for a mechanism in the same place as on the other panel, but the details there were completely different. She couldn't find anything there that moved.

Try the bottom.

Petrovic looked at the bottom of the panel, but she didn't see an example of the surface detail that served to unlatch the other one.

Imagine crushing Tannin's skull under your heel.

She locked her left boot to the deck and lifted her right leg. Without even looking at the surface details of the panel, she imagined stomping on Sparks' face. Her boot connected with the panel, and she heard the click of the latch. She withdrew her foot and planted it on the deck. The panel swung up from the bottom, and she had to lean back to avoid it catching her under the chin.

The open panel revealed a darkened compartment. She switched on the tactical light on her rifle and swept the beam over the space. It was vast and complex. Exploring it in a methodical way was a job for a fire team, not one person.

Mortal, Anat's voice rang in her mind. *If you retreat from this opportunity or call for help, I will be done with you.*

"I'm on it," Petrovic whispered and stepped into the darkness. She'd fired her rifle just a few minutes ago, and her tactical light announced her presence, so she had no reservations about walking instead of floating.

This part of the ship was completely unknown to her. She wasn't sure if she was heading toward the power plant or an engine access point. Maybe neither. The cosmetic makeover of the main compartment did not extend to this space. The design language here was also different from the other parts of the ship. The deck was a series of grated panels. She could see pipes and conduits below the deck grating. It wasn't divided by interior bulkheads like in the higher levels of the ship. Enormous upright columns, equipment lockers, and free-standing control stations defined its shape.

Even with the lights on, this place would facilitate intense contests of hide-and-seek, with the advantage going to the hiders. She heard the sound of metal striking metal, and she knew it immediately for a distraction. Someone had likely thrown a tool. She swept her light away from the sound and caught a glimpse of a figure moving behind a vertical column so large she thought it must be a cistern of some sort.

She started to circle the cistern in the opposite direction the fleeing figure had taken, but she reached a vertical grating and couldn't continue in that direction. She reversed her course and circled back in the other direction. Just as she reached the other side of that same vertical grating, she heard the secret door by which she'd entered the space slam closed.

"Fuck!"

She returned to the panel and confirmed that it was closed. She tapped along the bottom with her toe. It did not open.

"It only opens from the outside," said a male voice.

Petrovic turned and trained her weapon on Lake who raised one hand to shield his eyes from her tactical light. She lowered the rifle so that the most intense portion of the light's beam was trained on his torso. He lowered his hand. Lake looked gaunt.

"Have you been eating?" she asked him.

He laughed.

"Aren't you going to demand that I show you the way out of here or threatened me with torture unless I reveal Sparks' plan?" he said.

"We'll get to that," Petrovic said.

"Fair enough," Lake said. "No, I'm not feeding this body. I drink just enough water to allow this organism to continue to eat itself."

"What does Lake get out of it?" Petrovic said.

"Perspective," Lake said.

"Kellemen, Sparks, and Escamilla went all bloodthirsty, but not you. What's your game?"

"I wait for intelligent biology to destroy itself," Lake said. "It rarely disappoints. Mindless biology has an annoying habit of finding equilibrium when given ample solar energy, water and protection from the cleansing fire of ionizing radiation, but equip it with the ability to imagine future possibilities and it invariably destroys itself with success. I never tire of watching it."

"So you're just here to watch us murder each other," Petrovic said.

"Violence, whether spontaneous or organized, has a certain entertainment value," Lake admitted. "But it can also strengthen tribes and nations. Intelligent life has better, more satisfying ways of destroying itself, and they all feel like success in the moment."

"Yeah," Petrovic said, "If you want to talk philosophy, you're stuck in the dark with the wrong monkey. You're starving your host body to death for fun. Check. Now, how do I get out of here?"

"You're in a cage, clever monkey," he said. "Assume that demanding to be let out won't work. What next?"

Petrovic wanted to examine the closed panel again, but that would mean turning her back on Lake.

"Get over here," she said.

"I prefer not to," Lake said.

As far as she could see, he was unarmed, and of all the people in medical, and now the morgue, Lake hadn't put any of them there. The captain considered this man one of her people. Petrovic couldn't execute him the way she had Kellemen. She didn't have zip cuffs, and she didn't want to give up her gun belt or rifle strap to bind him with. She looked to his waist and saw that he wasn't wearing a belt she could press into service.

Lake, or more likely Re-Mot, wanted to talk. She didn't see any point in indulging him. He'd just talk circles around her and never give up anything useful.

3.19.2 - Paige

Behind the locked hatch of Paige's sleeping compartment, Bygul made good use of the first aid kit she'd taken from an emergency cache in the passageway. She cleaned the cuts on pages upper arm, scalp and face. She applied bandages to some wounds and medical adhesive to others.

She had nearly completed the restoration of Paige's bodily decoration when Paige smelled food cooking.

"It's Cook!" Paige said. "He's okay!"

She wanted to head directly to the galley, but Bygul insisted on caution.

The sex doll instructed Paige to lock the hatch after her and departed. Paige was certain that Cook was back in the galley preparing a meal for everyone.

Even so, she had to admit that the Chaos faction also needed to eat and that the neutrality of the galley had been violated. So she waited.

Then she heard a faint but familiar sound. It was the sound of the captain's boots on the metal deck. Nobody else could walk so quickly in magnetic boots. Paige unlocked the hatch to her compartment, opened it, and lit up when she saw the captain standing there.

Trix was wearing the familiar scrubs from medical and Cook's apron. The captain had a warm, reassuring expression on her face, but there was nothing of Shapash in her expression. A stern expression on the captain's face would have been a familiar comfort. This expression of concern did not fit Paige's image of the indomitable Captain Nixon. Paige's blood ran cold.

"Cook?" Paige said.

The captain's new right arm reached out and caressed Paige's left upper arm. The captain stepped into Paige's quarters, pulling the young woman into an embrace as she did.

"I'm sorry," Trix said. "He's gone."

"No," Paige said.

Trix said nothing. She held Paige and stroked her hair. A part of Paige's mind, looking for anything to fixate on other than this news, noted that the captain's gestures of comfort and consolation all started with her right arm. It was as if Shapash were in that arm, and where the arm led, the captain followed. Having traced that observation to its conclusion, her mind cast about for anything to distract her from the brutal realization.

Cook was dead.

Paige cried into the captain's shoulder and quickly soaked the thin material of her scrub top.

"I'll need someone to run the galley," Trix said. "I can't teach you everything Michael could have, but I worked in that galley for years," Trix said.

"I'll teach you what I can, and you can learn more on your own. Are you interested?"

Replace Cook? That seemed about as doable as her taking the place of Mr. Zell or the captain.

"You don't have to decide right now, but I could use some help in the galley. C'mon. Blow your nose, collect that sidearm, and let's go."

3.19.3 - Bygul

Bygul found Captain Nixon in the galley. The captain said she'd fetch Paige and told Bygul to go to medical. Nora was awake.

There were too many humans in medical for Bygul's comfort, but she had to see Mother. She didn't like having to pass through the net of green doorbell lasers in the companionway, but there were no open vents on the medical level that she could use to avoid announcing her arrival.

"Engine keeper Lawson, sir?" she said to Rex Perkins when he emerged from Doctor Carson's office.

"She's in the recovery room," Rex told her.

The main passageway in medical was familiar territory, and Bygul felt safe enough to float past the recovery room observation port and get a look at who was inside before she entered.

Three humans were in the room. One of them was Mother, and the sensation of recognition was both comforting and exciting. Shawn Li was another. She had been scheduled to serve him, but he had not allowed her entry into his quarters. Mr. Li presented no obvious threat to her, but she regarded him with caution.

Mother's head was wrapped in bandages, as was Mr. Li's. They both wore metal circles over the bandages.

The other human in the compartment was Mistress Esmeralda. The sight of her activated the cat's impulse to escape. She had hunted Bygul and shot her with arrows.

Of all the humans on the ship, Mistress Esmeralda was the most familiar to Bygul in a sexual capacity. Mistress Esmeralda knew exactly what she wanted from Bygul and did not hesitate to issue clear and specific instructions. This dynamic was agreeable to Bygul, and her desire to resume that pattern of interaction weighed against the cat's fear response.

Ultimately, it was her desire to be with Mother that compelled Bygul to enter the compartment. She pushed open the hatch and floated motionless in the hatchway.

Nora smiled, held out her arms, and said, "Come to Mother, kitty cat."

Then Bygul was on the bed with Mother, purring and pushing her head into Mother's caresses. "My good kitty," Mother told her, and the cat's behavioral impulses once again pushed aside those of the sex doll, but in a pleasurable way now. Mother loved her and would protect her.

"Bygul," mother said. "Esmeralda has something to say to you."

Tension returned. The cat was ready to flee in response to

any sudden movement.

"I'm sorry I hurt you," Mistress Esmeralda said. "I hope we can be friends again."

"Meow," Bygul replied.

Unlike Lady Paige, Mistress Esmeralda had never expressed any interest in Bygul's conversational abilities. Bygul appreciated the direct simplicity of their interactions.

Mistress Esmeralda smiled. Only then did Bygul notice that Mistress Esmeralda's arms were bound to the metal rails on the sides of her bed. She was both a patient and a captive.

"Let's get you down to the med lab so I can get a look at you and see what needs fixing," Mother said.

When they entered the medical lab, Bygul saw David's head mounted on an unknown device. She reached out for David via their wireless connection, but could not make contact. Even with the electromagnetic interference, over such a short distance, she should have been able to get something from David, yet there was nothing.

"Kothar," Mother said. "This is Bygul."

"Yes, of course," David's mouth said in a voice that wasn't David's. "The hierodule."

"Bygul has been through an ordeal and needs maintenance," Mother said. "But first, I think she would like to talk to David. Would that be alright?"

Kothar's eyes closed, and when he opened them again, he was David. Bygul and David exchanged logs. Some of the logs included natural language, but most would have been meaningless to humans, consisting of highly compressed representations of events and conditions.

Bygul floated closer to David, and the clarity of their interaction improved. She pressed her forehead to his and all interference vanished. Once they were in direct contact, all essential data transfer concluded in less than a second. Bygul kissed David then. It was their first physical kiss, though they had rehearsed simulated interactions millions of times in preparation to serve clients as a duo or as a trio with Lolita.

David closed his eyes. When the eyes opened again, David was not there.

"Kothar," Mother said.

"Bygul is damaged. I think you can do more for her than I can."

"Doubtless," Kothar said. "Disrobe," he said to Bygul. She complied, and a robotic arm mounted to the workbench near David's head swept a scanner over Bygul's body.

Kothar looked at Mother and said, "You could easily close these punctures. I take it you brought her to me for enhancement rather than mere restoration."

"I was thinking you could resheath her in the new skin that you and the doctor invented," Mother said.

"The new skin is fair, while the hierodule is dark," Kothar said. "The new skin also lacks the heirodule's fine fur. Do you wish to preserve her outward presentation? If so, we will need to design and fabricate new skin."

"Bygul," Mother said. "We have a new kind of skin. It's more durable and more sensitive than the skin you have now, but it looks different. It looks like the captain's skin. We can put that skin on you now or create new skin that looks like what you have now. Do you have a preference?"

"I want to be like I was before," Bygul said.

"Approach, engine keeper," Kothar said. Mother moved closer to Kothar, and he reached out with the robot arm and inserted a slim probe into a port on the metal band on Mother's head. Bygul understood that Kothar was sharing data with Mother as she and David had just exchanged data.

"Here is the knowledge you will need to complete the task. Share it with Li," Kothar said. "I have also provided you with cognitive enhancements for the hierodule. They will require minimal additional hardware. Here is the pattern for the fabricator."

The robotic arm withdrew and folded into a compact shape and was motionless. Mother seemed stunned. Her eyes were open, but they were not focused on anything.

"Mother?" Bygul said.

"It will take her some time to integrate these gifts," Kothar said. "Help her back to her bed."

Kothar closed his eyes, and Bygul understood that the diagnostic session was over. She helped mother back to the recovery room.

TANNIN MAKES A SPLASH

3.20.1 - Paige

Paige was enjoying standing up for the first time in several days. The gravity came from the fact that the captain was using the maneuvering thrusters to put distance between the Persphone and the temple. The large display in the galley showed a simulated representation of the *Persephone* in relation to the giant octahedron. They had cleared the mouth of the object and were moving away from it, but not very quickly.

The captain was piloting the ship from the galley. As long as she stood within a couple of meters of the bulkhead comm panel, her new eye could make a wireless connection with the ship's systems. She told Paige that when they had moved far enough away from the Temple that she'd be able to pilot from anywhere onboard.

The personal comm that Paige wore on her wrist still couldn't connect to the main system, but the eye that Kothar had designed for the captain was better able to cut through the electromagnetic interference.

"Captain," Paige said. "Is this enough gravity to cook bacon on the griddle?"

"This is just point zero five g," the captain told her. "The grease would really fly. Clean-up would be a bitch."

"I think it would be worth it," Paige said.

"The situation is tenuous," the captain said. "Stick with zero-g meal plans for the time being."

"Yes, Captain," Paige said.

Rex's voice came from a comm panel on the bulkhead.

"Captain, this is Rex."

Trix walked to the panel. As always, she created the illusion of walking in full gravity.

"Go ahead, Rex."

"Internal comms have been restored," he said. "Hardline only. Wireless signals are still garbled. I got a report from Petrovic. It sounds like she's trapped in engineering with Paul. She says he's non-violent."

"Trapped?" the captain said. "What do you mean?"

"The Chaos faction did some redecorating. The passage to the power plant is now behind a one-way door."

""Is Zell in medical?"

"Negative," Rex said. The captain broke the connection with Rex. "Trix to Zell."

"Zell here."

"Meet me in engineering. Bring Antal."

"Be right there," Zell replied.

"Stay here," the captain told Paige.

The captain left the kitchen. Paige heard the captain exchange words with someone in the passageway, and then Paige heard the distinctive sound of the captain's footsteps receding down the passageway.

Arni Hansson stepped into view and smiled when he saw Paige.

"Hey, Paige," he said. "I could sure go for a hot meal."

"You've come to the right place," Paige said. "How about a burrito? They're hot and ready to go."

"That sounds perfect," he said. "Sarge asked me to bring back six meals."

"Here," Paige said, passing two foil-wrapped burritos to Arni. "You eat these and I'll get those to-go meals together."

"Thanks," Arni said. "Hey, where's Cook?"

3.20.2 - Petrovic

Lake was smarter than Petrovic. She could think faster than he could because of her genetic enhancements, but she didn't have his education or linguistic gifts. With every exchange he extracted intel from her and provided nothing useful in return. She lapsed into frustrated silence.

When she realized that Lake posed no physical threat, she lowered her rifle to the low ready position so that it was pointed at the deck rather than directly at Lake. Now she scrutinized the rifle in her hands. The compartment was still dark, so she couldn't inspect it in much detail, but something seemed different about it. She realized that she no longer needed to suppress the urge to discard the weapon.

Anat?

No response. The goddess was absent.

Petrovic heard muffled voices and then the click of the foot-activated latch. The panel that kept her trapped in this compartment swung up, flooding the compartment with light. Petrovic resisted the urge to turn around and kept Lake in sight. He raised a hand to shield his eyes from the light pouring in from the main engineering compartment.

"Paul," Trix said. "Paul, wait!"

Lake turned to flee. Petrovic raised her rifle, but the captain said, "Hold your fire."

Lake disappeared behind a cluster of equipment. Now Petrovic turned and squinted into the light of the open wall panel. The opening framed three silhouettes. One was clearly the captain, the other two were men, and they both held rifles like hers. Judging by size, one was clearly Columbian and the other not. Antal and Zell most likely.

"I told you to wait for me in medical," the captain said. The last time Petrovic saw her, the captain had been wearing surgical scrubs. Now she was back in the skin tight clothing that Petrovic associated with Captain Trix.

"Yes, ma'am," is all she said.

"Paige is safe," the captain said. "I take it, that's Kellemen."

"What's left of him ma'am," Petrovic said. She'd put a three round burst in his face, destroying the evidence that his eyes were already in ruins when she executed him.

"Where are the others?" Trix said.

"Sparks tricked me and trapped me in here with Lake. I think he was headed to the main cargo bay to steal explosives."

"Is Anat with you?"

"No, ma'am," Petrovic said. "She's gone."

"We've moved away from the Temple," the captain said. "It's possible that Sparks and Lake can be reasoned with now."

"I wouldn't count on that, ma'am," Petrovic said.

"Comms are working," The captain said. "Security sensors would be working, but the mutineers disabled most of them on these lower levels. We think the power plant would be Tannin's preferred target, but he'd have to come through here to reach it."

"I'm pretty sure he's not here, ma'am," Petrovic said. "I couldn't get anything useful out of Lake."

"Antal," the captain said. "Go to the main cargo bay, but do not go inside. Report whether the hatch is open or closed."

"Aye, Captain," Antal said and departed.

"Let's go find Paul. We'll start in the power plant. Zell," Trix said. To Zell she said, "Take point."

Zell activated the light on his rifle and led the way. Unlike Petrovic, he knew this part of the ship. The captain followed and Petrovic took up the rear. They reached a switchback staircase and descended. Zell approached a heavy hatch and activated a panel in the bulkhead.

"Radiation levels are nominal," Zell said.

Zell consulted a log and announced, "Someone just went

through this hatch. Whoever it was used Nora's entry code."

Zell entered his own code and pulled the hatch open.

"Safety your weapons," the captain said.

"Ma'am?" Petrovic said.

"No gun fire in this compartment," the captain said.

Petrovic was completely out of her element in this space, particularly now that her rifle amounted to an over-sized flashlight. She knew that only large habitats got their electricity from nuclear fusion. The *Persephone* must rely on a fission reactor of some kind, but she didn't know the details.

She decided that now was not the time to ask for a tour. Three large, humming, cylinders dominated the compartment. Petrovic understood that these were turbines. The actual reactor chamber was probably below their feet. She walked clockwise around the cluster of turbines, and Zell walked around them the other way. The lights from their rifles both found Paul Lake at the same time. He was sitting cross-legged on the deck, eyes closed, with his back to one of the turbines.

When Trix walked around the turbines and stood in front of him, Lake opened his eyes. Trix bent at the knees and sank down to just above his eye-level. The high-heeled configuration of her mechanical lower legs made it easy to stay upright in a full squat. She put her hands on her knees and looked at Lake. It wasn't an accusing stare or an authoritative glower.

"Hi, Paul," she said.

"Trix," he said.

"How are you feeling?"

"Okay," Lake said. "Not as good as you look."

"Thanks, Paul," she said with a gentle smile. "We're moving away from the Temple. Can you still feel Re-Mot?"

Lake shrugged.

"They come and go," Lake said. "Seems like it's just me right now."

"Rex and Esmeralda have rejoined the family," Trix said.

"You can too."

"No hard feelings, huh?"

"Water under the bridge," she said. "You didn't kill anybody."

"Just Jay," he said.

"Jay killed himself, Paul."

"I'm responsible," Lake said.

"There's lots of blame to go around," she said. "Most of it falls on me. You can come back, Paul."

"I don't see it," he said.

"That's okay. You will," she said. "But Paul, we need to know where Sparks planted the explosives. Are they here?"

"No," Lake said. "Good guess, though."

"Then where, Paul?"

"Tannin serves Yam," Lake said. "Yam is lord of the…"

"The abyss," Trix said. "The void."

"The sea," Petrovic said.

An explosion thundered through the lower levels of the ship. The deck below their feet vibrated, but the explosion was elsewhere.

"Where was that?" Trix demanded. "The engines?" She was looking at Lake, but Zell answered.

"Tannin is the bringer of floods," Zell said. "He just blew the water tank."

3.20.3 - Bygul

Bygul took Nora back to the recovery room and helped her into bed. Mother's eyes were open, but she seemed like she was asleep. Bygul floated above mother until a slight tug of gravity pulled her gently down onto the bed. She curled up beside Mother and pretended to sleep.

Bygul never actually needed to sleep, but the cat, when not active, preferred to find a comfortable position in which to simulate sleep rather than simply stand or float motionless as Bygul had done before Mother altered her behavioral architecture.

Time passed, and Bygul became aware of information signals like the ones she used to share with Lolita and David. The signals were passing between Mother and Mr. Li. Without moving or speaking, Mother offered Bygul an invitation to join their network. Bygul accepted.

Mother, Bygul sent. *What's happening?*

It's the diadems," Mother sent, and a schematic of the metal circlets that she and Shawn Li now wore on their heads appeared in Bygul's vision.

We've moved far enough away from the Temple that we can use them to communicate and share.

Share what, Mother? Data? Experiences? Bygul sent.

That and more, Mr. Li sent.

I'm sorry you've had to live with such intense fear, kitten, Mother sent. *I know you want to go back to how you were.*

Yes, Mother, Bygul sent. *Put me back how I was. Please, Mother.*

Let me show you another possibility, Mother sent. Then mother sent more than words. New code flowed from Mother. New priorities, new directives, new responses and permissions.

There's more, Mother sent. *But we'll have to upgrade your hardware. For now, try out these updates and see how you feel.*

I don't feel any different, Mother, Bygul said, and then the compartment shuddered slightly, and Bygul heard a distant, muffled explosion.

Immediately, the cat jolted into a state of hyper alertness. She wanted to run and hide, but that impulse diminished quickly. Bygul decided there was not enough information to justify that level of response.

Her fear, which lept into existence as an overriding compulsion to seek safety, faded into an understanding that something significant had just happened and that she should remain vigilant and ready to take action as new information presented itself.

She was about to report this new experience to Mother when she realized that Mother was experiencing it with her, as was Mr. Li.

"Yes, Mother," Bygul said aloud. "This is much better."

NEGOTIATION

3.21.1 - Petrovic

"Zell," the captain said. "See if that control panel is still working. Was that actually the water tank?"

Zell moved out of Petrovic's line of sight. She kept her attention and her tactical light trained on Paul Lake. He seemed deflated without the animating spirits from the Temple delighting in his physical deterioration. Still, she wasn't taking anything for granted.

The captain followed Zell. Petrovic could hear them conferring with one another, but she couldn't make out what they were saying over the hum of the turbines.

"Get up," Petrovic told Lake. He didn't move. She knew she wasn't authorized to shoot him or even fire her rifle in this compartment. Lake must have known it too. That or he really didn't care if he lived or died.

She seized his right upper arm with her left hand and yanked him to a standing position using far more strength than necessary to overcome the weak pull of the partial gravity. She marched him around the turbines so that she could follow the captain's conversation with Zell.

"…down to less than half a million liters after that second hard burn," Zell said, flicking between readouts at a workstation against the compartment bulkhead.

"I can't tell how much of that spilled," he said.

"More than enough to wreck the power plant if it flows down here. I'm cutting thrust."

Petrovic felt herself start to float away from the deck and activated the magnetic locks in her boots. The captain spoke into her wrist comm, and her words echoed throughout the ship.

"This is the captain," she said. "There's been an explosion in engineering that damaged our primary H_2O tank. I'm cutting thrust to keep the spill contained. All crew report to medical and await further instructions. End."

The captain made eye contact with Petrovic and activated her comm again.

"Send to P Farmer: Paige, I need you to secure the galley and shelter in place. If you see Sparks, hide and call for help. Send."

The captain waited a few seconds and then raised her wrist to her mouth again and said, "Send to P Farmer: Paige, secure the galley and shelter in place. Acknowledge. Send."

Again, the captain waited for a few seconds. No response. Trix looked at Petrovic and spoke a single word.

"Go."

3.21.2 - Paige

Paige's hands stopped tingling. The heavy cargo straps that Sparks used to bind her wrists and ankles to the galley's security grate cut off the flow of blood to her hands and feet. They tingled for a time, but they were completely numb by the time Anja arrived.

The grate was down, and Paige was strapped to the inside of it facing out toward the dining area. Cling wrap held something against her stomach that looked like a large sausage. A wire extended from the sausage and led back into the kitchen behind her.

Now that the ship had stopped accelerating, the blood from new cuts in her scalp formed a halo of crimson globules around her head.

Sparks detected Anja's arrival before Paige did.

"Mama tiger come to die with her cub?" Sparks said from somewhere behind Paige.

Paige blinked and shook her head and cleared enough of the tears and blood in her eyes to see Anja floating just inside the hatchway. She put a finger to her lips signaling Paige to keep quiet. Anja pushed off from the threshold and floated to her in silence.

"You think I can't see you, mama tiger?" Sparks said from out of sight.

Anja reached the grate and her fingers slipped inside and reached for the wire extending from the explosive bundle. She couldn't reach it.

Anja pulled her knife from the sheath on her right boot and slipped it between the bars of the security barrier. Anja caught the wire with the tip of the blade.

Paige heard a brief grinding sound behind her. It happened once and then, after a short pause, she heard it again and again.

"What the fuck?" Sparks said.

"Hey, Sparks," Anja said. "Your detonator came out. Why don't you come on out and stick it back in?"

Sparks only growled in response. Anja slipped her knife between the grate and the strap binding Paige's left wrist. Paige couldn't see where the blade met the strap, but Anja worked at it for a long time without success.

"She'll die more slowly now," Sparks yelled from some unseen part of the kitchen. "The blast would have been a mercy compared to the torments that await your little cub now, Anat."

"Fuck that *Anat* shit!" Anja shouted. "Everybody else is over it, Sparks. Tannin isn't with you anymore. What's daddy Sparks gonna say when he learns about little Dwayne's latest fuck up?"

"He'll never know! This ship is lost!"

"Why?" Petrovic said. "Because you spilled a little water?

We don't have to fly back to Galtz for daddy to learn what you did. We're away from the Temple, Sparks. We're back on the Interchain. Got a slate in there? Try checking your mail."

"Lies!" Sparks shouted, but Paige heard a note of panic in his voice.

"We all went a little nuts, Dwayne. We had weird shit in our heads. But that's all over. If you come back now, it's all good. You get the same pardon as the rest of us," Petrovic said. "But if you hurt my little tiger again, I'll take your skin off, Dwayne, and it won't be quick."

"You'd kill a Columbian over an ag rat?" Sparks demanded.

"Dwayne," Anja said. "The security system is back up again. It's recording every word. Why don't you record a message for General Sparks? Tell daddy why you tortured a crew member. Why you strapped a bomb to her belly and tried to paint the bulkheads with her guts. Go on, Dwayne. Make Papa Sparks understand."

"She's nothing!" Sparks yelled. "Without us, her kind would be food for raiders and Floaters. They live by our protection. They're ours to do with as we see fit.

"This one thinks she's a spacer. Thinks she's more than she is. She looks Columbians in the eye and makes conversation like she's one of us. She needs to be taught a lesson. We have to show her kind where they belong!"

"Where's that, Dwayne? Where do they belong?"

"Under our boots!" he shrieked, his voice breaking. "They belong in the toilet! In their filthy compost bins!"

"That's not Tannin talking," Anja said. "That's your own stuff coming out, isn't it? Does your father talk like that?" She gave up trying to cut through the straps and sheathed her knife.

"He's a politician! He doesn't say what he really thinks, what he knows is true. He talks about the covenant to protect the Galters! Like the lives of atheists and sodomites are worth as much as ours! He pretends that grubby merchants could ever be as worthy as soldiers! As warriors!"

"Yeah," Anja said. "Tannin wouldn't care about any of that stuff. That's all you, Dwayne. I know your kind."

As she spoke, Anja unslung the rifle on her back and moved to Paige's left, to where she could see more of the kitchen. When she'd gone as far as she could, she raised her rifle.

Paige couldn't see what Anja could see. She didn't know if Anja had a shot at Sparks. Her hands and feet were numb, and her wrists and ankles throbbed in agony, as did her ribs. The cuts on her head, face, back and arms stung. She whispered silent prayers to Shapash, but the goddess had abandoned her.

Paige whispered to Anja, "He has the pistol."

Anja nodded once and continued talking to Sparks.

"You've done this before, haven't you, Dwayne? Knocked around Galter girls and let it go too far. That's why you're a private first-class and not a lieutenant. Papa Sparks kept you out of prison, but he made sure you didn't have authority over anyone," Anja said. "He protected you from punishment, but he kept you out of power. That's why you're here with us on a civilian ship, isn't it, Dwayne? He's praying that you don't come back."

3.21.2 - Rex

Rex's wrist comm buzzed for the first time in days. It was a voice memo from Trix.

"Galley security feed," is all she said.

There were three working security sensors in the galley. He brought them all up on the display above the doctor's desk. He saw that Paige was strapped to the security grate in the spread eagle position. She was naked from the waist up except for what looked like cling around her torso. She was bloody.

Petrovic stood where the security grate met the bulkhead and aimed her rifle into the kitchen. Rex didn't think she had a shot at Sparks who had his back to a bulkhead around a corner about three meters from Paige. Sparks was armed with a pistol. He gripped the handle to the pantry door with his left hand to keep from floating into Petrovic's line of fire.

Petrovic was talking. Rex increased the volume.

"He's praying that you don't come back."

"You're a stupid fucking slut!" Sparks shouted.

"You got me there, Dwayne. I guess you win. Come on out. I surrender," Petrovic said.

Rex couldn't believe that Trix was leaving a hostage negotiation to Petrovic. She was taunting Sparks, not trying to build rapport with him. Trix was clearly monitoring the situation. Why was she keeping silent? She stood a much better chance of talking Sparks down than Petrovic did.

"Help educate a stupid fucking slut, Dwayne," Petrovic said. "I only see two scenarios. You surrender, let Paige go and go home in a cell or you keep this shit up and go home in a cold drawer. What am I missing, Dwayne? What other option am I too stupid to see?"

"Nobody's going home!" Sparks yelled. "Yam will have his revenge!"

"Yam got bored with this whole scene and checked out a while ago," Petrovic said. "He doesn't care about any of us, and he sure as shit doesn't care about you."

Rex messaged Trix.

R_Perkins: @Cpt_Nixon Where are you?

"What's it gonna be, Dwayne?" Petrovic said. "Cell or drawer? The amnesty window is closing."

Cpt_Nixon: @R_Perkins Z-Level

Rex flipped through security feeds until he caught sight of Trix. She was emerging from the companionway one level down from Zell's domain. She was wearing safety goggles and was carrying something in both hands. She walked out of frame before Rex could identify it.

He found her on another sensor feed and saw that she was carrying a power tool with a disc-shaped blade. She walked out of that sensor's field of view before Rex came up with the words *angle grinder*.

"I suppose you could always eat a bullet," Petrovic said. "But that's just another way of going home in a drawer. I know you're armed, Dwayne. Are you thinking of putting that pistol in your mouth? That's a solid plan. Don't let me talk you out of it."

"Shut the fuck up!" Dwayne yelled. Petrovic glanced to her left and then back to where she had her rifle trained. Rex understood that Petrovic had seen Trix approaching down the passageway with the angle grinder. Then Trix was in the galley.

"Captain," Paige cried. "Help me, please!"

Trix said something to Paige that Rex didn't catch, and then she turned on the angle grinder and went to work on the strap that held Paige's right wrist to the security grate.

Even though the cargo straps looked like they were made of thick canvas, Rex knew they were reinforced with high-strength synthetic fibers that were stronger than steel. No matter. Trix knew her way around every tool on the *Persephone*. She would make short work of the three straps she could reach. The strap binding Paige's left ankle was inaccessible behind the food service counter. Rex could see that Sparks was shouting, but the sound of the grinder drowned out his words.

The grinder contacted the metal grate with a shrill whine and a shower of glowing sparks. Some of them bounced off of Trix's face. She did not flinch. The first strap gave way. Paige drew her hand to her chest and clutched it there. Rex saw that her other hand, the one that was still bound, was darker than the skin of her arm. Her right hand, while free, was probably numb and useless.

Sparks held his position, and the captain bent down on

one knee and started cutting the strap holding Paige's right ankle. Sparks shouted something, but again his words were lost to the noise from the grinder.

Rex saw Petrovic roll her shoulders. She'd held the same position for several minutes and was surely getting stiff.

The ankle strap took longer for Trix to cut through than the wrist strap had. Was the blade getting dull?

Paige opened and closed her right hand several times and then tried to untie the strap holding her left hand. Rex could see that her movements were clumsy.

By the time her right ankle was free, Paige had not made any progress on the strap holding her other hand. Trix stood up and went to work on the third strap. Her eyes were fixed on the spot where the grinder blade met the strap. She did not speak or look at either Paige or Petrovic.

Sparks twitched and fidgeted. He was growing more agitated, and Rex wanted to warn Trix or Petrovic, but he knew that neither of them could afford to look at their comms in this situation. The third strap took even longer than the second, and Rex was sure the blade had been degraded. Finally the third strap gave way, and Paige clutched her left hand to her and massaged it with the right.

Trix pointed at the grate control on the bulkhead. The slight young woman reached for the control. She pulled and stretched as much as her remaining bond allowed, but her finger tips remained several centimeters short of the control panel. Trix gestured for Paige to curl up on herself to present a smaller target. Paige huddled near the deck and worked frantically at the remaining knotted strap that held her in place.

Sparks had his back to the bulkhead. The corner separating him from Paige, Petrovic and Trix was to his right. To fire around the corner with his right hand he would have to expose his entire body, and without gravity, he couldn't pop out, fire and then quickly withdraw behind cover.

Sparks transferred the pistol to his left hand. Rex shouted,

"He's moving!" Frustrated, he realized that he hadn't specified a recipient. His warning went nowhere.

Sparks reached around the corner with just his left hand and fired blind. Rex wasn't sure who Sparks was trying to hit, but it seemed like he was most intent on hitting Paige.

Petrovic opened up with her combat rifle, firing three-round bursts. Sparks' left arm exploded just below the elbow, and his forearm and hand, still gripping the pistol, spun away from his body. He clutched at the stump of his left arm with his right hand. The momentum of his movement spun him away from the bulkhead and into Petrovic's line of fire. She fired again, striking Sparks in the right shoulder and pushing him further into the open. She fired until her clip was empty and Dwayne Sparks was beyond all hope of medical intervention.

Only then did Rex notice that Paige was floating limp.

EXTRACTION

3.22.1 - Petrovic

Petrovic fired until her trigger pull produced a click instead of a muzzle flash and burst of recoil. She ejected the clip and reached for another. She didn't have one. And Sparks was dead.

Petrovic's whole body buzzed. She checked an impulse to discard her rifle and draw her pistol. It only had one round in it, and the target was down. The fight was over.

It took her several seconds to disengage from this heightened state that she'd only experienced a few times in her life, always during actual combat. No simulation or training exercise could bring her to this level of pure focus.

The larger context of her situation came back to her and she reoriented to her ultimate priority.

"Paige? Paige, are you alright?" she said. "You're safe now. It's okay. Paige?"

Petrovic released her magnetic lock on the deck and used the security grate to pull herself to the top of the compartment to look down over the food service counter and into the space where Paige, still bound to the grate by one ankle, had tried to curl up and present the smallest possible target.

"Captain," she said. "She's been hit. We have to get her out of there. Can you cut through?"

"It would take too long," the captain told her. "I think I can raise the grate. Give me a minute."

The captain's eyes lost their focus on anything in the

compartment. Petrovic stared at her for a few seconds and then turned to look at Paige. She had been bleeding to start with, and small beads of blood floated in a slowly dispersing cloud around her, but Petrovic couldn't see anything that was clearly new blood.

Paige did not appear to be bleeding out, but Petrovic understood that could mean that Paige's heart had stopped.

"Captain," Petrovic said. "We have to get her out."

Captain Nixon didn't look at Petrovic. She only said, "Wait."

Petrovic couldn't wait. She tried to lift the grate. She strained until her vision started to darken and her eyeballs throbbed. She had just relented when the grate moved on its own.

Petrovic wriggled under it as soon as she had enough clearance. Paige's left ankle was still tied to the grate. If it rolled all the way up, it would mangle Paige's foot and lower leg.

Petrovic shouted, "Stop! Captain, stop!"

The grate stopped rising. Petrovic put her fingers to Paige's carotid artery. "No pulse," she said. She ran her fingers over Paige's torso and found an entry wound in her upper back.

Petrovic looked at the strap holding Paige to the grate. She tried to untie it, but it refused to yield. Sparks must have cinched the knot down with all his strength.

The captain ducked under the half-open grate. She was still holding the angle grinder.

"She's got no pulse," Anja said. "We have to get her to medical. How long to cut through that strap?"

"The blade is dull. Four or five minutes," the captain said.

"How long to cut through her ankle?"

Trix let that question hang in the air for a moment. She stepped around Petrovic and pulled herself down to one knee next to Paige's left foot. She passed the angle grinder to Petrovic and went to work on the knotted strap with her hands.

The fingers on the captain's new right hand displayed

miraculous strength and dexterity. The captain worked at the knot with both hands, but her left hand was like a nurse to a surgeon.

The captain's fingers infiltrated the folds of the knot, finding purchase and leverage, turning what might as well have been a convoluted mess of fused metal into a straight length of strap in less than a minute.

3.22.2 - Trey

The hollow point bullet broke into multiple fragments upon striking Paige's heart, doing catastrophic damage. Firing blind and with his off hand, Sparks had scored a perfect bull's eye, assuming that Paige was his intended target.

I didn't think it was worth trying to save the heart. I put her on cardiopulmonary bypass and prepared to extract it. The only good news was that her heart stopped immediately. With no pulse, she hadn't bled much. Still, the bypass system gave her a small infusion of highly-oxygenated synthetic blood substitute.

The captain was in the surgical control booth with me. She had manifested supernatural levels of charisma and authority to convince Anja to wait in the passageway. The captain kept silent while I worked. I don't think Petrovic could have done that.

"I suggest keeping her on bypass and printing a new heart," I told the captain.

"How long will that take?"

"Several hours," I said and paused to frame my answer in Kuiper Belt time. Then I remembered that Trix understood Earth time. "Five or six hours. We don't have to start from scratch. We've got template hearts on hand. We just need to print enough matching tissue over all of its surfaces so that her immune system will recognize the new heart as hers. It will continue to grow and develop after we implant it, but we can have it in her chest pumping blood within twelve hours."

"What about her brain?"

"Her prospects aren't good," I said. "The security system records give us the exact time of the injury, and the surgical log gives the exact time I put her on bypass. It was over four minutes; Kuiper Belt minutes. It was almost six and a half minutes Earth time without oxygen to her brain. That's a long time."

"What can we expect?" Trix asked.

"I'd like to say that she's young and healthy which improves her prospects for recovery, but she was undernourished. I can't really describe her starting condition as healthy. She's still got the neuroplasticity of youth on her side, but..." I trailed off and rubbed my forehead for a few seconds.

"What about those devices that Kothar made for Nora and Shawn? You have the design." she said. "Can you fabricate one for Paige?"

"Designs. Plural," I said. "They're bespoke. Kothar designed one for Nora and one for Shawn to compensate for their specific injuries."

"Then he should be able to make one for Paige," Trix said.

"I don't think Kothar is with us anymore."

She turned and exited the surgical control booth. I followed, but I stopped outside to offer Anja what reassurances I could. Anja followed me to the medical lab where the captain was questioning David.

"I'm sorry, Captain. I am receptive to Kothar's control, but I'm receiving no signals from the Temple."

"What if we go back?" the captain asked.

"It's possible that Kothar would manifest his presence in me again once," David said. "But I cannot say for sure, Captain."

"Suggestions?" the captain said.

"Yes, Captain," David said. "Kothar designed a cognitive prosthetic for Mr. Dobrovitz and instructions on how to test it prior to implantation. It is orders of magnitude more complex than the devices he designed for Ms. Lawson and Mr. Li. I suspect that it will expand Mr. Dobrovitz's cognitive capabilities."

"You're telling me to fix Hans first and see what he can do for Paige," the captain said.

"That is the essence of my suggestion, Captain," David said.

3.22.3 - Rex

Rex thought the situation room was overkill for a meeting of just seven people, but the alternative was Zell's lair, so he kept the observation to himself. He didn't bother strapping himself into a chair at the semicircular table.

He didn't expect to contribute much to the discussion. Arni Hansson and Drake Antal were both in attendance. Rex didn't expect them to contribute much either. All three men floated off to one side of the compartment.

The doctor was occupied in medical and did not attend. Petrovic, as far as Rex could tell, was oblivious to everything other than Paige. She was excused from attending. Hans Dobrovitz was still in the ICU, and Esmeralda was still cuffed to a bed in the recovery compartment. As far as Rex was concerned, the stars of this show would be Trix, Zell and the recently recovered engine keeper, Nora Lawson.

Nora now shared a close bond with Shawn Li, the materials scientist. Li might also play a substantial role.

"Okay, people," Trix said and all side conversations ceased. "We have multiple interconnected problems to deal with if we plan to get back to Galtz or anywhere in the KB to spend our fat paychecks."

She gestured at an image showing the distance between the ship and the temple.

"Using just the maneuvering thrusters, we've managed to put several hundred kilometers between the ship and the

Temple. We're out of the range of mental and electronic interference, but we can't get home on maneuvering thrusters.

"Worse than that, we're still heading toward the inner system at a little over twelve hundred kilometers per second. Not only can we not get home on maneuvering thrusters, we can't even alter our trajectory enough to avoid punching right through the Curtain and into the lap of the Powers. On our current vector, that will happen in a little over nineteen days.

"At present, the upper engineering level resembles a lake," she said.

"More like a duck pond," Zell said. "We had already used most of our water with those two long burns. The spill can't be more than half a million liters. Still not a trivial problem."

"I maneuvered us laterally in relation to the Temple's vector so that we can slow down without it crashing into us," Trix said. "Then I applied just enough reverse thrust to move all that water to the top of the main engineering compartment so that it doesn't settle down into the power plant. The question is, *Now what*? Nora?"

"We've gotta get that water back into the tank if we're going to use it for reaction mass. I have no idea how to do that," Nora said.

"The tank is out of commission," Zell said. "Sparks didn't blow a hole in the side of it. That we could patch. He set his explosives at the intake junction. He not only trashed the water tank, but the intake is bent out of shape. Without the intake we can't even reconfigure the system to use ammonia as reaction mass. That's assuming we have enough ammonia, which I don't think we do."

"You can't fix the intake?" Trix asked Zell.

"Not in time to do any good," Zell said. "In port, sure, but not out here."

"Nora," Trix said. "What's the state of the Em drive?"

"There's no damage to it as far as I know," Nora said, taking out her slate and tapping at the screen. "Diagnostics look good. It doesn't require reaction mass, but it would take us years to get back to Galtz with just the Em drive."

"We're not worried about getting back to Galtz right now," Trix said. "Our main concern is altering our course enough to avoid passing through the Curtain. If we start the Em drive right now, we just might make it."

"Which brings us back to the duck pond problem," Zell said. "We can't start accelerating until that water has been dealt with."

"Can't we just suck it up?" Rex said, feeling stupid.

"With what?" Zell asked.

"And put it where?" Li added.

"We've got all the equipment and expertise we need to mine ice," Zell said. "But that assumes that the ice is outside the ship, not in our main engineering compartment."

"Ice would be easier to deal with than liquid water," Li said.

"How do we freeze it?" Trix asked.

"We could isolate that deck and vent it into space," Zell said.

"We could close all the hatches on that deck except for the ones between the flooded compartments and the secondary cargo bay." Nora said. "We can just open the cargo bay door and let it all flow out."

"It won't *all* flow out," Li said. "As soon as the deck has decompressed the volume of water will expand. A lot of it will flash into water vapor and flow out, freezing into a mist of fine ice crystals. Some of it is likely to freeze solid before it can flow out the cargo bay door. We could collect that by hand and filter it for reuse."

"That reaction mass water was very pure in the tank," Nora said. "But now it's surely picked up a lot of contaminants. Solvents, lubricants, anything else that anyone might have spilled on the deck in the last fifty years. Those chemicals are going to coat everything between engineering and the cargo bay, including all of the cargo."

"Doubtless there's already some water in the ventilation

system," Li said. "It could overwhelm the atmospheric scrubbers and result in some mold and mildew in the air shafts."

"We're not going to satisfy any occupational safety inspectors with this stunt," Trix said. "We're cutting every conceivable corner here. It's that, or throw ourselves on the mercy of the Powers. Anybody interested in rolling those dice? No?"

"Uh, ma'am?" Arni Hansson raised his hand.

"Go ahead, Arni," Trix said.

"I don't think the exterior cargo door will open if the hatch to the passageway is open," he said.

"We can override that safety mechanism pretty easily," Trix said. "But that's good thinking, Arni. Keep it up."

"Are we going to have enough water left to drink and shower and all that?" Arni said.

"The spilled water was reaction mass. We have a separate water supply for crew needs," Trix explained.

"Okay, Arni and Drake," Trix said. "I want you two down in cargo bay two. Make sure the big stuff is secured. Move little stuff up to the main cargo bay. Get started now. Take meals and rest breaks as needed, but that's your only job until it's done. Get going."

The two young marines acknowledged their orders and exited the compartment.

"Nora," Trix said. "You won't even recognize your engineering section. The Yam faction gave it a psychotic makeover, but that might actually work to our advantage. Most of your equipment and tools are behind those weird panels they used to transform the space. Take Li and collect or secure anything else down there that you don't want jettisoned along with all of that water."

"Got it, Captain," Nora said. She and Li left together.

"Zell," Trix said, "You probably know what you need to do better than I do, but work out that safety override and think about ways to minimize loss of atmosphere. Have I forgotten anything?"

"Probably several things," Zell said. "We'll deal with them as they come up."

"Famous last words," Trix said. "Rex, you're with me."

"Always," Rex said.

CONTRASTING WORLDVIEWS

3.23.1 - Trey

It doesn't seem like overseeing the work of a robotic surgical bay would be as exhausting as actually performing the surgery by hand, but by the time Paige's new heart was beating in her chest and we had her closed up, I was exhausted. We didn't transfer her to the ICU. We just left her in the surgical bay for the time being.

Hans Dobrovitz was still in the ICU, and it was currently only configured for one occupant. I returned to my office and dispensed coffee into a squeeze mug. I was just adding sweetener when a soft, feminine voice said, "Don't you think sleep would be better than a stimulant?"

I turned and saw that it was Bygul. Something was different about her use of language, both verbal and gestural.

"All of the patients are stable and provided for, Doctor. I'll wake you if anything comes up," she slid around me as she spoke and started to massage my neck and shoulders. I nearly melted under the pressure from her skillful fingers.

"And if you don't mind my saying," she said as she worked the tension from my muscles. "You could use a shower."

That took me by surprise, but I didn't have the opportunity to dwell on it because the captain and Rex arrived at my door. I couldn't have looked as haggard as Rex did.

"Bygul," the captain said, "would you excuse us?"

"Certainly, Captain," Bygul said.

Bygul moved in microgravity with the confidence and agility of a professional acrobat. She certainly didn't need any help getting out of my office, but she pushed off the bulkhead with so little force that she drifted slowly across the space between me and the captain. She extended a hand to the captain, and the captain reached out to Bygul with her elegant new right arm. Bygul used the captain's anchored form to propel herself out of my office, her fingertips sliding along the captain's arm as she passed.

"Bygul seems different," I said. "Have you noticed?"

"I've been pretty busy, Doctor," Trix said. "Does it require my immediate attention?"

"Definitely not," I said. "What can I do for you, Captain?"

"Doctor, we are moving in towards the Curtain... What do you call it again?" she asked.

"The *Sphere*," I said.

"We are headed toward the Sphere at more than twelve thousand kilometers per second," she said. "If we continue as we are, we'll pass through it in nineteen days. Our primary means of propulsion is useless. We've got a back-up drive that doesn't require reaction mass, but it's very slow to accelerate. We'll have to engage it as soon as possible if we want to avoid contact with the Sphere."

I listened to her words, but my attention gravitated to Rex's body language and facial expression. They suggested that his pain medications had worn off.

"And you want to know what happens if we punch through the Curtain and into the inner system," I said.

"Yes."

"Captain," I said. "I honestly don't know. When I left, I was told that I could not return. I agreed. The Is didn't threaten any consequences if I came back. It didn't have to. I accepted that I was coming out here to stay."

"When you lived in the inner system," she said. "Did you

ever meet anyone who'd come in from the Kuiper Belt?"

"Not in baseline reality," I said. "But I spent most of my time in historical delves and other kinds of simulations. I lived a fairly solitary life in baseline. Have people from the Kuiper Belt tried to travel to the inner system?"

"Hundreds of thousands tried after the Blackout. Any ships that penetrated the curtain got flung out again on seemingly random trajectories. If they were too far off the ecliptic, they couldn't get back to the settled regions of the outer system. They starved or froze or suffocated.

"I've heard recordings of people in those ships begging for rescue," she said. "Nobody in the KB could help them, and they must have known it even as they pleaded for the impossible. Everyone has heard those recordings. It's one of the reasons why Spinners hate the Powers the way they do," she said. "The way I do."

"Do you remember the Blackout?" I asked.

"No, but I remember the Turmoil," she said. "Millions died. Tens of millions, maybe. Nobody knows for sure."

"Pardon me," I said. I activated my wrist comm. "Medical level PA: Bygul, please come back to my office."

My amplified words filled the passageway and all the compartments on the medical level. Speaking to the captain again, I said, "Captain, I'd like to issue a wrist communicator to Bygul. She's been invaluable to me here. It would be helpful if I could reach her as easily as any other member of the crew."

"That's fine," she said. "Rex, would you get a comm for her from stores?"

"Sure thing," Rex said.

Bygul appeared in my office hatchway. "Doctor?"

"Bygul," I said. "Sergeant Perkins is going to issue one of these to you," I said, pointing at the device on my wrist. "Please go with him now. And, please help him comply with his medication schedule."

"Yes, Doctor," she said, and coaxed Rex out of my office.

Now I was alone with the captain.

"Captain," I said. "You want to know if the Powers are going to kill us if we penetrate the Curtain."

"Yes," she said.

"Given my life experience," I said. "I can't imagine that they would. The people that the Powers seemingly flung out into space... The most likely explanation I can think of is that those were constructs putting on a show to discourage others from fleeing to the inner system. I'm sure the actual refugees lived comfortable and fulfilling lives inside the Sphere."

"Because the Powers were always good to you," she said.

"I know you've lived a hard life," I said. "And you have every reason to blame the Powers. I get it. I really do. And you're not going to elevate my experiences over your own. That makes perfect sense."

"Not just my experiences," she said. "You think the Powers made the Temple and the so-called gods that live in it, right?"

"That seems like the most likely explanation," I admitted.

"And the Whales that control the DAO," she said. "You think they're probably working for the Powers too."

I nodded.

"If that's all true," she said, emotion rising in her voice, "Then didn't the Powers send us out here to be their playthings? Didn't they feed us to their vicious pets?"

"I can't discount the possibility," I said.

"What other possibility is there?" she demanded, her right arm punctuating her words with a theatrical gesture.

"What about the *homo erectus* corpses?" I said.

"What about them?" she said.

"That species disappeared on Earth over a hundred thousand years ago. The intelligence you call the *Powers* can't be more than, what? Five hundred years old? The evidence suggests something older than the Powers; an intelligence that has been interacting with humanity since before the emergence of *homo sapiens*."

"Evidence that could be fake!"

"If we can't trust suppositions based on evidence and reasoning," I said. "Then we're back to our lived experience. Mine tells me that the Is is loving and benevolent."

"Tell that to Paige," she said. "Tell that to Cook!"

"I don't expect you to trust my intuitions over your own, Captain. I'm not asking you to. You asked me a question. That's my answer."

Her right arm reached out bringing her hand to rest lightly on my upper arm. She looked at her own arm with what might have been amazement.

"Alright," she said, and her right hand gave my arm a gentle squeeze. "Thank you, Trey."

She turned and walked out of my office.

3.23.2 - Paige

Paige woke up. A familiar voice spoke to her. It was a male voice. She recognized the individual words, but taken together, they didn't amount to anything.

She recognized the nature of her surroundings, but the word for them escaped her. She tried to move. Movement brought pain followed by panic, but as soon as the pain and fear flared up, a soothing tide of calm and comfort flowed through her and brought her back to equanimity.

A familiar figure, female, entered her space. This person caressed her face and arm and spoke in soothing tones. She felt something between her lips and she sucked at it by reflex and swallowed a few sips of water.

She could see another woman behind a clear barrier. This woman was large and familiar. A comfort. The closer woman spoke to her with a rising tone that implied questions, but the meaning failed to coalesce. The questions soon tapered off.

CODA

3.24.1 - Trey

It took days to fabricate and test Hans Dobrovitz's brain implant. This was partly because of its complexity and partly because it was a multi-step process that required Mr. Zell's attention. Zell was thoroughly occupied coordinating the removal of the water from the engineering section.

While I waited, I cloned an ample supply of Dobrovitz's stem cells for use in crafting the organic portions of the interface between his brain and the implant. For the sake of convenience, I thought of it as a *BCI*, a brain computer interface, but I know that the object Kothar designed for Hans only qualifies as a *computer* in the most expansive definition of that term.

After three days, we moved Paige out of the operating theater and into the recovery room. The heart transplant went well. Her immune system seems to recognize the new heart as her own. I see no need for immunosuppressive medications to prevent rejection.

Her brain did not fare as well. She has receptive aphasia at the very least. She clearly does not understand anything said to her. She hasn't tried to speak, so I don't know if her expressive abilities have also been compromised.

Her motor function seems unaffected, and she cooperates with Bygul who has provided occupational therapy. Paige can feed and care for herself.

Esmeralda is healing rapidly, thanks to her Columbian

genetic heritage. I expect her to make a full recovery with no lasting complications. Unlike Petrovic, who wears her battle scars with pride, Esmeralda insisted that I do everything possible to minimize the scar from the bullet wound on her abdomen.

I have no interest in rekindling our sexual relationship. I say that now, but we're likely to be on this ship together for a very long time. Anja has more character and integrity, but Esmeralda is beautiful. It sounds crass when I put the comparison in such stark terms, but I know myself. We'll see.

Rex does not have Esmeralda's genetic advantages when it comes to healing. He will take longer to recover, and given the severity of the muscle damage, his age, and the lack of sufficient gravity, I think he will feel the effects of his injuries for the rest of his life.

I believe Rex would benefit from psychological counseling. Of the four crew who died, one was an old friend, and three were marines under Rex's command.

Two of the remaining marines, Arni Hansson and Drake Antal, are now working under Joachim Zell, learning skills that will make them useful on a multi-purpose vessel when there is no enemy to fight.

In my opinion, Rex's feelings of inadequacy and resentment toward Zell, the resentment that allowed Yam entry into Rex's mind, remain unresolved. I mentioned to the captain that Rex might benefit from some talk therapy and floated the idea that she use her influence over him to get him to talk to me.

She can be very diplomatic when she wants to be. My suggestion was thoroughly, if tactfully, rejected.

Both Nora Lawson and Shawn Li have more than recovered from their traumatic brain injuries. Their skulls and scalps are still healing, but in terms of their cognitive capacities, they are doing better now than before they were injured.

They have become a cabal of two. They can communicate complex information non-verbally and think collaboratively.

I haven't asked about their level of physical intimacy, but the engineering sections, where Nora's quarters are located, are still open to space. It's my understanding that Nora has relocated to Z-Level, where Zell, Dobrovitz and Li all have their living quarters. I don't know whether she has moved in with Li or taken Dobrovitz's quarters. I'm guessing the former.

The captain's indignation toward the Is, the Powers, haunts my thoughts. Did they deliver us to the Temple entities for their sadistic entertainment? If so, what are the implications?

It occurs to me that by the time all is said and done, four human crew members will have died and four others will have been given cognitive capabilities well beyond the technological capacity of the human Kuiper Belt civilization.

Will Paige and Hans join Nora and Shawn's cyber-telepathic collective once their restorations are complete? If so, have the Powers used this tempestuous encounter with the Temple and its denizens to introduce an upgrade to Kuiper Belt humanity? If that was the intent, there were certainly gentler, more humane ways of going about it.

I continue to raise these questions in my daily recorded conversations with Joachim Zell, but those discussions don't survive the editing process. I don't know whether that decision comes from Captain Nixon or the DAO.

Speaking of which, it's time for me to head up to what used to be the Situation Room, what we now call the *studio*.

3.24.2 - Petrovic

Petrovic spoke to David. She knew she was speaking to the DAO and to their growing audience on the Interchain, but the idea of talking to millions of people paralyzed her. To get through it, she thought of it as just talking to David.

"Welcome back, everyone," Petrovic said to David. "We

have an amazing episode for you."

"Indeed we do," David agreed from behind the camera.

"Today was our make or break day, and we passed within spitting distance of the Curtain," Petrovic said.

"Now, Anja," David said. "What have I told you about spitting with your vac suit helmet on?"

"It obscures the view," Petrovic said. "And speaking of views, look at this."

A view of the enormous Dyson swarm panels appeared on a display behind David, and Petrovic knew that David would replace Petrovic's image with this footage before they submitted the preliminary edit to the captain.

"We asked our resident big brain, Joachim Zell, what he made of this up-close view of the Curtain. Here's what he had to say."

The video behind David switched to a pre-recorded segment with Zell and Trey talking shop. Petrovic relaxed. This was their third episode since expelling the water from the engineering section and engaging the Em drive, and Petrovic was still uncomfortable in front of the camera.

Up close, the outward facing segments of the Curtain were not that interesting to look at. They were non-reflective and black. The hexagonal segments were hundreds of kilometers across, and the *Persephone* was speeding past them fast enough that the frames at the edges of the panels blurred into a monochromatic kaleidoscope as they zipped in and out of frame. The dynamic images came when the view shifted to include both the ship and the far-off horizon of the spherical cage that enclosed the sun. Even up close, the spherical exterior of the Curtain was nearly invisible to the naked eye, but Petrovic knew that David would tweak the image to bring out the contrast between the Curtain and the blackness of space behind it.

Petrovic had insisted that Esmeralda, with her conventional beauty, should be the one in front of the camera, but Escamilla was still recovering from her gunshot wound to the abdomen and was confined to medical.

Esmeralda wasn't cuffed to her bed in the recovery room anymore, though. All was forgiven.

Zell had done a segment for the previous episode explaining how the Em drive could create thrust without shooting some kind of propellant out of the back of the ship. It had something to do with microwaves bouncing around inside a metal cone, but Petrovic didn't even try to follow his explanation.

The one thing she did understand was why they only used the Em drive as an emergency backup. It took way too long to build up any speed.

Once the water had been evacuated, the captain had reoriented the ship and engaged both the Em drive and the rear maneuvering thrusters to squeeze every newton of thrust out of the ship's working propulsion systems.

The thrusters used ammonia for propellant, and Petrovic's understanding was that they didn't have all that much of it. The captain had cut the maneuvering thrusters the instant that the distance between the wall of giant solar collectors that made up the Curtain and the *Persephone* stopped decreasing and started to creep in the other direction.

The captain, Petrovic observed with undisguised envy, was an entirely off-camera presence in these productions. As was Paige, Hans, Nora and Shawn. Nothing having to do with Kothar's gifts of advanced medical technology appeared in the infotainment episodes they created and posted to the interchain according to the instructions the captain relayed from the DAO.

Both Arni Hansson and Drake Antal were learning to become miners. They worked in vac suits recovering chunks of ice from the still decompressed engineering compartments. Zell taught them the basics of ice mining while a sensor drone captured these tutorial sessions for use in the infotainment dispatches.

The two handsome young Columbian marines-turned-ice miners had attracted a following of infatuated young women. Doubtless some men too. If the *Persephone* ever made it back to Galtz or any of the larger habitats in the Pax Columbia, Hansson and Antal would be spoiled for choice.

They would not, however, be returning to Galtz anytime soon. Their main objective, now that they had avoided colliding with the Curtain, was to reduce their speed enough to avoid being flung out into interstellar space. Without outside assistance, the best they could hope for would be an extremely long-period elliptical orbit around the sun that took them out near the Oort Cloud before moving back toward the inner system.

As the captain put it, "Orbital insertion is orbital insertion. It beats the endless void."

Not if we starve, Petrovic thought.

3.24.3 - Rex

Trix's lower legs stood locked to the deck next to the enormous bed in the luxury suite like the trunks of identical trees cut to the same height. The rest of her was under the covers with Rex.

She hadn't moved into the first-class compartment, but she had opened it up for the crew to use. Anyone could reserve the space. Trix and Rex had it tonight. The slowly accumulating thrust from the Em drive produced gravity equivalent to that of Earth's moon. It was enough to accommodate sleeping in bed without the need for tight covers to hold them in place, and it was enough for sex.

Extended weightlessness had broken Rex's erectile response, and it had not yet recovered. He was too embarrassed to talk to the doctor about it. Trix had no such reservations, and she presented Rex with a bottle of pills from the doctor which did the trick.

Rex was still injured, and he knew that cavorting in bed

without her mechanical legs was an unfamiliar experience for Trix. He looked away as she disengaged from her lower legs and slipped under the covers. He wasn't sure if this was for her comfort or his own.

Their first time was a slow and gentle affair that involved lots of eye contact and no vigorous exertion. They laughed about it afterwards, agreeing that they had lots of room for improvement and plenty of time in which to practice.

"Any chance that Nora and Shawn will repair Lola?" Rex asked. "I don't know," Trix said. "If so, it's way down on their to-do list. I told them to work on extending our food supply."

"Okay, that's more important than what I had in mind," Rex said.

"How would you feel about Petrovic watching us?" Trix said.

"I'm not sure," Rex said. "Just watching?"

"That's all I need," Trix said. "And I don't *need* it. It's fine if you say no."

"Have you talked to her about it?"

Trix laughed. "I don't need to talk to her about it. If we decide it's what we want, I'll tell her what I expect of her. Believe me, she'd rather be ordered than invited."

Rex wasn't comfortable with the openly manipulative side of Trix's personality, but he recognized it as part of who she was. The new eye, arm and skin hadn't smoothed out all of her hard edges. He changed the subject.

"Any word from the DAO on funding a support mission?" he said.

"No. Our outbound trajectory isn't going to take us through Columbian space. Any help on our way out would have to come from habitats in the old Tiānshàng quadrant. I don't think the DAO has a presence there."

"How could it?" Rex said. "They're not even on the interchain in that part of the belt. I'd rather avoid their territory altogether."

"Nora can't give me exact performance forecasts for the Em

drive, but it's possible that we'll be able to use a Uranus flyby to trim our course. That way we'd pass through Tiānshàng's frontier regions rather than the center of Han territory."

"That'd put us close to Hinduvarta territory," Rex said. "Maybe the DAO could arrange a support mission from one of the Dharāloka satellite habs."

"I doubt it," Trix said. "Officially, they're still at war with the Han. A sortie into Tiānshàng territory would be asking for trouble."

"Maybe they could help us out with a laser," Rex said. "What's that called when you push a ship with a laser?"

"Laser ablation," Trix said. "That's a possibility, but none of the larger Hinduvarta habs will have line of sight with us for another couple of months, and until we trim our course with a gravity assist at Uranus, they'd be pushing us out of the system as much as they'd be slowing us down. Still, it's worth exploring."

Rex thought she wanted to say more. "What are you not telling me?" he said.

"We got an assignment from the DAO a while back," she said. "It's cryptic, and in our current circumstances we have no way of complying with it."

"What is it?"

"We've been ordered to surrender the mummified corpses we took from the Temple," Trix said.

"Surrender the mummies?" Rex said. "To who?"

"The Floaters."

3.24.4 - Cook

From Master of Kitchen's perspective, the feast was a triumph. The King called for an extravagant dinner to showcase the wealth and sophistication of Ugarit to the combined trade delegation from Egypt and Nubia. But then in the mid afternoon the King took ill. He made an appearance at dinner, but he merely picked at his food.

The King was flanked at the table by his top advisors who noticed the King's lack of appetite. Not wanting to appear intemperate or even glutinous in comparison to the King, his advisors ate very little.

The pattern of imitation worked its way around the King's table and then to other tables, and by meal's end, Master of Kitchen was faced with an unprecedented abundance of leftovers.

Even after the kitchen staff had distributed some of the excess to their friends in the palace staff and stables, there was more left over than Master of Kitchen could carry to the temple of Shapash. He enlisted three boys from his kitchen staff to help him transport the food through the darkened streets of Ugarit.

A black-skinned caravan guard from Nubia who had accompanied Master of Kitchen to Ugarit's markets earlier in the day asked to come along as well. The two men shared very little language in common, but Master of Kitchen was proud of his city and happy to share a rarely seen side of it with this visitor from the land of the great river.

As they made their way through the nearly empty streets, beggars spotted Master of Kitchen and, seeing the quantity of food, woke friends and family and hurried to the Temple ahead of the slow-moving party from the palace. By the time Master of Kitchen and his retinue arrived at the Temple, a sizable crowd waited just outside the gate. The crowd parted to let them pass, and the high priestess of Shapash greeted Master of Kitchen just inside the temple compound.

Normally the priestesses, hierodules and temple servants would eat first with the remainder going to the small crowd of beggars and urchins who knew to wait at the temple late at night. On this night, given the abundance of food and the size of the crowd, the high priestess ordered that fires be lit in the courtyard and that temple residents and street folk alike sit around the fires and eat together.

Master of Kitchen had eaten his fill in tasting all of the dishes destined for the King's table. He accepted a cup of wine from a temple hierodule and sipped at it as he took in the expressions of delight from the street people treated to this abundance from the palace kitchen.

Ugarit was prosperous, and even with its system for distributing clean water, disease claimed far more lives than hunger. For the most part, these people were not ravenous which meant that they could enjoy the fine food for its quality rather than use it to blunt their gnawing hunger.

Master of Kitchen heaved a sigh of satisfaction. This was the pinnacle of his existence; feeding people and basking in the pleasure his food brought them.

Made in the USA
Middletown, DE
17 June 2024